Classical Chinese Tragedies (Chinese-English)

中国古代悲剧故事（汉英对照）

Golden Boy and Jade Maiden

娇红记

Meng Chengshun

孟称舜（明）

Adapted by Zhang Xuejing

张雪静 改编

Revised by Liu Yousheng

刘幼生 审订

New World Press
新世界出版社

First Edition 2002

Translated by Paul White
Edited by Zhang Minjie
Book Design by He Yuting

ISBN 7 – 80005 – 645 – 7

Published by
NEW WORLD PRESS
24 Baiwanzhuang Road, Beijing 100037, China

Distributed by
NEW WORLD PRESS
24 Baiwanzhuang Road, Beijing 100037, China
Tel: 0086 – 10 – 68994118
Fax: 0086 – 10 – 68326679
E-mail: nwpcn@public. bta. net. cn

Printed in the People's Republic of China

娇娘

娇红记

飞红

娇红记

王文瑞

娇红记

Foreword

The romance *The Golden Boy and the Jade Maiden* is a love tragedy that has been handed down since the Ming Dynasty (1368 – 1644). Its author was Meng Chengshun, styled Ziruo. His hometown was Shanyin (today's Shaoxing, in Zhejiang Province), and the exact dates of his birth and death are unknown, although his dramatic creation was mainly accomplished during the Tianqi and Chongzhen reign periods, towards the end of the Ming Dynasty. Apart from the present work, Meng also wrote two other romances, *The Story of Zhenwen* and *The Story of Erxu*, as well as six *zaju* or poetic dramas, including *The Peach Blossom Beauty*. *The Collection of Famous Dramas Ancient and Modern*, which Meng edited, contains 56 plays from the Yuan and Ming dynasties, and was a valuable contribution to the work of collating and publishing dramas of that period.

The story of the love between Wang Jiaoniang and Shen Chun, which is the theme of *The Golden Boy and the Jade Maiden*, is an ancient folk tale which has been passed down and appeared in over a dozen versions in the form of novels or *zaju*. Meng Chengshun elaborated and developed the story on the basis of those works when he composed his romance.

In the latter part of the Ming Dynasty, the feudal ruling class placed great stress on the ideology of Neo-Confucianism, which advocated "subordinating human desires to the Heavenly order." But the images of Shen Chun and Jiaoniang represent in the ideological field the budding of capitalism in the feudal economy, through their striving for liberation of the individual, which was an essential product of that budding. Jiaoniang's "soul mate" view of love and Shen Chun's view of life, which rejected honor and rank and stressed that a person should follow his inclinations, were in opposition to the dominant feudal ethics of that time, and represented a break from the orthodox stress on utmost loyalty and filial piety, and the acquisition of titles and honors.

The overall theme of *The Golden Boy and the Jade Maiden*, that of advocating free choice of marriage partner, was influenced by the romances *The Romance of the Western Bower* and *The Peony Pavilion*. But in its depiction of the ideal hero and heroine, whose standard for "free choice of marriage partner" is to "share a house during life and a tomb after death," *The Golden Boy and the Jade Maiden* is much more progressive than *The Romance of the Western Bower*, in which the standard is simply that the hero should be talented and the heroine should be beautiful. And so, the former standard has a more modern flavor, as it is built on a foundation of a common way of thought. It expresses an enlightened democratic longing to take control of one's own destiny by shaking off the fetters of feudal ethics.

In delineating the images of the two lovers as victims of feudal ethics, the author shows their great courage in breaking out of the restrictions of the traditional mores, and their rebellious spirit as they pursue a beautiful love. Jiaoniang sincerely loves Shen Chun. She pledges her love to him, and offers herself to him in marriage. By doing so, she shows the typical yearning for love of a girl sequestered in a boudoir in feudal times, and her contempt for feudal ethics, and at the same time reveals the iron will beneath her soft and yielding exterior. When her stern father breaks off her engagement to Shen Chun, and the young man himself proves weak and vacillating, she rounds on the latter fiercely, reminding him that since she is pledged to him she is his forever, and "the only way I can repay your kindness is by my death. " This is a vivid illustration of how doggedly opposed she is to feudal marriage concepts and how much she is committed to constancy in love. When, despite all her resistance, she proves powerless to change her fate, she consummates her struggle against feudal ethics and her quest for true love by boldly accepting death.

The contradiction between love and worldly success is employed by the author to deepen his characterization of Shen Chun. From ancient times, worldly success, or the gaining of honors and rank, had been advocated by the feudal ruling class as the right — indeed, only — way for a man to measure his social status. All desires and ambitions were supposed to be channeled in this direction. In the early part of the story, Shen Chun is a typical young Confucian scholar with his sights firmly set on achieving success. But as soon as he sets eyes on Jiaoniang, his calculating ambition flies out the window, thereby showing the hollowness of the ideology of the ruling class, which falls at the first blow when it comes into conflict with real human nature. The trenchant satire here is skilfully applied. Shen Chun's view of love, which rejects worldly success, is in contrast to that of Master Zhang Sheng, the hero in *The Romance of the Western Bower* and Liu Mengmei, the hero in *The Peony Pavilion*, of which such success is an integral part. It is a vigorous defiance of the doctrine of "subordinating human desires to the Heavenly order" promoted by the ruling class in the closing years of the Ming Dynasty, and reflects the ongoing awakening of young intellectuals to objective knowledge towards the end of the feudal period. In Shen Chun, we can get a glimpse of Jia Baoyu, the protagonist of the classical novel *A Dream of Red Mansions*, in embryo.

Of course, *The Golden Boy and the Jade Maiden* is not without its flaws. There are still some backward and negative elements in the characters of Shen Chun and Jiaoniang. Bound by the limitations of their time, they cannot see the social roots of their frustrated love affair; in ascribing their tragedy to the machinations of fate, they are echoing the ideological limitations of the author. When the lovers turn into mandarin ducks (a symbol of constancy in love) after their deaths, this is a metaphor for people's beautiful aspirations. It is the same literary device as is used in *The Bride of Jiao Zhongqing*, when Jiao Zhongqing and Liu Lanzhi turn into birds, and in *Liang Shanbo and Zhu Yingtai*, when Liang Shanbo and Zhu Yingtai turn into butterflies. But this idea of lovers who are sundered during life but united after death has had the negative effect of leading many young men and women who were disappointed in love to suicide, hoping to be together in the next world.

The techniques of characterization are different in novels and drama. In the adaptation of the story, efforts have been made to remain as faithful as possible to the original theme and basic plot. However, there are 50 old versions of the story, and most of them are tediously wordy. Moreover, the characters and scenes change in a bewildering fashion, and dialogs are rambling. So the time, place and plot sequences have been arranged into ten chapters, using a more accessible style of language. This has involved cutting out some minor episodes which have little or no connection with the main story, and adding details to make the development of the narrative more credible and make the characters more distinct both in their actions and their psychology.

We hope that we have made a contribution to the transmission of classical Chinese drama. We are conscious that there may be shortcomings in this work, and sincerely hope that readers will point them out and offer advice.

前　言

　　明代传奇《娇红记》，是一部流传久远的爱情悲剧。作者孟称舜，字子若。明会稽山阴(今浙江绍兴)人，生卒年不详。他的戏剧创作活动主要在明末天启、崇祯年间。除本剧外，还撰有《贞文记》、《二胥记》两部传奇和《人面桃花》等六种杂剧。他所编的《古今名剧合选》收入了元明两代的杂剧五十六种，对元明杂剧的整理刊布作了有益的工作。

　　《娇红记》中王娇娘和申纯的爱情故事，在民间早有流传，曾被编写成小说和杂剧，版本至少在十种以上。代表作有刘兑的杂剧《金童玉女娇红记》和无名氏的小说《娇红传》。孟称舜在这些作品的基础上加以丰富发展，写成了传奇《节义鸳鸯冢娇红记》。

　　明朝末期，封建统治者大力提倡程朱理学，宣扬"存天理，灭人欲"的封建正统思想。而申、娇形象的出现，是封建经济的资本主义萌芽在意识形态领域里提倡个性解放的必然产物。娇娘"同心子"的爱情观和申纯"弃功名、存人欲"的人生观，是对封建礼教统治的反抗，是同封建统治尽忠全孝进取功名思想的决裂。全剧主题受《西厢记》、《牡丹亭》的影响，强调择偶应"自择"，"与其悔之于后，岂若择之于始"。男女主人公理想中的择偶标准是"生同舍，死共穴"的"同心子"，将《西厢记》所提出的郎才女貌标准大大向前推进了一步，其实质是建立在共同思想基础上的爱情观，带有很强的现代情爱色彩,表明了反对封建礼教束缚,希望主动掌握自己命运的带有启蒙性质的民主思想。

作者在本剧中着意刻画了两个封建礼教牺牲者的形象,表现他们大胆冲破传统礼教禁锢,追求美好爱情的反抗精神。娇娘真挚地爱着申纯,一经定情,便主动以身相许,表现出一个封建深闺女子对爱情的渴望和对传统礼教的蔑视,从而凸现出在她纤弱外表下所具有的刚烈性格。当她父亲惧威悔婚,而申纯又表现得软弱无能时,她愤而言道:"妾身不可再辱,既已许君,则君之身也。""事不济当以死谢君。"表达了她对爱情的忠贞不渝和反抗封建婚姻的决心。当一切抗争都无法改变自己的命运时,就毅然自绝,最终以死完成了对爱情的追求和对封建礼教的反抗。

作者在刻画申纯时,有意识地加进了"爱情"与"功名"的矛盾冲突,借此深化了这一形象的意义。自古以来,封建统治者都把"功名"作为男性立身处世的"理"加以标榜,要求一切欲念都必须服从之。申纯开始也是个刻意追求功名的儒生,但当他见到娇娘后,便"功名之心顿释",把统治者所鼓吹的"理"在人的本性面前不堪一击的虚伪本质充分暴露出来,讽刺得巧妙犀利,恰到好处。申纯弃功名、存人欲的思想与张生、柳梦梅热衷于功成名就的爱情观截然不同,它是对明朝末期统治者宣扬的"存天理,灭人欲"的有力鞭挞,反映了封建社会末期青年知识分子对现实认识的不断深化和觉醒,从申纯身上已可以隐约窥见《红楼梦》中贾宝玉的雏型。

当然,《娇红记》并非白璧无瑕,在娇娘与申纯身上还存在着落后与消极的因素,他们受时代的局限,看不到爱情不能实现的社会根源,把它看作是命运的捉弄,也反映了剧作者思想的局限。申、娇死后化为鸳鸯,上承焦仲卿、刘兰芝化鸟,梁山伯、祝英台化蝶的手法，表现了人民的善良愿望，但这种生前仳离，死后团圆的结局，往往导致一些在爱情上绝望的青年男女走上双双殉情的道路，有其消极影响作用。

由于戏剧与小说表现手法的不同，改编者在力求忠实于原著主题的基础上，保存了基本情节。但由于原作品长达五十出，冗长拖沓，人物场景转换频繁，对话描写枝蔓横出，因而在改编时对原作的时序、场次、情节作了必要的合并调整，分为十章，并删除了一些与主要情节关系不密切甚至无关的枝节，又适当地增添了若干生动的心理和细节描写，使故事发展更为可信，人物形象更加鲜明，语言更加通俗易懂。

我们希望能为中国古典戏剧的传播做一些有益的工作，但由于水平有限，在改编过程中一定存在着许多不足之处，敬请方家批评指正。

Contents
目　录

娇红记

Chapter One
Shen Chun Meets Jiaoniang

It is said that towards the close of the Song Dynasty (960-1279), in the city of Chengdu, in Sichuan Province, renowned as a "land of plenty," there lived a gentleman named Shen Qing. He was also known to his close acquaintances as Ziyu. He belonged to a clan that had once been illustrious, but, as the saying goes, "the influence of men of virtue lasts no more than five generations," and the Shen family fortunes were now at a low ebb. Finally, disheartened by constant setbacks, Shen Qing had no recourse but to wander from place to place in search of ways to earn a living, accompanied only by his page Shen Cheng. In the city of Jinjiang, he sought assistance from an old friend of his family called Wang Ziyou, a wealthy man from Chengdu. Mindful of benefits bestowed on the Wangs by the Shens in the past, and holding Shen Qing's talents in high esteem, Wang Ziyou took him on as his manservant. Back in Chengdu, Shen Qing took advantage both of his native wit and his master's influence to go into business on the side on his own account. After a few years, he had built up a tidy bit of property, and had so impressed Wang Ziyou with his steady ways that the latter was convinced that he had inherited the sterling qualities of his predecessors, and betrothed his daughter to him.

Miss Wang was of a virtuous disposition, and had a shapely figure and comely features. She and Shen Qing were a perfectly matched couple, who treated each other with respect and courtesy. After one year, a child was born to them, whom they named Shen Wan. But the universe is unpredictable, and both disaster and fortune lurk between dawn and dusk; before

第一章　申娇初会

　　话说北宋末年，素有"天府之国"美誉的四川成都府，有位员外，姓申名庆，字子余。祖上本是诗书世宦簪缨之族，应了句老话"君子之泽，五世而斩"，到他这辈根基已尽，家道中落，人口凋零，只剩下他孑然一身。因为屡次求取功名未就，不免有些心灰意冷，看着坐吃山空，无以为生，只得带着家生小厮申成，琴剑飘零来到锦江城，投奔世交王子由。王子由乃成都富豪，念在申庆祖上对自家有些恩德，又爱申庆才高，将他收留，从此主仆二人流寓成都。申庆天资聪颖，依仗着王子由的势力，做些小本经营，数年后也置下些产业。王子由见申庆办事沉稳，颇有祖上遗风，便将女儿许配与他。

　　这王氏性情贤淑，品貌端妍，知书达理，与申庆夫唱妇随，琴瑟和谐，相敬如宾。

　　次年得一子，取名为申纨。不料天有不测风云，人有旦夕祸福，申纨不满一岁，便被一场伤寒夺了性命。申庆夫妇为此痛不欲生。

　　又过数载，王氏接连生下二子。一个取名申纶，

he was one year old, little Shen Wan died of a chill. His parents were inconsolable for a long time, but after a few more years two more boys were born — Shen Lun, also known as Wensheng, and Shen Chun, also known as Houqing. Having suffered the pain of losing one child, Shen Qing considered himself doubly blessed, and personally oversaw their education, full of confidence that some day his sons would score high marks in the imperial examinations and become officials, adding luster to their ancestors and kin.

The younger boy, Shen Chun, was outstanding in ability and intelligence. At the age of eight, he had mastered the Six Classics; at the age of ten, he could write essays, and had mastered the lute, chess, calligraphy and painting. In addition, he was fond of riding and archery, and practiced martial arts in intervals between lessons. On account of all this, he was his parents' favorite.

In the flitting of an eye, it seemed, the Shen boys attained manhood. They were strapping youths with a graceful and elegant bearing. In the third year of the Xuanhe reign period (1121), they went together to take the imperial examinations, but both failed.

Their parents were deeply disappointed, but turned their attention to finding brides for the boys. Eventually, after much toing and froing of matchmakers, Shen Lun consented to marry the daughter of a gentleman of substance named Zhou. The couple were suited to each other in every respect — a talented husband and a beautiful wife. Shen Chun, however, was ambitious and proud. He vowed that he would not marry until he had made a name for himself, and his parents resigned themselves to his stubbornness.

Now it happened that their mother had a brother, Wang Li, whose style was Wenrui. This man was serving as a magistrate in the city of Meizhou. He had two children — a son named Shanfu, aged six, and a daughter named Jiaoniang, aged 16. Jiaoniang had been known from her childhood for her beauty and intelligence, and her aunt had always been particularly fond of her. In fact, she had long been thinking of her as a

字文绳;一个取名申纯,字厚卿。申庆曾遭丧子之痛,故对申纶、申纯二子倍加呵护,亲自启蒙课业,盼望有朝一日二子科场高中,腰金衣紫,耀祖荣亲。

其中单说那幼子申纯,天资卓绝,聪颖过人,八岁通六经,十岁能作文,琴棋书画样样精通。生性又喜欢鞍马弓箭,常于习书之余演练一番武艺,因而愈受父母宠爱。

光阴似箭,岁月如梭,转眼申氏兄弟长大成人,皆出落得丰姿俊逸,仪表堂堂。宣和三年,兄弟二人同赴选场,不料秋桂未折,双双落第而归。

申庆夫妇见二子失意功名,终日郁郁寡欢,心中十分焦急,便张罗着为儿子操办婚事,一时间提亲说媒的踏破门槛。不久,申纶便迎娶本地周员外的小姐,郎才女貌,夫妻恩爱,倒也美满。只是小儿申纯心高气傲,立志不得功名誓不成家,也勉强不得,只能随他去了。

却说王氏有个胞弟,名理,字文瑞,现为眉州通判。他膝下有一对儿女,儿子唤作善父,年方六岁;女儿名叫娇娘,年已二八。此女自幼才貌端妍,聪明伶俐,深得姑母欢心。王氏早就有心聘她与申纯做媳妇。只因这几年王文瑞远在眉州,往来不便,故一直未曾遣媒说合。如今眼看儿子长大了,这事也该着手办理,只是申纯尚未成就功名,兄弟不知是否同意这

bride for her younger son, but as the families were living far apart and it was difficult to keep in touch, she had not sent a go-between to arrange the matter. Now that Shen Chun was already a grown man, she decided that she should start doing something about it. However, Shen Chun had still not achieved success in life, and so had put marriage out of his mind, and besides she did not know what her brother's attitude would be. But as luck would have it, just at this time Shen Chun was on vacation from his studies. Why not sent him to his uncle's to give him a chance for relaxation, and at the same time sound out Wang Wenrui's thoughts on a possible marriage between his daughter and Shen Chun? She consulted her husband, who approved heartily of the idea. After they had discussed the details, they called Shen Chun before them. Shen Qing said, "My boy, I have long had it in mind for you to go and pay your respects to your uncle, who, as you know, is an official in Meizhou. I did not want to distract you from your studies before, but now that you are on vacation, this is a suitable time to go. For one thing, you will be able to see your uncle and aunt; for another, your uncle will be able to give you guidance on writing documents; and for another, you really ought to see a bit more of the world and broaden your horizons. As the old saying goes, 'Read ten thousand books and walk ten thousand miles.' What do you say?"

The young man was overjoyed. He had heard of Meizhou's reputation as a place of great scenic beauty, and longed to see it for himself. He was also keen to see his uncle again after so many years. So he responded with alacrity: "I would be delighted to go, Father."

His mother was pleased, too, that her scheme had got off to a good start. "Now, when you meet your uncle and aunt again, be careful to mind your manners," she exhorted Shen Chun, "and show your cousins the proper respect." Shen Qing then gave his son a few words of advice, and ordered arrangements to be made for his journey.

The following morning dawned fair and bright. Shen Chun bade farewell to his parents, his brother and his sister-in-law, whipped his horse

门亲事。好在这段时间儿子有暇，不如先让他去舅父家散散心，顺便探询兄弟的态度。王氏遂将自己的想法与丈夫说了，申庆当下赞同。

老夫妻商议已定，便将申纯叫在面前，申庆慢慢说道："儿啊，你舅舅现在眉州为官，我与你娘早有心思让你前去问安，只是你学业功名要紧，不宜分心。如今场事已过，你可乘暇去眉州走一遭。一则看望你舅父、舅母；二则请你舅父在文章上给你指点指点；三则古人有云：读万卷书，行万里路。你也该出去开开眼界，长长见识。不知你以为如何？"

申纯闻听此言，心中好生欢喜。自己早就听人说眉州山青水秀，风景如画，极欲游览一番。再说舅父在外做官，多年不见，也想去看望一下，便爽声应道："孩儿愿往。"

王氏见申纯答应前往，心中十分高兴，连声叮嘱道："我儿见了舅父、舅母，休要缺了礼数，在弟弟妹妹面前也要有个做兄长的样子。"

申纯点头道："孩儿记下了。"

申庆又再三再四地将路上小心等话头嘱咐了一番，便为申纯打点行李，安排上路。

次日一早，风和日丽，申纯拜别爹娘兄嫂，扬鞭策马前往眉州。一路上但见青山叠翠，碧水拖蓝，野

to a canter, and rode off in the direction of Meizhou. The road was lined with rolling green hills and flowing blue waters. The wild flowers were in full bloom, and the birds chirped merrily. Farming folk were busy plowing and planting in the fields, and in the suburbs of Chengdu, parties of sight-seers were enjoying poetry-and-wine picnics. The boundless brightness of spring left room for nothing but delight in the heart of Shen Chun, now in the full bloom of youth. At a whim, he would spur his horse to a gallop, hallooing wildly, and then allow it to slow to an easy trot, as he intoned verses and hummed tunes — just as the mood took him. In this carefree manner, he arrived in the vicinity of Meizhou on the second day. Entering the city, the young man gazed in awe at the opulent mansions that lined the streets. His eyes were dazzled by the banners that fluttered from the multi-tude of taverns and teashops, and his ears were captivated by the strains of flutes and pipes that wafted from the courtesans' quarters and the motley cries of the market vendors. Inquiring his way among these thoroughfares teeming with prosperity, Shen Chun finally came to the mansion of the magistrate, in the western section of the city.

This residence had emerald hills at its back, and its vermilion gate with steep steps leading up to it faced a stream — bespeaking an auspicious situation. A rose-colored wall surrounded the mansion, topped with green tiles. Beyond the wall could be glimpsed lofty and spacious pavilions, ter-races, halls and towers. Behind was a splendid garden with luxuriant trees and tall bamboos, artificial mounds and exotic rocks. At the gate stood an old janitor, with a shock of white hair and white whiskers. Shen Chun went straight up to him, and announced who he was and where he had come from. The old man immediately went inside to report.

Wang Wenrui had been born to Wang Ziyou's senior wife. From an early age, he had set his sights high. He studied diligently, and was re-warded with success in the primary civil service examination at the age of 17, in the provincial-level examination at the age of 20, and later in the highest examination. He then entered on an official career. He was diligent

花烂漫,百鸟啼鸣。田野上农人村妇插秧耕作,郊原上诗朋酒侣相携踏青。申纯毕竟是少年心性,置身于无限春光之中,心中块垒早已化为乌有。一会儿纵马疾驰,狂呼呐喊;一会儿缓缰慢步,吟诗唱词。真正是随心所欲,畅快无比。不过两日,已到眉州地面。进得城中,只见大街两旁华屋林立,酒肆茶坊幡招飘扬,青楼勾栏笙簧迭奏,市场上叫卖声此起彼伏,一派繁华景象。申纯左顾右盼,一路打听,来到了城西通判府。

只见这通判府背依青山,门傍绿水,粉墙碧瓦,朱门高阶。隔墙望去,里面亭台楼阁,峥嵘轩敞,后面一带花园里茂林修竹,假山怪石,景物粲然。申纯来到门前,见有一位须眉皆白的老院公,不免上前通名报姓。院公听说是成都来的申官人,急忙进去通报。

王氏之兄王文瑞,本是王子由的嫡子,少年老成,刻意功名,萤窗雪案,发奋读书,十七岁中秀才进府学,弱冠中举,而立之年进士及第,从此开始了仕宦生涯。他勤政爱民,为官清正,在朝中颇有廉名,而今调任眉州通判已两年有余。夫人赵氏乃蜀中名门之女,仪容端庄,贤达明理,相夫教子,恪守妇道。膝下一双儿女,都是聪明孝顺。一家人尊卑有序,和睦度日,倒也其乐融融。王文瑞素与姐丈申庆意气相

in his work, and showed care for the common people. His administration was noted even at the imperial court for its honesty. He had been the magistrate of Meizhou for two years by this time. His wife came from the prominent Sichuan family of Zhao. She was a woman of great poise and tact. She was also a fine helpmate for her husband and teacher for her children, in short, a paragon of wifely virtues. Their two children were intelligent and impeccably behaved. So the family was harmonious and happy. Wang Wenrui had always been fond of his brother-in-law Shen Qing, and admired his nephews' literary talents. In recent years, as he had felt old age creeping up on him, there had formed in his mind a desire to give a helping hand to Shen Lun and Shen Chun in their careers by taking them into his own service. But the young men were adamant in continuing to study from morning till night, and entering for the examinations, all to no avail. When he heard that She Chun had come to pay him a visit, Wang Wenrui was delighted. He ordered that his nephew be shown in immediately.

The old gatekeeper hurried back. Putting Shen Chun's horse in the care of a lad, the old man led the way to the reception room. They passed through a spacious courtyard lined on either side with covered corridors, and then through a central hall in which there was a screen made of purple sandalwood and marble. Rounding the screen, they traversed a small hall, and emerged into the main courtyard. In the middle of the courtyard was a large rockery made of layers of exquisitely carved stones from Lake Taihu. It was covered with climbing plants and creepers, between the leaves of which shone flowers of every hue, making the whole glitter like a brocade mantle. Beyond the rockery were long trellises of roseleaf raspberry plants. Further on, they came to the main hall, an imposing and splendid building with carved beams and painted rafters. Suspended under the central part of the eaves was a horizontal signboard bearing the words "Cherishing Spring Hall" in gold characters on a black background. On both sides were covered walkways and outbuildings. As they approached, Wang Wenrui and his wife, dressed in their best clothes, appeared at the top of the steps and came down

投，且非常赏识两个外甥的才华。近年身体老迈，常思将申绾、申纯接到任所来做些帮衬，为自己分担家务。无奈两个外甥都在朝经暮史，读书进场，总不能如愿。现在听说外甥申纯到来，心中非常高兴，忙传命请进。

老院公返回府门，说声老爷、夫人有请，将申纯骑来的马匹交与身边一个小厮，自己在前边为申纯带路。申纯随院公进得府门，就见偌大的庭院，两边是游廊，正中是穿堂，穿堂当地安放着一个紫檀架大理石屏风，转过屏风是小小三间厅房，厅后是正房大院，院中太湖石砌就的假山玲珑剔透，数枝青藤攀缘其上，叶间各色小花星星点点，灿若锦屏。绕过假山，是一排长长的荼蘼架。从架下走过，正面是五开间雕梁画栋的中堂，檐下正中悬块黑底金字大匾，上书三个大字"熙春堂"。中堂两旁是穿山游廊厢房。尚未走近中堂，就见舅父一身家居服饰，与夫人赵氏迎下阶来。

申纯疾走两步，上前施礼道："舅父、舅母在上，容小甥一拜。"

王文瑞忙伸手相扶，眯起眼睛上下打量申纯一番，感慨万分道：

"贤甥，快快免礼。久违音讯，今日骤见贤甥，使老夫有不胜之喜。想不到几年不见，贤甥已是一表人

to meet them. Shen Chun quickened his pace, bowed deeply, and said, "Uncle, Aunt, please accept greetings from your humble nephew."

Wang Wenrui extended his arms to raise the young man up. He then directed a piercing gaze at him, and sighed deeply. "Nephew," he said, "you don't have to stand on ceremony. It's been so long since I've heard any news about you. I'm quite overwhelmed with delight to see you here. You've grown into quite a grand young man in the years since I last saw you. I'm sure that if I met you somewhere else I wouldn't recognize you. I trust your father and mother are well?"

"Quite well, thank you sir," replied Shen Chun. "I hope you and my aunt are also well."

"We are, we are," said Wang Wenrui.

"My dear," his wife interrupted, "why don't you bring our nephew inside for a cosy chat? What are we doing standing in the courtyard?"

Wang Wenrui, his eyes moist with emotion, hurriedly: "I'm sorry, my boy. I am so happy to meet you again that I had quite lost my wits. Come, come inside and take your ease." Turning to the gatekeeper, he said, "Wang Zhong, hurry to the kitchen, and tell them to prepare a feast to refresh our young traveler here."

Wang Zhong scurried off, beaming, while Shen Chun followed his uncle and aunt into the main hall. On the wall facing the entrance there hung a painting by State Artist Guo Xi, titled "At Ease in a Mountain Villa." It showed a fascinating scene of a mountain retreat surrounded by winding streams and sheer precipices, thick woods and soaring peaks around which strings of mist and cloud threaded. The picture was flanked by a couplet composed by Wang Wenrui himself, which read: "The gurgling of the stream at night chills my pillow/The beauty of the mountains in the morning dyes my very garments emerald." On a purple sandalwood table stood a bronze tripod vessel and incense burner shaped like an animal's head and from which exuded a heady fragrance. There was a large table and two armchairs made of hardwood and inlaid with marble. Around a tea table

材。若陌路相逢，老夫还不敢相认呢。厚卿，你父母近来可好？"

申纯道："托舅父、舅母的福，我父母安然无恙。舅父、舅母想来一切都好？"

王文瑞答道："还好，还好。"

"老爷，还不让三哥儿进里边叙话，直在院里站着做甚么？"赵夫人一旁说道。

王文瑞眼中湿润，忙道："看我高兴糊涂了，厚卿，快快进堂叙话。王忠速去厨下传话整治酒席，准备接风洗尘。"

王忠应了一声，笑嘻嘻地去了。

申纯随舅父、舅母进了大堂，见正墙迎面挂着本朝国手郭熙所绘《山庄高逸图》，回溪断崖，树隐山斋，峰峦秀起，云烟缭绕，端的是气势不凡。两边是王文瑞手书的一副对联：溪声夜涨寒通枕，山色朝浓翠染衣。紫檀条几上摆着青铜鼎彝和一个兽头香炉，篆烟袅袅，香气馥馥。楠木八仙桌和一对太师椅皆是大理石嵌面，多宝格尽头立着云龙高几，几上一对冰纹胆瓶内插着云帚。两侧茶几旁设着香楠雕花的小杌。申纯见堂中布置得超凡脱俗，心中暗道主人胸中大有丘壑。

款款落座后，申纯便问道："表弟、表妹都好吗？"

were small stools carved with designs of *nanmu* tree blossoms. The out-standing elegance of the furnishings made Shen Chun think that the mansion's owner must be a man of superb taste. As soon as he had seated himself, he inquired, "Are my cousins well?"

"They are," said his aunt. "They are spoiled and are being very naughty right now, but Shanfu has come to greet his cousin." With that, she pulled a little boy out from behind her back, and pushed him towards Shen Chun. The boy's hair was arranged in two buns on the top of his head, and he wore a pink gown over a pair of trousers of the same color. On his breast there hung a longevity key. He was an attractive child, with delicate features, red lips and white teeth. Shyly, he bowed to his older cousin, and said some formal words of welcome. Then, without waiting for Shen Chun to reply, dashed back behind his mother, from which vantage point he peeped at the visitor. Shen Chun beamed at the little fellow, and said, "He's certainly well-mannered for his age. You are bringing him up well, Uncle and Aunt." He then beckoned to Shanfu. "Come here and have a chat," he urged.

But Shanfu hid himself behind his mother, who laughed, and said, "He's hopeless, I'm afraid. He's afraid of strangers." She turned and pretended to scold the child. "Shanfu, from now on you must learn how to behave from your grown-up cousin."

Shen Chun gave an understanding smile. He looked around the room for Jiaoniang, and when he found that she was not present, inquired after her.

"Jiaoniang is very well," her mother replied. "She's still upstairs in her chambers."

Shen Chun found himself at a loss for something to say. Eventually, he stammered, "I wonder, er, well ... how old Miss Jiaoniang would be now?"

"She's 16 this year," her mother answered. "I'm sure you must remember how the two of you used to play so happily when you were chil-

"都好，只是娇生惯养，不成器。善父还不过来见过三哥。"赵夫人说着从身后扯出一个小男孩。只见这孩子梳一对丫髻，着一身粉色裤褂，胸前挂一个长命锁，眉清目秀，唇红齿白，煞是喜人。这孩子却有些害羞怕人，慌里慌张地躬身一揖道："三哥好。"不待申纯答话，一溜烟又躲到赵夫人身后，却露出头来偷眼观瞧申纯。

申纯心中欢喜，说道："表弟年纪尚小，便如此懂礼，全是舅舅、舅母教导有方。"说罢，向善父招手道："表弟过来叙话。"

善父却缩在母亲身后不肯出来。赵夫人笑着说："这孩子没出息，怕见生人，真没法子。"回转身佯怒道："善父，以后多向你三哥学学，不要这样不懂礼数。"

申纯笑了一笑，扫视堂内，却不见娇娘，便问道："娇娘妹妹可好？"

赵夫人道："噢，她也好。还在绣楼上没有下来。"

申纯一时不知该说些什么，搭讪道："不知娇娘妹妹于今芳龄几何？"

赵夫人道："今年一十六岁了。厚卿莫非不记得小时候你们在一起玩耍么？"

申纯回想起当年在外祖家与表妹坐卧不避、嬉笑无间的情景，讪笑道："那时候小甥尚不懂事，常惹

dren. "

A scene of Jiaoniang and himself romping and laughing all those years ago in his grandparents' house flashed into the young man's mind, and he said, with an embarrassed laugh: "I was a little terror in those days, and I was always making Miss Jiaoniang angry. I believe that she has grown into a very intelligent young woman. "

Wang Wenrui was unable to conceal his pleasure at hearing these words. He stroked his beard in a self-satisfied way, and said, "She has made some progress in her studies, it is true. She is also a sensible girl. "

"I suppose she has a suitor?" The words were out of Shen Chun's mouth before he could control his tongue. His face flushed scarlet.

Wang Wenrui, however, did not seem to notice. He looked at his wife, and sighed, "It's my fault, I know. I've been serving as an official away from home for so long that a suitable match has been impossible to find. " Turning back to Shen Chun, he added, "It's a great worry for us. "

"What kind of person are you looking for as a husband for Miss Jiaoniang, Uncle?" Shen Chun probed.

Wang Wenrui laughed in spite of himself. "Well, the ideal son-in-law would be someone like you, my boy, " he said.

The words were spoken light-heartedly, but they had a great effect on the hearer. Shen Chun's heart felt like it had just consumed a dollop of the sweetest honey. "Miss Jiaoniang and I have not seen each other for ages; I wonder if she would still recognize me?" he remarked.

His aunt understood exactly what this hint meant. She turned to a maid servant: "Feihong, go and ask Jiaoniang to come down and meet her cousin. "

With a swift glance at Shen Chun, Feihong scurried off. Shen Chun could not help admiring the maid servant's pretty features and slender figure as she left.

It was not long before she was back, but without Jiaoniang. Feihong

表妹生气,听说这几年她愈发聪慧了。"

王文瑞掩饰不住内心的欣喜,捋须说道:"倒还说的上是知书达理,秉性温良。"

"可曾许聘人家了吗?"话一出口,顿觉失言,申纯脸上刹时腾起一片红云。

王文瑞却未留意,看了夫人一眼,叹道:"唉!只因老夫这些年宦居他乡,尚未遇着可意的姻缘,如今也是一桩为难的心事。"

申纯试探道:"不知二老欲将表妹许与何等样的人家?"

王文瑞失笑道:"要想称心如意,除非那东床的人材似贤甥这等模样。"

说者无心,听者有意。申纯闻听此言,心中顿时如同吃了蜜糖一般,道:"我与表妹多年未见,不知表妹可还认得我么?"

赵夫人听出申纯的话外之意,微微一笑,对身边侍立的一个大丫头道:"飞红,你去请小姐来见三哥。"

飞红丫头瞥了申纯一眼,应声而去。申纯见那丫头星眼蛾眉,杏脸桃腮,黛眉樱口,削肩细腰,不由暗忖道:"舅父家的一个丫环也长得这般齐楚。"

不多时,飞红返了回来,身后却不见娇娘的身影。只见那丫头快步走到赵夫人身旁,俯耳道:"夫人,小慧说小姐刚刚出浴,未曾梳妆,不便见客。"

said to Shen Chun's aunt, in a low voice: "Madame, Xiaohui says that the young lady has just had a bath, and has not yet combed her hair. It is not convenient for her to meet the guest right now."

The other frowned, and said, "Shen Chun is one of our family. There is no need for her to get all dressed up just to meet him."

Shen Chun put on a diffident smile. "I have no pressing business," he said hastily. "I will be perfectly happy to wait."

His aunt also smiled, but said, "My daughter is quite old enough to know right from wrong. I will trouble you, sir, to wait just a little while longer." Then, turning to Feihong, she said, "Our visitor is no stranger in this house. Tell your young mistress to come down right now."

Just at this moment, Wang Zhong entered with the food and wine for Shen Chun's welcoming banquet. Wang Wenrui ordered it to be set out in the middle of the room, saying to his nephew, "I have prepared some snack, as you can see. Let us refresh ourselves as we talk."

Shen Chun's aunt waved to the maid servants to bring bowls of water and towels for washing. These were placed before them. After cleaning his face and hands, Shen Chun took his place at the table, his uncle ushering him to the seat of honor.

Wang Wenrui sat opposite his wife, and Shanfu sat next to his mother. An empty place was left for Jiaoniang. The first thing that Shen Chun did upon sitting down was to propose a toast to his uncle and aunt. In his pleasure at seeing his nephew, who had traveled a long distance specially to meet him, Wang Wenrui drained his goblet in one gulp. He immediately ordered a maid servant to refill Shen Chun's cup, and the two of them drank heartily, perfectly at their ease.

After the third toast had been drunk, Feihong returned, escorting a gracefully slim girl. Right before Shen Chun's eyes appeared a vision of loveliness: Her eyebrows were arched like mountains in spring; her eyes were like limpid pools in autumn; her nose was as fine as a goose's claw; without a spot of rouge, her lips were perfectly red, and without a tinge of

赵夫人眉头一皱,说道:"三哥是自家人,便不梳妆,出来见个面,又有何妨?"

申纯在一旁听了,忙笑道:"小甥左右无事,就等一会子,也不妨事。"

赵夫人遂含笑道:"娇娘大了,知道害羞了。贤甥且稍等片刻。"转过脸对飞红道:"自家兄长又不是外人,你去告诉她快些过来就是。"

正在此时,王忠回禀,酒宴已经备妥。王文瑞吩咐丫环婆子就于中堂设宴,回头又对申纯道:"贤甥且先用些便饭,咱们一家人边吃边聊。"

赵夫人招一招手,小丫头当即将洗面铜盆和手巾端了过来,放在面前。申纯洗手净面,然后入席。

王文瑞安排申纯在客座上落坐,自己与赵夫人打横,善父跟在母亲身旁,下首空着一座,自然是给娇娘留着的。申纯坐定,抢先举杯向舅父、舅母敬酒。王文瑞因外甥远道而来,心中高兴,一饮而尽。接着吩咐丫头为甥少爷斟酒,主客就此开怀畅饮起来。

酒过三巡,忽见飞红扶着一位袅袅婷婷的丽人来到中堂。只见那丽人眉颦春山,眼横秋水,腮凝新荔,鼻腻鹅脂,唇不点朱而红,肤不施粉而白,一头乌云松松挽就了一个坠马髻,髻侧簪一支颤巍巍凤头金步摇,上身穿一件蜀锦藕丝裳,下拖一条月白撒花百褶裙,真个娴静似娇花照水,行动如弱柳扶风。申

powder, her skin was alabaster; her black hair was done up in a cloud-like bun, adorned with a gold hairpin. She wore a jacket of Sichuan embroidery, and a pleated skirt of pale-blue silk, decorated with flower patterns. The girl looked as gentle and refined as exquisite flowers reflected in water, and she moved like a willow branch wafted by the breeze. Shen Chun paused, with his chopsticks hovering in the air. A flicker of memory from his childhood told him that this was his cousin Jiaoniang. For a moment, he was spellbound, until his aunt said, "Jiaoniang, come and greet your cousin!"

The girl, her eyes shyly downcast, uttered a few conventional words of welcome.

Shen Chun hastily rose to his feet, and thanked her.

Blushing, Jiaoniang took a seat at the foot of the table. Her mother, beaming with fondness, urged her to offer her cousin some more wine, which the girl did, holding the cup politely with both hands. Shen Chun accepted it, also using both hands and feeling immensely flattered by this attention, and drained the wine in one gulp.

Jiaoniang took this opportunity to glance cautiously at the young man. She was impressed by his dashing eyebrows, his shining eyes, delicate features, full red lips, and his refined and scholarly demeanor. "He's grown into such a fine gentleman in the years since I last saw him!" she thought to herself.

The very notion made her blush again, and she hastily lowered her head. Observing her confusion, Shen Chun forgot all about his duty to chat to his uncle and aunt, but sat with his eyes riveted on Jiaoniang. Whenever his uncle affably urged him to partake of more of the delicacies on the table, he would answer absent-mindedly, and yet not move his chopsticks.

In the end, his aunt offered him some choice dishes with her own hands. Only then did he realize how rudely he had been behaving. He stammered, "May I ask if the young lady drinks wine?"

纯见了，不觉停箸细瞧，依稀辨出尚有幼时的影子，料想这丽人便是表妹娇娘了。霎时间不觉目摇心荡，魂飞魄扬。

赵夫人在一旁招呼道："娇娘，快快见过三哥。"

娇娘垂首敛衽，翩翩道了个万福，娇声道："三哥远来辛苦，小妹这厢有礼了。"

申纯急忙起身还礼道："多谢表妹。"

娇娘粉面微红，款款坐到下首。赵夫人疼爱地看看女儿，轻声道："三哥远道而来，我儿可把酒劝哥哥一杯。"

娇娘依言斟满一杯酒，捧到申纯面前，莺喉鹂啭地说道："三哥，请饮一杯薄酒。"

申纯受宠若惊，慌忙起身双手接过酒杯，说道："多谢妹妹。"遂一饮而尽。娇娘这才轻抬眼帘，看了一眼申纯，只见他剑眉入鬓，星眸流辉，面若傅粉，唇若涂朱，风神儒雅，气韵天成。心中不觉吃了一惊，暗道："几年未见，三哥已长成丰姿韶秀、风流俊逸的美男子了。"

想到此，不由红了粉面，忙又低下头。申纯一见娇娘便心猿意马，魂不守舍，早忘了与舅父、舅母攀谈，一双眼睛只是在娇娘身上打转。王文瑞心情舒畅，不时劝申纯道："贤甥多吃一些。"申纯一心只在娇娘身上，口里答应，却不动筷子。赵夫人以为申纯拘束，亲手为他布菜。申纯这才发觉自己失态，不免

"Oh, Jiaoniang doesn't touch wine," her mother answered.

Shen Chun glanced at Jiaoniang, who happened to be dabbing lips with a silk handkerchief. Their eyes met, and then parted abruptly, leaving them both red-faced.

To break the awkward silence that ensued, Jiaoniang's mother said, "Feihong, more wine for the young gentleman!"

On dainty feet, Feihong hurried to where Shen Chun was sitting, filled his cup and coquettishly urged him to drain it.

Shen Chun shot an awkward glance at his aunt. "Forgive me," he said. "I know that it is against etiquette to refuse a gift from a superior, but the fact is that I am oppressed with a sense of failure at not having yet made my mark in the world. I feel that it is not right to accept another cup of wine."

Hearing this, Jiaoniang tugged Feihong's sleeve, "Master Shen cannot take much wine," she said in an undertone. "Don't force him."

Feihong snorted, and replied, with a smile: "How do you know him so well, Miss? You've only just met him."

Overcome with shyness and annoyance, Jiaoniang glanced at Shen Chun. Then she glared at Feihong, and growled, "You saucy little cat!"

Feihong concealed a smile as she glanced first at Shen Chun and then at Jiaoniang. Then she bent to whisper to the young mistress: "Miss, the weather is not at all hot today. Why is your face so flushed?"

Jiaoniang boiled with rage inside, but in front of the others she could not show it. There was nothing for it but to bite her lip and grip her sash tightly. Wang Wenrui noticed the mournful look on his nephew's face. "You've had a long and tiring ride, my boy," he said boisterously. "There's nothing like a few cups of wine for making travel fatigue vanish."

But Shen Chun was adamant. "I am sorry, Uncle," he said, "but I really cannot drink any more wine."

He stole a surreptitious glance at Jiaoniang, and caught her gazing at him with amorous eyes. His heart beat wildly in his breast, and his limbs

狼狈,支吾道:"敢问妹妹平日里可饮酒吗?"

赵夫人道:"娇娘天性不饮。"

此时,娇娘装着用手帕抹嘴,低头偷觑申纯,正与往这边瞟来的申纯打了个照面,二人又都忙不迭地避开,彼此的脸愈发红了。

赵夫人怕冷了场,便对立在身后的飞红道:"飞红,你去给三哥斟酒。"飞红轻移莲步,转到申纯面前,满满斟了一杯酒,扮出千娇百媚、风情万种的模样,道:"表少爷请满饮此杯。"

申纯看看赵夫人,面有难色,道:"舅母,按理说长者赐,不敢辞。只是小甥失意功名,心怀郁闷,不敢贪杯。"

娇娘闻言,伸手悄悄扯了一下飞红的衣袖,轻声道:"看三哥似不胜酒力,就不要勉强他了。"

飞红鼻子里哼了一声,笑道:"小姐初见表少爷,怎便恁般相知哩?"

娇娘含着带怨瞟了一眼申纯,又白了一眼飞红,低头嗔道:"你个多嘴的死丫头。"

飞红看看申纯,又瞧瞧娇娘,掩嘴一笑,俯身在娇娘耳边低语道:"小姐,这天气还不到热的时节,为何脸红如此?"

娇娘心中着恼,当着这么多人的面,也不好发作,只好紧咬下唇,手指儿绕着裙带,不吭一声。王文瑞见申纯面露难色,哈哈一笑道:"贤甥远路而来,鞍

trembled so violently that he knocked his wine cup over, the wine splashing over himself, which made him lose his composure completely. His aunt ordered Feihong to clean the young man up. At this point, Wang Wenrui came to the rescue, by saying, "I see you really must be tired, my boy. Perhaps you'd better go to your room and rest? Tomorrow, we can have a proper welcoming banquet for you, and a family chat."

His wife chimed in, ordering Feihong to escort Jiaoniang to her room.

The maid servant glanced back at Shen Chun as she helped her young mistress to her feet.

In fact, Jiaoniang had been wanting to stay a little longer, but she had no choice but to leave. Just as she reached the door, she could not help giving Shen Chun a backward glance. With the young man's eyes glued to their backs, Jiaoniang and Feihong disappeared from sight. Chagrined, Shen Chun turned to his uncle and aunt, and said, "It was in deference to my parents' wishes that I came to pay my respects to you. I may stay only two days before returning home."

Wang Wenrui was taken aback. "Oh, you've made a long and difficult journey, and found our house in veritable turmoil," he said. "I want you to stay here and help me to put the place in order. Let's hear no more talk about going home. Just you make yourself at home here. Consider yourself one of the family. If there's anything you need, don't hesitate to speak up."

Now that he had had a glimpse of Jiaoniang, the young man was all too willing to stay for a while, his ambition to rise in the world having quite vanished from his mind. So, hearing his uncle's exhortation, he responded with alacrity. "In that case, sir, I will respect your wishes," he humbly replied.

His aunt thereupon ordered Wang Zhong to see Shen Chun to his quarters in the study in the east wing.

Having moved into his uncle's house, Shen Chun spent his days examining the mansion and helping with household affairs. He saw Jiaoniang

马劳顿,多饮几杯,也好解乏。"

申纯推辞道:"小甥实在是饮不下了。"

说着又偷觑娇娘,见娇娘也不住地往自己这边瞧,秋波盈盈,似有情于己,胸膛里一颗心就禁不住狂跳起来,一时手忙脚乱,竟将酒杯弄翻,淋淋漓漓洒了一身,愈发窘迫不安起来。赵夫人忙命飞红为他擦拭。王文瑞便打圆场说:"贤甥一路劳顿,既然不能饮了,就先回房歇息。且待明日重摆酒宴,再叙家常。"

赵夫人对飞红道:"飞红,你送小姐先回绣阁去。"

飞红口中答应,瞥了一眼申纯,将娇娘扶起道:"小姐,咱们走吧!"

娇娘有心再呆一会儿,可又说不出口来,只得由飞红扶着起身,临出门时又忍不住回头看了申纯一眼。目送娇娘、飞红走出中堂,申纯也自觉有些失态,便对王文瑞、赵夫人道:"小甥领二亲尊命,前来拜候舅父、舅母,小住两日,便要返回。"

王文瑞道:"贤甥远来辛苦,况我府中事务繁忙,正欲唤你前来帮着料理,归去之话休要再提。你且安心住下,这里有我和你舅母、表妹、表弟,也是一家子团圆。你就把这里当作自家,需要什么但说无妨,千万不要见外才是。"

申纯一见娇娘,功名之心顿释,巴不得多住些日子,听到舅父挽留,忙答应道:"既然如此,小甥遵命就是。"

often, but whenever he did so there were always other people around, and so he had to observe the proprieties, the slightest suggestion of flirting being out of the question. He could not guess from the girl's demeanor towards him whether she was trying to be close or distant, warm or cold. Nor could he ever seem to find a chance to be alone with Jiaoniang so that he could pour his heart out to her.

As for Jiaoniang, she was after all a young girl. Although she was well read in *The Four Books* and *The Five Classics*, and had heard stories of chaste maidens and virtuous wives from her parents, nevertheless in her heart she secretly admired romantic heroines who eloped with their lovers or died for love, and so on. At the same time, she was horrified at the prospect of dying an old maid. Ever since she had set eyes on the grown-up Shen Chun, her heart had been all of a flutter. She had no doubt that this gentle and scholarly yet dashing young man was the person she wanted to share her life with. But she knew such a major event as her marriage was up to her parents to decide; she had no say in the matter at all. In the meantime, she spent most of her time lounging around her boudoir, listlessly playing chess or painting.

One morning, the spring rain came down in torrents, only clearing up after noon. When it did, though, it left the garden full of rosy fragrant clouds of apricot blossoms. Jiaoniang told her maid Xiaohui to take her embroidery frame out into the arbor. As she was at her work, a sudden gust of wind blew some apricot flower petals onto the embroidery. Jiaoniang stopped what she was doing, and picked the petals up. Suddenly there flashed into her mind an old saying about flowers fading after 100 days and youth fading fast away. A pang of sorrow pierced her heart, and tears welled up in her eyes. In this moment of agony, she heard a voice behind her saying, "Miss, what are you doing here, embroidering all by yourself?"

Jiaoniang hastily wiped her eyes, and, turning her head, saw that Feihong had crept up on her. "I was just passing the time with a spot of embroidery work," she said, lowering her head and flicking the flower petals

赵夫人于是吩咐王忠带申纯到东厢书房歇息。

申纯在舅父家住下后，整日周旋于堂庑之间，帮助料理府中事务，时常见到娇娘，可每次见面，四周总有旁人，只得依礼行事，并不敢露出半点轻狂。再暗暗看那娇娘对自己的态度，总是若即若离，不远不近，令人揣摩不透。虽想寻个两人单独相处的机会，向她表明心迹，却苦于无机可乘，心里不免如同这乍暖还寒的春天一般，时暖时凉。

却说娇娘正当妙龄，不由不思量自家的终身大事，虽说自小读了些四书五经，听爹娘讲的也是烈女节妇，但心中却暗慕那夜奔相如的文君，甘为情死的紫玉，自择佳配的莺莺。深恐红颜失配，抱恨终身。自打那日见了申纯，芳心不觉为之所动。暗忖道：三哥性情温良，风流倜傥，且又知根知底，倒是可托终身。只是这婚姻大事须由父母作主，自己又如何开口？因此上终日里情思绵绵，懒对妆台，无心棋画，郁郁寡欢。

这一日春雨霏霏，午后方晴，满院杏花纷飞，恍若香雪粉雾。娇娘让丫环小慧在廊下支起绣床，独自绣花解闷。正绣时一阵轻风吹来，几瓣杏花飘落下来，娇娘停针拈起花瓣，不由得想到花无百日好，人生能几春。顿时愁肠百结，珠泪盈盈。正在悲苦缠绵之际，就听身后有人说道："小姐好兴致，独自一人在

away.

Coming closer, Feihong noticed that her young mistress' eyes were tinged with red. She glanced at the embroidery. It was a picture of two gaily colored butterflies flitting on a white silk background. The girl guessed what was on Jiaoniang's mind. "Miss, I think you must be regretting the passing of spring," she said, teasingly.

Jiaoniang was horrified at the thought of others guessing what was tormenting her, and stammered, "I was concentrating on my embroidery. I was taking no notice of the spring or anything else. What on earth is there to regret?"

This did not fool the crafty Feihong, who then asked, meaningfully: "Well then, if it's not the passing of spring that pains you, why did you stop plying your needle and start dropping tears?"

"I was feeling fatigued, that's why I stopped working for a while," replied Jiaoniang, in a matter-of-fact tone. "And I don't know what you mean by 'dropping tears'."

The maid servant peered closely at Jiaoniang's face, and said, "Your eyelids are bright pink, Miss. You have been crying, haven't you?"

"Oh, that's just a chill from the wind," Jiaoniang quickly replied.

Afraid that her young mistress might get angry if she probed any further, Feihong changed the subject: "Those butterflies look very realistic, Miss!"

Jiaoniang was irked by the maid servant's chatter, and simply answered, "Really?"

"Oh, yes," continued the little chatterbox. "It's so charming the way they are flying together, don't you think Miss? There must be love in the heart of the person who embroidered them, mustn't there?"

At this, Jiaoniang snapped, "Stop this nonsense about love! You are more like a garrulous old woman than a young girl. You are so insensitive, and you have no sense of shame."

But Feihong was a headstrong girl, and not easy to browbeat. She and

这儿绣什么呢?"

娇娘拭泪回顾,却见是飞红逦迤而来,便说道:"解闷儿罢了,还能绣些什么?"说着低头将花瓣弹落。

飞红来到近前,见娇娘凤眼微红,又见白绫上绣着一对五彩翩跹的大蝴蝶,心中已明白一二,遂试探着问道:"小姐莫不是在伤春吧?"

娇娘惟恐心事被人察觉,忙遮掩道:"我只管绣花,不知春色何在,伤得哪门子春?"

飞红察言观色,狡黠地问道:"不是伤春,又为何停针落泪?"

娇娘冷冷道:"我因身子倦乏暂且歇手,哪里又落泪了?"

飞红紧盯着娇娘道:"眼皮都哭成了粉桃,还说没有落泪?"

"噢,是风迷了眼。"

飞红怕娇娘着恼,岔开话头道:"我来看看小姐绣的花样,呀,这两只蝴蝶翩翩跹跹,如同活了一般。"

娇娘无心与她多言,淡淡地道:"是么?"

"当然是了。你瞧这双双对对,好不令人羡煞,心中无情,焉能绣出此物?"

娇娘不悦道:"这里好像有只巧嘴八哥,鼓唇弄舌,说什么有情无情的,一个女孩子家,老皮老脸的,说个不停,也不害羞!"

Jiaoniang were about the same age. Besides, they were on intimate terms from being together every day. "Well, Miss, as a maid servant who comes from a humble family I may be insensitive — compared to a refined young lady like yourself. But young ladies with tender feelings do tend to sob out their feelings to the wind and feel anguish at the sight of the flowers fading."

Jiaoniang's cheeks turned bright red, as she hissed, "You impertinent little hussy! I'll stop that mouth of yours for good if I hear any more of your claptrap!"

Feihong simply laughed. "All right, all right," she said. "Why don't we take a stroll in the flower garden on such a nice day as this? Never mind embroidery."

But her young mistress was reluctant to stir. "The truth is, I don't feel like making any exertion," she said. "Besides, looking at flowers and grass would only be vexatious."

Feihong prattled on. "Please don't think that I'm poking my nose in where it isn't wanted, Miss, but of late I've noticed that your dresses have been becoming slack on you, and that your waistline has been narrowing. So I know there must be something on your mind. And now I come to think of it, it's strange that you should have such a careworn expression all the time, when you live here in the lap of luxury and your parents treat you like a precious jewel. If I were to hazard a guess, I would say that you are hearkening to the mournful cry of the cuckoo which misses its mate, and that you are anxious because the springtime of your youth is passing ... and you can't bring yourself to confess your feelings. Isn't that it?"

These words hit home, of course, but Jiaoniang remained perfectly composed. "The mournful cry of the cuckoo?" she drawled, in a tone of derision. "The passing of spring? What have such notions to do with me?"

Feihong retorted, eagerly: "Of course not, of course not. But you must be longing for someone to spill your heart out to ... there in your lonely boudoir. But it won't be long before your father starts talking about

"我们做丫头的生来下贱，比不得千金小姐，自是老脸老皮的。可那细脸细皮、嫩皮嫩肉的小姐，却会临风洒泪，对花伤怀。"原来飞红与娇娘年纪相仿，平日里相处惯熟，故任着性子揶揄打趣。

娇娘急了，红了香腮道："做死的小蹄子，再要胡言乱语，仔细撕了你那张花嘴。"

飞红笑道："好了好了，不说这个了。今日天气晴好，咱们何不到花园散散心，只管绣这些东西做甚？"

娇红推托道："我懒得行动，看那花花草草，愈添烦愁。"

飞红道："不是我多嘴多舌，我看近来小姐绣裙宽了三四褶，腰肢瘦了一两围，就知你心中有事。转念一想，小姐每日里锦衣玉食，老爷夫人又视若掌上明珠，哪里会有什么难事，惹得你这样愁上眉梢？我猜呀，小姐定是听了那子规悲啼，怕春光老去……可又说不出口来，是也不是？"

娇娘闻听此言，触动心事，却冷着脸道："什么子规悲啼，春光老去，与我何干？"

飞红不待她说完，便接言道："是哩，是哩，是与小姐无干。不过闺阁中形单影只，身边也该有个说体己话的姐夫了。待老爷发话，定有人来说亲，只不知……"

arranging a match for you. It's just that. . . ."

Jiaoniang angrily cut her short. "For Heaven's sake, you little scatter-brain," she yelled. "Stop talking utter nonsense!"

But there was no stopping the maid servant once she got an idea into her head. With a silly grin on her face, she carried on: "I wonder what sort of a man would take your fancy. Perhaps you could give me just a tiny hint?"

Her young mistress was crestfallen. She blushed and lowered her head, at a complete loss for words.

Feihong could not help noticing her embarrassment. Looking around carefully, she tiptoed up to Jiaoniang, and whispered in her ear: "There is nobody her, Miss, but the two of us. You may speak freely, and I promise that I will help you in any way I can."

At this moment, Jiaoniang felt that she really needed to confide in someone. Looking up at Feihong's open and honest face, she was ready to pour her heart out to the girl, but the words somehow seemed to get stuck in her throat.

Feihong was astute enough to know that the one matter of supreme importance to a young girl was not one she could lightly unburden herself of even to an intimate acquaintance. She smiled, and said, "Well, let me make a suggestion. Which one do you like best: Master Li, the son of the prefect head or the son of Squire Zhao?"

Jiaoniang wrinkled her nose in disdain. "Those coxcombs?" she snorted. "They just trade on their families' wealth and power. They have no education, and are simply dressed-up dunderheads. If I were to marry a playboy like that, I would be like a delicate flower that has been plucked by a rustic boor."

"So, I suppose you prefer gallant young men of talent?" Feihong kept on probing.

Jiaoniang gave a mirthless laugh. "Oh, no," she said. "Men of talent have no attraction for me at all."

娇娘怒气冲冲地打断飞红的话头，嗔道："死丫头还不住口，只管胡乱说些什么！"

飞红却不肯罢休，嬉皮笑脸地道："嗯……不知小姐心上想要什么样的人？可能向婢女略说一二？"

娇娘一听，羞得双颊飞红，粉颈低垂，心想："我一个女孩儿家，这事儿教我怎么说得出口？"

飞红见小姐娇羞难当，一言不发，就知她不好意思说，便四下里看了看，走近前来，俯耳道："这里就你我两人，小姐但说无妨。说出来，我也好替你周全周全。"

"这……"娇娘此时的确想找个人倾诉心事，见飞红一脸真诚，便有心说出来，可话到嘴边，还是咽了回去。

飞红知道这有关终身大事的话，让小姐自己明明白白地说出来，比登天还难，便笑了笑，说道："我来替小姐说，这一郡之内，像李太守的衙内，赵员外的公子，这些泼天价富贵的子弟可好么？"

娇娘鼻子里哼了一声，道："都是些纨绔子弟，仗了爷娘老子的权势银钱，个个不学无术，不过是些纸鸳凤，草麒麟，金玉其外罢了。若嫁与这般子弟，那才叫好花输与村郎折。我是断不肯答应。"

飞红见娇娘一脸不屑，进一步试探道："那小姐是要拣个读书风流的才子了？"

娇娘冷笑道："那也不见得，就说那才子，也有不

"Why not?"

"Sima Xiangru of the Han Dynasty was reckoned to be a great genius of all time. But as soon as he became famous, he looked down on his old literary companions of the taverns. No, gallant young men of talent have shallow emotions and lack sincerity. They bend whichever way the wind blows; one can't rely on them."

Feihong pretended to be angry. "You turn your nose up at wealth and power, and talent and a fine appearance are not to be trusted!" she exclaimed. "What on earth do you want?"

Jiaoniang sighed, and said, "Beautiful women have always had tragic fates. A fine flower tends to get snapped off easily. I would be quite content to find a soul-mate with whom I could share my life and feelings."

No sooner were the words out of her mouth than she realized that she had been indiscreet. She hastily covered her blushes with a handkerchief. The meaning of this had not escaped Feihong, however, who smiled and said, "Marriages are in the hands of fate. You, Miss, never leave this house. You will have to depend entirely on your parents and the efforts of a matchmaker. How can you find your soul-mate, as you call him? But there is a young man not too far away who has splendid talent and a fine appearance. Besides, you have known each other since childhood. I think you are destined for each other."

These words hit the nail on the head, but to conceal her confusion Jiaoniang made a show of indignation. "What kind of disgraceful talk is that?" she shrilled. "The person I assume you are referring to and I stand in the relation of brother and sister. Marriage is quite out of the question!"

Feihong thought gleefully to herself: "Aha, so you've let the cat out of the bag!" Then said aloud, "But what harm is there in mentioning it? That would make you even closer; it would be an even more wonderful match, wouldn't it?"

Jiaoniang rose to her feet, her face grimly set. "You mischief-making little hussy!" she snarled. "Don't you know that walls have ears? Are you

同。"

"怎么不同？"

"就说那汉代的司马相如才高八斗，也算得上是古今第一才子了。可一旦驷马高车得坐，还不是将随他当垆卖酒的文君轻弃了吗？唉，风流才子大多薄情寡义，见异思迁，哪里又靠得住了！"

飞红闻言，假做发愁道："有钱有势的不好，有才有貌的又靠不住，这可如何是好？"

娇娘轻叹一声道："自古红颜薄命，好花易折。但得个同心子，生同舍，死共穴，相知相重一辈子，也就知足了。"

说罢自觉失言，忙用绡帕捂住羞红的粉面。飞红心中明镜似的，笑道："姻缘本是命中注定，小姐大门不出，二门不迈，只能靠父母之命、媒妁之言了，焉能得个同心子？哎，眼前倒有个人才貌俱佳，又是与小姐自幼相知，恰是天生地就的一对儿。"

娇娘被飞红一语道破心事，顿时娇羞难当，佯怒道："你一个小妮子家，净说些没羞没耻的话，我和他兄妹排连，怎能姻亲相结？"

飞红心想，我还没说出是谁，你倒不打自招了，便道："这也是好事，说说何妨？况且亲上加亲，岂不更美？"

娇娘变了脸起身，压低嗓子道："死丫头，就不怕

trying to vex me to death?"

The maid servant realized that she had gone too far, and, anxious not to bring further trouble upon herself, waved her hands. "Oh Miss, I'm so sorry. It's all my fault for being such a busybody. I know I talk too much. Well, it's getting late, and I have to go and attend to your mother."

As she turned to go, she thought, "I know just about everything that's going through your mind, Miss. You can't hide it from me!"

At this point, the reader must be wondering what kind of a girl this Feihong was, she was on such familiar and jesting terms with her young mistress. In fact, she was about the same age as Jiaoniang. She had been born the only child of a scholar's family. Her father had tutored her from an early age in the arts of the lute, chess, calligraphy and painting, and she was particularly accomplished at composing poetry. So she was almost as educated as Jiaoniang. However, her life, from the first, had been dogged by misfortune. At the age of 12, she had lost both parents. Unable to afford the funeral fees, she had offered to sell herself into service to earn the money to bury her parents. Just at that time, her noble gesture had come to the notice of Wang Wenrui, who arranged the funerals out of charity, and took the girl into his household. Quick-witted and personable, she soon rose in her employers' esteem above the ranks of the other maid servants, and she became the personal attendant of the mistress of the house. In the past year or two, she had become aware of the relations between the sexes, and she had secretly been harboring a desire to repay with her body the kindness the old master had shown to her. But she was thwarted in this ambition by the knowledge that Wang Wenrui's wife, although kind-hearted and genial in other ways, would not brook the introduction of a concubine into the household. She was instantly attracted to the suave young scholar Shen Chun, when he came to visit, but as he was far above her station she could do nothing but pine for him from a distance. Now, seeing Jiaoniang so pensive and distracted, Feihong guessed that she too had fallen in love with the dashing young man. By various indirect questions and hints, she had

隔墙有耳暗中听了去?可是要找死么?"

飞红见小姐认真起来,也怕再说下去自寻没趣,连连摆手说道:"算了,算了,全怪我多管闲事、多嘴多舌,行了吧?时候不早了,我且看看夫人去。"

随即转身就走,心中暗道:"你五分心事,我已知三分,何须抵口遮藏,死不承认!"

说到此处,诸位看官不免要问这飞红是何许人,怎敢与小姐调侃说笑。原来这飞红与娇娘同龄,本是一位老秀才的独生女儿,自幼受父亲教诲,琴棋书画样样来得,尤擅填词,文才与娇娘不相上下。只是生来命苦,十二岁那年父母双亡,因无钱殡殓,只得自卖葬亲。正巧被王文瑞碰上,为其孝心所动,当下令人厚葬了老秀才夫妇。飞红无依无靠,从此在通判府中当了个大丫环。她心灵眼活,讨人欢心,不久就成了赵夫人的贴身丫头,自比别的丫环要有些脸面。这两年渐懂男女之事,暗暗感念老爷葬父埋母之恩,便思以身相报。可那赵夫人虽然贤慧敦厚,惟独对老爷纳妾之事存着戒心,故飞红不敢到老爷面前有所表示。风流倜傥的申纯一进通判府,飞红一眼便相中了他。不过尊卑有序,空想无望,只能是望梅止渴罢了。近来见小姐日日魂不守舍,忽忽若有所思,想是与那申家公子有关,便以微言试探,可小姐守口如瓶,不露痕迹。适才从厨房安排晚饭回来,路过此处,

tried to discover if this was so, but Jiaoniang had remained as tight as a clam. It had been quite by chance that, returning from the house, where she had been arranging the evening meal, she had come across Jiaoniang weeping, with her unfinished embroidery on her lap. Suspecting that a matter of the heart was the cause of this, she had probed a little too deeply, and met with a stinging rebuff. Nevertheless, she began to hatch a crafty plan. "Well, Miss," she thought to herself, "you may prefer to pine in secret, just like the heroine in *The Romance of the Western Bower*, but just see if I don't act as your matchmaker!"

Meanwhile, dusk had fallen, and the moon had risen. Jiaoniang sat locked in gloom and frustrated longing. Suddenly, she was aware of a light footfall behind her. She whirled round, to see Shen Chun standing there, dressed in his scholar's cap and gown. Her heart began to pound, and she turned back in confusion.

The young man had been strolling that way, when he caught sight of Jiaoniang bent over her embroidery and sighing. Glancing around and seeing that there was nobody in the vicinity, he thanked Heaven for this rare opportunity to reveal his true feelings to Jiaoniang. In a low voice, he said, "Miss, why are you sighing in the moonlight? Are you tormented by some worry or longing?"

Jiaoniang did not know how to reply. She hung her head, and uttered not a word. After a while, she recovered her composure, and said, "Sir, where have you come from? It is already dark, and the spring evenings are chilly. You really should be resting."

Shen Chun knew that these were evasive words, and he pressed his advantage, saying, "Although the spring chill may be severe, it can't freeze spring thoughts."

Jiaoniang stared at the young man. She was going to say something, but stopped herself in time. Turning on her heel, she stalked off. Shen Chun was at a loss what to do: He couldn't cry out to her, nor could he pursue her. All he did was sigh, "Ah, Jiaoniang, Jiaoniang, what really is

见娇娘停针落泪，料得是有心事，这才凑到近前与她说说体己话，不料反落了个没趣。心想："小姐呀小姐，你虽暗恋情深，我亦颇知佳趣。果然你要做那莺莺，只怕少不得我这红娘为你穿针引线。"

再说娇娘被飞红道破心事，愈发情思绵绵，不觉已是暮云四合，月兔东升，思量春夜良宵，独坐寂寥，不由长叹一声。忽觉身后有脚步轻响，惊得回头观望，却见申纯儒巾青衫翩然而至，芳心早突突跳作一团，慌忙把头转回来。

申纯本是路过此处，一眼瞥见娇娘倚着绣床儿颦眉凝睇，悄然长叹，似有动情之意。看看左右无人，心中暗自庆幸，天赐良机，何不就此上前向她表明心迹？便趋步来至近前，低声问道："妹妹为何对月长叹？是心有所思，还是意有所念？"

娇娘一时不知如何对答，埋头不语，半晌稳住心神，凝妆正色道："三哥这是从何处而来？天色已晚，春寒逼人，也该歇息了。"

申纯见娇娘乱以他语，岔开话头，只得逼进一步道："春寒虽重，春意却浓！"

娇娘看看申纯，欲言又止，忽地转身而去。申纯喊不得追不得，茫然不知所措，不禁心中悲叹："娇娘啊娇娘，真不知你心中是何主意？难道看不出我情有所钟吗？只可怜我这单相思实实害煞人也。"

in your heart, I wonder? Surely you can see that my affections are fixed on you. I fear that I will die of unrequited love!"

A sudden gust of night wind chilled Shen Chun to the marrow. He shivered uncontrollably, and hurried back to his room. But he found himself so dispirited that he could neither sit nor stand. Finally he unrolled a scroll of Tang Dynasty poetry, and began to read it to comfort himself. In the silence of the dreary night he heard the sound of midnight being signaled from the drum tower. "How will I ever get through this chilly night," he groaned. But before he knew it, he had fallen into a deep sleep slumped over the table.

He had the hazy feeling that he was taking a stroll along a corridor, when he suddenly came to a beautiful spot. At first, he thought it was the flower garden in his uncle's mansion, but when he looked more closely, he discovered that it was not. Filled with confusion, he suddenly saw, in the midst of the flowers, Jiaoniang looking radiantly beautiful and smiling shyly at him and stretching out her loving arms towards him. Overcome with joy, Shen Chun rushed towards her, oblivious of all else. He clasped her tightly to his chest. Her warm and fragrant body was so soft as if it had no bones. Jiaoniang yielded to his caress, saying, "My darling, I know how you have suffered!"

Shen Chun was intoxicated with happiness. He mumbled words of love. He was just about to kiss Jiaoniang's perfumed lips, when he heard the warbling of an oriole. At that moment, the girl tore herself from his arms, and fled. Shen Chun cried out in distress and indignation. He was about to give chase, but he suddenly realized that Jiaoniang had vanished. "Jiaoniang!" he was shouting when he woke up. Rubbing his eyes, he saw the rising sun peeping through his window, and heard a pair of orioles twittering in the treetops. It had only been a dream, after all! For a long time, Shen Chun sat disconsolate. Eventually, he wandered out, making his way to the flower garden.

The garden was a fairly large one. On the left of it there was the Cher-

一阵夜风袭来，侵肌彻骨，申纯不禁打了个寒颤，只得回到书房。他坐也不是，站也不是，万般无奈，于孤灯下展卷吟诵唐人诗赋，聊以自慰。一个人凄凄凉凉，听得谯楼响了二鼓，心道："这寒夜如何捱得到天明也！"不觉伏案沉沉睡去。

恍恍惚惚中觉着自己信步走出游廊，来到一处好景致，乍一看好似通判府的后花园，可仔细一看又不是。正在狐疑之际，忽见百花丛中，蝉首蛾眉的娇娘巧笑含羞，正在春情脉脉地向自己频频招手。真是喜从天降，当下不顾一切奔了过去，紧紧将娇娘抱在怀中。这妙人儿果真是软玉温香，柔若无骨。娇娘也不相拒，只说："三哥，小妹想得你好苦啊！"

申纯心如中酒，口中喃喃道："巧笑倩兮，美目盼兮……好个多情的妹妹。"说着便欲吻那香唇，忽听得黄鹂儿鸣唱声声，娇娘挣脱怀抱便走。急得申纯心中直骂："泼毛贼，坏了你家少爷的好事。"抬腿欲追，可娇娘转眼间就不见了踪影。申纯口中大呼"娇娘"，一时惊醒，揉眼一看，哪里有什么娇娘。只见窗外红日高照，枝头儿一对黄鹂正叽叽喳喳地唱和，方知是黄粱一梦，心中十分懊恼。怔了半晌，无法排解，便漫步来到后花园。

通判府的后花园占地不小，左有"惜花轩"，右有"凝翠轩"。惜花轩前又有一处"天香圃"，种满了牡

41

ish the Flowers Pavilion, while on the right was the Lush Greenery Pavilion. In front of the former was the Heavenly Fragrance Garden, which was full of peonies, and beside this was a stretch of artificial mountains and a man-made lake. In the lake was a small pavilion, called the Viewing the Stream Pavilion. From here, there was a view of lush and fragrant trees of all descriptions.

Shen Chun walked deeper into the garden, following a cobblestone path. He saw the Cherish the Flowers Pavilion in the distance. And there, leaning on a balustrade in an upper window of the pavilion, he espied Jiaoniang! The girl was clad in a silk gown of magnolia color, and her eyes were filled with tears. Shen Chun's own eyes lit up at the sight. The first thought that occurred to him was that his dream had been a message, summoning him to this sequestered spot for a lovers' tryst. Fighting back an impulse to rush to her, for fear he might frighten her, he proceeded slowly and calmly.

Jiaoniang had been too careworn to sleep well the previous night. After breakfast she had listlessly tried to do some needlework in the company of her maids, but soon gave that up and wandered into the flower garden in search of solace. But everywhere she looked the very blossoms seemed to form pairs, not to mention the butterflies dancing in the air in couples, and this only served to deepen her gloom.

"You seem to find the scenery here absorbing, Miss."

Startled, Jiaoniang whirled round, her heart thumping, for she recognized the voice as that of Shen Chun. She glared at him in indignation, and then averted her gaze and hung her head in modesty. The young man reproached himself for his impetuousness, bowed hastily, and said, "Miss, I seem to have frightened upon you. Please forgive my presumption."

Jiaoniang looked at him with an expression full of meaning, but said not a word. Awkwardly, Shen Chun said, "May I ask why you are all alone in this place?"

The girl did not reply, but demurely turned to view the peonies. This

丹。天香圃旁是一带叠石连绵的假山湖水,湖心上曲栏红槛,卧着一个翘角飞檐玲珑剔透的小亭,题为"望溪亭"。放眼园中,万木争春,姹紫嫣红。

申纯沿着鹅卵石砌成的小径向花园深处走去,远远望见惜花轩上一身玉兰色蜀锦衣裙的娇娘正在独自凭栏凝睇,顿时眼睛一亮,心想适才梦中佳兆,指引自家来此与娇娘幽会。本想拔脚奔过去,可又怕惊吓了娇娘,只得轻手轻脚缓缓走近。

却说那娇娘满腹心事,也是一夜辗转难眠。早饭后,安顿丫环们做针线,自家则来到花园散心。触目都是花儿并蒂,蝶儿成双,反到愈添愁绪,不禁连连叹息。

"对景悠悠暗自吁,妹妹好情致呀。"

娇娘不提防此处有人,惊得芳心乱颤,回头见是申纯,含怨带嗔剜了他一眼,复又侧脸垂颈不语。申纯心中自责不迭,匆忙一揖到地,说道:"妹妹不要惊慌,恕愚兄冒昧。"

娇娘面沉似水,一语不发。申纯搭讪着道:"请问妹妹独自一人在此做什么?"

娇娘不睬,转脸去看轩外牡丹。申纯觉得好没意思,本想赌气走开,可又一想女孩儿总是怕羞些,况且机会难得,于是在脸上堆笑道:"妹妹,你看这园中牡丹,欲开未开,似有惆怅之意。愚兄不揣愚陋,想以

made Shen Chun even more embarrassed. His first instinct was to beat a hasty retreat, but on second thoughts he realized that Jiaoniang was shy, and, besides, this was a rare opportunity. So he wreathed his face in smiles. "Just look at the peonies, Miss," he said. "See how they long to blossom, but cannot. They seem so sad. At the risk of making myself look foolish, I would like to compose a poem on this subject. I hope you will refrain from laughing at my poor versifying."

Without waiting for Jiaoniang to reply, he thereupon recited extempore:

"Whisps of whitewash are stirred as you lean on the wall,
The rising sun is reflected in your red gauze shawl.
Your heart is crushed by a ponderous weight.
Spare a thought for the pining man at your gate.
To beauty and grace distressed by the spring.
What anguished thoughts does this season bring?
Anguished at the absence of your longed-for swain,
Cherish the Flowers Pavilion is filled with pain."

He then took up pen and ink, and with expert flourishes wrote the poem he had just composed on a sheet of the finest paper. With both hands, he presented it to Jiaoniang.

The girl had been impressed by his masterly verse making, and by his charming voice ardent with emotion. Her heart had already been warmed by the thought that he was a person who could understand her feelings, and now that she had seen with her own eyes how graceful his brush strokes were, her admiration for him increased even further. However, she was loath to betray any sign of this, in case Shen Chun lost respect for her. All she did was to give him a quick glance, and continue gazing at the scenery as before, without taking the paper. The young man was mortified. He felt as though he had been doused in icy water, and shuddered from head to toe. At a loss what to do, he thought to himself, biting his lip hard: "You heartless slip of a girl! How dare you humiliate me like this? If you won't

此为题吟咏两句,还望妹妹不要见笑。"

说罢不待娇娘发言,便朗吟道:

"乱惹祥烟倚粉墙,绛罗轻卷映朝阳。

芳心一点千重束,肯念凭阑人断肠?

娇姿质艳不胜春,何意无言恨转深。

惆怅东君不相顾,空余一片惜花心。"

吟罢,就着轩中的文房四宝,援笔挥毫,将二绝写于薛涛笺上,双手捧与娇娘。

娇娘见申纯出口成章,且句句关情,心中暗喜,已将申纯认作知音。及至目睹笺上字迹龙飞凤舞,笔如云烟,更添了几分爱慕之意。可又不愿表露出来,生怕申纯将自家看轻了,故而扫了一眼,却不伸手去接,依旧转脸观景。申纯见娇娘无动于衷,如同冰水灌顶,一下子从头凉到了脚。不禁咬牙暗道:"好个无情的妹妹,也就是在你面前,我才如此低三下四。今天你若不接这诗稿,我便撕了它,立即回成都去,再不见你也就是了。"

想到此,伸着手朗声说道:"请妹妹不吝赐教。"

娇娘也觉得再不接过诗稿,实在让申纯下不了台阶,便转过身来抽笺在手,垂首观看,本想对说几句话,一时间万语千言如鲠在喉,竟化作几滴泪珠儿

accept my poem I'll rip it to pieces, and go straight back to Chengdu, and never see you again!"

He tried again. Coaxingly, he said, "Please don't spurn my gift."

Jiaoniang was reluctant to hurt Shen Chun's feelings, so she turned and took the paper. As she bent her head to read the poem, a thousand things she wanted to say welled up inside her, but the words stuck in her throat and turned into teardrops, which rolled down her cheeks. A warm glow seemed to suffuse Shen Chun's heart when he saw Jiaoniang take the paper, but the sight of her tears put him back into a state of alarm. Just at that moment, they heard a voice calling, "Miss, Miss! Your mother wants you." It was the maid servant Xiaohui.

Jiaoniang glanced at Shen Chun. Her lips started to part, but then a frown creased her brow, and she said nothing. Stuffing the poem into her sleeve, she hurried away. Shen Chun, who had been agog to hear what she had been on the point of saying was left standing like a wooden pillar, stupefied at the way this fortuitous meeting had suddenly ended in a fiasco. Downcast, the young man made his way back to his study.

滚落下来。见娇娘接过诗笺，申纯当下心暖血热，忽见娇娘对笺落泪，不免重又慌张。正在犹豫之际，就听见小慧直着嗓子呼喊："小姐，小姐，夫人叫你呐。"

娇娘瞅瞅申纯，芳唇欲启，又轻轻一蹙蛾眉，什么都没说，低头将诗笺藏于袖中，转身飘然离去。申纯原想娇娘总会有所表示，可她连一个字都没出口，看来今日这场相会又是枉然，痴立半晌，只得怏怏回到书房。

娇红记

Chapter Two
Pledge Made in a Cosy Room

Jiaoniang had been ready to open her heart to Shen Chun when they met unexpectedly in Cherish the Flowers Pavilion, and he had made her a present of his poem. But she had been forestalled by the call from Xiaohui, and, fearing a scolding from her mother if she delayed, had left immediately.

That night, she did not sleep well, and in the morning she felt heavy-headed and unsteady. She was gloomy and out of sorts. After paying her morning call on her mother, she sat down to her needlework. But her fingers were sluggish that day. Seeing that her maids Xiaohui and Ziyan were playing truant, Jiaoniang furtively took out Shen Chun's poem from its hiding place in a cosmetics case. She had unfurled it and just started to peruse it, when in tripped Feihong. Jiaoniang quickly put the paper away, and turned to find Feihong looking at her archly. "What are you doing sitting here dully all by yourself, Miss?" the girl asked. "The other maids have sneaked off, and are fooling around," she said in a tone of reproach. "It's all your fault, Miss. You really mustn't allow this sort of thing to go on, you know. You should exercise stricter control of them."

When her young mistress remained silent, Feihong went on, "The master has accepted an invitation to a friend's house, and the mistress is asleep. So I have some free time to come and cheer you up."

"It is kind of you to be so anxious about me," Jiaoniang replied.

Seeing that Jiaoniang was still careworn, Feihong suggested a stroll in the central courtyard.

"Aren't Mr Shen's chambers next to the central courtyard?" Jiaoniang

第二章　暖阁结盟

再说娇娘与申纯在惜花轩相遇，又看了他的赠诗，本欲应答几句，却听小慧呼唤，怕回得迟了母亲怪怨，只得舍他而归。

夜里回到绣房，满腹心事沉沉，哪里能睡得安稳。早上起来，头重脚轻，心中愈发不爽。待到去母亲处问安回来，见小慧、紫嫣溜出去玩耍，自己一个人却待拈针铺绣，又懒得动弹，便从钿盒中取出诗稿展看，正欲细细品味，就见飞红袅袅婷婷走了进来，急忙将诗笺收了起来。飞红来到近前，眼儿斜睨着娇娘道："小姐怎么一人在房里闷坐？小慧她们必是偷跑出去玩耍，这都是小姐惯下的毛病，长久下去可怎么了得？这些小蹄子也真该管束管束了。"

说罢，见娇娘不答，又说道："今儿个老爷出门应酬去了，这会子夫人也睡着了，我得空来陪你说会儿话解解闷。"

娇娘道："难为姐姐挂念着。"

飞红见娇娘仍是少情无绪，道："咱们到中庭散散步可好？"

had blurted it out before she could stop herself.

Feihong thought to herself: "So, you're still hankering after him, are you?" Aloud, she said, "Mr Shen accompanied the old master when he went out today."

"Well, all right," agreed Jiaoniang, "I'll go for a stroll with you."

"Miss, your trouble is that you are too cautious. Why are you so afraid of the young gentleman? He is one of the family, after all."

"The sexes should keep a respectful distance from one another," retorted Jiaoniang. "It is somewhat inconvenient him being here."

Feihong shot her a quizzical glance. "Inconvenient?" she cried. "So long as one harbors no ulterior motives, I don't think there's any need for anxiety. As they say, if you stand straight you don't have to worry about your shadow slanting. So a pure-minded person should not fear gossip."

Jiaoniang was piqued at this. "Who harbors ulterior motives?" she pouted.

Feihong made a wry mouth, smiled, and said, "Well, that's all right then. Let's go."

With studied indifference, Jiaoniang complied, and off the two of them went to the central courtyard. As they stepped out of the covered walkway into the courtyard, a sudden gust of wind made the corner gate creak. Jiaoniang clutched her maid servant's sleeve in alarm. "What was that noise?" she gasped. "Perhaps someone came in?"

Feihong thought to herself: "What are you so afraid of that you have to go imagining things?" She smiled, and said, "No stranger is going to be blundering in to the courtyard of a mansion like this. It was only a sound made by the wind. Please calm down, Miss."

As they drew level with the eastern study, Jiaoniang peeped through the gauze-covered window. "Feihong, have a look, and tell me if you think the young gentleman's come back yet."

The maid servant also took a look through the window, and said, "No, he's not back yet. Miss, why don't we go inside?" and within wait-

娇娘脱口道:"中庭外那申家哥哥可在么?"

飞红心想:"你也掂记着他呀。"口中忙应道:"申家哥哥陪老爷出去了。"

娇娘想了想,道:"哦,这等我就依了你,且去园中走走。"

飞红道:"小姐也忒谨慎了,自家兄长怕个什么?"

娇娘道:"总是男女有别,不太方便。"

飞红瞧瞧娇娘,说:"有何不便,只要自家心中无事,身正影直,怕他做甚?"

娇娘心中发虚,口中犟道:"谁心中有事了?"

飞红撇一撇嘴,笑道:"没事就好,小姐快走吧。"

娇娘懒洋洋地答应,二人相随着往中庭走去。刚转出游廊,一阵风吹来,角门吱吱响了两声,惊得娇娘一把抓住飞红的衣袖道:"呀,是什么声音,敢是有人来了?"

飞红心说:"哪有这么娇贵的,装模作样。"嘴上却笑道:"咱这深宅大院能有什么人闯入,是风吹门响,小姐直管放宽心就是。"

二人来到东厢书房外,娇娘隔着纱窗向里张望了一下,悄声道:"飞红,你看,是不是三哥已经回来了?"

飞红也贴近纱窗看了看,道:"他还没回来哩。小

ing for Jiaoniang to object, dragged her young mistress into the study.

Inside, the room was spick and span. On the desk were arranged the "four treasures of the study" — writing brush, ink stick, ink slab and paper. A sprig of plum blossom, like a rosy cloud, was in a porcelain jar on a side table. Hanging on the eastern wall was a precious sword, and resting on a stand was an antique lute made of purple sandalwood. On the western wall hung several scroll paintings bearing poems, the work of Shen Chun. Suddenly, Feihong pointed out a poem written in a fine flowing hand on the wallpaper of the western wall.

The poem read:

"Sunshine bathed the steps as I drowsily awoke,

The noon wind scattered the coils of chimney smoke.

At the notes of a flute did my love cares abate.

Or was it the cry of a phoenix calling to its mate?"

Jiaoniang's eyes were glued to the verses in admiration. She thought to herself: "That allusion to the phoenix and its mate is a subtle hint of his loneliness!"

Feihong, too, was greatly impressed by the poem, but she pretended otherwise. With a sardonic smile, she said, "What a silly pedant, showing off his so-called talent like this! He thinks he's the center of the universe. But I'll bet you could get the better of him in a poetry contest any time, Miss." And so saying, she laid out some paper and began to prepare ink.

Feihong's flippant remarks left Jiaoniang speechless. But on second thoughts, it occurred to her that by writing a reply to his poem she could reveal her feelings for him in an indirect way. So she moistened the brush, and after a pause for thought, she wrote, following the pattern of the poem on the wall:

"Spring anguish filled my dreams, sad I greeted the day.

Strange looked the sun, the wind so high and far away.

In an abyss unable to soar was my poor, shattered soul,

On a branch bereft of blossoms sang a sweet oriole."

姐,咱们何不进去看看?"

说着不由分说拉着娇娘推门进入房中。只见室内窗明几净,书案上排列着文房四宝,案头瓷瓶中插着一枝粉桃,艳若红霞;东墙上悬一柄青龙宝剑,琴几上横一张紫檀古琴;西壁上挂着几轴自书的诗画。忽然,飞红指着西窗道:"小姐快看,窗纸上题有一绝。"

娇娘抬头看去,果见西窗上有数行行草,写得龙蛇飞动:

"日影蒙阶睡正醒,篆烟如缕午风平。

玉箫吹尽霓裳调,谁识鸾声与凤声?"

娇娘看了题诗,一时不忍移目,潜心玩味,自忖道:"三哥果真才高八斗,诗思奇妙。其中暗喻求鸾求凰之意,又感慨曲高和寡,无人知音。"

飞红心中也为申纯的才华倾倒,却故意装出一副不以为然的样子冷笑道:"这酸丁卖弄才学,却不知天外有天,人外有人。小姐和他一首,将这酸丁压下去。"

说着就铺纸研墨。娇娘口中不言,心中却恼飞红多嘴,转念又想,和诗便和诗,要他也明白我的心。略微沉思,润笔挥毫依韵和道:

"春愁压梦苦难醒,日迥风高漏正平。

魂断不堪初起处,落花枝上晓莺声。"

"A fine match, a fine match," chirped Feihong. A sly glance at Jiaoniang's reddened cheeks confirmed what she was already quite sure of. "Miss, this poem of yours expresses your inner sentiments entirely. It matches Master Shen's word for word — a perfect couple of couplets, so to speak. Wait till he gets back and sees it: I've no doubt the Weaving Maid will be treading the Milky Way tonight!" [A reference to the legend of the Oxherd and the Weaving Maid, who fell in love and were turned into stars. They were allowed to meet in the Milky Way only once a year. — *Trans.*]

"What on earth do you mean by that?" snapped Jiaoniang, feigning anger.

"You don't know?" replied Feihong, with another crafty glance at her young mistress.

"Don't talk nonsense!" cried Jiaoniang. "It was you who urged me to write it. I just scribbled a few lines for fun, and now your tongue's running away with you. Fancy, uttering such rubbish!"

"You're right, Miss. I've touched you on a sore spot. It's all my fault." And Feihong burst into peals of laughter.

Just then, a parrot started cawing from his cage under the eaves. Feihong stopped laughing. "It must be nearly noon, Miss," she said. "And your mother will be waking up from her nap. Besides, the young gentleman will probably be coming back soon. It will be embarrassing if he finds us here. We'd better go quickly."

Jiaoniang agreed, and the two of them scurried out of the study like frightened deer.

Shen Chun arrived back at the mansion just after noon. He read Jiaoniang's poem in reply to the one he had written on the wall, and trembled with joy as he appreciated the meaning in every word and the sentiments in every phrase.

Towards evening, a colleague of Wang Wenrui came to call. A banquet was arranged for him, to which Shen Chun was invited. The gathering did not break up until the moon was high in the sky. Wang Wenrui saw his

"和得好,和得好。"飞红在一边连连称赞,暗地里偷觑娇娘的神色,见娇娘红飞双颊,心中愈发明白,续道:"小姐这诗题红怨绿,将满腹衷肠表白得清清楚楚,且字字同声相和,与申家哥哥的诗珠联璧合,正好是一对儿。待他回来见了此诗,必道今宵织女空渡银河了。"

"飞红,你说的这是什么话?"娇娘佯怒道。

"小姐说这是什么话?"飞红一脸顽皮地瞅着娇娘。

娇娘嗔道:"好生荒唐,是你让我和诗,我也不过玩耍子胡乱应和了几句,你却说什么珠联璧合,什么织女银河。我看是你这个小蹄子心动了吧?"

"哟,倒是我胡说了。小姐自家心虚,只管编排起丫环来了。"飞红说着,嘻嘻笑个不住。

这时,只听檐下笼中的鹦鹉叽叽喳喳叫个不停。飞红忙止住笑声道:"日近晌午了,夫人昼睡将醒,再则申家哥哥回来,多难为情,还是快回去吧。"

娇娘点点头,与飞红悄悄带上房门出来,心中无缘无故似揣了小鹿般一阵狂跳。

却道申纯午后归来,见到书案上娇娘的和诗,字字有意,句句含情。不觉喜形于色,手舞足蹈起来。

当天傍晚,王文瑞同僚来访,府中开宴,邀申纯陪客。直到月上中天方才散了,王文瑞送客后回房安

guest off, and retired to bed. Shen Chun was left alone in the Hall of Radiant Spring. He was just about to return to his study, when he suddenly heard the tinkle of jade pendants outside, and saw Jiaoniang and the maid Xiaohui come tripping lightly towards the hall. He felt a surge of happiness well up inside him, as he hastened to meet them.

Jiaoniang looked to neither left nor right, as if she were entering an empty room. Seeing a pile of ash in the incense burner, she took a golden pin out of her hair, and started to clean out the vessel. Shen Chun was eager to speak to her about her poem. But when he noticed how deadpan her face was, the words stuck in his throat. He felt awkward, and felt an impulse to leave, but his feet would not obey him. Seeing Jiaoniang still intent on stirring the ashes, he managed to take a few steps towards her, and say, "Miss, it is late, and most people are in bed. Why are you busying yourself so?"

Jiaoniang replied in a monotonous tone, and without raising her head or stopping what she was doing: "Incense is precious and everlasting. How can I neglect it, even in the dead of night?"

Shen Chun knew immediately that "incense" signified "love." Gazing straight at Jiaoniang, he said, meaningfully: "If incense has a heart, it ought to be content."

Instead of replying to this, the girl replaced the golden hairpin, and walked to the window. Pulling aside the brocade curtain, she gazed up at the moon. Outside, the moonlight was shining as bright as day. Jiaoniang whispered, "Xiaohui, Xiaohui."

"What is it, Miss?" the girl quickly replied.

"Look at how beautiful the moon is tonight," Jiaoniang said. "I have not seen such a fine moonlit night for a long time."

The maid servant was a frivolous girl by nature, and seeing her mistress in a romantic mood she egged her on, saying with great alacrity: "Oh, that's right, Miss. The moon is so round and bright. Miss, why don't we go out and enjoy it?" And taking her mistress by the hand, the

歇，熙春堂上只留下申纯一人。正欲起身回书房，忽听堂外一阵环佩叮咚，就见娇娘小慧主仆二人翩翩而入，心里不由一阵狂喜，忙迎上前去。

娇娘目不斜视，如入无人之地，见几上香炉内香灰堆积，便径直走过去从云髻上抽出金钗整理余香。申纯本想上前与娇娘搭话，就便提起和诗的事。可看到娇娘神情冷冷的，话到嘴边又咽了回去，只觉得自己走也不是，留也不是，好生尴尬。又见娇娘只顾拨弄香灰，趋前两步搭讪道："现在已是夜半人寝，妹妹安用如此费心？"

娇娘头不抬手不停，冷冷地说道："香贵长存，怎能以夜深为由而弃之？"

申纯听出娇娘一语双关，以香喻情，双眼紧盯着她意味深长地说道："香若有心，也该知足了。"

娇娘却不答话，将金钗往云髻上一插，走到窗前，掀开绣帘仰头望天，只见玉兔当空，月色如昼，便柔声唤道："小慧，小慧。"

小慧忙应道："小姐，何事？"

"你看今夜月色这般美好，很久没有看到这么好的月亮了。"

小慧本来贪玩，见小姐突发兴致，马上来了劲，急忙说道："是呀，是呀，多大多圆的月亮呀。小姐咱们索性痛痛快快玩上一会子，好么？"

impulsive maid servant pulled her out of the hall and down the steps.

Shen Chun followed them. Outside, the scenery reminded him of the perfect moonlit nights in novels, on which lovers hold their trysts. He began to recite a line from Su Dongpo's poem, *The Red Cliff*:

"The silvery moon and the charming breeze,
What night could be as fine as this?"

His sentiment was not lost on Jiaoniang. But she gave a scornful chuckle, saying, "I really can't think why Master Dongpo was so enamored of nights like this."

The young man hastily replied, "The silvery moon and charming breeze reminded the poet that life is short and full of grief, and fine nights are few. So when he gazed on a scene such as this, he could not help feeling breathing romantic sighs. Don't you think that's what he meant, Miss?"

Jiaoniang gave him an arch look. "I dare say you are right," she conceded, "but people tend to get too wrapped up in sentimentality. It is strange, but perhaps I was too obtuse to have such sensitive feelings."

With a sad smile, Shen Chun murmured, "It seems to me that you do indeed have feelings, Miss. Otherwise, what could be the meaning of what you wrote in your poem today: 'Spring anguish filled my dreams'?"

As he said this, he glanced sideways at Jiaoniang, who was pleased, shy and annoyed at this remark of Shen Chun's, which had pricked her to the heart. She was pleased because the young man plainly understood her feelings; shy because she was, after all, a woman and diffident when it came to tender emotions; and annoyed because Shen Chun had spoken out rashly in front of Xiaohui. Luckily, she thought, it is night, and they can't see my blushes. She then looked up into the sky, pretending to be interested in the constellations. Carelessly, she said, "People often talk about the Weaving Maid and the Herdboy. I wonder which stars they are. Do you happen to know, sir?"

Shen Chun also looked up at the stars. Pointing at Jiaoniang, he said,

说着手拉娇娘下了台阶，申纯也跟着出堂，觉得眼前情景倒有些像《会真记》中张生月下会莺莺。心中不禁感慨，朗吟《赤壁赋》中的句子道："月白风清，如此良夜何？"

娇娘在一旁听了，已知其意，冷笑一声道："真想不通苏学士为何如此钟情这月白风清之夜？"

申纯听娇娘搭话，忙道："东坡居士见月色皎洁，清风徐来，便觉人生苦短，良夜无多，由此不禁触景生情，遂发慨叹。妹妹莫非是说他想的不对么？"

娇娘白了一眼申纯道："三哥所言，倒也在理，不过世人皆如此缠绵悱恻，这情也用得太多太滥了。真是奇怪，也许是小妹生来迟钝，怎么偏偏就没有这么多情呢？"

申纯低声调笑道："依我看妹妹实为有情。如若不然，今日诗稿中所谓'压梦苦难醒'者，又是何物呢？"

说着用眼角斜觑娇娘。娇娘被申纯一语道破心事，又喜又羞又恼。喜的是三哥已明白自己的心意；羞的是毕竟自己是女儿家，情面上有些过不去；恼的是三哥出言莽直，当着小慧说这种话，也太放肆了些。好在是夜里，自己脸红面热旁人也看不见，忙假意仰头观星，问道："人常言的织女、牛郎二星在哪里？三哥可知道么？"

申纯仰头观望，指点着对娇娘道："妹妹你瞧，那

"I think this is the Weaving Maid, right here."

Jiaoniang smiled, and said, "Sir, you are so learned that you know both Heaven and Earth. So you should know which star is the Weaving Maid. But is that really the Weaving Maid, I wonder?"

Shen Chun felt that he left himself open to a jibe, and his face burned. He was at a loss how to reply. To Xiaohui, listening on the sidelines, the other two seemed to be talking in riddles, and she became bored. She urged her mistress to retire to bed: "It's getting late, Miss, and there's a chilly wind."

Looking at Shen Chun from under her eyelids, Jiaoniang said, "Well, I must be going now," and she and Xiaohui threaded their way through the flowers and willows to the rear courtyard. Watching them go, Shen Chun paced back and forth alone in the moonlight. Mulling over the scene that had just passed, the young man concluded that the few words he had exchanged with Jiaoniang had not been entirely devoid of significance.

First thing the following morning, he hit on the idea of using the excuse of thanking Jiaoniang for her poem to call upon her and sound out her feelings for himself still further. He found Xiaohui outside Jiaoniang's boudoir, playing with the birds.

The maid servant greeted the visitor cheerfully.

"Is the young lady at home, Xiaohui?" Shen Chun asked.

"Yes, sir, she is engaged in her toilet. Please go in," said Xiaohui, holding aside the door curtain for him.

As he stepped across the threshold, a whiff of perfume caressed his nostrils. Inside, he saw that the furniture was made of ornamented purple sandalwood, elegantly arranged. By the ivory-inlaid bed, stood a four-paneled sandalwood screen, on which were placed four volumes of Tang Dynasty poems — "In Praise of Willows" by He Zhizhang (659-744), "Bamboo Stem Odes" by Liu Yuxi (772-842), "Cicadas" by Yu Shinan (558-638) and "Snow-Bound River" by Liu Zongyuan (773-819). These four volumes hinted at the four seasons, and impressed

颗就是织女星。"

娇娘莞尔一笑道:"三哥博古通今,上知天文,下晓地理,还认得织女星。原来那就是织女星呀。"

申纯受了一通奚落,方知自己上了圈套,当下脸上发烫,不知如何应对。小慧在一旁听了半晌,弄不清这两个猜什么谜,一时没了兴致,便催促道:"夜深风凉,小姐该回房歇息了。"

娇娘瞥了一眼申纯,道:"那就走吧。"二人遂穿花度柳,转身回后院去了。申纯目送娇娘主仆二人离去,独自漫步月下,回味适才的情景,觉得今夜与娇娘说了这许多话,也算不虚此行。

第二天早上起来,申纯便思量着何不以谢诗为名,到娇娘处看看,也好再探探虚实。来到娇娘绣阁外,就与廊下逗鸟的小慧打了个照面。

小慧喜盈盈地招呼道:"表少爷早哇。"

申纯道:"小慧姐姐,你家小姐起来了吗?"

"正在梳妆呢,快进去吧。"小慧说着为申纯挑起了门帘。

申纯甫进绣阁,就觉香气扑鼻,但见房中一式紫檀木雕花家具,摆设讲究,布置精雅。牙床之侧有四扇檀香木屏风,上书唐诗四首,分别是贺知章的《咏柳》,刘禹锡的《竹枝词》,虞世南的《蝉》,柳宗元的《江雪》,暗喻春夏秋冬四季,足见主人的情

the viewer with a feeling of good taste.

Jiaoniang was painting her eyebrows seated before her dressing table mirror when Shen Chun entered. She saw his reflection in the mirror. Her heart skipped a beat; however, she allowed no trace of her emotion to show on her face. Shen Chun stepped forward, made a low bow, and said, "Excuse my intrusion, Miss, but I came specially to thank you for your kind present of a poem. I could see from it that your literary talent far outshines the accomplishments of Ban Zhao (49-120, a historian of the Eastern Han Dynasty) and Su Hui (a female poet of the Former Qin Dynasty)."

Jiaoniang put down her eyebrow pencil, stood up, and bowed. "You do me too much honor, sir. If I ventured to wield a brush, it was merely to 'blow on the flute in front of the master flautist Xiao' or 'chip away with an axe in front of the master carpenter Lu Ban.' I am afraid you must have laughed at my poor effort."

"You are far too modest, Miss," the young man assured her. "Your reply to my poem was far better than the original. Moreover, upon reading it carefully, I could detect that it expressed the tender feelings of a young woman. How could I hope to match it?"

At this daring mention of "tender feelings," Jiaoniang pouted. "I do believe you are making fun of me, sir," she said. "How could I possibly write a fine poem? And as for things like 'tender feelings'...."

Fearing that he had overstepped the mark, and made Jiaoniang angry, Shen Chun hurriedly changed the subject. "Er, this eyebrow lacquer you were using just now," he said quickly, "is it made from candle snuff?"

Forgetting her annoyance, Jiaoniang softened her tone, as she replied, "No, it's made from lamp cinders."

Shen Chun stepped forward to inspect the cosmetic more closely. "It's fine stuff, indeed," he murmured. "And it's luckier than I am."

"What do you mean, sir," asked Jiaoniang, puzzled, "by 'luckier' than you?"

Shen Chun gave her a meaningful look, and, with a mournful counte-

致不俗。

娇娘正对着菱花镜描眉，从镜中看见申纯进来，心中一喜，脸上却不露出来。申纯上前深深一揖道："愚兄特意前来谢妹妹赐诗。妹妹才过班姬，字超苏蕙，堪称女中才子。"

娇娘放下眉笔，起身还礼道："惭愧，惭愧。还是三哥才调高雅，字字见出风标，小妹在萧史面前弄箫，鲁班门上耍斧，倒让三哥见笑了。"

"妹妹过谦了。妹妹的和诗，超出原诗百倍，细细读来，只觉幽情暗生，芳心如见。愚兄怎能比得！"

娇娘听得"芳心如见"四字，粉面含羞嗔道："三哥莫要嘲讽，小妹哪里能作出什么好诗？更谈不上什么芳心……"

申纯见她娇羞难当，便不再提起，转而见梳妆台上的青黛色泽滋润，不比寻常，问道："妹妹适才描眉所用黛膏，是烛花么？"

娇娘稍稍平静下来，柔声答道："不是烛花，乃灯烬所积。"

申纯凑近观看，赞道："好灯花呀，想愚兄倒不如它。"

娇娘不解其意，问道："三哥此话怎讲？"

申纯看了一眼娇娘，哭丧着脸道："愚兄说不如它自有道理，它也日傍妆台为你画眉，它也曾夜入帐

nance, explained, "Well, you see, by day it adorns your face, and at night it lies beside you in your cosmetics box. It is rubbed gently by your delicate fingers and preserved carefully. That is why I say it is luckier than I am. "

These subtle words, filled with the young man's ardent passion, delighted Jiaoniang. But she lowered her head, and said nothing, twisting her girdle tightly with her hands. Perceiving that Jiaoniang grasped his meaning, Shen Chun thought to himself: "Buddha be praised!" He then pushed his luck a little further, saying, "Miss, I would greatly appreciate it if you would give me a little of it. I can use it to make ink to write a letter home. "

Jiaoniang nodded. "Please help yourself, " she said.

The young man reached out, to take a pinch of the eyebrow lacquer. Then he hesitated, and said, "But surely you would not trouble your guest, I think. Are you too shy to hand it to me yourself?"

"Are you afraid of getting your fingers dirty, " Jiaoniang said teasingly. Thereupon, she took half of the lacquer and handed it to Shen Chun, and put the rest back in the cosmetics box. As she did so, she wiped her fingers on the young man's gown. Then, pointing to the stain, she asked, "Are you going to clean that now? "

Tingling with excitement, Shen Chun answered, "Oh, no. Definitely not! Since it was given to me by your own fair hands, I shall preserve it as a keepsake. "

At the mention of the word "keepsake, " Jiaoniang's expression froze. Her eyebrows shot up, and her eyes became glaring saucers. In a trembling voice, she said, "I had no such intention, sir! It is impertinent of you to deliberately poke fun at me. What kind of a person do you think I am? Let me remind you that our relationship is that of brother and sister, so how can you talk of such things as 'keepsakes'? I am not one of those 'roadside willows' or 'flowers dangling from the wall' who may be toyed with at will. I shall go straight to my parents and report your effrontery. "

With a contemptuous flourish, Jiaoniang rose, and started to stride

帏亲近芳泽,它是兰指亲调,用心收留,久积而成。我哪里有这个福份,所以说我不如它。"

娇娘见他语含深情,出口珠玑,心中着实喜欢,便捻着衣带低头不语。申纯见状,心中直念"阿弥陀佛",试探道:"妹妹,能否分一半给我,也好书写家信?"

娇娘点点头道:"请三哥自家取用就是。"

申纯见娇娘同意了,便将黛膏拈起来,欲取不取,说道:"妹妹既然答应送与我,怎好意思让客人亲自动手呢?"

娇娘伸出葱指拈了过来,说道:"既许三哥,何惧沾手?"说着掰下一半递与申纯,又将剩下的一半放回眉盒里,随手牵了申纯的衣襟将手指擦净,复又指着衣上的油污顽皮地说道:"我想三哥得此,还能做那袖手无事人吗?"

申纯听了她的话,不由得心花怒放,嬉笑道:"岂敢,岂敢!妹妹亲手所赠,愚兄必将留作信物。"

谁知娇娘听见"信物"二字,顿时变脸,只见她柳眉上挑,凤目圆睁,颤声说道:"我本无他意,三哥为何出口无礼,成心将人奚落,把我当成什么人了?我与你本是兄妹排连,有什么可以做信物的?我可不是那路柳墙花,随人取笑,任人欺负。我这就去禀告爹娘,告你无人处尽情轻薄戏弄。"

说着一甩手站起来向外就走。这突如其来的变

away. Shen Chun was stunned at this unexpected turn of events. His heart thumped in his breast, and he broke out in a sweat. In a complete dither, he flopped down onto his nerveless knees, and clutching at the departing Jiaoniang's gown, he pleaded piteously: "Oh Miss, have mercy. Please forgive me! I did not mean to offend you."

The young lady waved him away with a flourish of her sleeve: "It was quite clearly intentional; how can you deny it?"

"Oh no, oh no! I assure you, Miss. Please forgive me, I beg."

"What if I don't?"

"Then ... then ... I'll stay here grovelling on my knees."

Jiaoniang saw that the young man was really afraid of his conduct being reported to his host, Wang Wenrui. She did not have the heart to cause him such trouble, so, with a sigh, she turned and helped him to his feet. At this, Shen Chun was carried away by a surge of happiness. On an impulse, he reached out to embrace Jiaoniang, who jerked herself away from him. Her cheeks flaring and her heart palpitating, Jiaoniang gasped, "Sir, I must insist that you stop playing tricks to frighten me, and I advise you not to think of me in the wrong way any longer!" Whereupon, she hurriedly turned her face away from him. The young man was plunged into an agony of embarrassment, and fell upon his knees once more.

After a while, Jiaoniang turned back, and seeing Shen Chun in this abject attitude, in a low voice, in which were mingled both annoyance and pain, she said, "Get up, you blockhead! What will people think if they see you like this?"

This came like a reprieve to a man on the gallows to Shen Chun, who hastily rose to his feet. Standing respectfully to one side, he cast a glance at Jiaoniang. The young lady, for her part, kept her expression strictly under control. Shen Chun found Jiaoniang even more captivating when she was angry; so much so that he could not bear to tear himself away from her presence. He made a deep bow, and said, "Miss, your magnanimity in forgiving the dolt who stands before you will remain forever in his heart."

化，把申纯弄懵了，心跳汗出，手足无措，双膝一软跪在当地，一把扯住娇娘的衣袖苦苦哀求道："妹妹开恩，妹妹开恩，饶过愚兄这回吧！我不是故意的。"

娇娘一甩衣袖道："分明是故意的，你还敢抵赖？"

"不敢，不敢。好妹妹饶了我吧。"

"我若不饶呢？"

"那…那…愚兄就一直跪在这里。"

娇娘见申纯当真怕了，心中又有些不忍，叹了一口气，转身相扶。申纯见娇娘伸手相扶，欢喜欲狂，伸出双臂就势去搂抱娇娘。惊得娇娘闪身退后两步，双颊飞红，一时心悸不止，喘息道："三哥起来，休要装模做样吓唬人，我劝你今后休将小妹看歪了。"说着将脸背了过去。申纯窘得无地自容，低着头仍跪在那里。

半晌，娇娘转过脸来，见申纯呆呆跪着，又疼又气，低声道："呆子，还不快些起来？让人看见才称意么？"

申纯如同得了赦令一般，忙站了起来，立在一旁，偷眼瞧着娇娘。娇娘紧绷着脸，对申纯瞧也不瞧。申纯见她生气的样子越发可爱，不想离去，便一揖到地，说道："谢妹妹担待，饶了愚兄这一回。愚兄感恩戴德，铭记在心。"

He wanted to blurt out some more cajoling words, but Jiaoniang's expression was inscrutable, and he feared that her anger might not yet have dissipated, and he might make another blunder. Besides, if he stayed any longer somebody might come by and notice the scene, giving rise to gossip. So he hastily muttered, "I have caused you offence, Miss. I will now take my leave." With this, he picked up present of eyebrow lacquer, lifted the door curtain, and withdrew.

It pained Jiaoniang to see Shen Chun leaving with his tail between his legs like this. She thought to herself: "Oh, you poor young man! I well know your innermost feelings. But do you know mine, I wonder? It must have been distressing to hear my harsh words just now. I don't know how you will get through the torments of this night." As she pondered this, tears sprang to her eyes.

The following morning dawned to the patter of raindrops. Jiaoniang sat alone in her boudoir. She held a book in her hands, but was loath to direct her eyes to the page. Driven by a moaning wind, the rain lashed the latticed window. An early spring chill pervaded the room. Jiaoniang told Xiaohui to fetch her embroidered cloak. When that failed to keep out the cold, she went behind the partition to where the stove was.

The glowing charcoal gave off a fragrant scent. Xiaohui helped her young mistress to take off her cloak, and sat her down by the stove to warm herself. The maid servant noticed that Jiaoniang's brows were creased in a frown, and her eyes looked full of gloom. Xiaohui recalled that Jiaoniang had been downcast for the previous few days, and couldn't help asking, "Miss, why are you so morose these days?"

Jiaoniang did not reply for a while, and then she sighed, and said, "I don't know myself. This depression has settled on me like a shadow. It won't leave me even for a single minute. It twines round my heart and vexes my mind without ceasing."

Xiaohui blinked in utter confusion. There was no way the muddle-headed girl could understand her young mistress' mental torment. Pout-

申纯还想再说些好话，却见娇娘面沉似水，像是真的生气了。他生怕画虎不成反类犬，弄巧成拙，况且也担心时间久了，让人看见，惹出闲话来，便搭讪道："愚兄唐突妹妹，多有得罪，告辞了。"

说罢拈着那块灯烬，掀帘退了出去。娇娘见申纯怏怏而去，心中好生不忍，暗忖道："三哥呀三哥，你的衷肠我已尽知，我的衷肠你可明白？你被我抢白了几句，想是此时心中如盐撒刀割，不知今夜里你将怎生难过。"想着想着，不禁滴下泪来。

且说第二日一大早，淅淅沥沥下起雨来，娇娘独坐闺中，手中拿着一卷书，却怎么也看不在心上。风挟雨丝抽打窗棂，沙沙作响，房中愈发春寒逼人。遂令小慧取来红绣氅披了，可仍抵不住寒冷，便由小慧扶了来到暖阁。

暖阁中香气馥馥，炭火红红。小慧为娇娘解下大氅，安顿娇娘坐在绣榻上拥炉取暖。转脸看见娇娘蛾眉微颦，凤眼含愁，不言不语，想起这几天来，小姐一直怏怏不快，便问道："小姐为何总是这般愁眉不展的？"

娇娘沉吟半响，方叹道："我也说不清为了什么，这愁绪便像影子似的片刻也不离人，缠得人心烦意乱，不得安宁。"

小慧眨眨眼睛，不解地看看娇娘，嘴儿一噘道：

ing, she said, "Well, Miss, I wait on you hand and foot from morning till night, so I can't imagine what you have to complain about. Honestly, it beats me why you have to wear that moping expression all the time, it really does!"

"You silly little creature!" snapped Jiaoniang, who longed to be alone with her thoughts, "You are so annoying! Go to my mother at once, and don't come back unless she sends for me."

Xiaohui was only too pleased to have a chance to go and play with Xiang'e, Luying and the other maid servants. She gave a sprightly assent, and tripped out to the main courtyard. Along the way, she muttered to herself, "Well, I hope I never find out what this thing called 'depression' is as long as I live, I really do!"

When she had disappeared, Jiaoniang couldn't help envying girls of Xiaohui's age. They seemed to have no knowledge of love. They had not a care in the world, and were always cheerful. But there was no turning the clock back; she would never be so carefree again. Then it occurred to her that there must be many girls like herself in the world — racked with cares and anguish, and all because of that one word "marriage." Indeed, how did it come about that "marriage" could so make itself the master of a girl's life? Just then, Jiaoniang heard the sound of footsteps outside the door. Then, a hand bearing a sprig of pear blossoms lifted aside the door curtain, and Shen Chun stepped inside. Her heart in a tumult, Jiaoniang modestly lowered her head.

Having accepted the eyebrow lacquer the previous day, Shen Chun had been too excited and perturbed to sleep that night. The next morning, after breakfast, he looked out of the window, and noticed the rain. It occurred to the young man that the plum blossoms would look particularly appealing after being washed by the raindrops, so he ventured out into the courtyard. The sight of the bunches of snow-white plum blossoms gladdened his heart. He snapped off a twig which sported a particularly bounteous array of the flowers, and was just about to return indoors to put it in a vase when a gust

"小慧从早到晚服侍小姐,不知愁是什么,为何小姐整日价嘴边老挂着个愁字?"

娇娘心里烦乱,想静坐一会儿,嗔道:"小丫头,你晓得什么。且到前面看看夫人去,若是夫人寻我,便来说与我知道。"

小慧巴不得出去和湘娥、绿英等小丫环耍一会子,高兴地应了一声,便一路小跑往前院去了,边走边嘀咕:"小慧我但愿这辈子不识得愁是个啥东西。"

娇娘见小慧风风火火地去了,心中不由羡慕起来,像小慧这等年纪的小妮子,不谙情为何物,无忧无虑,倒也快乐。只是时光不能倒流,自己再没有这样的快乐了。转而又想,这世间女子,似自己这等愁肠百结的,必定不少,说不得都是为了这"婚姻"二字。可这婚姻又如何能由得女儿家自己做主?正在思量间,听得门外有脚步声响起,就见申纯手持一枝梨花掀帘走进,心中一阵慌乱,忙把头低下。

申纯昨日分得灯烬,心里七上八下,一夜未眠。早饭过后,见窗外细雨朦朦,思量雨中梨花一定楚楚动人,便起身踱入后园。看了会儿剪云堆雪的梨花,心境开朗了许多,就拣了一枝花朵繁茂的折下,准备回屋插瓶。此时雨已停了,一阵凉风吹过,侵肌刺骨,不禁打了个冷战,正巧路过暖阁,便想进来暖和暖

of wind sprang up, and chilled him to the marrow. The rain had stopped by this time, but the wind, penetrating his damp garments, caused him to shiver violently. It happened that he was passing a room which he knew had a heated area inside, so he decided to step in and warm himself up. As soon as he did so, to his great surprise and joy, he saw Jiaoniang there, huddled around the stove. Immediately, the memory of the scene the previous day returned, causing his heart to beat furiously. Shen Chun was at a loss whether to stay or go. But he plucked up courage, thinking to himself: "The worst that can happen is a repeat of yesterday's debacle — and then I'll have to go down on my knees again. But anyway, I'll get a definite answer out of her." Seeing that Jiaoniang still sat there with her head bowed, not saying a word, Shen Chun silently resolved: "Well, Miss, I know how to make you open your mouth." Whereupon, he dropped the rain-washed plum blossoms at Jiaoniang's feet.

Startled, the girl raised her head. Seeing the purposeful resolve in Shen Chun's countenance, she felt her heart quiver. She quickly looked down once more, her eyes coming to rest on the plum blossoms at her feet. After a while, she picked up the twig with trembling fingers, and, in a tone of suppressed indignation, asked, "Sir, why did you throw these plum blossoms down here?"

Shen Chun snorted, "Flowers blossom and wither in their own good time. Who can know their intentions? And so I threw them away."

Jiaoniang realized at once that the young man was trying to sound out her real feelings for him. And so, she replied, "Everyone knows that flowers bloom in the spring so that people can admire them. Why wear yourself out with anxiety about them? Look how these flowers brim with tears, and how thin and weak the twig is. Perhaps they too are afflicted with spring longing? That would explain the twig's frail appearance. People often compare a person's face to the countenance of a flower, but I am afraid that a person's beauty cannot withstand the blasts of the wind and the battering of the rain."

和。谁知进门看见娇娘拥炉而坐，真是喜出望外。可思量起昨夜分烬之事，心中又翻腾起来，不知该走该留，愣在当地。转念一想，给自己打气道："大不了又似昨日，也无非是再跪一次，一定要讨得娇娘一句准话。"

申纯打定主意，见娇娘低头不语，他自己也不急不恼，心想你不说话，我非要逗着你开口。眼珠儿一转，计上心来，随手将那枝带雨梨花掷在娇娘脚下。

娇娘被惊得一怔，抬头看了一眼申纯，见他面若秋霜，心里禁不住发颤，复又低下头去凝视脚下的梨花，半晌，颤颤地拾起花枝来，含怨问道："三哥为何弃掷此花？"

申纯鼻子里哼了一声，道："花儿自开自谢，谁知其意何在！所以弃之。"

娇娘听得申纯话里有话，是在试探自己对他有情无情，便道：

"花自有心，春开一枝，以供玩赏，人也该知足了。三哥又何苦求之过深过急呢？你看这花泪盈盈，花枝瘦弱，想它也是为春而伤情，才害得这样瘦骨伶仃。人常言'人面花容'，只怕是人面犹不及花容长久，更经不得风吹雨打。"

不待娇娘说完，申纯已一揖到地，说道："幸蒙妹

She had hardly finished before Shen Chun made a deep bow, and said, "Since you have given your promise, Miss, I hope you will not go back on your word."

"What promise?" Jiaoniang asked, astonished and annoyed.

"Please think," Shen Chun answered, without a moment's hesitation.

A blush spread over the girl's face, as she realized that Shen Chun had grasped the message of love hidden in her words. After a long time, she finally raised her head once more. This time, she deliberately changed the subject of the conversation. "Sir, the weather at this time of year is very fickle, and today is colder than yesterday. You must be careful not to catch cold. Please sit down and dry your clothes; they are wet-through."

These unexpected kind words sparked a jolt of delight in Shen Chun. His annoyance vanished in an instant, and he said, beaming with joy: "That is very kind of you, Miss." Thereupon, he seated himself sideways next to Jiaoniang. The girl reached out, and felt his robe with her fingers, saying timidly: "Sir, I fear your clothes are too flimsy to withstand the spring chill."

Shen Chun was now sure that since she was so solicitous about whether he was warm enough, she must also care for him in her heart. He felt a warm glow suffusing his breast, and at the same time a welling up of tears in his eyes. Choking with sobs, he gasped, "Miss, you are so concerned about the thinness of my apparel; perhaps you can also pity my broken heart."

Jiaoniang hid a smile with her hand, and replied, "Sir, I do not know how you come to have a broken heart. However, perhaps if you were to tell me the details of this ailment I could suggest a remedy."

Perceiving that the opportune moment had arrived. Briskly wiping away his tears, and assuming a solemn expression, he said, "A gentleman does not speak flippantly, so I will tell you the honest truth. Since the very first moment I saw you, Miss, on this visit to Meizhou, my heart has not been mine to command. Day and night I have been longing to explain my

妹见诺,还请万勿翻悔。"

娇娘嗔道:"我见诺什么了?"

申纯眨眼道:"妹妹自想。"

娇娘心知自己方才一番言语中所含真情,已被申纯领悟,羞得满面绯红。半晌方抬起头,岔开话题道:"这时节午暖还寒,今日较昨夜更冷,三哥衣衫都湿了,还不快坐下烤烤,当心着凉。"

申纯听了娇娘这知冷知热的几句话,真是受宠若惊,不觉心花怒放,乐颠颠道:"小生遵命。"说罢侧身坐在娇娘身旁。娇娘伸手捻一捻申纯的衣襟,轻声道:"不知三哥衣裳厚薄,可能抵得住这春寒相逼?"

申纯见娇娘嘘寒问暖,想是她心中惦念自己,否则怎会这么体贴入微?心里一热,鼻子一酸,忍不住滴下泪来,哽咽道:"妹妹既体恤为兄的衣裳单薄,怎么就不可怜我这柔肠寸断呢?"

娇娘掩口失笑道:"不知何事能使三哥断肠,不妨将其中原委一一道来,容小妹为三哥谋一善策。"

申纯见时机已到,一抹眼泪,正色道:"君子无戏言,那我可照实说了。此番来到眉州,自与妹妹见面那一刻起,愚兄便魂飞魄扬,不能收摄。寒夜苦长,终宵不寐,日夜欲求向妹妹一诉衷肠而不得。我暗自看妹妹的言语态度,也不像是无情之人,可每当与妹妹言及情字,你便翻脸变色,将人奚落。不知妹妹是

feelings for you, but no chance presented itself. My nights are cold, sleepless and endless. Every time I have come close to speaking tender words, you have rebuffed and mocked me. I do not know whether this arises from your lack of understanding of such things, or whether it is just pretence. Sometimes I think that I am too boorish to express fine sentiments — an ordinary earthbound creature like myself dare not aspire to be the consort of an immortal fairy. If you would only make clear to me your true emotions today, it would once and for all relieve the agony in my heart."

Having got this out, Shen Chun felt as though a great weight had been lifted off his chest, and he breathed a long sigh. Jiaoniang, meanwhile, had listened to his impassioned plea with a mixture of delight and consternation. This time, it was her turn to shed tears. Finally, she gasped, "But, Sir, since you do not trust me, what is the use of me saying anything?" Ignoring an interruption by the young man, she continued, "I have long known of your kind feelings. Moreover, in the past few days I myself have been unable to cope with things because of this. My sleep is troubled, and my food and drink untasted."

"But, Miss," Shen Chun burst out, "if this is so, then why have you kept me at arm's length?"

Jiaoniang retorted brusquely: "Sir, since you are an accomplished scholar, I would have expected you to be acquainted with the proprieties concerning relations between the sexes. If you really did have an honest affection for me, you would go home to report this to your parents. They would then send matchmakers. A casual relationship would be most improper."

In a tear-choked voice, Shen Chun asserted, "Miss, I am in the throes of love-sickness. I am in a dither from morning to night. I will return home and ask my parents to allow our marriage. If they refuse their consent, I will not dare to return to face you. And then, I do not know what will become of me!"

"Oh, please do not talk so," Jiaoniang urged him. "We must be

当真不谙世事，还是故意装出这样给人看的？想是愚兄丑陋之质，不足当雅意，凡夫俗子做不得神仙伴侣。今日为兄厚颜吐露心曲，也算了结了一桩心愿。"

说罢，如释重负，长长吐了一口气。娇娘见申纯如此动情，知他对自己属意已久，心中又喜又惊，早已滚下泪来，许久方轻叹一声道："三哥如此信不过娇娘，那还有什么可说的？"

"这……"

"小妹早已尽知兄长心意。这些天来，小妹也是万事儿做不到心上，寝梦不安，饮食俱废，三哥又哪里知道？"

申纯道："妹妹既有心意，为何总是拒人于千里之外呢？"

娇娘嗔道："三哥知书达理，岂不知男女婚姻当图长久。三哥既对小妹有情，就当返回故里禀告双亲，三媒六证派人前来说合才是，怎能只图眼前苟且？"

申纯带着哭腔道："我已染上这相思病，朝不谋夕，往返求婚，动须累月。况且倘若议亲不成，我有什么脸面再来，往后又如何自处！"

娇娘只得劝道："三哥休做小女子之态，只要你我心坚如石，好事定谐。事若不济，小妹当以一死以

strong, you and I, so as to secure our lifelong happiness. But if fortune does not smile upon us, the only way to repay your loving kindness would be for me to seek my death."

Greatly moved, the young man replied, with a voice full of fervor: "These words of yours will remain forever engraved deeply on my heart."

Jiaoniang was silent for a while, and then she said, haltingly: "There is still one thing which I have not unburdened myself of...."

"What is troubling you?" Shen Chun asked without hesitation.

"Just this," Jiaoniang replied. "From ancient times, it has been a well-known tragedy for a maiden to be hopelessly in love with a cold-hearted man. I fear that you may not prove constant, but abandon me to a life of solitary mourning."

Shen Chun flung himself to his knees, and swore a passionate oath: "I assure you, Miss, that I will never forsake you. Should I do so, Heaven bears witness, may I suffer a violent death!"

Feeling as if a huge stone had been lifted from her heart, and that there were no longer any barriers to sharing a lifetime of love with Shen Chun, Jiaoniang was overcome with emotion. Her face turned a bright red, putting her in a state of the utmost confusion. Her agitation was not lost on the young man beside her. Glancing round, and seeing that there was no one else present, he plucked up his courage, and edged closer to Jiaoniang.... But just as he did so, Xiaohui was heard calling from outside: "Miss, Miss, come quickly! Your mother wants to talk to you at once!"

Shen Chun hurriedly shifted back to where he had been sitting before. Jiaoniang, gazing at him with a look full of tenderness, said, "Sir, I must go. My mother has sent for me. Please stay awhile here, and warm yourself."

So saying, she left. Shen Chun felt deliciously intoxicated. The only thing stopping him being perfectly happy was the thought of that wretched creature Xiaohui, who had spoiled everything just as he and Jiaoniang were getting so affectionate. But now that he and Jiaoniang had pledged their

谢三哥深情。"

申纯闻言，动情地道："娇娘此言，为兄此生当铭记肺腑。"

娇娘闻言低头，嗳嚅半晌道："小妹尚有一事放心不下……"

申纯盯着娇娘，急切问道："妹妹所虑何事？"

娇娘道："自古人言痴心女子负心汉。小妹着实担心三哥不能始终如一，将来令小妹有白头之叹。"

申纯见娇娘仍然心存疑虑，当下跪地发誓道："妹妹不必过虑，申纯倘若有负于你，天地不容，定遭横死之灾。"

娇娘心里有如一块石头落地，猛地想起自己情不自禁，与申纯私订终身，不由红晕上脸，又急又愧。申纯见娇娘此时眼润息微，娇羞难状，禁不住心旌摇荡，又视左右无人，便大了胆子往前凑到娇娘身边。猛听小慧在门外嚷道："小姐，小姐，夫人叫你过去叙话呢。"

申纯见有人来，慌忙躲在一旁。娇娘粉面含春，深情地看了申纯一眼，道："娘唤我，我先走了，三哥且暖暖身子再去。"

说罢，起身出门去了。此时申纯心中如饮蜜汁，如醉醇酒，美中不足的是正要与娇娘亲热一番，密订佳期，却让小慧这死丫头给搅黄了。如今，自己与娇

81

love to each other, the memory of the previous painful few days vanished into thin air. Truly, he thought, Heaven does not forsake those who struggle on in the face of all odds!

Following this chance encounter, which turned out so fortuitous, Shen Chun did not see Jiaoniang for two anxious days. Unable to bear being parted from his beloved, at dawn on the third day, Shen Chun threw on his clothes, and went out, determined to find some way of meeting her once more. He was reluctant to go straight to the back courtyard, in case the maids were alerted. So he pretended to be heading for the flower garden to take a stroll. As he passed by Jiaoniang's window, he walked close to the wall, reciting a line from a poem: "Don't wake the neighbor's cackling hens, and disturb my hometown dreams."

Jiaoniang, who was sitting at her dressing table, recognized this quotation from Su Dongpo. "So he is feeling homesick," she mused. "But what is the foolish young man doing getting up at this early hour to recite poetry for? I only hope he doesn't cause some kind of commotion."

Raising her head, she noticed a flickering shadow of a man, whom she knew to be Shen Chun, on the window paper. She stepped quickly to the window. Shen Chun moved next to the wall, and said, "Miss, why are you up so early?"

Jiaoniang simply said, "Sir, you seem to be sorely missing your home."

"It is profitless for me to linger here broken-hearted," the young man replied. "Yesterday I heard a cuckoo hastening the spring along with his song, and it seemed to me to be saying 'Better go home, better go home!' And so I think I must hasten back to my native place."

Jiaoniang's tone changed abruptly. "Sir, since you seem to have so little regard for me, what was the purpose of the words you spoke the other day?"

"So little regard!" Shen Chun exclaimed. "Miss, what can you mean? The fact is that since you speak only empty words to me, it is in vain for

娘私定了终身，这段日子的相思之苦，总算没有白受。正是皇天不负苦心人。

申纯自在暖阁中巧遇娇娘，表情订盟，却连着两天没见她的影子，心中好生牵挂。这一日，天刚放晓，他便揽衣而起，思谋着寻机会与娇娘见上一面。待到进了后院，恐怕丫环发觉，便装作到花园散步的样子，走近娇娘窗前，边走边吟道："为报邻鸡莫惊觉，更容残梦到江南。"

娇娘正在房中对镜梳妆，猛听得申纯在外高声吟诵，听出是苏东坡的思归之句，心中便是一惊，心想："这个呆子，一早起来到这里吟什么诗？可千万别生出什么乱子来。"

抬头看见窗纸上有人影晃动，知道是申纯来到窗外，便急步走到窗前。申纯见是娇娘，贴近窗子道："妹妹起得这么早？"

娇娘隔窗问道："三哥为何思归之心如此迫切？"

申纯道："满腹衷肠断尽，在此空留无益，昨日里听得催春杜宇声声唤'不如归去'，看来为兄只得先回家去了。"

娇娘语声陡变，道："三哥既无意于小妹，前日所言，却是为何？"

申纯听出娇娘生气了，道："我岂无意于妹妹？但妹妹空言相调，愚兄再住下去也是枉然，所以欲图归

me to remain here, and so I pine for home. However, if your love for me were true, then I would be content to stay here for a hundred years."

Jiaoniang realized that Shen Chun was demanding an unequivocal answer. However, it would soon be broad daylight, and other people would start to stir. If they saw the young man hovering beneath her window, it would raise eyebrows. So Jiaoniang whispered, urgently: "Listen. There are too many prying eyes in the daytime. It is impossible for us to meet then. Wait until after dark, and climb out of the western window of your study. Make your way past the raspberry trellis to the Bright Spring Hall. Few people go there, and the foliage is thick. I will be waiting for you there. But go now, quickly!"

"Do you ... do you ... really ... mean it?" the young man hardly dared to believe his ears.

"If you don't trust me, then don't go," came the crisp retort.

"I trust you. I trust you. Miss, I will do as you say. I will go now. Please, whatever you do, don't break your promise." With a fluttering heart and soaring spirits, Shen Chun gave two low bows to the window, and scuttled off back to the study.

The young man spent the whole day waiting impatiently for nightfall — now peeping out of the window to see if the sky was getting any darker, now dashing outside to see if the sun was any lower. The latter perverse villain seemed to be glued in position, and only moved an inch at a time after Shen Chun, in his agitation, had made a groveling bow. He thought of the common saying: Heaven will always comply with good intentions. "But now that what I want is the most wonderful thing in the world, Heaven seems to be deliberately against me," he reflected. Finally, having waited in an agony of impatience for the sun to set, Shen Chun began to dress himself for the evening's expedition. But just as he was doing so, a wild wind began to blow, and black clouds rolled across the sky. In an instant, huge raindrops started to pelt down, as if the very Milky Way was pouring down from the skies. The desperate young man could do nothing but pace

计。倘若妹妹果有真情,我便在这里住上一百年也使得。"

娇娘心中明白,若不给申纯一个明确的答复,他必不肯走。此时天已大亮,一会儿人们都起来了,见他立在自己窗下,成何体统?便道:"你听我说,白日里人多眼杂,无法相会,待到天黑后,你可从书房里西窗跳出,穿过荼蘼架到熙春堂下。那里人稀花密,我在那儿等你。现在你快快去吧!"

"此话当……当真?"申纯有些不敢相信自己的耳朵。

"不信你就别去。"

"我信,我信。好妹妹,愚兄全听你的,这就回去,你千万不可爽约。"申纯心花怒放,神驰意荡,冲窗子拜了两拜,这才蹑足潜踪回到书房。

这一天,申纯只盼着天黑,一会儿从窗中探出头来望望天,一会儿奔出门来看看太阳,只见那金乌似用鳔胶粘在天上一般,半晌挪不了一寸,急得他直冲天上打拱作揖。心想人常言:人有善愿,天必从之。可我欲成就百年之好,这天就是不黑,想来是老天也故意与我作对。就这样魂不守舍盼到了红日西坠,整束衣衫准备去赴约。忽然狂风大作,乌云滚滚扑天盖地而来,霎时大雨滂沱,似天河决口一般。申纯又急又恨,对着一庭苦雨跺脚叹道:

to and fro in despair, and bemoan his tragic lot.

But, fret as he would, there was nothing for it. The rain fell, now furiously, now softly. But it refused to stop — as if it were deliberately pitting its will against his. Sitting by the light of a single guttering candle and listening to the pattering of the raindrops, Shen Chun finally poured out his anguish in a poetic composition.

The rain did not stop until cockcrow. With the coming of daylight, Shen Chun wended his way listlessly to pay the usual early-morning call on Jiaoniang's mother. He happened to find Jiaoniang there at the same time. The two young people glanced at each other, and then quickly averted their eyes. After exchanging a few commonplace remarks with Jiaoniang's mother, Shen Chun excused himself. He sauntered along the passage outside, pretending to be absorbed in the window and door carvings, while he waited for Jiaoniang to emerge. It was not long before he heard the patter of soft footsteps behind him. Sure enough, it was his beloved! The young man hastily drew from his sleeve the poem he had written in his desolation the previous night, and handed it to her.

Jiaoniang, too, had been in a state of great vexation the previous night, since her first clandestine assignation with Shen Chun had been frustrated. She had been wondering how he had endured the long hours of tedious longing. Of course, in her mother's presence, they had been unable to exchange so much as a word. But, taking note of how hurriedly Shen Chun had extricated himself, she guessed that he would be waiting outside for her. So she too made an excuse, and hurried out of her mother's chambers. Spying Shen Chun in the corridor, she looked around carefully to make sure that there was nobody else about, and followed him at a prudent distance.

Taking the poem, she looked it over, and then carefully tucked it into her sleeve. Then, pursing her lips in a smile, she said, "Sir, the course of true love never runs smoothly. You should not keep your feelings bottled up in your heart. I have already made my inclinations known, and so you may

"时来风送滕王阁，运去雷轰荐福碑。申纯啊申纯，你好命苦也！"

可再急也没办法，那雨一会儿急，一会儿缓，就是不停，好像成心跟他较劲。万般无奈只能是独对孤灯听雨声了。遂将满腹怅恨渲于笔端，援笔写下一首《玉惜春》。

直到鸡唱三遍，雨方住了。天亮后，申纯无情无绪，照例到赵夫人处请安，恰巧娇娘也在房中。二人对视一下，忙又将目光移开。与赵夫人闲话了一会子，申纯便告辞出来，有意放慢脚步，装做欣赏堂前窗扇木雕，想等娇娘出来。不多时便听到身后有碎步弓鞋声响起，回头看时，正是心上人。申纯忙从袖中取出夜里所写词章，双手递与娇娘。

娇娘昨夜也是心急如焚，初次相约天公就不作美，想三哥定是坐立不安，这一夜不知他如何熬过。刚才在母亲房里遇到申纯，当着母亲的面不便言语，见他匆匆别了母亲出去，知他定在外面等候，忙托故告辞出来，见申纯朝熙春堂走去，左右瞧瞧见四下无人，便慢慢跟了过去。

此时，她接过词笺看罢，款款收到袖中，抿嘴笑道："好事多磨，三哥不必往心里去。小妹既以心相许，迟早总会有机会的，当乘间别图。"说罢匆匆离去。

rest assured that there will surely be another opportunity." With that, she hurried away.

The young man watched her retreating figure, as if in a daze. "Another opportunity," he said to himself. "Yes, but when? In the far distant future, it seems to me." But there was nothing for, he knew, but to wait in feverish impatience.

It so happened that on that very day, a fellow-graduate of Wang Wenrui, who had reached the age of 50, was giving a banquet. So, Wang Wenrui sent Wang Zhong to invite Shen Chun to join them to go to congratulate. And the young man, thinking that perhaps the entertainment might dispel his gloomy mood for a while, consented to go. But the wine which he gulped back did nothing to lift his spirits, and eventually, he mumbled his regrets, and made his way with a heavy head and wobbling legs back to his study. There he fell onto his bed, and was soon in a drunken slumber.

That evening, as the lamps were being lit, Jiaoniang sent her maids Xiaohui and Ziyan to attend to her mother. She herself then sneaked along the corridor to the study. Tapping on the window brought no sound of movement within, so she called out to Shen Chun in a low voice. When that failed to elicit any response, she peeped through the window, to see Shen Chun sprawled on the bed, fully clothed and sound asleep. She could not help thinking, "He's deliberately ignoring me and pretending to be asleep, because he's angry about our rendezvous of last night being put off. Oh Shen Chun, you really are being petty! It wasn't my fault, you know...."

Her thoughts were interrupted by a snore from inside the room. "Oh, you're making a good pretense of being asleep, all right!" Jiaoniang said to herself, in indignation. "It has long been said that young scholars have shallow emotions and are always playing tricks. Well, I have treated you with sincerity, but you have trifled with my affections. Oh, how I wish I could really open my heart!"

申纯呆呆地看着娇娘的背影，自忖道："这一乘间别图，却是何时？想是遥遥无期了。"心中好生不快，可是万般无奈，也只能耐着性子等待。

恰巧这日王文瑞有位同年做五十大寿，派王忠到书房来请申纯同去祝寿。申纯心想出去正好散散心，便换了衣服，陪舅父前去赴宴。席间，申纯因心中不爽，借酒浇愁，多贪了几杯。

午后回到通判府，只觉得头重脚轻，昏昏沉沉，挣扎着与舅父聊了几句，就告退回了书房，一进门便倒头酣睡。

掌灯时分，娇娘将小慧、紫嫣支到夫人那里，自己则悄悄沿游廊转到书房外的小窗前，轻轻弹响窗棂，却不见动静；又低声唤道："三哥，三哥。"也没有人答应，透过窗纱隐隐看见申纯合衣而卧，猛地翻了个身向里睡去了。娇娘不禁心中一动："敢是因昨日之约惹恼了他，故意让我在此难堪，假装睡着了。申纯啊申纯，你真是小肚鸡肠，昨夜之事怎能怪我……"

正思量间，听申纯呼呼打起了鼾声，心中道："你倒装得真像呀！人都说书生自古多薄情，惯会逢场做戏。我诚心实意待你，你却虚情假意待人。恨只恨自家怎么便把一片真情全都对他讲了。"

想到此，悔恨难当，心抽胸闷，头晕目眩，几欲支撑不住，眼泪便似断线的珠子扑簌簌掉了下来。也顾

At this point, she was overwhelmed by an unbearable feeling of sadness. Her head swam, and her eyes glazed over. For a moment, she thought she was about to collapse. Tears streamed down her cheeks as she stumbled back to her boudoir.

The sun was high in the sky when Shen Chun finally awoke. He felt refreshed by his long slumber. He arose, and looked out of the window. It was a bright, sunny day, and the young man felt his spirits rise. After washing and having a bite to eat, he helped his uncle with some trifling matters, and then strolled over to the back courtyard and entered Jiaoniang's apartments. There he found her alone, sitting on her bed and wiping her eyes. He stepped forward in concern. "Miss, what is the matter?" he cried.

The sight of Shen Chun brought forth a loud wail from the girl.

Shen Chun was taken aback. "Miss, aren't you feeling well?" he cried. "Shall I fetch a doctor?"

Jiaoniang turned her face away, and made no reply. The tears continued to fall. Shen Chun began to panic. "Miss, please tell me if there is something that displeases you," he urged her.

Whatever Jiaoniang wanted to say stuck in her throat. Not a word could she utter through her choking sobs. Shen Chun paced up and down in a fit of agitation. Finally, he pleaded, "What on earth is the matter? You know that the two of us are of one heart and mind. If there is something I should know, please do not keep me on tenterhooks, with an aching heart, but tell me straight out!"

"Pah!" Jiaoniang muttered, wiping her tears away at last. "What would you know about aching hearts? It has been said since ancient times that scholars have shallow feelings, and now I consider that my eyes have been well and truly opened to the truth of this."

Hearing this, Shen Chun was flabbergasted. "Good Heavens," he croaked, "where did you get such a notion? I? Shallow feelings? How on earth have your 'eyes been opened,' as you say? I really am in a daze. I

不得苔湿径滑，一路踉跄回绣阁去了。

再说申纯一觉醒来，已是天光大亮日上三竿，真是一场酣睡。起来后，见窗外风和景明，艳阳高照，心情豁然开朗。洗漱完毕，吃了些点心果子，帮助舅父料理了一些琐事后，便向后院娇娘绣阁走去。一进门，见娇娘正坐在床前独自抹泪，急上前问道："妹妹为何伤心？"

娇娘见申纯来了，心中愈发委屈，呜呜咽咽竟哭出声来。

申纯莫名其妙，又转到娇娘对面问道："妹妹莫非身子不爽，待我让院子去请太医。"

娇娘扭转身子不理他，仍旧垂泪不止。申纯心急火燎，又问道："妹妹是有什么不顺心的事么？到是说话呀。"

娇娘满腹话语鲠在喉间，却吐不出一字来。申纯急得在地上团团乱转，半晌又道："到底是怎么回事？你我心心相印，有什么事总该让我知道，别叫我这样心焦才是。"

"呸！"娇娘拭着脸上的泪，轻轻地啐了一口，道："你还知道心焦呀？自古秀才多薄幸，我今儿算是开了眼了。"

申纯闻听此言，如坠五里雾中，痴呆呆道："这话从何说起？我又如何薄幸了？妹妹又开什么眼了？我

don't know for the life of me where you got this fantastic idea from!"

"Oh, in a daze, are you?" Jiaoniang snapped back. "You know perfectly well what I mean; don't pretend to be 'in a daze,' as you say."

The young man was getting more and more frantic. "Pretending to be in a daze? I haven't a clue what you mean," he wailed. "Please tell me plainly what the matter is — even if it kills me, I must know."

"Huh, don't talk about it killing you," Jiaoniang snorted. "I don't want to hear such nonsense. Yesterday, after dark, I went to ... I went to...." Suddenly, she choked with sobs, and was unable to continue.

His eyes wide with amazement, Shen Chun asked, "Where? Where did you go?"

"To ... to your study," the girl gasped. "To see you."

Shen Chun could scarcely believe his ears. "What? Did you really go to my study to see me," he hurriedly asked.

"Are you still pretending to be dazed?" Jiaoniang inquired, in a huff. "I called and called to you, but you took absolutely no notice. How could you be so heartless? Tell me! Tell me!"

"Oh, good Heavens! Why are you always setting yourself up against me?" the young man moaned, in a paroxysm of agitation.

"Who's always against you?" came the tart response. "Why must you always be the one suffering injustice?"

The attempt to suppress his indignation turned Shen Chun's face bright red. "Injustice? Injustice?" he stammered. "Heavens above! If you must know, Miss, I drank too much yesterday, and passed the whole night in a drunken stupor. How was I to know that you would come to see me?"

"You are quibbling again," Jiaoniang said, this time quite coolly. "Everyone knows that even when a person is drunk the mind remains clear. You are simply making an excuse. You came here today to play your old tricks, little suspecting that I had seen right through you, eh?" Having delivered herself of this withering observation, Jiaoniang covered her face with her sleeve, and recommenced weeping.

可真是糊涂了，这究竟是哪一出呀？"

娇娘愤愤道："你糊涂？你心里明镜似的，愣装什么糊涂？"

"装糊涂，我怎么装糊涂了？妹妹说个明白，让我死也做个明白鬼。"

"休要死呀活呀的，我不想听。昨日天黑时，我去……去……"蓦地一股委屈兜上心头，娇娘哽咽着说不下去。

申纯瞪大眼睛问道："妹妹去哪里了？"

娇娘哽咽道："去……去书房看你。"

申纯不敢相信自己的耳朵，追问道："什么？什么？妹妹你昨晚去书房了？"

娇娘愤愤道："你还在装糊涂么？我千呼万唤，你就是不理，你安得什么心？你说，你说呀。"

"啊呀，天啊，天啊，你为何总是要和我申纯作对？"申纯急得手足无措，失声叫道。

"你喊什么？谁和你作对了？莫非冤枉了你不成？"娇娘不依不饶道。

申纯脸憋得通红，连声道："冤枉，冤枉，天大的冤枉！妹妹，我昨日贪杯醉酒，昏睡了一夜，哪里想到你会去？"

"你还要狡辩！谁人不知酒醉心明，你分明以此推诿。今日里来这儿故伎重演，想不到我早已看透了你。"说着娇娘掩面抽泣起来。

At his wits' end, Shen Chun seized a pair of scissors from a needle-work box. He then dropped to his knees, pulled the bone hairpin from his hair, seized a hank, and snipped it off. Hearing the clack of the scissors, Jiaoniang looked up in astonishment. In silence, she watched as Shen Chun offered her the lock of hair, humbly using both hands. With his eyes filled with tears, the young man intoned, "If I should ever forsake you, may this happen to my head!"

Shen Chun's sincerity moved Jiaoniang to thinking that perhaps she had done him an injustice, after all. She hastened to help the young man to rise, saying, "Please don't kneel before me; it distresses me so."

Realizing that he had been pardoned for whatever crime Jiaoniang had imagined him to have committed, Shen Chun got up from his knees. With the help of a mirror, he re-arranged his hair. In the meantime, the girl picked up the lock of hair Shen Chun had lopped off, tied it with gaily-colored thread, and tucked it in her bosom. Later, she made a special perfumed sachet to keep it in.

The passing of the storm clouds was a great relief to Shen Chun.

Two days later, as Shen Chun was sitting alone reading in his study the gatekeeper Wang Zhong brought him a letter. It turned out to be from the young man's father, and it brought somber news: The nomads from across the western border had invaded. They were already pressing hard on Chengdu, and the situation was desperate. A general mobilization order had gone out, summoning all able-bodied men to the defense of the city. His father wanted Shen Chun to return with all speed. Shen Chun was thunder-struck at this turn of events, but before he had time to collect his thoughts, he heard the voice of Wang Wenrui outside, calling, "What news from home, young man?" The next moment, his host entered, followed by his wife and several of the local notables. Without saying a word, the tearful Shen Chun proffered the letter. It seemed that the gatekeeper had informed his master and mistress of the arrival of the missive.

Having scanned the letter, Wang Wenrui said, "Do not be unduly

申纯急得不知如何是好，一把操起床上针线盒中的剪子，跪倒在地，猛地抽掉头顶骨簪，揪起一缕头发，"咔哧"一声剪落下来。娇娘闻声急抬脸看时，当下惊得目瞪口呆，吐不出半个字来。申纯将那缕头发用双手捧着，递与娇娘，两眼蓄泪道："娇娘，我若有负于你，此头有如此发。"

娇娘见状，心想也许真是冤枉了他，当下将申纯搀起来，道："三哥快些起来，男儿膝下有黄金，怎能叫你今儿一跪，明儿一跪的，折煞小妹了。"

申纯见娇娘原谅了自己，这才起来，对着铜镜重新挽好发髻。娇娘忙把这缕青丝用七彩丝线扎紧揣在怀中，后来又专门绣了个香包盛了不提。

申纯见满天的乌云散了，一颗心方才落下。

过了两天，申纯在屋中独自看书，老院公王忠送来一封书信。申纯拆开观看，是老父手书。信中道，小西番国的土鲁们发兵来攻成都，兵临城下，形势危急。城中守将帅节镇下令三丁抽一，把守城池。老父要自己速回成都。申纯哪里经过这种事，一时毛发耸立，茫茫然不知所措。这时就听外面响起王文瑞的语声："厚卿家中来信有何事？"说话间王文瑞与赵夫人带着几名家人已鱼贯而入。申纯忙将书信递了上去，自己一句话也说不出来，眼里不禁落下泪来。原来老院公王忠先给申纯送了信，又急去报知老爷、

alarmed. I heard of this invasion a few days ago. You have lived the pampered and sheltered life of the scholar; not for you the clash of steel and the whinnying of warhorses. There is no point a person such as yourself volunteering to serve as cannon fodder. And while I would not urge you to flee from the flames of battle, it would be foolish to act like a moth attracted to a candle flame. However, I am worried about your mother and father; not to go to take care of them in these troubled times would be unfilial. It was because I knew that it would put you in an awkward position that I was loath to inform you earlier of the situation in Chengdu. Now that your father has summoned you to return, I suppose there is nothing else you can do."

Wang Wenrui's wife joined in, with, "Please don't distress yourself. The tides of war are unpredictable. Please send word to us by anyone who comes here from Chengdu, to relieve our worries about you and your family. And then when the fighting is over, you must come and stay with us again."

After discussing various contingencies with Shen Chun, Wang Wenrui and the others left him alone. His mind was in such a turmoil as a result of this latest development that he could neither sit nor stand. He was worried about his parents, so much that he wished that he could sprout wings and fly straight to them. But then the image of Jiaoniang intruded on his thoughts. Oh, why did those wretched nomads pick this time — of all times — to invade, and ruin his wonderful dream come true? Upon careful reflection, he decided that he had no choice but to return to Chengdu as quickly as possible. But how could he face Jiaoniang, and get her understanding for his grievous decision, as well as a token of her love as a keepsake? Shen Chun was still wrestling with this problem when he heard a sound in the doorway, and in rushed the girl herself, with tears streaming down her cheeks. The young man rushed forward to greet her. Jiaoniang, choking back her sobs, gasped, "I heard that you received a letter summoning you home. What on earth is the matter?"

夫人。

王文瑞看了书信，说道："贤甥莫急，番兵进犯早有传闻，老夫前几日就已知晓，只是想贤甥是一个文弱书生，金戈铁马疆场厮杀，并非你所擅长；权作民夫，充做炮灰，有你不多，无你不少；常人远避战火惟恐不及，断没有飞蛾扑火之理。但又虑及你严父、慈母尚在水深火热之中，不去守护，也是不孝。舅舅实在为难，故一拖再拖，不肯告你成都近况。如今你父唤贤甥回去，舅舅也不好再说什么了。"

赵夫人接着道："三哥儿此去勿要心慌，城外军情变化莫测，一切当随机应变，切记不可硬闯。倘若有成都来的人，捎个话来，以免我们惦念。日后战火停息，勿忘再来舅家。"

王文瑞又把一切应变事宜再三再四地叮嘱一番，便偕家人去了。

申纯独在房中，坐也不是，站也不是，一时间心乱如麻。心中惦念父母，恨不得肋生双翅飞回成都；又思想娇娘，只恨小西番为何此时来犯，坏了自家的好事。思来想去，还是快回成都为上，只是怎么与娇娘会上一面，讨她个准话，要个信物。正思量间，忽听屋门一响，进来一个泪人，正是娇娘。申纯忙起身相迎，娇娘忍悲问道："小妹闻姑母家中寄来书信，要三哥回去，不知是何急事？"

Shen Chun explained briefly to her the situation in Chengdu, and his parents' urgent summons. "As soon as I arrived here, I fell in love with you," he sighed. "I was so happy and grateful. But now the barbarian invaders have shattered our dream of wedded bliss."

Jiaoniang assured him, with fervent words: "The vow made by the stove will remain forever engraved on my heart. In life and in death, I am yours."

"For the past two months," Shen Chun rejoined, "although I have been separated from you in person, my heart has not for an instant left your side. My only wish is to cherish you from morning till night. But now, out of the blue, I find we have to part. Who knows when we shall meet again?" At this point, Shen Chun was unable to hold back his tears any longer.

"I share your feelings about parting," Jiaoniang said. "And I have a farewell poem for you." So saying, she choked back her sobs, and recited as follows:

"The verdant leaves shed shadows deep,

The sparse flowers hide in their shade.

My scholar lover cannot but weep,

As the cuckoo pipes in the glade.

The bird is bidding the spring depart,

And my love, who is bound far from me.

He takes with him a broken heart,

And tear-soaked sleeves for company."

Shen Chun wiped his eyes, and said, "You are too kind, Miss. I must match your gracious verse." He thought for a little while, and then recited:

"Amid the thick leaves the butterflies dance,

And on the drapes of the bridal bed.

The fear summer's advent, perchance,

By the returning swallows led.

Oh that the heart of my scholar swain,

申纯便把成都形势及父命速归等事详说一番，又道："愚兄初来，即蒙妹妹错爱，甚是感激。无奈小西番之乱，惊了你我一对鸳鸯。"

娇娘泣道："拥炉之约小妹铭记肺腑，生死与兄同心。"

"两月以来，虽未获身侍妆台，可是我的心却无时无刻不在妹妹身上，惟愿与妹妹朝朝暮暮长相守。如今匆匆别去，不知何年再逢？"申纯言罢，悲泣不能自持。

娇娘道："别后离情，妹有同感。妹有诗一首，为兄赠别。"遂忍泪吟道：

"绿叶荫浓花正稀，声声杜宇劝春归。
相如千里悠悠去，不道文君泪湿衣。"

申纯以袖拭泪道："感谢妹妹厚意，愚兄愿和诗一首。"略思片刻，吟道：

"密叶重帏舞蝶稀，相如只恐燕先归。
文君为我坚心守，切莫轻抛金缕衣。"

吟罢紧锁双眉，欲言又止，半晌方嗫嚅道："愚兄还有一言，不知当讲不当讲？"

Will maintain its constancy,

And that my keepsake he'll retain,

And not set my heart free."

Finishing his recitation, Shen Chun closed his eyes tightly. He wanted to say something, but the words would no longer come. Finally, he stammered, "I have something more to say, but I do not know whether it would be proper to say it."

"Please say it," Jiaoniang urged him.

"You and I have reached marriageable age," the young man explained. "But we have not been formally engaged. I dare to think that Heaven is not unmindful of us. But hearing you mention the 'deep shade cast by the green leaves' [reference to a woman who marries young and bears many children — *Trans.*] I could not but begin to have doubts. I fear that the next time we meet you may be married to another."

It had happened that Jiaoniang had taken her inspiration from luxuriant green leaves and the scanty red blossoms that set them off in the garden. It was just coincidence that these things were a poetic conceit standing for perfectly matched lovers. In no way was she hinting that she intended to marry another. Piqued at Shen Chun's tiresome sensitiveness, she said, "You have a very shallow understanding of my feelings, sir. A rapid profusion of green leaves is out of the question. The flower will be the same even after ten years have passed."

So saying, she drew from her sleeve a gauze pouch, and handed it to Shen Chun. "This is a little keepsake from me," she said. "Every time you look at it, I hope you will remember the donor."

Shen Chun peeped inside the pouch, and then tucked it carefully in the breast of his gown. Jiaoniang, weeping once more, helped him make preparations for his journey.

Arriving back in Chengdu, Shen Chun joined the defenders of the city, both military and civilian, and took his turn patrolling the city walls, night and day, and guarding the gates. Daily martial exercises soon made him an

娇娘道:"但讲无妨。"

"小生与妹妹正及婚时,喜的两下未曾聘定,窃谓老天不为无意。适闻妹妹'绿叶荫浓'之句,使人未免生疑。我只怕他日重逢,红花飘谢,绿叶成荫,别嫁东风。"

娇娘只是见庭中绿肥红瘦,因景而成句,焉有别嫁东风之意。听了申纯的话,心中甚是委屈,嗔道:"小妹此心三哥还不知晓吗?休道三年绿叶成荫子满枝,便是十载也花依旧。"

说罢从袖中取出一方罗帕包儿递与申纯道:"此乃小妹一缕青丝,送与三哥为念,望兄睹物思人,莫忘了小妹。"

申纯展开看罢,小心翼翼揣进怀间。娇娘含泪帮着清点路途应用之物不提。

申纯回到成都后,与驻守官兵及城中百姓,昼夜轮番在城墙上巡逻,把守各个城门。因他素日里也曾操练些武艺,此时颇觉游刃有余。不久,小西番兵临城下,全城军民奋力抵抗,死保家园。那小西番国王攻城无功,久围城下,恐怕大宋援兵来到,自己腹背受敌,反倒吃亏。且此次进兵,掳获颇丰,于是见好就收,下令在城郊大搜三日,而后满载而去。

帅节镇见番兵忽然退去,心中甚是疑惑,待要追击,又怕其中有诈,忙派探子出城去观虚实。待探子

expert swordsman. The people of Chengdu put up a stiff resistance to the invaders, until the latter, tiring of the long-drawn-out siege, and fearing to be trapped by a relief force sent by the Song emperor, took what plunder they could from the surrounding countryside, and withdrew.

Puzzled at first, the garrison commander was inclined to follow in hot pursuit. But, fearing a trick, he took the precaution of dispatching scouts to ascertain the truth of the matter. When the scouts reported that the invaders were indeed in retreat, the garrison commander had the main gate of the city thrown wide open, and led the forces under his command in splendid array hard on the heels of the invaders. However, he was cautious enough not to risk close-quarters combat with the enemy, and was satisfied just to harry them back across the border. The troops then returned to Chengdu in triumph, to the sound of songs of victory and rolls of drums.

The people of the city sprinkled the streets with water to keep down the dust, and thronged to welcome the victorious heroes with jugs of wine and plates of mutton. A swift rider was sent off to report the glad tidings to the imperial court. Officials flocked to the garrison commander's gate, hoping to share the glory and rewards for this splendid achievement. The commander himself held a grand celebratory banquet for his men.

Before long, a decree was issued by the emperor, raising the garrison commander to ministerial rank. A glorious and honored career lay before him, but we will say no more of this.

With the threat from the western nomads lifted, the people of Chengdu returned to their normal occupations, and peace descended once more on the city. Shen Chun, however, startled his parents by appearing to fall ill. His face turned sallow, and he lost weight. It was assumed that the alarms and travails of the siege had taken their toll on the young man, and that a few days of rest would see him fully recovered. But when two weeks had passed, and he showed no signs of improvement, doctors were sent for from all quarters of Chengdu. It turned out that none of them could diagnose the origin of his ailment, the general consensus being that he was suf-

报说番兵真的退去，这才大开城门，率领所部人马追出，做出一番乘胜追穷寇的样子，却不敢上前厮杀。走走停停，一直尾随番兵出境，这才整顿军容，唱着凯旋歌，敲着得胜鼓，雄赳赳气昂昂返回成都。

城中百姓清水泼街，黄土垫道，担酒牵羊，欢迎帅节镇凯旋归来。军中师爷急写庆功表快马向朝廷报捷请功。一时朝中内外大臣，皆想趁机借名升赏，帅节镇府门前车马喧腾，人声鼎沸。帅节镇大摆太平宴席，犒赏三军。

不久圣旨下，加封帅节镇为太尉。帅太尉春风得意，安民庆功诸事甚多，在此不提。

且说番兵退后，成都百姓重操旧业，依旧过起太平日子来。

只有申纯面黄肌瘦，恹恹害起病来。家里人只当他惊恐忧虑，劳累过度，休息几日便会痊愈。不料半个月过去，没有一点儿起色。四下求医，众郎中也说不出个病因来，只道身体虚弱，将养几天便好。可就是迟迟不见其好转。

其实申纯害的是相思病，自家心里最清楚不过。自打离了眉州，心里便在牵挂娇娘。只是大敌当前，昼夜巡守，容不得多想。待到番兵退去，无事可做，娇娘的音容笑貌无时无刻不萦绕脑海，浮现眼前。以致睡不安寝，食不甘味，人前还得强打精神应

fering from physical debility, and that all he needed was tonics to build up his strength again. Nevertheless, as time went on the young man showed no sign of a turn for the better.

The fact is that Shen Chun's complaint was love-sickness. He had sorely missed Jiaoniang ever since he had been compelled to leave Meizhou. While Chengdu was under threat from the western nomads, the night-and-day emergency patrols had left Shen Chun little time for brooding. But as soon as the invaders departed, and he found time hanging heavy on his hands, he was continually haunted by the vision of Jiaoniang's smiling face. The result was that sleep would not come to his weary body, nor would food and drink refresh it. He found it an effort to carry on normal dealings with other people. In private, he would finger the lock of hair that Jiaoniang had given him as a keepsake just before they parted, and let out heartfelt sighs, wishing that he could mount the wind and fly back to her in an instant. What was worse was the fact that he felt that there was no way he could open his heart to his parents. The result was that his love-sickness got progressively worse.

One sunny day, caressed by a balmy breeze, Shen Chun lay on his bed with his eyes closed drowsy and trying to calm his spirits, he started to feel that his body had become as light as a leaf. His lissome form was wafted to a place where peach and apricot trees intertwined. Blossoms blazing crimson and white adorned them, and bees buzzed and butterflies flitted in and out. Above, orioles sang and swallows darted; below, azure waters wound lazily. Clouds and mists hovered. Lost in wonder, Shen Chun suddenly saw Jiaoniang, her eyes shining with love, floating slowly towards him. The young man hurried forward to meet her, joy surging within him. Making a low bow, he asked, "Miss, did you come here specially to meet me?"

Suddenly, tears poured from the girl's eyes. It seemed that she wanted to say something, but could not. Shen Chun, too, wanted to speak some words of comfort to her, but no words came....

He was awakened by a voice calling him. Opening his eyes, Shen

付,背地里则握着娇娘临别所赠青丝长嘘短叹。恨不得缩地驭风前往眉州,只是无缘无故,怎好向爹娘开口?因此这相思病便一日胜似一日地沉重起来。

这日,日暖风恬,花明柳媚。申纯昏昏沉沉倚在软榻上闭目养神,朦胧中自己身轻如叶,飘飘摇摇来到一处,桃杏间杂,重葩叠萼,如火如荼,其间蜂飞蝶绕,莺歌燕舞,四周碧水环绕,云雾飘渺。正在纳闷,只见娇娘美目传情,款款走来。心中好生欢喜,便疾步上前深施一礼道:

"妹妹在此是专为等候愚兄吗?"

娇娘忽然泪眼婆娑,欲言又止。申纯正欲安慰几句,就听耳旁有人呼唤:

"三儿,三儿。"

睁眼一看,爹娘兄嫂环绕榻前,都是一脸焦急,方知自己适才是南柯一梦,不禁叹了一口气,挣扎着向父母问安。

王氏见儿子昏昏沉沉,真是心痛万分,坐在榻前抹泪道:

"孩儿,你怎么会成了这个样子?为娘看你日见憔悴,心都要碎了……"

"孩儿,你身上到底是哪里不舒服?"申庆也急切地询问。

申纯叹道:"这病连我自己也不知因何而得,反

Chun found his whole family standing at the foot of his bed, all wearing worried expressions. Realizing that he had been dreaming, the young man groaned. With great difficulty, he struggled to greet his parents. Distressed to see his son in such a pathetic condition, Shen Chun's mother sat by his bedside, and wiped her son's tears away. "My boy," she said, "how did you come to waste away like this? Our hearts are breaking to see you in such a woeful state. . . . "

"Where does it hurt?" asked his father Shen Qing in a tone of great concern.

"I myself don't know how it came about," replied Shen Chun. "All I know is that my whole body is racked with pain. I am afraid that there is not a physician in all of this great city of Chengdu who can cure me. My only hope lies in Meizhou, where there are eminent doctors who specialize in curing unnamed sicknesses. If one could be called to examine me, perhaps there might be a chance of improvement."

His brother Shen Lun objected: "But Meizhou is a long way from here. It is not likely that a doctor would come all this way. I think it would be better if you went there for a consultation."

But Shen Chun's mother had her doubts. She suspected that some of the horrific scenes of warfare during her son's period of duty with the city garrison during the siege might still be haunting him. In this case, regular herbal medicine would be useless. Frowning, she said, "Those ordinary doctors kill more people than they save. It seems to me that what is needed here is a witch who can exorcise the demon that is troubling the boy."

Her husband shook his head, and protested, "As the old saying goes, 'Trust in sorcery is the road to ruin.' No, a doctor is needed to treat an illness. But I am afraid that Shen Chun is too frail to withstand among journey on horseback."

Hearing that his father was in favor of sending him back to Meizhou, Shen Chun was overjoyed. He felt as if his illness was half cured already. "A child receives his body from his parents," he said, "and so if the body

正是浑身上下不舒服，可恨偌大个成都竟没个像样的郎中，倒不如眉州那边有几个惯治无名之症的太医。不如请一位来看看，或许有些起色。"

申纶道："眉州那么远，就是请到太医，人家也不一定来。依我说还是你去就医的好。"

王氏闻言心里直犯嘀咕，想是儿子在城上巡守，经了些拼搏厮杀的场面，说不定是哪个冤魂野鬼缠身，所以草药不起效用，便一皱眉道："这些庸医，医死的人多，医活的人少。依我看，还是请个师婆来驱驱鬼，定有效验。"

申庆摇摇头说："古人云：信了巫，卖了屋。有病治病，还是就医的好。但孩儿病体虚弱，怎能经得住一路上的鞍马劳顿？"

申纯闻听此言，恰似吞了一粒仙丹，顿时心花怒放，欣喜若狂，觉着五脏六腑通泰了许多，病便去了大半，当下道："身体发肤受之父母，孩儿因病求医，也只得强打精神，挣扎前行。只是爹娘在家，孩儿怎忍相离？"

申纶道："爹娘自有为兄照料，三弟只管去治病要紧，不必挂念。但愿弟弟此去眉州好好医病养神，日常多写些信来，以免家中惦念。"

申纯急忙点头不止。申家二老见小儿愿去求医，心中也略感宽慰，择吉日派管家申成驾了轿车，送申

is afflicted it is the child's duty to seek a cure. But how could I bear to be parted from my dear parents?"

His brother Shen Lun consoled him, saying, "I will remain to look after our parents; you must only concern yourself with finding a cure for your illness. Hurry back to Meizhou, but please make sure that you write every day, so that we will not worry about you."

Shen Chun nodded eagerly in assent. His willingness to consult a skilled healer in Meizhou was a great consolation to his parents, and, upon a lucky day being appointed, they sent him back to Meizhou in a special carriage driven by the family retainer Shen Cheng.

纯前往眉州诊病。

娇红记

Chapter Three
First Taste of Passion

Every day since their pledge of love and tearful parting, Jiaoniang had pined for Shen Chun. At first she had been fearful that if the invading nomads captured Chengdu, her brave lover would lose his life in the destruction of the city. Then, when she learned of the attackers' retreat, she had been greatly relieved, but as the days went by and there was no sign of Shen Chun returning, she had grown peevish and fretful. Before she knew it, spring had departed, and summer had arrived.

One day, as Jiaoniang was sitting alone in her room, listlessly picking at some embroidery, Feihong pranced in, her face wreathed in smiles. "Miss, Miss! I've some wonderful news for you!" she cried.

"What's got you so all worked up?" Jiaoniang drawled, not showing much interest.

Feihong stepped close to her, and whispered in her ear: "Master Shen's here. Your mother wants you to go and meet him straightaway. Isn't it marvellous?"

Jiaoniang's heart thumped in her breast at this news, and a rosy flush spread over her cheeks. Keeping her voice steady with an effort, though, she said, "Really? I hope you are not making a story up."

Feihong pouted. "How would I dare do such a thing?" she asked, indignantly. "Anyway, what would be the point of playing a trick on you? Well, if you don't believe me, don't go."

Not caring to bandy words with the maid servant, Jiaoniang put her embroidery down, and went and sat before her dressing-table mirror to paint

第三章 初试云雨

　　且说王娇娘自与申纯结盟泣别后，日日为申纯担忧。先是怕贼兵攻破成都，玉石俱焚搭送了性命。后知贼兵退了，心中略安，便日思夜想盼着申纯再来，可又不见他来，不由生出几分怨恨。转眼间，已是春去夏来。

　　这日，娇娘正在房中刺绣，飞红喜眉笑眼地进来，道："小姐，小姐，告你一件天大的好事。"

　　娇娘漫不经心地问道："什么事值得你这么张张狂狂的?"

　　飞红凑到耳边道："申家哥哥来了，夫人请小姐相见哩。这不是喜事么?"

　　娇娘听了不禁芳心狂跳，霞飞双颊，脱口道："果真是他来了?你休要说谎。"

　　飞红一撇嘴道："我哪里敢说谎?再者说，我骗小姐做啥?小姐如若不信，不去也就是了。"

　　娇娘也顾不上与飞红斗嘴，忙停了手中针线，到菱花镜前描眉点唇，略整衣裙，便随飞红快步来到熙春堂。

her eyebrows and lips. Then, hurriedly adjusting her dress, she was accompanied by Feihong to the Cherishing Spring Hall.

The first thing Jiaoniang noticed when she entered the door was how pale and sallow Shen Chun looked as he sat in conversation with her mother. In the presence of the old lady, the two young people could do no more than exchange a few conventional words of greeting, and covertly signal their affection with their eyes, keeping all expression of their real feelings in check.

This time too, Shen Chun was housed in the study in the eastern wing of the mansion. The young man's heart was filled with joy at the thought that he would be able to see Jiaoniang every day. But when several days passed, and there was no sign of her coming to call on him, he began to lose his appetite once more and to have trouble sleeping again. Feihong often dropped by for a chat, but, needless to say, that did not help to lift Shen Chun's spirits much.

One day, when he was feeling a little better, he decided to try to shuffle out into the rear courtyard and try to catch a glimpse of Jiaoniang. But when he finally got there, there was not a soul to be seen. He sat down on a stone bench to rest, leaning his back on a pillar. He gazed at the crabapple trees in courtyard. They were in full bloom, a riot of color. Butterflies flitted among the branches, and bees buzzed as they hovered over the blossoms. In the midst of this tranquil and enchanting scene, the young man felt a strange sense of desolation creep over him. Then, just as he thought he was in the depth of despair, he heard a light cough behind him. He turned his head, and to his astonishment and delight, found Jiaoniang standing there. "Miss," he cried out, "I have been here for several days, but you have never once come to see me. I thought you must have forgotten all about me!"

"How could you imagine such a thing?" the girl replied. "It has been a little inconvenient, that's all. If you think that I could forget you, you must be naive indeed! Today I managed to give my maid servants the slip

进门就见申纯一脸憔悴，正与赵夫人叙话。娇娘上前寒暄几句，碍着母亲的面，也不便多言。二人只能眉目传情，暗致心意而已。

此次申纯重来，依旧住在东厢书房。满以为可与娇娘日日相见，心情畅快了许多。可住了几日，并不见娇娘前来探视，倒是飞红时常走动，或说些宽慰话，或调侃一阵子。那也无济于事，越发食不甘味，寝不安眠。

这日，申纯觉得略有些精神，强撑病体踱出门来，到后园中探头探脑，指望看到娇娘，不想园中一个人影也没有。只得倚廊柱坐在石凳上小憩，望见庭中数株海棠，争奇斗艳，花开正浓，花间蝶飞蜂绕，好不热闹，一时倍感凄凉无助。

正在发痴之际，忽听身后一声轻咳，转过头来见娇娘不知什么时候已立于自己身后，一时惊喜万状道：

"是妹妹呀，愚兄到此多日，也不过来看望一下，敢是妹妹心上不记得我了？"

娇娘忙道："怎么会呢？只是不便过来，你若说我忘了，则只有头上的苍天知道。今日也是瞒过丫头们，偷着来看你。三哥怎么越发消瘦了，还不及才来的时候丰润些。须解开愁怀，勉加餐饭才好。"

specially to sneak out and look for you." She added, in a worried tone: "But you have grown so thin — a far cry from the sleek youth who came here the last time! You must stop worrying, and eat some proper meals. Then you'll be fine."

Shen Chun uttered a deep sigh. "How can I dispel my worries?" he moaned. "I'm lucky I still have my life."

It pained Jiaoniang to hear this. "But my father has summoned so many eminent doctors. Why is it that they cannot find a cure for what ails you?" she asked.

Shen Chun shook his head. "No doctor can cure the ailment that is afflicting me," he said, gloomily. "Only you can do that."

"But I don't know anything about feeling pulses and writing prescriptions," protested Jiaoniang, puzzled. "How can I cure you?"

"Surely, you haven't forgotten the words said as we parted, about 'deep shade cast by the green leaves.' Perhaps you have already broken your vow?"

This last cutting remark brought tears to Jiaoniang's eyes, and she retorted, "How on earth could I so lightly forget those parting words?"

"If that is so," the young man countered, "how can you stand there looking on as I suffer the torments of love-sickness, and not extend a helping hand?"

Jiaoniang took a quick look around, and, as nobody else was near, whispered, "Are you mad? In a public place like this there are too many prying eyes. But if you have a mind to, come to my chamber tonight."

Shen Chun blinked his understanding, but inquired, "What about your maid servants? Won't that be somewhat awkward?"

"I'll think of an excuse to send them on some errand or other tonight. On the western side of the Cherishing Spring Hall there is a wicket gate which connects with my boudoir. I will leave it open for you."

Shen Chun was overcome with joy, but then, remembering how a rain shower had ruined the previous solemn tryst, smiled ruefully, and said,

申纯长叹一声道："我愁怀怎生得解？没送了性命就是万幸了！"

娇娘心疼地说道："为何爹爹请了这许多医生来家，也治不好三哥的病？"

申纯叹道："我的病太医怎能治得？只有妹妹可以救我。"

"小妹又不会把脉开方，何以救你？"

"妹妹难道忘了临别之言吗？真可谓应了'绿叶荫浓'之语，妹妹已尽改前盟了。"

这一句话说得娇娘泪眼婆娑，委屈万分，道："临别之言，小妹岂敢忘却？"

申纯道："既然如此，妹妹为何坐视愚兄相思成疾，而不加援手呢？"

娇娘看了看四下无人，悄声道："大庭广众之下，十目所视，你要死呀！三哥若是有意，今夜可到我房中来。"

申纯心领神会，眨眨眼道："当着丫环们多不方便呀！"

娇娘道："今夜里我寻个理由将丫环们支走，熙春堂西边有一个小角门通着绣阁，我给你留着。你尽可放心。"

申纯听了喜出望外，转念想起上次密约为暴雨所阻，苦笑道："不知今夜有无风雨，但愿莫像上回那

"Who knows? There may be another rainstorm tonight that stops us meeting, like last time."

"I am sure that Heaven is not opposed to us," Jiaoniang said coyly.

Shen Chun took her by the hand, and after hesitating for a while, said, "But if we meet at night, and someone chances to come upon us and reports us to your parents, the consequences could be serious."

Jiaoniang gave a dismissive wave of her hand. "Why are you so beset by misgivings at such a crucial moment? I often reflect that life is fleeting — like the glimpse of a white steed racing past the crack in a door. Ours is a love that will through all eternity. If we are discovered and foiled, I am quite willing to face death."

Shen Chun had never expected such an impassioned outburst from Jiaoniang. He was completely taken aback. His face turned purple, as he spluttered, "Well, if that's the case, I too will fear nothing!"

Jiaoniang, after whispering a few more words of instruction, departed. Shen Chun felt his confidence returning and his spirits buoyed up. He returned to his quarters to watch the moon climb up the sky. As soon as all was quiet in the mansion, he climbed out through the west window. Everywhere he looked he saw ghostly swaying branches and flickering shadows of the flowers. Disquiet filled his mind, but he plucked up his ebbing courage. "You must not go back now," he told himself. So, accompanied by the chirping of insects all around, he tiptoed forward with hesitant steps through the foliage and willows. The young man's heart was palpitating, and he was panting for breath as he groped his way forward. Finally, the side gate to Jiaoniang's boudoir came in view. It swung open at the touch of his hand. Thrilled to the marrow, Shen Chun slipped inside, closing the gate softly behind him. As he inched his way into the garden, suddenly he was grabbed from behind. He stood stock still, except for his knees, which started to tremble violently. Beads of sweat started to trickle down his body. In his mind he was screaming in anguish. After what seemed like an age, and there was no further movement behind him, Shen Chun, timidly

般阻人赴约。"

娇娘羞答答道:"老天总不会总与你我作对吧!"

申纯拉住娇娘的手,犹豫半晌,说道:"深夜相会,倘若被人撞见,告到舅父舅母那里,不是要子。"

娇娘甩脱他的手道:"事到临头,三哥怎么反倒畏首畏尾起来? 我常想人生一世,如白驹过隙,你我彼此钟情,生死同心,事情倘若败露,小妹当以死继之。"

申纯没料到娇娘如此痴情刚烈,一时羞愧难当,无地自容,满脸紫胀道:"既如此,我乃身长七尺的须眉男儿,还有什么可怕的!"

娇娘又叮嘱了一番,方才离开。申纯顿觉身上的不适都化为乌有,精神为之一振。回房后看着月上中天,府中安静下来,这才从卧室西窗越出。只见四下里树枝轻摆,花影摇曳,不由得心里惶恐,转念一想,事已至此,断没有回去的道理。于是蹑足潜踪,穿花度柳,来到熙春堂。一路上听得草虫儿唧唧鸣唱,更觉心慌气促,鬼鬼祟祟摸了半天,才找到通往绣阁的小角门。轻轻一推,虚掩的门扉随手而开,心中一阵狂喜,闪身进来,仍把门轻轻掩上,踮起脚尖走了几步,忽觉有人从身后扯住了衣襟,申纯登时吓得两腿发颤,冷汗涔涔,心中叫苦不迭,呆立在当地不敢行动。立了半晌,不见动静,慢慢回头一看,哪有什么

turned his head. With a gasp of relief, he realized that there was nobody behind him, after all. The hem of his robe had caught on a bush. Muttering "I've got to pull myself together," he bent down and unhooked himself from the bush. Creeping further into the garden, he spied a gleam of lamplight. Soon he had arrived before Jiaoniang's boudoir. The window was wide open, affording him a view of Jiaoniang seated at a table with her chin propped up in her hands. She was dressed in a flimsy nightgown, and was gazing at the moon. To the young man, she looked as enchanting as the Moon Goddess herself come down to earth. At that moment, Shen Chun threw off all restraint. Tucking up the skirts of his gown into his waist sash, he stood on tiptoe, put both hands on the window-sill, and vaulted lightly into the room, startling the girl out of her reverie.

Shen Chun wasted no time. He took Jiaoniang in his arms. "My dear, I miss you very much!" he said.

Recovering from her fright, Jiaoniang accepted his embrace with a low moan. For a while, the two were locked in each other's arms, whispering endearments. Shen Chun was transported with delight, gazing on his beloved's perfectly arched eyebrows, fascinating mouth and coy expression. An all-consuming and uncontrollable passion blazed up inside him, and he whispered in Jiaoniang's ear: "My dear, the night is already half over. I fear that the hours are fleeting, and it will too soon be morning. Why should we not taste to the full sweetness of our love right now?"

Startled at this abrupt suggestion, Jiaoniang attempted to push the ardent youth away. "Although I am pledged to be yours," she protested, "the betrothal formalities have yet to be gone through. Besides, I have not even obtained my parents' consent. Any closer union between us is out of the question." But, despite her protests, the hands which pushed at Shen Chun's chest seemed to be losing their force of their own accord — until finally, they went limp.

Shen Chun made no answer, but held Jiaoniang even more tightly, and kissed her passionately. The girl felt as if their lips, glued together, were

人？原来是被一丛灌木勾住了衣裳下摆，这才松了口气。暗想道："这张生会莺莺的事，实在不是好做的。"低头将衣襟摘开，前行数步，便看到一缕灯光，转眼来到绣阁前。只见阁中窗扇洞开，娇娘着一身轻纱，倚几托腮，凝眸望月，飘飘然不啻嫦娥降临人间。申纯此时已忘了顾忌，来到窗下，把前襟往腰中一挽，双手一撑窗台，脚尖轻轻点地，便翻身跃进了绣阁，把个正在痴想的娇娘吓得浑身一颤。

申纯不管三七二十一，上前一把搂住娇娘，道："好人，你可把我想煞了！"

娇娘回过神儿来，嘤咛入怀，二人紧紧抱在一起，唧唧哝哝说起话来。申纯玉人在抱，又见娇娘柳眉笼翠，檀口含丹，媚眼如丝，娇羞难状，一时间心旌摇荡，情热似火，无法自持，附在娇娘耳边道："夜漏过半，良宵恨短，你我何不共赴巫山，初试云雨？"

娇娘闻言一惊，推拒道："小妹此生必属三哥，而今媒妁未通，父母未允，佳礼未成，怎能先行苟且？"说着便欲推开申纯，无奈身饧息微，半点儿力气也使不出来。

申纯双臂一紧，并不答话，却深深地吻在娇娘的朱唇上。娇娘只觉一股热流忽地窜上脑门，四片嘴唇紧紧地粘在了一起。许久之后，申纯才将娇娘稍微放

igniting a flame inside her. After what seemed like a long time, Shen Chun slackened his embrace, and whispered again: "Since I caught this love-sickness, you have been the only person who can save my life. If we wait until all the formalities have been completed, I am afraid that I will be as dead as a rotten fish on a street stall."

Jiaoniang could no longer control her passion. Her face a fiery red, she averted her gaze as Shen Chun half-carried her to the bed. There, they disrobed, and became as one.

But just as the butterfly was alighting on the bloom, and the lovers were mounting the clouds and riding the mist, two people were whispering to each other outside the window. The two were none other than the maid servants Feihong and Xiang'e. The fact is that Feihong was always poking her nose into other people's affairs. This time, she had been extremely curious about what Shen Chun was up to, and when she noticed that Jiaoniang had sent her own maids away that night to attend to her mother, she suspected that some intrigue was afoot. She found an opportunity to visit Xiang'e, and told her: "The old master's away from home tonight, and the old mistress is not well. Well, what do you think? The young mistress has taken advantage of this to get rid of her maids. She's sent them to look after her mother, but she herself won't go. Now isn't that fishy? But that's not all. Xiaohui told me that the young mistress and Master Shen Chun were talking as thick as thieves in the rear courtyard this afternoon. It's as plain as daylight that they were arranging a rendezvous."

Xiang'e almost jumped with gleeful outrage. "Let's go and have a look," she suggested.

This was just what Feihong wanted, but she pretended to be shocked at such impropriety. "The very idea!" she snorted. "What do you think I am? If you want to go, then go. I am above such vulgar goings-on. Well, what are you waiting for? Off you go!"

So saying, she pushed Xiang'e out of the door. The latter, as she stumbled into the courtyard, pulled Feihong with her, pleading, "It's for

松些，依旧附在耳边恳求道："好妹妹，你三哥得了这个相思的症候，只有你才能救我一命。若是等到合卺礼成，妹妹只能索你三哥于枯鱼之肆了。"

娇娘此时已经情不自禁，莲脸凝红，粉颈低垂，只得任由申纯半拥半抱共入罗帐。两人解带宽衣，握雨携云，成了好事。

正当二人蝶上花枝，腾云驾雾之际，哪能想到窗外却听麻了两个人。这两个不是别人，正是丫头飞红和湘娥。原来，飞红心思细密，又对申纯有意，平日里有事无事总在注意。今晚入夜后，飞红见娇娘将房里的丫环都打发到夫人房中来，心中就有几分怀疑，瞅空将要好的湘娥找到房中，悄声道："今日老爷不在家，夫人身子不爽，小姐偏偏叫房内的丫头都去陪伴夫人，自己是嫡亲的女儿却不去，能不叫人起疑？我听小慧讲，申官人下午在后园与小姐说话，分明是两个白日里约下了。"

湘娥听了，跃跃欲试道："既然如此，咱们何不去看看？"

此话正中飞红下怀，可她却拿起架子道："你把我看成什么人了？要去，你去。我可不做那下三滥的事。你去吧，快去，快去！"

说着就往外推搡湘娥。湘娥急忙拉住飞红央求道："好姐姐，这还不是为了小姐好，怕小姐被人欺

the young mistress' own good. We have a duty to go and watch out for her, in case she is taken advantage of. Don't you see? So long as the young mistress gets into no harm, we won't get into trouble later. Otherwise there'll be ructions in this house."

Feihong, pretending reluctance, finally said, "Well, all right. But wait until the old mistress is asleep, and then come and call me. Then we'll go to the rear courtyard together. We don't want to leave the young mistress unattended all night, do we?"

Sure enough, at midnight Xiang'e came to fetch Feihong. They found the main gate to the rear courtyard locked. Xiang'e said, disappointed: "It's locked. I don't suppose Master Shen could jump over the wall. The young mistress probably isn't feeling well, and so stayed at home. Let's go back."

Feihong was not at all inclined to leave the matter at that, and as the two girls were hesitating they suddenly heard the creak of a door from the western side of the rear courtyard. Feihong remembered the side door, which was seldom used. She tugged at her companion's sleeve, and whispered, "I just heard something on the western side. Let's go and have a look."

They followed the courtyard wall until they reached the path that Shen Chun had taken to Jiaoniang's boudoir. Entering the side gate, they saw that there was a bright light shining inside. The window was tightly closed, but, putting their ears close to it they could hear Shen Chun and Jiaoniang exchanging ardent words of love, followed by the commotion as they tumbled onto the bed. "Did you hear that?" Xiang'e hissed excitedly in Feihong's ear. They're up to something they shouldn't be getting up to. Our young mistress pretends to be so prim and proper during the day, and carries on in this vulgar way at night! It really is enough to make you blush for shame. And that Master Shen — he's a nasty piece of work. We should grab the rascal and march him off to the old master to face the music for his disgraceful behavior. That would be the right thing to do, don't you

负,过去看看何妨? 但愿小姐没事,将来咱们也能脱得干系,否则老爷的家法可是难捱。"

飞红这才半推半就地随口应道:"这还算是人话。一会子等夫人睡了,你过来喊我,咱们到后院看看去,别让小姐孤零零的夜里害怕。"

待夜半时,湘娥果真来唤飞红,二人相随来到后院,发现门已上锁。湘娥扫兴地说:"门锁着,申官人总不能跳墙吧? 也许小姐是不舒服,没有到前院来,咱们回去吧。"

飞红心里可不这么想,也不愿就此做罢。正在这时,西边传来一声"吱呀"的开门声。飞红顿时想到了平时无人出入的角门,便一拉湘娥低声道:"西面好像有响动,咱们过去看看。"

二人遂绕过院墙,沿着申纯经过的路线来到绣阁外。 见阁内红烛高烧,门窗紧闭,俯耳静听,只听得里面申纯正与娇娘互诉衷情,不多时,便听到二人拉拉扯扯地上了床。湘娥十分得意地对飞红耳语道:

"姐姐,你听到了吗? 真是要想人不知,除非己莫为。咱这小姐素日口强,却做下这等风流勾当,真是让人羞煞了。那申官人也不是什么好东西,咱们把这偷香窃玉的贼汉拿住,交与老爷发落,岂不是立了一功?"

think?"

But Feihong pulled her friend away, under the eaves of the building. "It's not Master Shen's fault," she told Xiang'e. "It's always the woman who lures the man; not the other way round. Thinking carefully about it, I've come to the conclusion that it was our young mistress who arranged this. But we'd better not cause a fuss. Because for one thing the young mistress will get mad at us; for another Master Shen's reputation will be tarnished; and thirdly if the old master and mistress find out, they will insist on a tight watch being kept on their daughter's movements, and that would be more work for us. No, we should keep out of the way, wait until Master Shen leaves, and then confront him and see what his explanation is."

Xiang'e agreed.

In the meantime, their passion spent, Jiaoniang and Shen Chun lay wrapped in each other's arms. Jiaoniang said, "Now that I have surrendered my body to you, I hope that you will be always constant and never forsake me."

"How could I abandon a love I never deserved should be mine?" the young man protested. As he spoke, his embrace tightened around his beloved, and he murmured an urgent request.

"Oh no, you must go quickly," Jiaoniang protested. "Dawn is not far off, and I am afraid someone might discover us."

The young man was most reluctant to tear himself away. "My dear, how can I bear to part from you?" he moaned.

"We have to make long-term plans," Jiaoniang said firmly. "Get up, quickly."

So the two of them arose, and began to dress. In the light of the lamp, Jiaoniang spotted a bright red stain on Shen Chun's sleeve. She swiftly cut the patch out of the sleeve with a pair of scissors. "I'll keep this as a souvenir," she said coyly.

Just then, the cock crew, and the dew began to gather. Jiaoniang straightened Shen Chun's cap and gown, and then said, "Remember that in

飞红忙拉着湘娥退到廊檐下悄声说:"这事怪不得申官人,世间只有女子偷的汉子,哪有男子偷的女子?仔细想来,这定是小姐约下的。我们若声张起来,一来小姐见怪;二来也坏了申官人的名声;三来么,即使老爷夫人知道了,必定护着自家女儿,我们做下人的往后如何做人。咱们且躲着,待申官人出来,上前捉住他,看他怎么说,再相机行事。"

"也罢,就听姐姐的。"

此时,绣阁中申纯、娇娘云收雨敛。娇娘依在申纯怀中含情道:"小妹此身已属三哥,惟愿三哥始终如一,不负我心。"

申纯道:"小生承娘子错爱,岂敢负心?"说着,又紧紧抱住娇娘道:"你我不妨再赴高唐。"

娇娘道:"更漏将尽,恐人发觉,你且去罢。"

申纯依依不舍道:"娘子,叫小生怎忍离去也?"

娇娘道:"三哥,你我应图长久之计,还是快快起来吧。"

二人披衣而起,灯影下但见申纯衣袖上猩红点点。娇娘拿起剪子将染血的衣袖裁下,含羞道:"小妹留此为他日之念。"

此时,雄鸡一唱,夜漏将残。娇娘为申纯整束衣冠,道:"这府里人多眼杂,此后一言一行皆当谨慎在意。"

this mansion there are many people and many prying eyes. You must be careful about every word and every action. "

"Please rest assured, my dear, " he said. "I will not do or say anything indiscreet. "

He held Jiaoniang close for a short while, and then pushed open the door and stepped lightly outside. After a quick look around, he left along the same path he had come by, through the side gate. Taking advantage of the cover of the bushes, he had not gone more than a few paces, when two figures ambushed him. Closing in from either side, they growled, "Aha! The old lady knows what tricks you've been up to!"

The young man was frightened out of his wits, and his knees turned to jelly. A cry of anguish welled up inside him, but found no outlet. But then he heard the mysterious figures giggling. Plucking up courage, he peered into the gloom of the dawn, and saw that his assailants were the maid servants Feihong and Xiang'e. "Knows? Knows what?" he spluttered.

Xiang'e blocked his way, her hands firmly on her hips. "Knows what?" she mimicked. "Oh you're a fine one you are. We were standing under the window, and heard everything that went on. "

Shen Chun felt as though his brain had suddenly exploded. He started to plead abjectly: "Oh, my dear young lady, I beg you not to say a word about this. "

Feihong sneered, "Master Shen, you are supposed to be a modest scholar steeped in sacred classics and righteous tomes. How did you manage to stoop to such disgraceful behavior? Scaling walls in the dead of night, consumed by insatiable lechery, well I never! When the old master finds out about this, he won't let you off lightly, you can be sure!"

At this, Shen Chun's heart dissolved within him, and his knees turned to jelly. He threw himself onto these unreliable joints in front of the two maid servants, and wailed pitifully: "My dear, kind, good young ladies, please don't let this matter come to light. "

Feihong snorted. "Just fancy, a scholar sneaking into boudoirs to steal

申纯道："娘子放心，小生怎敢妄言莽行，与人留下话把！"

说罢，又与娇娘温存一阵，轻轻推门出来。看看四周无人，依旧从来时路径出了西角门，借着荼蘼架遮掩身形，走了几步，不提防从斜刺里冲出两个人来，低声喝道："话把，话把，夫人已知道你做下的好事！"

申纯顿时惊得魂飞魄散，腿一软瘫在地上，心中暗暗叫苦不迭。又听见女子"哧哧"的笑声，这才壮起胆子，抬头看去，见晨曦中飞红和湘娥挡住前路，慌忙问道："知道，知道什么了？"

湘娥双手叉腰道："你说知道什么了？秀才你做得好事！我们在窗下都听见了。"

申纯脑子里"嗡"的一声，好似炸开了一个爆竹，急忙央求道："好姐姐，千万为我遮掩则个。"

飞红冷笑道："申官人，你是读过圣贤书的谦谦君子，怎能干出这种有辱斯文的勾当？黄夜跳窗，真是色胆包天。老爷夫人知道了，岂肯善罢甘休？"

申纯心惊肉跳，双膝发软，跪在地上哀求道："只求二位姐姐多多担待，为小生遮掩。"

飞红鼻子里"哼"了一声，道："你个秀才家偷香窃玉，岂能白白饶过你？"

a young lady's most precious treasure! How can you have the nerve to ask to be let off scot-free?"

Seeing that groveling was not going to get him anywhere, Shen Chun suddenly thought of a change of tactics. He straightened himself up, and said in a haughty tone: "As a matter of fact, I was finding the summer heat quite unbearable, and simply stepped outside in search of cooler air. At the same time, I was desirous of viewing the night scenery. It just so happened, quite by chance, that I came upon the young lady leaning on her windowsill, gazing at the moon and we just happened to exchange a few words. What's wrong with that? So, whether you make a big fuss or not, it's all the same to me."

This attempt by Shen Chun to brazen it out infuriated Feihong. "You shameless pedantic scoundrel!" she cried. "Taking the cool air and viewing the scenery were you. A likely story! In the young mistress' boudoir? Are you trying to deny that you forced yourself upon our young mistress, who's as pure as ice and as unsullied as jade...?"

Xiang'e chimed in with "That's right. Our good, kind young mistress. And what have you made of her, eh? How dare you bluster at us, you miserable bookworm? You're no better than a thief, and you'll get what's coming to you."

"It seems that you don't know the meaning of the word 'shame'." Feihong rejoined.

At this point Shen Chun realized that neither blandishments nor tough words would enable him to pacify the two girls. To add to his agitation, just then the cock crew, reminding him that the other people in the mansion would soon be up and about. In haste, he made a low bow, and said, in a low voice: "Please, young ladies, refrain from mentioning what we were talking about just now. Otherwise...."

"Otherwise what?" piped up the bold Xiang'e.

Shen Chun decided that he might as well fight fire with fire. "Otherwise, your young mistress will be in the position of Yingying, the

申纯见恳求无效，一时间情急生智，立起身来道："小生暑热难耐，散步纳凉，月夜观景。正巧遇着小姐倚窗望月，便在窗前闲话几句，有什么见不得人的？你们饶也罢，不饶也罢，又能将我怎样？"

飞红听申纯口气陡然强硬起来，变了脸斥责道："好个没脸的秀才，你纳凉观景，就观到小姐的闺房里去了？方才已经不打自招，如今反倒抵赖。我家小姐素来冰清玉洁……"

"好好一个小姐，如今不知被你弄成什么样子了，你个穷酸饿醋还敢嘴硬，这真是做贼的不让失主，反了你了！"湘娥不待飞红说完，也上前抢白。

飞红道："亏你还敢钢牙铁嘴地说这种太平话，真是不知人间尚有'羞耻'二字。"

申纯见二个丫头软硬不吃，耳听鸡唱二遍，稍待人多起来，更是无法脱身，只得深深一揖，低声下气道："如今什么话都不消说了，二位姐姐，肯休便肯休，不休……"

湘娥道："不休你想怎的？"

申纯索兴以毒攻毒，道："不休的话，少不得她做了莺莺，你们做红娘，勾引的名儿你们担着，咱们大家谁都脱不了干系。"

飞红、湘娥面面相觑，说不出一句话来。半晌，湘

amorous young lady in the drama *The Romance of the Western Bower*. And you two will be a pair of Hong Niangs — you remember, the maid who acted as the go-between for Yingying's illicit love affair. Then we'll all be mixed up in this affair."

Feihong and Xiang'e exchanged glances. After a long silence, Xiang'e pointed her finger at Shen Chun. "You sneaky, lecherous villain," she said, in a grating voice. "Don't you dare try to put the blame on us. So, if we do decide to go easy on you just this once, how will you reward us?"

The young man spread his palms in a gesture of helplessness. "I am just a poor stranger who has wandered here from afar. I own nothing but my body. How do you suggest that I repay you for your kindness?"

"What can we do with your body, if that's all you have?" asked Xiang'e.

"You tell me," said Shen Chun.

"How should I know?" the naive Xiang'e cried in exasperation. "Anyway, which one are you going to reward first?"

Shen Chun blinked in feigned innocence. "Perhaps I should reward you to that the same time?" he said. "That way I wouldn't playing favorites."

Feihong spat in disgust, and hid her face for shame. "You deserve to die for the disgraceful way you treat people!" she hissed.

Seizing his opportunity, Shen Chun made a low bow, and wheedled, "My dear young ladies, I trust you to avoid indiscretion. You shall be amply rewarded, I assure you."

Xiang'e dismissed him with a wave of her hand. "Enough of your nonsense!" she snapped. "If you have any conscience at all you will burn incense and pray for long lives for us. Now, off you go!"

Hearing the last three words, Shen Chun felt as relieved as if he had received an imperial pardon. He lost no time scuttling back to his study. The following day, he sorted out some small presents, and sent them to Feihong and Xiang'e to seal their lips. From then on, the girls were content to keep their mouths shut, and to keep their old master and mistress in

娥指着申纯骂道:"看这惯偷老婆的贼汉子,还会倒打一耙。我们如今权且饶过你这一次,你说该如何谢我们呢?"

申纯双手一摊道:"我远来客居,别无长物,就只有这光光一个身子,你说我拿什么谢你?"

湘娥道:"你道只有光光一个身子,我们要你身子做什么?"

"你说呢?"申纯知道湘娥单纯鲁直,便放肆起来。

湘娥直着嗓子嚷道:"我哪里知道?你只管说,先谢哪个?"

申纯眨眨眼笑道:"最好是一齐谢了,免得厚此薄彼。"

飞红"呸"地啐了一口,羞得捂了脸,转过身骂道:"酸秀才,作践人,不得好死。"

申纯见时机已到,又深深施了一礼道:"小生恳请二位姐姐莫向人前闲话,小生日后定有重谢。"

湘娥一摆手道:"休闲饶舌头了,你要有良心,今后有空在花下烧香拜祝我们长寿便是了。快走吧!"

申纯听了一个"走"字,像是得了皇帝的赦令一般,慌忙逃回书房。次日捡出两样东西,分别送给飞红与湘娥,封住二人的口。这两人得了好处,也绝口不提此事,故而王文瑞夫妇一直蒙在鼓中。申纯却寻

the dark about the affair, while Shen Chun continued his nocturnal visits to Jiaoniang's boudoir, as happy as if had reached Heaven. Luckily, no one spotted him either coming or going on these expeditions.

Feihong, however, who was the same age as Jiaoniang, 16, could not help feeling envious of the bliss of the two lovers as she sat alone in her room while they held joyous trysts. Whenever she had spare time, she would visit Shen Chun on some pretext or other, and make fun of him. The young man, for his part, knew that Feihong had a hold on him, and so had no choice but to put up with her teasing.

机便到娇娘绣阁幽会,快活好似神仙。如此来来往往也有几十遭,幸喜再无旁人撞见。

只是飞红见他俩相亲相爱,共效于飞之乐,而自己年逾二八,独守空房,未免有些牙酸。因此得空便无话找话来撩拨申纯,申纯有把柄捏在她手中,也只得逢场做戏,应付几句。

娇红记

Chapter Four
A Matchmaker Rebuffed

Ever since their son had left for Meizhou to seek a cure for his illness, Shen Qing and his wife had waited anxiously for him to return home with his health restored. They never expected that they would not hear from him for half a year. The autumn wind was sighing and the leaves were tumbling from the trees when they finally decided to send the servant Shen Cheng to Meizhou with a message demanding that Shen Chun come home immediately. The young man dared not disobey. His uncle and aunt, too, were well aware that they could detain him no longer against the wishes of their close kinfolk, and forthwith set about arranging a farewell banquet for their guest. Needless to say, Jiaoniang was heartbroken at the news. A cloud of sadness hovered over her continually, but she was able to utter no word of complaint. She stood behind her mother in constant attendance, nursing her lacerated heart and swallowing her bitter tears. Shen Chun strained every nerve to find one last chance to be alone with his beloved, and finally managed to sneak into her boudoir, where, on the tear-soaked pillow and under the lamplight, unbreakable and everlasting vows and oaths of fidelity were sworn.

Nevertheless, parting was inevitable. Although the young man begged to be allowed to stay one more day, Wang Wenrui feared that if he delayed Shen Chun's departure any longer it would mean offending Shen Qing, and urged his young guest to start packing right away. And so, early the following morning Shen Chun and Shen Cheng headed eastward towards Chengdu.

第四章　遣媒遭拒

申庆夫妇自申纯去眉州看病后，日夜盼望儿子痊愈，早些归来。谁知他一走就是半年，没有一点儿音讯。眼看着秋风萧瑟，木叶纷落，便派申成持信往眉州去催促申纯回家。

申纯接到爹娘的家信，不敢不从。王文瑞夫妇见是姐夫来信催促，亦不便强留，便摆宴为申纯饯行。娇娘知申纯将归，一时柔肠百结，惆怅如天，又不便多言，只是站在母亲身后，心中滴血，苦水暗吞。

申纯好歹找了个机会，深夜摸入娇娘所住的绣阁，二人灯下枕上，也不知说了多少山盟海誓的言语，流了多少黯然别离的眼泪，这才分手。

第二天一早，申纯还想再留一日，无奈老管家催促上路，申纯也怕舅父舅母看出破绽，只得草草收拾行李，与申成一起策马东归。

二老见儿子精精神神回来，病是全好了，心中自是欢喜无限。申庆欢喜之余，颇有些不满，道："你原说病愈后就回来，为何一去就是半载？也不怕我和你

Shen Qing and his wife were delighted to see their son return hale and hearty, his illness completely cured. The old man, however, was somewhat peeved that Shen Chun had stayed away so long. "You said that you would return as soon as you recovered your health. But you were away for half a year. Did you not realize how much your mother and I worried about you? It seems that the older you get the more careless of propriety you become, and the more negligent of other people's feelings."

Shen Chun murmured, "Father, I have been undutiful, causing you worry and anger. But I had many duties in my uncle's household. Besides, my aunt and uncle were at pains to make me stay longer — I could hardly refuse. And so, you see, I was delayed until now. I humbly beg forgiveness."

His father was not yet mollified, however. "If I hadn't sent that letter summoning you back, I suppose you'd have forgotten about your real home completely," he yelled.

Shen Chun's mother, fearing that her husband would go too far and be too hard on the boy, and being completely taken in by the lad's story about helping his uncle, tried to mediate. "Oh, please, my dear," she cooed, "he's here now, and that's all that matters. Besides the Wangs are not exactly strangers, are they? There's no need to go on and on about it." Then, turning to her son, she said, "As a matter of fact, the reason why we were anxious to have you back was that we worried that you were neglecting your studies. Another reason is that you are of marriageable age, and we wish to find a suitable wife for you. Now, the last time you returned from Meizhou you mentioned Jiaoniang was also not married. Your father and I had it in mind to propose a match between the two of you. What do you think?"

Hearing this, Shen Chun felt as though he had drunk of the sweetest honey and had been drenched in spring sunshine. Nodding eagerly, he intoned, "I will of course accede to my respected parents' wishes." To himself, he thought, "My parents really do understand where my heart lies, after all!"

Shen Qing and his wife smiled, seeing how eager the young man was.

娘担忧?倒是越大越不知礼,越大越不省心了。"

申纯低声道:"孩儿不孝,惹爹娘生气挂念。因为舅父公务繁忙,府中事务皆托于孩儿,舅母又苦意相留,孩儿实在不好推辞,故此滞留到今,望爹娘恕罪。"

"不是我去信唤你,你把家都要忘了。"申庆怒气未消,仍然大声训斥。

王氏见丈夫没完没了地唠叨,心疼儿子,又听说儿子是为自家兄弟料理事务,便在一旁打圆场道:

"罢了,罢了,回来就好。况且舅舅家也不是外人,值得你这样絮叨。厚卿,我们唤你回来不为别的,一则是怕你客居在外荒废了学业;二则是你的年纪也不小了,尚未成家,打算着为你寻一头亲事。上次你从眉州回来,提起娇娘尚未订亲,我和你爹早有意请人做伐,将她说与你为妻,不知我儿意下如何?"

申纯乍闻此言,如沐春光,似饮甘露,忙点头道:"孩儿的婚事皆由爹娘做主。"心里却想道:"真乃知我者父母也。"

申庆和王氏相视一笑,知道儿子是千愿万肯。王氏便道:"如此就寻个媒人前去说合。"当下申庆就差院公出去寻找媒婆。

Shen Chun's mother said, "We'll send for a matchmaker straightaway." And the servant Shen Cheng was dispatched on this errand.

A couple of days later, Shen Cheng returned to report success in his mission. He brought with him a woman in her late thirties. A straight-backed woman with large eyes, a prominent nose and thin lips, her name was Li, and she was popularly known as Flowermouth Li. She had been in the matchmaking business for many years, and had a reputation for a glib tongue which could charm the birds down from the trees.

"Congratulations, Squire Shen," she gushed, "and felicitations too to your good lady here. What do you think was the first thing I heard when I woke this morning? A cuckoo! Now, as you know, that means a happy event, doesn't it? It's about a wife for Master Shen, isn't it? Well, you've sent for the right person, I can tell you. There isn't a young couple in this city whom I haven't brought together. I can even make a head of stone nod in agreement. And as Master Shen is so talented and handsome, I can't imagine any family which wouldn't be eager to marry its daughter off to him."

As she rattled on, Shen Qing managed to get her to sit down and take tea. "Yes, indeed. It is about arranging a match for my son that I asked you to come," he admitted.

Flowermouth Li beamed, as if this were the most pleasant surprise in the world to her. "Aha!" she cried, clapping her hands in triumph. "I knew it! Well, if I can be of any assistance in arranging a happy union for Master Shen, I shall count it as equal to the blessings of three lives rolled into one and a store of merit that will ensure me passage to Heaven. Er, do you, sir, and your lady wife have any particular girl in mind?"

Shen Qing explained, "My wife's brother serves as an official in Meizhou. He has a daughter, Jiaoniang by name, who is of marriageable age. I would trouble you to go there and discuss a match between our children."

Flowermouth Li slapped her thigh. "Excellent! Wonderful!" she cried.

不两日，申成带着个媒婆回来复命。这媒婆夫家姓李，人送绰号李花嘴。只见她三十已过，四十不到，长得眼大鼻直嘴唇薄，模样颇为周正。因她做这媒婆已有数年，一张嘴能说得清水点灯，嫦娥思春，可谓伶牙俐齿，巧舌如簧。

"恭喜老员外，贺喜老安人，今儿一大早起来就听得枝头喜鹊鸣叫，便知有好事来到。老员外、老安人唤老媳妇来，定是为三官人说媒。老媳妇走东家串西家，没有我说不成的亲事，就是那石头人，也要让她点头。何况三官人年少多才，相貌出众，任她是谁家的女儿，岂有不愿意的？"到底是媒婆，一进门就请安施礼，喋喋不休地说起来没完。

申庆请她坐下，吩咐家人沏茶，道："妈妈说得很是，请妈妈来正是欲为犬子说媒。"

李花嘴双手一拍，满面春风道：

"啊呀呀，我早就有心为咱三官人说上一桩好亲事，能为老员外、老安人效一点儿微劳，便是老媳妇三生有幸，积了阴德。不知老员外、老安人相中哪家的小姐？"

申庆道："是厚卿的舅家，今在眉州为官，他膝下有一女儿，正当芳年，名唤娇娘。烦劳李妈妈去说合说合。"

李花嘴一拍大腿道："好好好！亲上加亲，锦上添

"Marriage ties between kinfolk add flowers to the brocade, as they say. Anyway, who would not fall in love with a man of such superior looks and accomplishments as Master Shen? I knew that a successful match was assured as soon as I walked in the door!"

This greatly pleased Shen Chun's mother, and she said, ingratiatingly: "Madame Li, we are putting you to no end of trouble."

"Please leave everything to me, and put your mind at rest," the other assured her, patting herself on the chest in a show of confidence and self-satisfaction. "You will soon be hearing wedding bells, mark my words."

Shen Qing then said, "Our two families are very close. If we could form marriage ties between us, that would be even better than the celebrated alliance between the ancient states of Qin and Jin. When you go there, Madame, I would like you to first give my regards to my brother- and sister-in-law. We will wait hear in eager expectation of your speedy return with good news."

"You can be certain of a generous reward, you know," his wife chipped in. "By the way, when do you intend to set off?"

Flowermouth Li reacted as if the idea of a reward for her services were the silliest thing she had ever heard. "Oh, please do not mention the word reward," she protested. "It is my bounden duty to do my utmost. Meanwhile, it so happens that today is an auspicious day for this kind of undertaking, and so I am quite prepared to start straight away."

"We rely entirely on your expert judgment, Madame," said Shen Chun's mother. Abruptly turning to Shen Cheng, she ordered him to prepare a donkey for Flowermouth Li to ride, and invited that worthy lady to begin her journey.

Shen Cheng did as he was ordered, and Flowermouth Li mounted the donkey with an air of giddy self-importance. She started on her way to Meizhou. Before she reached the city gate, however, she heard someone behind her urgently calling to her to halt. Turning in surprise, she saw

花。咱家三官人才偕宋玉，貌比潘安，谁人不爱见？老媳妇上门，包准一说一个肯。"

王氏闻言喜上眉梢，客气道："李妈妈，这就辛苦你了。"

"老安人只管放心，包在老媳妇身上！这红丝两下里一系，您就等着听好消息吧。"李花嘴说得来了兴致，拍着胸脯大包大揽下来。

申庆道："老夫和舅爷素相知己，若能再缔秦晋，更是锦上添花。妈妈去了，须先代老夫问舅爷、舅奶奶好。我们这里专候你的佳音，望尽早说成回转。"

王氏道："只要说成此事，我们定要重谢妈妈，青蚨红绢都不在话下。不知妈妈何日启程？"

"老安人勿要言谢，老媳妇就该做的，敢不尽力？今日便是吉日，老媳妇这就启程。"

"那么一切就都仰仗妈妈了。"王氏说罢，转头吩咐院子备驴，请李家妈妈去眉州辛苦一趟。

申成当下于院中为李花嘴备好一头毛驴，李花嘴抱着必得之心，喜气洋洋地骑驴上路前往眉州。尚未出城门，只听后边有人高喊："李妈妈慢行！李妈妈慢行！"李花嘴回头一看，只见一匹快马四蹄如飞来到近前，马上之人正是申三官人，便惊奇地问道："呀！三官人赶来做甚？"

申纯道："小生有密情相告妈妈。"说着翻身下

Shen Chun on horseback pursuing her at a gallop.

"Madame Li, I have something of a confidential nature to impart," the young man gasped, as he leapt from his panting steed and made a deep bow. "But first I must extend my gratitude to you for undertaking this mission. I rely completely on your diligence."

Flustered at this strange interruption, Flowermouth Li slid down from her donkey, and said, "There is no need to instruct me further, young sir. I will, naturally, do everything in my power to ensure your future happiness."

Shen Chun drew the go-between to one side, and said in a low voice: "I will be perfectly honest with you. The young lady in question, Jiaoniang, and I have already secretly pledged our love to each other, swearing oaths that bind us in the lives past, present and future. So there will be no objection on her part. This is what I came to tell you, Madame. I am sure that your efforts will pay off. And when they do, you can be sure that you will have earned my affection and gratitude. I vow that you will be amply recompensed." As he spoke, he drew out a letter from the breast of his robe. "Please deliver this to the young lady for me," he added.

Flowermouth Li was well practiced in the business of passing love notes back and forth. As she tucked this one away, her face was wreathed in smiles, and she said, "I will deliver this safely into the hands of your beloved, young master. Now that I know that you two have made your vows under the moon and before the flowers, I am sure that, with the help of the tender feelings which I am sure you have enclosed in this letter, I will be able to get you united in wedded bliss."

Shen Chun then pulled out a handful of silver, which he pressed into the matchmaker's hand. He thanked her yet again, and reiterated his promise of a handsome reward when she came back with good news.

As she mumbled a few polite words, Flowermouth Li silently counted the silver in her palm, calculating that there must be at least five or six ounces. This discovery fueled an even brighter smile, and she said, "Put

马，深施一礼道："小生先行谢过大媒，全仗妈妈周全。"

李花嘴慌忙跳下驴来，还礼道："不消三官人吩咐，老媳妇自当尽力。"

申纯将李花嘴拉到路旁，悄声道："真人面前不说假话，我和那小姐娇娘早已私定终身，发下三生誓愿，想小姐无有不肯。特来告知妈妈，请妈妈到时相机行事。"

李花嘴一听笑出了声，戏言道："那新人只怕已成旧人了吧？"

申纯俊脸一红，道："为此专望妈妈鼎力促成此事，果然成就了我俩百年爱眷，深恩大德，定当后报。"说着从怀中掏出一封书信道："我这里修有书信一封，求妈妈私下里捎与小姐。"

李花嘴专会做这花媒莺使，捎书递笺那是个行家。她将书信接了揣在怀中，眉飞色舞地说道："这个使得，老媳妇一准送到你那心上人手中。你们两个倒是才子佳人，情分不浅，早就月下花前结好盟约。有你这一幅锦笺暗传心事，我再把红线两下里系牢，管教你两人称心如意，配成鸳鸯。"

申纯又掏出一块银子塞在李花嘴手中，道："多谢李妈妈费心，事成之后，另有重谢。望李妈妈早去早回。"

your mind at ease, young master. Good news is what you shall hear."

She then mounted her donkey, said good-bye to Shen Chun, and continued on her way to Meizhou. Three days later, she arrived at Wang Wenrui's mansion. Giving her name to the gatekeeper, she asked to see the master of the house.

Wang Wenrui was surprised to hear that a matchmaker had come all the way from Chengdu to see him, and he ordered that she be shown in immediately.

In the course of her business, Flowermouth Li had visited the homes of many officials and other important persons, and she had a keen sense for sizing up situations. As soon as she was led into the main hall, she guessed that the two middle-aged people sitting stiffly in the places of honor there were Wang Wenrui and his wife. Wang, she noticed, was about 50 years old. In his official robes, he looked dignified yet kindly. His wife was tastefully dressed, and there was an appealingly matronly air about her. Without waiting to be introduced, Flowermouth Li stepped forward, and offered a polite greeting to the pair.

Wang Wenrui gave a nod of acknowledgement. "Please be seated, and take a cup of tea to refresh yourself," he said.

Flowermouth Li followed her host's gesture, and sat down on a small stool on his right. Xiang'e brought her a bowl of tea. With a friendly smile, Wang Wenrui's wife said, "Madame, may I inquire on whose behalf you have honored us with this visit?"

Flowermouth Li took a sip of tea, dabbed her lips with a handkerchief she took from her sleeve, and replied, "I have come to plead the suit of the Second Master of the Shen family."

Wang Wenrui leaned forward eagerly. "Which Shen family?" he asked. "Surely you don't mean that of Squire Shen of Chengdu?"

Flowermouth Li brought her hands down sharply on both thighs. "The very same!" she cried. "Your brother-in-law and his good lady entrusted me with this errand. I was commissioned specially by the Shen family to

李花嘴口中客气，手里暗暗一捏，便知这块银子少说也有五六两重，当下脸上笑成一朵花，洋洋自得地说道："三官人，你就听好吧。"

说着上了驴背，两腿一夹，别了申纯上路。一路之上晓行夜宿，自不必说，三日后来到眉州通判府，向院子通名报姓，要见老爷夫人。

王文瑞听院子通报说有媒婆自成都来府，心中一动，吩咐院子请进来。

李花嘴随院子进了中堂，见堂上两人端坐，右面是一位五十上下的老爷，身着官服，面目慈祥而不失威严，想这就是通判老爷了。左面坐的是一位衣着华丽、气度雍容的中年妇人，这定是夫人。李花嘴整日里在官宦人家里走动，是个见过些场面的人，不待引见，就上前道了个万福："老媳妇见过老爷、夫人。"

王文瑞微微颔首道："看坐，上茶。"

李花嘴道谢后坐在下首的小机上，湘娥端上一碗茶来。赵夫人微笑道："不知妈妈为谁家所差？"

李花嘴呷了口茶，从腋下拈出帕子在嘴唇上抿了抿道："老媳妇专为申家儿郎前来问亲。"

王文瑞探身问道："哪个申家？该不是成都申庆申员外家吧？"

李花嘴双手一拍大腿道："正是，正是。就是老爷的姑爹家那个三官人啊。老媳妇受申员外、老安人之

propose this marriage to you sir. In fact, Squire Shen's wife said that the match would bring the Wang and Shen families closer together, and that it was destined by Heaven that their talented son and your beautiful daughter should be united. "

This speech startled Wang Wenrui. He glanced at his wife, and said, slowly and carefully: "Madame, my wife and I are deeply touched by your kindness in coming here and proposing this marriage. But the fact is that our daughter and Master Shen have a relationship as close as elder brother and younger sister. How can they become man and wife?"

It was Flowermouth Li's turn to be startled, but she quickly recovered her wits, and said, "Oh sir, that should make no difference. As you both know, Master Shen is talented and intelligent. Such a son-in-law would be far from a disgrace to your eminent family. "

Wang Wenrui nodded gravely. "It is true that the young man is outstandingly talented. His deportment is impressive. He has a pleasingly steady demeanor, and he is most cultured. Deep in my heart I know that I could not wish for a better son-in-law. . . . "

Hearing this, Flowermouth Li beamed once more, and exclaimed, "Absolutely right, sir! Such a fine son-in-law as he would make would be hard to find indeed! "

Wang Wenrui looked somewhat put out by the interruption. He coughed drily a couple of times, and then continued, "However, the imperial court has laid down strict laws about these matters, and the fact is that people so closely related may not marry. It would be scandalous if I, a court-appointed official, were to openly flout the laws of the imperial court, would it not? I was of course pleased when my nephew honored us with a visit. He was a great help to me during the few months he stayed here. But I am afraid that the court regulations make a marriage between him and my daughter out of the question. "

Flowermouth Li was completely taken aback by this blunt refusal of Wang Wenrui to even entertain her suit, and citing some stuffy court rules

托，特来老爷、夫人处提亲。老安人说申、王两家亲上加亲，三官人与小姐郎才女貌，是天生的一对，地成的一双。"

王文瑞听了这话，心中一震，与夫人对视一眼，缓缓道："妈妈专为小女婚事而来，我与夫人着实感激。只是小女和厚卿乃是兄妹连排，怎可做夫妻匹聘？"

李花嘴闻言一愣，忙道："这有什么关系？申官人才俊聪明，老爷、夫人平素是知晓的，招这样的女婿也不算辱没门楣。"

王文瑞点点头道："三哥儿才俊出众，仪表堂堂，且历练老成，稳重有余，老夫打心里头愿意招得这样的佳婿……"

王文瑞话音未落，李花嘴喜笑颜开，眉飞色舞插嘴道："说的是呀，三官人可是打着灯笼也难找的好女婿。"

王文瑞有些不悦地干咳两声，打断了李花嘴的话，继续说道："但我朝立法，内兄弟不许成婚。老夫身为朝廷命官，总不能公然违背朝廷法令吧？前辱三哥惠访，留住数月，甚能为老夫分劳，又是自家外甥，实在喜欢，只是碍于朝廷条例，故不敢成此姻亲。"

李花嘴万万没有想到王文瑞会以朝廷王法为理由，冠冕堂皇地推辞这门亲事，便道："老爷说得不无

into the bargain! "Of course, what you say is perfectly correct, sir," she wheedled. "But as the saying goes, 'The sky is high, and the emperor is far away.' People don't take much notice of these things. Besides, I can assure you, sir, that I have arranged many marriages for families of official rank, and not a few of them have involved cousins. There again, who would dare to gossip about the affairs of an exalted house such as yours? The fact that you give permission should be good enough for anybody. Master Shen is well known throughout the whole of Chengdu and its ten prefectures. His prospects are unlimited."

Wang Wenrui frowned, and said, "You don't have to praise my nephew to the skies before me, Madame; I know his good qualities well. And I am very well aware that he will carve out a brilliant career for himself. Nevertheless, my daughter's fate is not linked with his. I am afraid you have had a wasted journey."

"But, sir...." The matchmaker began to protest, but an impatient wave of Wang Wenrui's hand silenced her.

"The subject is closed, Madame," he snapped. "And now, if you will excuse me, I have duties to attend to. Forgive me for not escorting you to the door." So saying, he rose, and left the hall.

The matchmaker sat stunned at this turn of events. Her face changed color several times, before she finally gave a dry cackle, turned to Wang Wenrui's wife, and said, "Actually, the Shens were hoping that you yourself would handle this matter. After all, isn't it always the girl's mother who takes care of her betrothal? Master Shen and your daughter would make a perfect couple, you know. Why don't you take the lead in bringing them together?"

"To tell you the truth," the other replied, "our two families are perfectly suited in terms of social standing, and there has long been a desire on both sides for a marriage alliance. But it is entirely up to Jiaoniang's father to arrange such things. No matter how many people there are in a family, there is only one head. If I were to take this matter into my own hands,

道理,只是天高皇帝远,谁人去管这些闲事?老身说合过多少官宦人家的亲事,其中颇有表亲成婚的,况且老爷府中的事谁敢多嘴?只要您老人家允诺了就成。申三官人的才名在成都十郡谁人不知,哪个不晓,今后的前途真是不可限量。"

王文瑞一皱眉,道:"我自己的外甥,我自己清楚,不劳你饶舌。厚卿才华横溢,他日定能鲤跃龙门,仕途得意。怎奈我家小女福薄,无缘与他相配。只好空劳妈妈跑这么远的路了。"

"老爷……"李花嘴还想劝说,就见王文瑞不耐烦地一摆手,到了嘴边的话又强咽了回去。

"不必多言,老夫衙门中还有事,就不奉陪妈妈了。"说着,王文瑞起身出堂去了。

李花嘴坐在那里,脸上红一阵、白一阵,十分的不自在,干笑两声,又转过头来对赵夫人道:"申家官人求亲,专望夫人做主了,谁家女儿的婚聘,不是当娘的做主?那申官人是天上仙桃,府上小姐就是日边红杏;申官人是人中之凤,府上小姐就是女中之凰。凤凰并影,那可就是占尽了人间的佳胜。夫人何不成就了这门亲事?"

赵夫人道:"说起来,我们俩家倒也门当户对,谈婚论嫁也在情理当中。但儿女婚姻大事还须听从老爷的安排,家有十口,主事一人,我做娘的怎能将老

bypassing my husband, what would people say?"

Thereupon, Flowermouth Li drew close to Wang Wenrui's wife, and said, "Just before I set out, your sister-in-law bade me deliver her special compliments to you. . . . "

But she was interrupted, with "Please tell my sister-in-law not to trouble herself over this marriage proposal. A girl's marriage is a matter for meticulous planning and preparation. Besides, as my husband said, we are restrained by the court regulations. We cannot do just as we please. "

Flowermouth Li clapped her hands in frustration. "Oh, good Heavens!" she cried. "The arranging of this marriage brooks no delay; and here you are quibbling about some silly 'court regulations'!"

All afternoon, Flowermouth Li used every argument she could think of to bring Wang Wenrui's wife round to her way of thinking, but all to no avail. Towards evening, the latter ordered a banquet to entertain her visitor, and ordered that Jiaoniang be present. Jiaoniang, however, was in no mood for feasting; she stood in attendance at her mother's side, mute and with her head bowed. When she had heard, earlier in the day, from Xiaohui that the Shens had sent a matchmaker, her joy had known no bounds. She lost no time dispatching the maid servant to the main hall, to eavesdrop on the proceedings there. But when she learned that her father had refused the matchmaker's suit, she was devastated. All her happiness of that day vanished as suddenly as it had arrived. So when the summons to the banquet came, she had to steel herself to attend simply because she could not go against her mother's wishes. When the feasting came to an end, Wang Wenrui's wife went out for a stroll, accompanied by Feihong and Xiang'e. Xiaohui and Luying cleared away the dishes, and took them to the kitchen, leaving Jiaoniang and Flowermouth Li alone. The matchmaker, looking round carefully to make sure that no one could overhear, drew near to Jiaoniang, and whispered, "Miss, do you know everything that has gone on?"

爷撇在一旁,自行其事,别人听着也不像呀!"

李花嘴往前凑了凑道:"老身临来时,姑奶奶再三拜上夫人……"

赵夫人忙打断李花嘴的话,道:"你去回复姑奶奶,休要忙着做姻亲,儿女的终身大事,还要端详仔细些。况且老爷说了,上有朝廷法令拘管着,也不是父母可以随便做主的。"

李花嘴一拍手道:"哎呀,我的舅奶奶!这头亲事不消迟疑,又去说什么朝廷法令?不过是夫人一句话的事。"

整整一个下午,任凭李花嘴怎样巧言说合,赵夫人始终不肯吐口。到了晚上,赵夫人设宴款待李花嘴,娇娘盛装而来,呆呆地侍立于赵夫人身旁,低垂粉颈不发一言。早间,娇娘就听小慧说起申家遣媒议婚,一时欣喜若狂,忙令小慧再到中堂探听消息。不料得知父母拒婚,犹如晴天一个霹雳,将一天高兴打得云飞雾散。傍晚时分,赵夫人令她出来陪宴,娇娘全无心情,可又不敢违背母亲,只好强打精神硬撑着出来。

酒罢宴散,赵夫人由飞红、湘娥扶着出去散步,小慧、绿英等忙着收拾碗碟送往厨房,堂中只留下娇娘和李花嘴。李花嘴见左右无人,忙凑到娇娘身边低声道:"小姐全都知道了么?"

Trying to hold back her grief, Jiaoniang uttered an affirmative moan, accompanied by tears. Flowermouth Li's eyes also reddened and large globules of tears rolled from them in sympathy. While dabbing the corners of her eyes with a handkerchief, she said, in a low voice: "What a shame! What a shame! Two lovers are kept apart. But Master Shen entrusted me with a letter for you."

She drew the letter from inside her robe, and pressed it into Jiaoniang's hand. The girl did not dare to open it and read it right there in the hall, so she hastily tucked it in her sleeve and sat bolt upright as if nothing had happened. As soon as her mother returned, Jiaoniang said, "Mother, I feel a little dizzy. I think I'll retire early tonight."

Her mother noticed that she was looking haggard and careworn, and thereupon ordered Xiaohui and Luying to escort her to her quarters, and sent Feihong to tell the cook to prepare a bowl of tonic soup made out of lotus seeds, and send it to Jiaoniang.

Watching the woebegone girl leave, Flowermouth Li was determined not to leave her mission in this unsatisfactory state. So she broached the subject of the marriage once more with Wang Wenrui's wife, saying, "You know that that elegant Master Shen would be the ideal mate for your daughter. Besides, Jiaoniang is at the right age to marry. I beg of you, do not let this chance of acquiring a perfect son-in-law slip through your fingers."

Wang Wenrui's wife forced a smile, and replied, "I am in perfect accord with you, Madame. I indeed pains me that my daughter is at the age to be married, and yet there is no prospect of such a happy event. We will just have to wait and see."

These evasive words made Flowermouth Li grit her teeth in exasperation. But she assumed a smiling countenance, and declared, "Tomorrow I intend to make on last appeal to your husband. I hope I can count on you to support me."

With that, she followed a maid to the chamber that had been set aside for her.

娇娘听了，忍悲答应一句，禁不住泪随声下。李花嘴也跟着眼圈一红，落下几滴浊泪，抽出腋下帕子拭拭眼角，低声叹道："可怜呀可怜，一对有情人竟不能如愿！我们三官人有手书一封，着我私下里送与小姐。"

说着从怀中掏出书信塞到娇娘手里。娇娘不敢在堂上展视，忙揣入袖中，端身正坐。待赵夫人返回，娇娘道："母亲，孩儿有些头晕，想早些回去歇息。"

赵夫人见女儿脸色不好，便吩咐小慧、绿英等丫环道："你们且扶小姐回房歇息。飞红，你叫厨娘做一碗银耳莲子汤给小姐送去。"

飞红应声而去，小慧也来扶娇娘起身。李花嘴见娇娘不胜悲苦地离去，委实不愿就此罢休，再次提起话头来，说道：

"小姐果真是玉貌花容，和那锦心绣腹的申家官人正好是一对儿。况且小姐已芳年及笄，夫人休错过了这门好姻缘。"

赵夫人勉强笑道："谁说不是呢？只怨女儿虽值韶年，未行花运，只能再等等看了。"

李花嘴见赵夫人所言全无诚意，心里恨得直咬牙，但也只好满脸堆笑道："明早待老媳妇再向老爷恳求一番，还望夫人从中斡旋，成就好事。"

说罢，随丫环到客房歇息不提。

In the meantime, Jiaoniang had waited in her boudoir for her maids to fall asleep, and then lit the lamp shaded with crimson gauze that stood on her dressing table. She spread out the letter written by Shen Chun, and began to read it. Its protestations of love and longing brought tears once more to the girl's eyes, and she had difficulty sleeping for the rest of the night.

The following morning, Flowermouth Li again sought Wang Wenrui. But the latter was adamant in his refusal. "Madame Li, I told you before that such a match is out of the question, so there is no need to detain you. Please convey my answer to my brother- and sister-in-law. Explain that it is not just a matter of my being stubborn. The young man has a promising future; some day he could rise to the highest rank, either military or civil. I am afraid that my daughter is not good enough to be his helpmate. He should look to some family of higher status than mine for a suitable marriage partner."

Seeing that matters had come to this pass, Flowermouth Li threw all caution to the winds. Pale-faced, she cried, "Sir, all you need to do is nod your head, and this marriage will come about without a hitch. In my opinion, they will make a perfect couple. As the saying goes, 'When kin are matched, the brocade becomes more splendid'."

Wang Wenrui, realizing that, if allowed to, the matchmaker would jabber on endlessly. So, with a dismissive wave of his hand, he said, "My mind is made up. Please do not broach this subject again."

Flowermouth Li spread her hands in a gesture of helplessness. "But, Your Honor," she pleaded, "if I return to report that I have failed in my mission after coming all this way to arrange a marriage, I will die of shame."

Wang Wenrui slapped the table, rose to his feet, and said, "Haven't you understood what I've been trying to tell you, Madame? A decent marriage must be in accord with the standards of morality. I explained to you yesterday that the rules of the present dynasty forbid marriage between people with kinship status as close as those of brother and sister. Therefore,

且说娇娘回到绣阁，待丫环们都睡下了，这才剔亮妆台上的绛纱灯，将申纯的信展开细读，竟是满纸的相思，满心的祈盼。看得娇娘珠泪涟涟，彻夜难眠。

天明后，李花嘴再次请见王文瑞。王文瑞一脸不耐，正色道："李媒婆，姻事不成，不好留你。你回去禀明姑老爷和姑奶奶，儿女婚姻不成，不是老夫有意作梗。三哥儿堪称人中之龙，前程不可限量，有朝一日，身价显贵，出将入相，怕我女儿区区陋质配他不上，还是让他别选高门，缔结良缘才是。"

李花嘴见事已至此，索性撕破面皮，抢白道："姻缘，姻缘，只要老爷点头就是。依老媳妇看，这姻缘正相当，俗语说亲套亲，锦上花。"

王文瑞见李花嘴喋喋不休地絮叨个没完，不耐烦地一摆手道："我意已决，不必再提。"

李花嘴双手一摊，拉开架式道："亲事不成，叫老媳妇怎生去回复？远行千里牵红线，今日空转回家门，岂不羞杀俺这作媒人？"

王文瑞一拍案几，站起来斥道："我说你这婆子，是不是听不懂人话？要结良缘，也得按人伦行事。昨日我已跟你说过，如今朝廷立法内表兄妹不许成婚，申纯与我女儿断不能成亲。你在成都想也跑动过不少豪门大户，回去自可为我外甥另寻佳偶，不要在这

Shen Chun and Jiaoniang may not marry. Go and find a suitable mate for my nephew among the gentry in Chengdu. Stop your coaxing and threatening around here. As for your dying of shame or not, that's not my business. Please be on your way as soon as possible. "

Flowermouth Li had no choice but to acquiesce. "Very well, Your Honor," she sighed. "I will go back and report what you have said to the Shens. I would just like to ask your lady wife to send for Jiaoniang, so that she can see me off in person. "

Jiaoniang's mother as reluctant to do so, but felt that it would be awkward to refuse. So she sent Xiang'e for Jiaoniang. When the girl appeared, the matchmaker stepped forward and addressed her, as if oblivious to the fact that her parents were present: "Miss, I am leaving today. Since your father refuses to countenance the offer of marriage I brought with me, I would like you to say what you think. "

Jiaoniang was flustered at this lack of propriety on the matchmaker's part in inviting a young girl to discuss marriage in front of so many people. She simply lowered her head, and said, "This matter is entirely up to my parents. "

Her father gazed at her with approval. Then, shooting a glance of triumph at Flowermouth Li, stalked out of the hall with a contemptuous flourish of his sleeve. His wife ordered wine to be brought. Toasting Flowermouth Li's departure, she said, "When you get back to Chengdu, please convey my deepest regrets to my brother- and sister-in-law. Ask them not to allow the unfortunate outcome of this marriage proposal to estrange us. "

"I quite understand," said the matchmaker, amiably, while muttering dark curses in her heart. "It cannot be helped. If it is not to be, then it is not to be. Of course, the closeness or otherwise of your family ties is not my concern. "

Saying, "We have put you to a great deal of trouble, I'm afraid," Jiaoniang's mother ordered Feihong to give Flowermouth Li some traveling expenses.

里软磨硬泡。你羞不羞杀，与老夫何干？还是及早回家去吧。"

李花嘴无可奈何地说："罢罢罢，说亲不成，我回去告知申员外、老安人也就是了。不过我想请小姐出来，亲自道别。"

赵夫人闻言不好推辞，便叫湘娥去请娇娘。不多时，娇娘来到堂上。李媒婆全然不顾王文瑞与夫人在旁，上前说道："小姐，我今日便要走了。既然老爷决意不肯成就婚事，小姐自家说一声也好。"

娇娘听了，又羞又恼，心里直埋怨李花嘴这事做得没分寸，叫我一个姑娘家怎么当着这许多人谈及婚事？只得低下头道："我一个女儿家，此事皆由爹娘做主。"

王文瑞满意地看了看女儿，又瞥了李花嘴一眼，一甩袍袖走了。赵夫人命人取酒来，为李花嘴饯行，道："妈妈回去后，多多劝慰姑奶奶和三官人，休以婚事不成为怪，终究还是嫡亲亲的一家子。"

"老媳妇晓得。"李媒婆口里应着，心里却骂道，"算了吧，不成便说不成的话，还装什么样子？我才不管你们亲不亲的事儿呢。"

赵夫人又道："枉劳妈妈往返奔波，我和老爷心里好生过意不去。"说着命飞红取银子送给李花嘴。

The maid servant then handed the matchmaker a purse containing some loose silver, which Flowermouth Li fingered expertly to determine how much it contained before stuffing it in her bosom. Knowing full well that Wang Wenrui had told his wife to get rid of her as soon as possible, the matchmaker, a ghastly smile on her face, took her leave. At the same time, Wang Wenrui's wife urged her to take care of herself on the road, and to come back and visit them again when she had time.

Jiaoniang escorted her to the gate, and when they got there said, "Madame, Master Shen and I are destined by fate for each other. But it looks like there is an insuperable obstacle in our way."

Flowermouth Li looked at the girl, and sighed, "Yes, your father is dead set against this perfect match. He is obstinately keeping you two love birds apart. Oh, it is such a crime!"

"Please don't say that, Madame," the girl pleaded. "Tell Master Shen that partings and meetings are predestined; everything is decided by Heaven. Time passes like flowing water, and the months and years must eventually have an end. He must not despair of our union. Tell him to visit me when he can."

So saying, she produced a letter from her sleeve, saying, "May I trouble you, Madame, to give this note to Master Shen? And urge him never in this life to forget his Jiaoniang." Then she burst into a storm of weeping.

Flowermouth Li thrust the letter into her own sleeve, and with a sigh of pity mounted her donkey and rode away.

In the meantime, the Shens had been anxiously awaiting the return of Flowermouth Li. Shen Qing considered that although his family had not distinguished itself in any particular way, he had always got on very well with Wang Wenrui; in fact, there had never been a cross word between them. Besides, Shen Chun was a young man of accomplishments and fine appearance, who would be the perfect match for Wang's daughter. How

飞红将装了几两散碎银子的绣袋递在李花嘴手中,李花嘴掂了掂,顿时眉开眼笑道:"老媳妇谢过夫人了,我这就起身回去了。"

赵夫人道:"妈妈一路多多保重,有空再来。"

李花嘴知道主人下逐客令了,便揣了银子,口中说道:"不送,不送,夫人留步。"脚下生风已出了中堂。娇娘跟了出来,快到大门时,悄声对李花嘴说:"妈妈,我与申官人也是命中注定,看来此生难结秦晋。"

李花嘴看了一眼娇娘,叹道:"好好一桩亲事,可老爷就是不肯,白白耽搁了你两个,真是罪过呀!"

"妈妈不要说了,请你转告三哥,离合缘契,皆由天定。时光似水,岁月有限,望他千万不要以婚事不成为念,有空便来看我。"

说着从袖中抽出一封书笺道:"烦劳妈妈将这封书信捎与三哥,告诉他今生休忘了娇娘。"说罢泪下如雨。

李花嘴急将书信袖了,口打唉声,骑驴去了。

却说申家自打发李花嘴前往眉州提亲后,老两口整日里都在惦念。申庆以为自家虽无功名,但与内弟王文瑞意气相投,向无嫌隙,加上申纯文才品貌俱佳,与娇娘郎才女貌,十分般配,王文瑞焉有不允之理?转念一想,如今王文瑞身浮宦海,又多年未见,不

could Wang possibly withhold his consent? On the other hand, he reminded himself, his brother-in-law now moved in official circles. He had not seen him for many years; perhaps he had changed in the meantime? It was possible that he wanted to use his daughter to form an alliance with a powerful and influential family. In that case, the proposed marriage between Shen Chun and Jiaoniang was far from certain, he worried.

His wife, however, had no such qualms. "My son is praised by everyone in Chengdu," she thought. "And although some of this may be mere flattery, nevertheless, there is no doubt that he is an outstanding youth. He did, it is true, fail the examinations the first time, but with his abilities he is sure, sooner or later, to be on the honors list of imperial graduates. My brother is a man of discernment; he will surely recognize his nephew's potential. Yes, a marriage alliance between our two families is assured." The more she thought of the prospect of Jiaoniang becoming her daughter-in-law, the happier she became.

As for Shen Chun, while his body was in Chengdu his heart was in Meizhou. He spent his days in a trance, dreaming of Jiaoniang, and every night he prayed to Heaven to ensure his eternal union with Jiaoniang.

Finally, the long-awaited day came when Flowermouth Li returned. Weary and dispirited, she recounted all the details of the Wangs' refusal to allow the betrothal of Shen Chun and Jiaoniang. Shen Chun's mother was crestfallen at the disappointing news, and said, "But I was sure that the match was almost certain. What is the matter with my brother?"

Shen Qing hastened to comfort her. "My dear, don't distress yourself," he urged. "Everything is pre-ordained, especially something as important in a person's life as marriage. We cannot force Providence."

But his wife was not so easily mollified. "That may be so, but I think that his refusal was just an excuse. My brother probably has his eye on a marriage alliance with some noble house, and looks down on us as having no influence. Naturally, I am deeply hurt by this."

知他是否还是当年性情？若是欲将女儿做了攀高结贵的敲门砖也未可知。这亲事成与不成，尚在两可之间，故此不免心事重重。

王氏却不以为然，暗想成都城里多人夸我儿乃人中之凤。虽说不免有点儿客气奉承，但也敢称是人中尖子。我儿虽一度秋闱失意，但依我儿才华，日后必有蟾宫折桂金榜题名之时。我兄弟自然是独具慧眼，识得我儿才学，这门亲事势在必成，我这姑姑做婆婆是拿稳了的。所以越想越高兴。

而申纯身在成都，心在眉州，日日梦魂牵绕，只想着娇娘。夜夜望天祈祷，求那老天爷务必成全自己与娇娘的婚事。

这一日，一家人千盼万盼的李花嘴终于回来，只见她疲惫不堪，无精打采，将王家拒婚之事一五一十说了。当下王氏一脸的喜气化成了愁容，道："我算定这亲事没有十分也该有九分的把握，我兄弟这是怎么了？"

申庆忙安慰道："安人切莫伤悲，凡事由来前定，何况婚姻乃人生大事，如今不成，也是天数，不能强求。"

"虽说如此，他那话分明是推托之辞，想如今兄弟是要拣豪门贵胄成眷属，把咱这没权没势的姐姐、姐夫视若等闲，我岂能不伤心？"说着王氏竟潸下泪来。

Shen Qing, too, was perturbed by the latest turn of events, but he took it in a more philosophical vein. "Please don't be too downcast, my dear," he said. "Remember the saying 'forced melons are never sweet.' It is not such a disaster for our son to be without a wife."

He turned to the embarrassed-looking Flowermouth Li, and said, "Madame Li, we are very sorry that we sent you on such a wild goose chase."

The matchmaker waved her disparagement of any apology, and said, "Not at all. It was due to my own incompetence that this happy event was not secured. And I have upset your good lady here. Besides, as we are close neighbors, you should not stand on ceremony with me."

Wiping her tears away, Shen Qing's wife asked, "What did my sister-in-law say about this matter?"

The matchmaker made a wry mouth, and replied, "She simply said that the marriage of her daughter was entirely up to her husband to decide."

Just then, Shen Chun, who had been eavesdropping outside the door, lifted the skirts of his robe, and strode into the room. "I find my uncle and aunt's words most offensive!" he cried abruptly. "It is clear that they do not think a poor scholar good enough to be their son-in-law. Why should scholars such as myself remain bachelors all our lives simply because we lack wealth and connections?"

His son's blunt words displeased Shen Qing, who frowned and demanded, "What kind of talk is that, young fellow? Have you taken leave of your senses?"

Flowermouth Li hastened to mediate in this tense situation. "Squire, it is perfectly understandable that Master Shen is upset. But I have a word of advice for him, if I may." And turning to Shen Chun, she said, "There is no need for a handsome and talented young man such as you to be love-sick for long, making a laughing-stock of yourself and undermining your own ambition. Just think of all the beautiful girls and grand officials

申庆虽然心中不满,毕竟城府较深,道:"安人言重了。俗话说强扭的瓜不甜。我们另作打算也就是了,我儿何患无妻?"

转过头来又对尴尬万分的李花嘴道:"李妈妈,叫你往来空走一场,我们好生过意不去。"

李花嘴摆摆手道:"这是哪里话? 都是老媳妇无能,没能将好事做成,惹得安人如此伤心。况咱们街坊四邻的,说这话就外道了。"

王氏拭了把泪,又问李花嘴道:"那舅奶奶怎么说?"

李花嘴一撇嘴道:"舅奶奶说,儿女婚姻,但凭老爷作主。"

这时,早在外面窃听的申纯一撩袍襟,跨进门来说道:"听舅父、舅母的话,真正是不堪入耳。分明是奚落我这个穷书生, 做不得他官宦人家的东床快婿。难道俺穷秀才们就当尽世儿独身?"

申庆听小儿子说话不中听,脸一沉道:"厚卿,你这是做什么?好没志气!"

李花嘴见状,忙打圆场道:"老员外,怪不得三官人埋怨。不过我倒有一句话相劝三官人:拿着官人这么个俊秀人物,不须为亲事长吁短叹,倒让旁人看了笑话,折了自己的志气。你想那京城中佳丽成堆,冠盖如云,多少王公贵胄都想招状元郎做女婿。你赌口

in the capital. The princes and gentry there would fall over themselves to get the Number One Scholar for their son-in-law. You should stop complaining, and aim to come top in the imperial examinations. Then you will not be single long!"

Shen Qing nodded, and said, "You are absolutely right, Madame. As soon as the young man has made a name for himself in scholastic circles, he will be able to take his pick of the daughters of princes, dukes, generals and prime ministers. He won't have to go to all the trouble of looking for a bride. It seems that the time is not yet ripe for his marriage, and there's no use trying to rush these things."

His wife, still wiping her tears away, agreed, "That's right. Madame Li, I know that it's not proper for a mother to boast about her son, but Shen Chun is the most outstanding youth for learning and talent in all of Chengdu and its ten prefectures." Turning to Shen Chun, she said, "What you must do now is concentrate on your studies, and a perfectly suitable marriage will come about of its own accord."

"Exactly, exactly, exactly," chimed in Flowermouth Li. "I myself will arrange a much better match for him in the future. In the meantime, it's getting late, and I must be going."

Shen Qing's wife hastily ordered the household steward to give the matchmaker some "tea money." Flowermouth Li made a big show of attempting to refuse, crying, "Oh, no, no, no! I couldn't possibly. After having failed in my mission, I'd die of shame if I accepted."

"Madame, you mustn't blame yourself," Shen Qing's wife urged, as she started to usher Flowermouth Li out. "We certainly don't."

"Please don't bother to see me out," protested Flowermouth Li, shooting a meaningful glance at Shen Chun. "I can find my own way out." The young man took the hint, and sprang forward to offer his services as an escort for the matchmaker.

Outside, the two of them found a deserted spot. "Madame, did you

气,中他个状元,还怕没个好媳妇?"

申庆点头称道:"李妈妈言之有理,只要我儿求得功名,王侯将相家的千金小姐任挑,不须自寻烦恼。想是我儿婚姻未动,若动时节,拦也拦不住。"

王氏拭泪言道:"谁说不是。李妈妈,按理说母不夸子,可我儿心藏锦绣,才情过人,也是成都十郡拔了尖的。儿呀,只要你发奋读书,自有美满姻缘。"

李花嘴连声道:"对对对!安人说得好,待老媳妇日后另寻一家更好的来替官人说合。时候不早了,我也该告辞了。"

王氏忙让管家取五两银子给李花嘴买茶。李花嘴假意推托了半晌,千恩万谢着收下,道:"多谢员外、安人,老媳妇恭敬不如从命了,实是受之有愧。罢!罢!罢!羞杀我这媒人了。"

"妈妈不必自责,我们都不怨你。"王氏说着起身相送。

"老员外、老安人留步,老媳妇告辞了。"说着李花嘴给申纯使个眼色,自己先出了门。申纯心领神会,知道李花嘴必有话说,便道:"我送送妈妈。"

跟着出来,二人找了个无人处站下。申纯忙问:"妈妈,我的书信可曾捎到?"

"受人之托,忠人之事,自然是捎到了。"

deliver my letter?" he asked eagerly.

"A person entrusted with an errand has a duty to honor that trust. Of course I did," replied Flowermouth Li.

"What did the young lady say?"

"Well, as soon as I mentioned you, she burst into tears. She beseeches you not to give up hope that the two of you will eventually be united. And when you get a chance, she wants you to visit her." As she related this, Flowermouth Li's eyes turned red at the corners.

"Oh, my poor Jiaoniang. . . ." Choking with tears, Shen Chun could not continue.

"Please don't cry, Master Shen," the matchmaker exhorted him. "Someone might hear you. Besides, I've a letter from the young lady for you." So saying, she produced Jiaoniang's letter, and handed it to Shen Chun. "Take it away and read it in private," she cautioned. "I must be going now."

With tears — of gratitude this time — filling his eyes, Shen Chun saw Flowermouth Li off and returned to his quarters. Alone, he perused the tear-stained letter. It was filled with vows of love and constancy, and reading filled the young man's mind with a turmoil of emotions. Restless, he jumped up from the bed, where he had been sitting, and sauntered out of the door. Looking up into the vast vault of Heaven, he saw that thin clouds were wafting across the moon, which now shone radiantly, and now was darkened. He could not make out the shapes of the Herdboy and the Weaving Maid, those starry symbols of everlasting love. Suddenly the thought that perhaps he and Jiaoniang were destined to be sundered forever stabbed at his heart, and he wept bitter and copious tears.

In this way, tormented by love-sickness day and night, Shen Chun could find no pleasure in anything. Winter passed into spring, and his debility turned into illness. One day, as he was shuffling painfully in search of some fresh air and relief from his stuffy sick room, he encountered Flowermouth Li. In utter despair, he begged the matchmaker to think of

"小姐怎么说?"

"唉,我一提起官人,小姐便哭成泪人一个。她说官人休以亲事不成为念,有空再去看她。"说着李花嘴的眼圈也发起红来。

"可怜我那娇娘……"申纯已泣不成声了。

"官人千万别哭,当心有人听见。小姐有回柬与官人。"说着李花嘴从怀中掏出书笺递与申纯,叮嘱道,"回去灯下好好看吧,我走了。"

申纯千恩万谢含泪送走了李花嘴,回到房中灯下展笺一看,笺上泪渍斑斑,写着两首绝句:

"云重月难见,风狂雨不成。

天书从寄意,倾泪若为情。

目断芳千里,情分役寸心。

藉君怜旧情,莫绝羽鳞音。"

读罢,申纯心乱如麻,坐卧不定,索性出门,只见天宇寂寂,薄云翳月,忽明忽暗,牛女双星,黯淡莫辨。心里想着今后与娇娘难偕鱼水,一时肝肠寸断,泪湿沾襟。

自此,申纯日夜相思,神魂颠倒,凡事做不到心上。冬去春来,竟恹恹成疾。一日,勉撑病体出外散步,正遇上李花嘴,说及婚事,十分扫兴。申纯央求李花嘴帮着自己出个主意,如何能与娇娘见上一面,还要瞒过众人。李花嘴到底老谋深算,见多识广,只见

some plan wherewith he might meet Jiaoniang once again, without anybody else knowing. Flowermouth Li had a wealth of experience with such liaisons, and it did not take long for her to conjure up a scheme to fit the bill, which she whispered in Shen Chun's ear before departing.

Shen Chun's illness worsened. He complained of headaches and loss of appetite. His behavior became odd: mumbling incoherently in broad daylight, breaking into fits of manic laughter and falling into comas. The whole household was in a state of alarm.

But before long, Flowermouth Li turned up at the Shen residence again, her face wreathed in smiles. She was no sooner inside the door than she started to gabble excitedly: "Squire Shen — and you too Madame — you know of course that I was devastated by my failure the last time to arrange a match for Master Shen. Well, in the last few days I've been running around here, there and everywhere to find a suitable girl, and I think I've found the very one. I heard that Squire Zhang's third daughter, Qiong, is as beautiful as an angel. She does excellent needlework, too. She would be the perfect wife for your son. It would be a match made in Heaven, I'm sure! Well, what do you think? Just say the word, and I'll go straight over there and get the girl's horoscope read. Then we can start the betrothal arrangements. Well, what do you say?"

Shen Qing and his wife had been so worried about Shen Chun's illness that the matter of his marriage had gone clean out of their heads. Shen Qing forced himself to explain their problem to the matchmaker. "Thank you, Madame, for your kindness," he said reluctantly, "and for your touching consideration for our son's happiness. But...."

"But what?" asked Flowermouth Li, bewildered.

With eyes reddened with weeping, Shen Qing's wife said, "Madame, there is something you do not know. Recently, our son fell ill. No doctor seems to be able to cure him, and so we have been far too worried to contemplate such a thing as marriage."

"Oh, no wonder I haven't seen him around recently!" said Flower-

她眼珠一转,计上心来,对申纯耳语了一番。

回家后,申纯就一日重似一日地害起病来,先还只呼头痛不思饮食,继而白日常出怪语,或似与人嬉笑,或昏睡不醒。一家人见状,不免乱作一团。

过了两天,李花嘴笑呵呵地来到申宅,进门便道:"恭喜老员外,贺喜老安人,老媳妇前番为三官人说亲不成,心里着实有些惭愧。这些日子,老媳妇为了给三官人寻个可意的佳人,走东家,窜西家地问寻。打听到张员外家的三小姐琼娘生得貌似天仙,且女红针黹件件精当,若与咱家三官人相配,倒是天生的一对,地造的一双,再合适不过了。不知老员外、老安人意下如何?倘若有意,老媳妇这就去讨那小姐的生辰八字来。"

申庆夫妇整日牵挂儿子的病,哪有心思再提婚姻之事,勉强应道:"多谢妈妈如此盛情,为我儿百般费心,只是……"

李花嘴问道:"只是什么?"

王氏眼圈一红,道:"妈妈有所不知,我儿近日重病在身,百医无效,正愁得没有办法,暂且顾不上谈论婚姻之事。"

"噢,怪不得老媳妇这些日子不见三官人在街上走动,敢是病了。不知得的是什么病,这等难医?"

"说来也怪,不烧不冷,只是常常说些离谱的话,

mouth Li. "But what kind of illness is it that is so difficult to cure?"

"We can make neither head nor tail of it," replied Shen Chun's mother. "He babbles nonsense from time to time. In fact, when he does it's not like our son talking at all. Madame Li, you are a woman of wide experience, what do you think...?"

"Oh dear," exclaimed Flowermouth Li, in a deliberately grave tone. "This is clearly a case of possession by flower nymphs and fox sprites. If we can't think of a way of ridding him of them quickly, I'm afraid the poor boy is doomed."

Shen Qing and his wife were stunned to hear this. The squire was not a believer in ghosts and suchlike, but his son's illness baffled him. Perhaps, he thought, there were evil spirits abroad after all. His wife was already nursing a grudge against him: She would have summoned an exorcist long ago, if she had not been afraid of Shen Qing's disapproval. Now, after hearing Flowermouth Li's opinion, she was sure she had been right in the first place, and found the courage to speak up. "Madame Li, are you sure?" she asked.

The matchmaker nodded sagely. "I'm afraid there's no doubt about it. It's the spring, you see. Everything is stirring and sprouting and coming back to life, including the spirits of the flowers and grass. Your son, too, is in the springtime of his life and has fallen in love. That's the very time when such spirits catch hold of young people. This is a very serious matter."

"But, what is to be done?" asked Shen Qing's wife.

Flowermouth Li clicked her tongue. "The only thing to do is to send for an exorcist to drive the evil spirits out of him," she said decisively.

"But, Madame Li, do you know of anyone accomplished in that art?" asked Shen Qing's wife. "Could you help us to find one?"

"Of course. Since we are close neighbors, you may rely on me to take care of this," Flowermouth Li said. "My adopted sister, Zhang by name, lives just outside the city, by the Wanghua Stream. She is the medium for

有时竟不像我儿的声音。李妈妈见多识广，你说这
是……"

"哎呀，这分明是花妖狐魅附了体，若不早想办
法，那可是要出人命的。"李花嘴故弄玄虚，夸张地叫
道。

申庆夫妇一听，惊得发呆。申庆虽不信这些鬼
话，可小儿子的病症，实难解释，或许这世上原本有
鬼也未可知。事到如今，还是宁可信其有吧。王氏则
暗暗怨恨老头子，自己早就有心请巫婆来跳神，只是
怕老头子不肯，此时经李花嘴这么一说，更证实了自
己的判断无误，因此缓了缓神儿道："妈妈，你敢肯定
么？"

李花嘴点点头道："定是无疑。这春月时节，万物
复苏，花妖草魅也都春心萌动，见咱家三官人青春少
年，爱慕不过，自然会缠上三官人，最是厉害不过。"

王氏急道："如此可怎生处置？"

李花嘴咂咂嘴道："这有何难？请个师婆来，捉了
鬼去便好了。"

王氏又道："那……妈妈可知哪里有法力高强的
师婆？帮我们请一位来可好？"

"老员外、老安人放心，咱街里街坊的，这事便交
给老媳妇去办。城外望花溪那儿有个张师婆是我的
干姐妹，现顶着九天玄女娘娘的真神，法力无边。明

the Black Lady of the Ninth Heaven. She has great and mysterious powers. I'll bring her here tomorrow. She'll drive the evil spirits out of your son in no time, and put your minds at ease."

"We are putting you to a great deal of trouble," gushed Shen Qing's wife, overwhelmed with relief and gratitude. Shen Qing himself, was forced to nod in silent acquiescence to the plan.

Looking very pleased with herself, Flowermouth Li then gave instructions concerning the preparations for the exorcism the following day, including the three types of sacrificial animals. With a brisk curtsey, she then flounced off.

In the meantime, Shen Chun had heard from the servants that Flowermouth Li had gone to fetch Zhang the exorcist, and he knew exactly what was expected of him.

The following day, as Shen Qing and his wife were standing by their son's bed, the former sighing and the latter weeping, the steward Shen Cheng announced that the matchmaker and the exorcist were waiting in the main hall, sipping tea. He was told to show them in at once. The two ladies duly appeared, and began to greet their host and hostess, only to be cut short by Squire Shen. "Don't bother about the formalities," he said brusquely. "Get on with saving my son's life." He then turned to a servant and ordered him to lead in the three types of sacrificial animals, which had been got ready the previous day. The animals were placed before Zhang the exorcist. Madame Zhang then asked that a table be brought. She prepared the table as an altar by spreading a yellow cloth over it. On the cloth she placed paper, cinnabar, a bowl of water, and pen and ink. She then lit incense sticks and candles.

The exorcism lasted for some two hours, as Madame Zhang rang bells, chanted mantras, whirled a sword and pranced wildly. At the end of the performance, Shen Chun slowly opened his eyes, and said, "I have had a good sleep. What time is it? Father ... Mother ... Brother ... Madame

儿个老媳妇便将她请来，施法驱鬼，可保三官人无虞。"

"如此有劳妈妈了。"王氏心中的感激之情实在是难以名状。申庆在一旁也不好说些什么，只能默许。

李花嘴满面春风道："那老媳妇就不叨扰了，明儿一早便请张师婆来捉鬼降妖，定保咱三官人平安无事。老员外、老安人可将福礼三牲及早准备停当。"说罢福了一福，便风风火火地去了。

再说申纯从侍女、院公口中听得家中要李花嘴去请师婆，心中就有数了。第二天早上愈发闹腾得比往常厉害些，将守在床边的王氏急得眼泪犹如断线的珠子掉个不停，申庆也不住地唉声叹气。

不多时，管家申成来报，说李媒婆领着张师婆来了，现正在堂上喝茶。申庆、王氏急命将师婆请进房来，救命要紧。不大一会儿，李花嘴与张师婆随申成进来，先给员外、安人请安。申庆此时已顾不得礼节，急道："不要讲究俗礼，快快作法禳解，救我儿性命。"又命小厮将昨日备好的福礼三牲抬进来，摆在张师婆面前。张师婆又令人抬了一张几案，蒙上黄布，上边放了裱纸、朱砂、水盂、笔墨，焚香点烛，立了法坛，然后披挂起来。一时间摇铃念咒，顶神作法，持剑砍杀，足足闹腾了一个时辰，方才收住。

这时，就见申纯慢慢睁开眼，道："好睡也，天色

Li ... What are you all doing here?"

Seeing his son in possession of his senses once more, Shen Qing was filled with a sense of relief and wonder. Hastily stepping forward, he asked, "My son, what strange things did you see in your dreams?"

In a perfectly clear voice, Shen Chun said, "I saw a divine general in golden armor enter the room, and drive out some goblin maidens."

His mother breathed a long sigh, and said, "Madame Zhang's magic skill is truly remarkable!"

Shen Qing looked thoughtful, and asked the exorcist: "What ·did the Black Lady tell you just now?"

"She said that the goblin maidens are products of Master Shen's previous existence. It is very difficult to catch them, and there is a danger that they may come back again. The Black Lady suggested that the young man may escape them by moving to a place several hundred *li* to the southwest."

Shen Qing frowned, and finally said, "Yes, that's all very well, but where in the southwest would it be best for him to go? I myself can't think of any place."

"Yes, where?" echoed his wife, her joy turning to worry once more.

Shen Lun looked at his parents, and then at his brother. Eventually, as if making a great effort, he said, "My uncle lives several hundred *li* to the southwest. Perhaps if I...."

The words were hardly out of his mouth when his father shook his head violently. "Oh no, no, no," he said. "Not after our failure to arrange a match for our son with his daughter last year! How could we send the boy there again without bringing shame upon ourselves?"

As a matter of fact, as soon as the exorcist had said that the Black Lady had suggested that Shen Chun should seek refuge in the southwest, his mother had immediately thought of her brother in Meizhou. However, she had been afraid to be the first to speak up. But since Shen Lun had brought it up first, she was emboldened to say, "I don't see why not. After all,

几时了？父亲、母亲、哥哥、李妈妈，你们如何都在这里？"

申庆见儿子神志清醒，心中暗道："奇了。"忙上前问道："孩儿，你方才睡梦中可有什么异样？"

申纯口齿清楚，朗声言道："只见一个金甲神将，进房中驱赶几个妖邪女子出门去了。"

王氏闻言长长舒了一口气，道："张师婆的符好灵呀！"

申庆若有所思地问道："适才玄女娘娘可曾说什么言语？"

张师婆道："玄女娘娘说，这些鬼魅是官人前生结下的，故不好捉拿她们，只怕日后还要重来。娘娘指点须到西南方向数百里外躲避，方可保得平安。"

申庆听罢眉头紧皱道："神人之言虽是，但西南方向何处可以躲避？老夫一时也想不出来。"

王氏也转喜为忧道："说的是呀，这可如何是好？"

申纶看了看父母，又看了看弟弟，半晌方惟惟诺诺地说道："只有舅父家在西南方数百里外，不如就去……"

话音未落，申庆头摇得拨浪鼓似的，说道："不可，不可，去年求亲不遂，怎好厚颜再去，岂不是自取其辱？"

其实，刚才张师婆说起玄女娘娘指点申纯向西

the boy's health is the most important thing, isn't it?"

"That's right, that's right," chimed in Flowermouth Li. "Although a new alliance between the two families has not been formed, the old one is still intact. And it's a very close one between the families of brother and sister. How could they refuse to help in a matter of life and death? Perhaps the squire is being over-cautious?"

These words were music to Shen Chun's mother's ears. "There is a reason in what you say, Madame Li," she affirmed, nodding all the while. Then she said to her husband: "The first thing to be considered is that our son is ill," she said. "If he can recover his health by going to his uncle's, then he should go, surely?"

Turning to Shen Chun, she asked, "What do you think, my son?"

The young man, who felt like bounding from the bed and racing off to Meizhou there and then, put on a show of meek resignation. "As Father said, the attempt to make a match for me with my uncle's family failed. Therefore, even if it cost my life I would not risk bringing shame on our family by seeking help there."

This pathetic speech brought tears rolling from his mother's eyes once more. She appealed to her husband: "You must think of a way! If any tragedy happens to my son, I will not wish to live...."

Shen Qing sighed in exasperation. No matter which way he thought about the situation, in the end his son's life was the most important thing; his own stuffy dignity could take a back seat. Finally, with a heavy heart, he said, "All right, send someone to ask my brother-in-law if he will give refuge to my son." Turning to Shen Chun, he said, "I must trouble you to make the journey, my boy." He then ordered that two ounces of silver each be given to Flowermouth Li and the exorcist Zhang.

The matchmaker winked at her crony, and with their faces wreathed in smiles the pair stepped forward to receive their reward and thank the squire and his wife.

Flowermouth Li then addressed Shen Chun, as follows: "Young Mas-

南方向避难时，王氏就想到了兄弟家，只是不敢先说出口罢了，此时见申纶提起，急道："这倒不妨，只要孩儿的病能好，怕些什么？"

李花嘴也在一边帮衬道："是呀，是呀，新亲不成，旧亲还在，况且还是嫡亲亲的舅舅，哪能见死不救？老员外过虑了。"

王氏闻听此言，十分入耳，频频点头道："李妈妈说得在理。老爷，当初孩儿有病，一到舅家便好了，如今毕竟去的是。"

转过头来又问申纯道："儿呀，你说呢？"

申纯此时一颗心恨不得马上就到眉州，可嘴上却说："孩儿为提亲之事，颜面都丢尽了，还是爹爹说的是，孩儿拼着一死，也绝不去自取其辱！"

王氏听了泪珠儿滚落下来，向申庆道："老爷，你看着办吧，纯儿若是有个三长两短，我也不活了……"

申庆见状连连叹息，思来想去还是儿子的性命当紧，自己这张老脸又算得了什么，心一横说道："如此就先着人去打个招呼，舅老爷若是答应，纯儿去避避也好。儿呀，只能委屈你了。"说罢，又命管家取二两银子谢了张师婆，另取二两谢过李花嘴。

李花嘴对张师婆一挤眼，二人笑逐颜开，欢欢喜喜上前接了谢礼，齐声说道："多谢老员外、老安人。"

李花嘴又对申纯道："三官人，老媳妇说句不当

ter, I hope you will forgive my impertinence if I say that the setback in your marital affairs is as nothing compared to the importance of the recovery of your health. Remember the saying, 'So long as trees grow on the mountain, there will always be firewood to burn.' Now flee from evil, and cure your illness, and I'm sure that everything will turn out for the best."

With tears in his eyes, Shen Chun thanked the matchmaker. "Madame, I will never forget your concern for me as long as I live."

Flowermouth Li winked again; this time at the young man. "When I undertake a task, I carry it out faithfully — especially a task entrusted to me by your parents! You must take good care of yourself."

She then excused herself and Zhang the exorcist to Shen Qing and his wife, saying, "If there is any other little service I can render, just mention it and it shall be done."

The squire and his wife escorted the two women to the gate, with fulsome expressions of gratitude. When they returned, they dispatched a messenger forthwith bearing a letter from Shen Qing to his brother-in-law.

That evening, Shen Chun's appetite returned, and he ate a hearty meal. This cheered up everyone in the Shen household, and they were full of admiration for the skill of Zhang the exorcist, which had brought about such a remarkable improvement.

说的话，不要太小家子气了，亲事不成，算不了什么，身子要紧，留得青山在，不怕没柴烧。好生去养病避难，定是大吉大利。"

申纯含泪谢道："妈妈搭救之恩，小生没齿不忘。"

李花嘴挤挤眼睛道："受人之托，必当忠人之事。既然员外、安人托付，老媳妇焉有不尽心尽力之理! 官人保养身体要紧。"

转过身来对申庆、王氏道："时候不早了，老媳妇姐妹就不叨扰了，以后有事，但凡用得着老媳妇的，言语一声就行了。"

申庆、王氏千恩万谢将李花嘴和张师婆母子送出宅外，回到府中即派一名小厮，持了申庆亲笔书信，星夜赶往眉州。

当天夜里，申纯便呼唤肚饥，索饭要汤，一顿饭吃了好多。申家老小自是高兴万分，都说张师婆法术高超，道行深厚。

娇红记

Chapter Five
Jiaoniang's Tribulations

Before three days were out, the man who had been sent to Meizhou came galloping back with the news that Wang Wenrui and his wife were deeply concerned about Shen Chun's illness, and urged that he be sent to them as quickly as possible to escape the trouble that dogged him. This was a great relief and comfort to the Shens, who hastily set about preparing the young man for the journey. The very next day, Shen Chun set off for Meizhou in a carriage driven by the chief steward of the house Shen Cheng.

It was the middle of spring. A warm easterly breeze blew, and the willows were just turning green. The orioles and swallows flitted and chirped. Azaleas bloomed scarlet all over the mountains and meadows, exuding a heady perfume. On the Jinjiang River, fleets of barges plowed through the swirling emerald ripples. In his carriage, Shen Chun felt as though he were sitting in a boat floating on a sea of flowers or voyaging through a picture landscape. He felt his spirits soar, and the depression and gloom of the previous few months miraculously disappeared. Traveling by day and putting up at inns by night, it took three days to arrive at Meizhou. As they approached the Wang mansion, Shen Chun felt his heart begin to pound like a drum, and try as he might he could not quiet it.

At the main gate of the mansion, Shen Cheng alighted, and raised the door curtain of the carriage, and helped Shen Chun out. The sight of the house just as it had been when he left it, stirred a welter of emotions in the young man. He thought, "I have worked a thousand stratagems to be once again with you, Jiaoniang. But what is my reception to be, I wonder?"

第五章　娇红生隙

不过三日，派往眉州的小厮已快马返回，说舅老爷夫妇十分关注三官人的病情，要其尽快动身前去避灾。申庆、王氏闻言心中欣慰，第二日便打点行装，令老管家亲自驾车送申纯前往舅家。

此时正当仲春，只见东风送暖，柳吐新绿，更兼莺啭簧声，燕啼韵笛。漫山遍野的杜鹃花，喷火蒸霞，芳菲烂熳；锦江上绿水奔腾，百舸争流。

申纯坐在车上恍如浮舟花海，穿行画间，精神不觉为之一振，数月来的忧愁苦闷一扫而尽。一路上晓行夜宿，只三日便来到眉州。待得临近通判府，申纯的心跳得像打鼓一般，无论如何静不下来。

车到门前，申成掀起车帘，搀申纯下来。抬头见门前风物依旧，不觉思绪万千，心道：

"唉，想我申纯为了娇娘，百计重来，却不知来了又将怎样？"

想着便上前叩门，老家院王忠应声出来，见是表少爷来了，忙开了大门，放车马进去安顿。申纯当下

With this weighing on his mind, he stepped forward, and knocked at the gate. Seeing who the visitor was, the gatekeeper Wang Zhong hastily opened up, ushered Shen Chun in and had the carriage and horses stowed away. When Shen Chun asked to be shown to his uncle and aunt so that he could pay his respects, the gatekeeper told him: "Sir, today the master and mistress have gone to the Tianning Temple to view the peonies, at the invitation of their neighbor Wang Sicheng. They will not be back until evening. Before they departed, they left word that when you arrived you should be housed in your old rooms in the eastern study." With that, he picked up Shen Chun's luggage and led him to his quarters. Seeing the young man comfortably settled, he took his leave.

The first thing Shen Chun did was to lie down on the bed and rest for a short while. Glancing round and seeing the furniture just as it had been the previous time he had stayed there, memories of that time came back to him in a flood of nostalgia. Eventually, feeling bored, he left the study, and wandered aimlessly towards the rear garden. Entering the garden, he gazed round at the luxuriant trees, the exotic flowers in riotous color, and the lake with its rockeries and sparkling green water. Truly, it was like an exquisite picture, as always, he thought. Among this exuberance, he noticed in the distance a girl in a pavilion. Wearing a red blouse and a white skirt, she was leaning on a railing, seemingly deep in thought. As he looked more carefully, Shen Chun gave a start. Wasn't that Jiaoniang, who had haunted not only his waking hours but his sleeping ones as well? Upon a sudden impulse, he started running through the willows and flowers towards the pavilion.

Ever since the failure of the matchmaker to secure a marriage between her and Shen Chun, Jiaoniang had been filled with despair. Every day seemed as long as a year. When the messenger from the Shen family arrived with an account of Shen Chun's illness, her heart had been consumed by a raging fire of anguish, of which of course she dared not reveal any sign. But when her parents agreed to allow the young man to come and re-

要拜见舅父、舅母，王忠道："三官人，今日老爷、夫人被隔邻王寺丞邀到天宁寺赏牡丹去了，须日落方能归来。老爷夫人临行时留下话，若三官人到了，仍旧到东厢书房安歇。"说罢，提着行李将申纯送入书房，安置停当，告辞去了。

申纯倚在榻上小憩，只见窗儿依然，旧日题诗墨迹如新，心中不禁怅然若失。歇息片刻，觉得独处无趣，便从书房出来，信步朝后花园走去。步入园门，但见佳木葱茏，奇花争艳，湖石叠翠，绿水生鳞，满园锦绣。游目四顾，远远望见秀溪亭上有一个红衣白裙的女子倚栏沉思。申纯仔细看了，心中一阵狂跳，那不正是自己日思夜想、魂萦梦绕的心上人娇娘么？当下穿花度柳，向亭中奔去。

自打议亲不成后，娇娘也是满腹苦水，度日如年。前几日申家小厮来送信时，正好她在中堂，闻得申纯有病，心中如焚似煎，又不敢有所表示。听得父母答应申纯来家调养，这才转忧为喜，几天来只盼望着申纯早些到来。

昨日王寺丞的家僮持帖子来请老爷夫人并阖家老小一道去天宁寺赏牡丹，娇娘心中有事，无意游春，推说身子不爽，留在家中。一大早，府中的人都欢天喜地地上车走了，只剩下几个粗使丫环和门子在家。

cuperate with them, her sorrow turned to joy. Ever since, she had been waiting eagerly for her lover's return. The previous day, a page from their neighbor Wang Sicheng had brought an invitation for the whole household to go and view the peonies at the Tianning Temple. Jiaoniang, however, had been too preoccupied with anxiety about Shen Chun to find any pleasure in the proposed excursion, and so had made an excuse that she was feeling unwell. And so, as the rest of the household set off in a gay cavalcade, Jiaoniang remained behind with only a few servants for company.

For some time, the girl wandered around the main hall, and finally walked out to the main gate. She waited and watched there for a while, until noon came and went, when she decided that there would be no visitors from Chengdu that day. She went and sat in the Beautiful Stream Pavilion, listlessly brooding. Then, alerted by the sound of footsteps on the zigzag bridge leading to the pavilion, she raised her head and saw Shen Chun tripping lightly towards her. She rubbed her eyes in disbelief. Could it be a dream? Even when the young man was standing right in front of her, she still stared at him in a daze. For a long time, the young lovers gazed into each other's eyes, without uttering a word. Eventually Shen Chun forced himself to say, woodenly: "Miss, I hope you have been well since we parted."

Jiaoniang noted Shen Chun's pale swallow features, and was pained at the thought of how much he must have suffered on the bumpy road. In a voice full of compassion, she said, "Oh, how could you come all this way in your weak condition?"

For what seemed like a long time, Shen Chun was too choked with tears of emotion to speak. Finally, he said, "We have not been parted long, but I was afraid that you had already forgotten me. You, though, have not been out of my thoughts for an instant no matter what I did, and no matter whether waking or sleeping. In the meantime, I even entrusted my hopes to a matchmaker, but Heaven turned its face away from my happiness. Now that I have strained every nerve to find a way to see you

娇娘无人说话，在中堂转转，又到门前看看，直到午后不见成都来人，想是三哥今日不来了，顿时少情无绪，独自一人坐在秀溪亭上想心事。忽听得曲桥上响起脚步声，抬头一看，来的正是翩翩申郎。忙揉了揉眼，一时不知是真是假，是梦是醒？及至申纯来到近前，仍是痴痴呆呆。两人四目相对，却都吐不出一个字来。半晌，申纯方揖问道："妹妹别来无恙？"

娇娘见申纯脸色苍白憔悴，又思量着他一路上风雨颠簸，病体难以支撑，心疼地说道："你既病着，何苦远道来此？"

申纯听了，当下心中凉了半截，顿时气噎泪流，说道："日月未久，妹妹敢是已将三哥忘记了么？自别离之后，愚兄行止坐卧，无一刻不在思念妹妹，中间请命于严君，寄望于媒妁。可恨苍天不从人愿，空辜负了金玉良缘。如今我费尽心机，百计重来，竟然换得你'何苦来此'之词！真令愚兄大失所望，悔恨交加。"

娇娘见申纯误解了自己，正欲解释，申纯却盯住娇娘道："莫非妹妹变心了不成？"

娇娘含泪道："既然三哥之心坚如金石，小妹矢死靡他，绝不变心！小妹只是担心三哥的身子，带病奔波道路，倘若有个三长两短，小妹怎能独生！"

again, you greet me with a cool 'How could you come all this way...!' This is a most bitter disappointment!"

Jiaoniang hastened to amend this misunderstanding, but met only a cold stare from Shen Chun. "Your feelings for me have changed, I am convinced," he said.

Holding back her tears, the girl said, "I am true to you, I swear it. It's just that I am worried about your health. I was alarmed that you had undertaken such a rigorous journey in your sickly condition. Oh, if any misfortune had befallen you, I would not have been able to carry on living!"

Moved by this confession of love, Shen Chun took Jiaoniang in his arms. Closing his eyes, he murmured, "My dear, I am to blame."

When Jiaoniang finally stopped crying, after much coaxing by Shen Chun, the young man explained to her the stratagem Flowermouth Li had devised: He had only been pretending to be ill, and Zhang the exorcist's performance and advice to seek refuge in the southwest had been aimed at tricking his parents into sending him back to Meizhou. In the end, Jiaoniang was laughing and crying at the same time.

Locked in a tight embrace, they related to each other how they had suffered during the time they had been apart. Before they knew it, dusk was falling, the moon was rising, and it was time for the Wang household to return from its excursion. So the two lovers regretfully parted, and went their separate ways.

Knowing that he had come to them to recover his health, Shen Chun's uncle and aunt showed him every consideration. On top of that, Jiaoniang sent to ask after him every day. Before many days had passed, the young man's spirits were completely restored. He thereupon made of show of trying to say good-bye, and reluctantly agreeing to stay when his uncle, who held his talents in the highest regard, importuned him. For over a month, he saw a great deal of Jiaoniang. Sometimes they would share appreciation of flowers and poetry; sometimes they would compose literary pieces or

申纯听了，动情地将娇娘拥入怀中，闭目喃喃道："妹妹，不要说了，是我错怪你了。"

娇娘嘤嘤而泣，申纯百般抚慰，方才止住。又问及申纯病情，申纯将李花嘴如何使计，自己如何装病，以及张师婆来家跳神逐鬼，假借神意远避西南的始末，详详细细讲了一遍。引得娇娘哭一阵，笑一阵。

二人相依相偎，互诉离别之苦，相思之情。不觉金乌坠落，玉兔东升，估计府中的人也该回来了，二人只得相携出了园子，各自回房。

申纯这次来舅父家避灾养病，王文瑞夫妇相待如初，加之娇娘日日问寒问暖，体贴备至，没几日就元气全复。申纯假意向舅父辞行，王文瑞觉得他做事历练老成，便苦意相留。申纯半推半就，也就安心住了下来，一晃便是月余。乘间与娇娘或是赏花和诗，填词作画；或是水边月下，谈情说爱，两人间的感情日加深厚。

这一日，申纯料理了府中事务，便悄悄过后院来找娇娘。进了绣阁，只见篆烟袅袅，馨香馥馥，紫纱绣帐低垂。申纯以为娇娘在帐中睡着，便蹑手蹑脚过来轻轻掀起帐帏，一看却是空的，锦衾角枕收拾得整整齐齐，枕畔却露出两弯小小的绣鞋，弯弯的似一对如意金钩。申纯如获至宝，轻轻拈起，置于掌心端详，

paint; and sometimes they would talk of love during moonlight walks. In this way, their fondness for each other steadily deepened.

One day, having completed his tasks for his uncle, Shen Chun took a stroll into the rear courtyard in search of Jiaoniang. Entering her boudoir, filled with the scent of incense and perfume, he noted that her bed curtain was hanging down. Thinking that the girl must be taking a nap, he tiptoed over to the bed, and gently lifted the curtain. The bed was undisturbed and empty. Beside the pillow was a tiny pair of embroidered shoes, delicately curved. As delighted as if he had discovered some great treasure, Shen Chun picked them up with the utmost care, and held them reverently in the palms of his hands. They carried rich patterns of flowers, stitched in eye-catching colors, and the heady scent from them titillated the young man's nostrils. He marveled at how light and exquisite they were. The more he looked at them, the more he was attracted by them. Looking round to make sure no one saw him, he thrust the shoes into his sleeve, and quickly returned to his quarters. He hid the shoes under his pillow, intending to fondle them late at night, when everyone else was asleep. He then went to see his uncle and aunt in the main hall.

No sooner had Shen Chun left the eastern study than Feihong slipped in. From the way her face was painstakingly made up, it was clear that she had come on purpose to visit Shen Chun. For the fact is that the maid servant had also lost her heart to the handsome young scholar, and she was burning to steal him away from Jiaoniang. Every time he went away, she was upset for days, and whenever he came she was both happy and consumed with jealousy. She was happy because she would have plenty of opportunities to see and flirt with the dashing fellow; she was jealous because Shen Chun had eyes only for Jiaoniang, and although she was his favorite among the maid servants, that was as far as it went. When Shen Chun left, she was both afflicted and triumphant: afflicted because her darling had departed and she suffered the pangs of love-sickness, and triumphant because her young mistress too was lovelorn, had lost her appetite and could not

见那鞋上的花样一层套一层，光彩夺目，花团锦簇，更有异香扑鼻，真是又软又轻又俏又柔。他越看越爱，见四下无人，便将那小鞋袖了，快步返回书房，将鞋儿藏在自家枕下，准备夜深人静之时在灯下仔细把玩。藏好小鞋，出来到中堂与舅父、舅母攀谈不提。

申纯前脚刚走，飞红后脚便到了书房。只见她施粉涂朱，刻意打扮了一番，专为来会申纯。原来飞红早被申纯惹得春心荡漾，恨不得从娇娘那里把申纯抢到自己手中。每次申纯来去，都令她数日不安。申纯来了，她又高兴又嫉妒，高兴的是，自己便可以经常看见这个风流倜傥的粉面郎君，不时与他调笑几句；嫉妒的是，申纯心中只有小姐，对自己虽然比别的丫头亲密些，却没有进一步的举动。申纯去了，她又悲伤又解恨，令她伤心的是，玉郎一走，自己暗下里倍受相思之苦；令她解恨的是，小姐也花容顿改，寝食难安，与自己一样受着煎熬。这次申纯避灾重来通判府，飞红几夜没合眼，费尽心思寻机与其相见，或言语调笑，或飞眼传情。申纯少年心性，不免对飞红渐渐语涉狎昵。飞红便自以为得计，觉得申纯与自己两下多情，心有灵犀，所以越发往书房走动得勤快些。

sleep at night. On the occasion of this visit, Feihong had stayed awake for the first few nights plotting and scheming how to find opportunities of meeting the young scholar, and of joking and flirting with him. On these occasions, the hot-blooded Shen Chun had come close to taking liberties with Feihong, and this had convinced the maid servant that she had won his affections, and that there was a secret understanding between them. The result was that she had begun to bend her steps towards the eastern study more often and more quickly.

This morning, finding the door to the young man's quarters unlocked, Feihong assumed that he must be inside, reading or composing essays. Beaming in anticipation, she gently pushed the door open. She was disappointed to find the room empty, but, reluctant to leave, sat down at the desk and began to leaf through some manuscripts of poetry. After a while, when Shen Chun had not returned, she lifted the curtain to his bedchamber and entered. With slow and deliberate steps she approached the bed, and sat on the edge of it. A sudden impulse made her stretch herself across the coverlet, thinking, "Oh, when will I ever share these quilts and pillows with Master Shen? I feel as if I have wasted half my life already." Tearfully she stretched towards the pillow, as if embracing Shen Chun, and just as she was feeling overcome with emotion her hands touched something silky and soft. Swiftly wiping her eyes, she discovered that it was a pair of dainty embroidered shoes. She picked them up and examined them carefully. She immediately identified them as belonging to Jiaoniang. But how did they come to be here? She thought. In a flash, Feihong's tender feelings vanished, to be replaced by a vindictive resentment. A sardonic smile spread across her face, as she murmured to herself: "So, my stuck-up little precious darling of a high and mighty family.... You put on an act of being prim and proper in front of the rest of the world. When Xiang'e and I heard you and Master Shen up to your disgraceful antics that time, you claimed that everything was above-board between you. A relationship like that between brother and sister, you said! Well, let's see you bluff your

适才早上起来，飞红见夫人陪着老爷在中堂说话，便悄悄溜出来，想看看申纯一个人在做什么。来到书房，只见门扉虚掩，想必是申郎在读书作文，便满面春风轻轻推门进来，房内却空无一人，不免好生无趣。一时间又舍不得离去，便坐在书案前翻看了一会子诗稿，仍不见申纯回来。又掀帘进了寝室，款步来到床帐旁边坐下，顺势一躺歪在锦被上，心想："我飞红何时能与申郎同衾共枕，这女儿身也不算枉活这一生一世了。"

想着想着，眼泪便淌了下来，伸手将绣枕抱起，想着如同拥了申郎一般。正在情不自禁之时，手指忽然碰着一件绵绵软软的东西，拭泪一看，呀！是一对娇小玲珑的绣花鞋儿，忙取在手中细看，这分明是小姐的绣鞋，怎么会在这里？飞红顿时柔情尽去，怨恨暗生，露出一丝冷笑道：

"哼，好个宦门千金，素日里只绷着个面孔对人，前番与湘娥听得你与申郎私通，不过一言半语地提醒你两句，你还一口咬定是兄妹排连，清清白白。如今连绣鞋都送了情郎，铁证如山，不怕你嘴硬。"

想到此，便用帕子将绣鞋包了，整好床铺，悄没声地溜出了书房，朝后院娇娘绣阁走去。

way out of this one. A gift of your embroidered shoes to your paramour is iron-clad evidence of sordid goings-on!"

Feihong lost no time wrapping the shoes in a piece of cloth and smoothing the bedclothes. Then she crept out of the eastern study, and made her way to Jiaoniang's rooms.

Earlier, just after she had completed her toilet, Jiaoniang had noticed that the flowers in the vase had faded. So she called Xiaohui and Ziyan to go with her into the garden to pick some fresh flowers. The two girls were in a frisky mood, and dragged their young mistress to see the pear blossoms, and then to view the plum flowers, and from apricot trees to plum trees. At the same time, they chased butterflies and teased birds. Picking a flowering apricot branch, Jiaoniang was ready to return. But the maid servants wanted to continue frolicking in the garden, and so she went back to her rooms alone. After she had arranged the blossoms in the flower vase, she looked down and noticed that her emerald-green pleated skirt and her phoenix-tipped embroidered shoes were soggy with dew. So she took off her skirt, and pulled back the bed curtain to find a new pair of shoes. There were clear signs that somebody had lain on the counterpane. She looked all over the bed, but nowhere could she see her other shoes. "This is strange," she thought to herself. "Where can they have got to? I distinctly remember that I left them beside the pillow this morning. Surely, they couldn't have flown away by themselves, could they?"

As she was sat on the bed, puzzling over this mystery, she heard someone lift the beaded door curtain. It was Feihong. The girl entered, and looking straight at Jiaoniang with a mischievous smile, said, "Miss, by this time you are normally outside, under the window, busy with your needlework. What are you doing sitting here all alone?"

Jiaoniang felt a strange sensation of alarm. She did not reply, but kept her head bent, still looking around for the shoes.

Feihong came nearer. "Are you looking for something, Miss?" she asked. It was seemingly an innocent question.

　　且说娇娘早妆已罢，见花瓶中花儿败落，便带了小慧、紫嫣到花园中折花。两个丫头贪玩，拉着娇娘看了梨花看桃花，看了杏花看李花，一会儿扑蝶，一会儿逗鸟，欢笑不已。娇娘拣了一枝杏花折下便要返回，小慧意犹未尽，不肯回来。娇娘只得任她们玩耍，自己持了花枝，独自返回绣房。进门将花插在瓶中，低头看见自己的湘翠百褶裙和凤头红绣鞋已被露水打湿，便将裙子脱下，揭了绣帐换鞋。却见绣枕似乎有人动过，满床上找遍了，也不见绣鞋的影子，心中暗忖："这真是奇了，我的绣鞋怎么会不见了？清清楚楚记得早上放在枕边，莫非它自家飞了不成？"

　　正在纳闷，听得珠帘一响，抬头一看，却是飞红进来。飞红似笑非笑地盯着娇娘说道："小姐日常此时早在窗外刺绣，今日怎么还在房内独坐想心事呢？"

　　娇娘心中着急，也顾不上回答，仍旧低头寻找绣鞋。

　　飞红近前道："呀，小姐你这是寻什么？"

　　娇娘早就看出飞红对申纯有意，时常当众搔首弄姿，纠缠申纯，因而心中对飞红十分不满。今天见飞红来追问不休，便故意不理她。飞红有把柄抓在手里，虽见小姐三番五次对自己不理不睬，却不气不

Jiaoniang had long been aware that the maid servant had a fancy for Shen Chun, and resented the way the girl flirted with him in public. Now Feihong's tiresome questions were especially annoying. Jiaoniang stonily ignored her. This, however, made no impression on Feihong, who knew that she had a hold over her young mistress. With the sweetest of smiles on her face, the maid servant said, "Oh, Miss, you look so worried! What can you have lost that has upset you so?"

Jiaoniang suddenly remembered that Feihong often asked to borrow her shoes, as their feet were about the same size. Whenever she made a new pair of shoes, the maid servant always insisted on trying them on. "She must have taken them while I was out," Jiaoniang thought, "and now she's playing the innocent." Aloud, she said grumpily: "Who's been in this room recently?"

Feihong uttered a mirthless laugh. "Who would dare to come barging into your boudoir, Miss?" she asked with forced incredulity.

"Then how is it that there is something missing?"

"What can be missing to get you so agitated, Miss?"

With a growing feeling of anger, Jiaoniang began to be convinced that it was Feihong who had stolen the shoes. "Somebody has definitely been in here," she hissed through clenched teeth.

Feihong's face twisted in a sneer. "I haven't seen anybody else come in," she said. "But judging by the way you are so flustered, Miss, I assume that you have lost something extremely valuable ... like a gold phoenix hairpin, perhaps, or a jade eardrop?"

"No, nothing like that."

"Well then, your green jade bracelet with gold wire, or perhaps your pearl hairpin with a cluster of gems?"

"No, not those either."

"In that case ... could it be that someone has stolen your broaded shoes?"

Jiaoniang's head jerked sharply upward. "Yes," she said, with an ac-

恼,微笑道:"哟,大小姐,瞧你这愁眉苦脸的,到底是丢了什么?"

娇娘猛然想起素日里飞红常来讨鞋样,因两人的脚儿一般大小,这双鞋才做好时,飞红就曾试过,想是她趁自己不在拿了去,故意拿自己开心,便没好气地说:

"适才谁到我房里来了?"

飞红冷笑道:"小姐的深闺,哪个敢轻易乱闯呀?"

"那,我房里的东西怎么不见了?"

"不见了哪件东西?看把你急成这个样子。"

娇娘心中含恨,又见飞红嘻皮笑脸,认定是飞红偷走了自己的绣鞋,道:

"定是有人来过我房中!"

飞红又冷笑一声,道:

"我可不曾见谁进来。小姐如此着慌,是没了金凤钗,还是不见了玉耳环?"

"不是。"

"那是丢了金丝翠玉镯,还是八宝攒珠簪?"

"不是,都不是。"

"那……莫不是有人偷了你那小绣鞋?"

娇娘猛地抬头道:"正是。看来你全都清楚,却在此明知故问,拿我开心,是不是?"

cusing stare. "You knew all along, and you just came here to bait me, didn't you?"

Feihong produced a cloth bundle from her sleeve, and unrolled it. "Are these the shoes?" she asked, archly.

Jiaoniang grabbed the shoes in great consternation. "Yes," she acknowledged. "How did you get hold of them?"

The main servant simply laughed. Then she said, "Miss, why didn't you say so in the first place, instead of working yourself up into such a state? I found them, and was bringing them to you."

"What do you mean, you found them? I put them by my pillow only last night. They were still there this morning. They haven't grown wings, so how could they fly out of here?" Jiaoniang was flabbergasted.

"It seems to me that you must have ... er ... given them to someone, Miss" was the sly rejoinder.

"What nonsense!" exploded Jiaoniang. "How could I have given my shoes away? I think you took them to trick me into being indiscreet. How preposterous?" And she turned her face away in a towering rage.

This treatment sparked resentment in Feihong. She thought, "You're lucky I didn't show these shoes to your parents; then, you'd really have been in trouble. I kept them to save you from disgrace, and here you are accusing me of some plot, and pretending to be offended!" Her face froze into a scowl. "There's no call for malicious slanders, Miss. Just give me the shoes back, and I'll return them to the person who took them."

With raised eyebrows and a brow like thunder, Jiaoniang intoned, "Somebody took them?"

Throwing caution to the winds, Feihong replied, "Well, if you didn't give them to the young gentleman, then he must have sneaked in here and taken them himself. Otherwise, they would still be safely tucked up beside your pillow. I don't think they ran over to the young gentleman's bed by themselves."

This announcement hit Jiaoniang almost like a physical blow. "What

飞红从袖中取出绢帕,展开往娇娘眼前一送,问道:"可是这双?"

娇娘急忙接过来,道:"正是。怎么会在你手里?"

飞红笑道:"小姐你何不早说,看把你急的。这是我拾到的,特来送还。"

"你拾到的?好生奇怪,这鞋昨晚我掖在枕侧,今早还在,它又没长翅膀,怎能飞出绣阁外?"

飞红又笑了笑道:"我想这鞋……是小姐送给一个人了吧?"

"胡说! 我的鞋儿怎能送人?想是你拿了去,寻我开心,现在倒打一耙说是我送人了,真正岂有此理!"娇娘猛地翻脸,怒不可遏。

飞红一听也恼了,心想我没把这双绣鞋交给老爷、夫人,已是给你留了天大的面子。如今你被我揭穿老底,恼羞成怒,竟反咬一口,往我头上栽赃起来。于是冷着脸道:"小姐可不要血口喷人,你且将绣鞋拿给我,我自去还给拿鞋的那人。"

娇娘柳眉倒竖,粉面含威,厉声道:"你说是谁拿去的?"

飞红到这时也顾不得许多了,道:"不是小姐私自送与那秀才,就是那秀才暗自偷了去。否则这绣鞋好好地藏在深闺,怎么能跑到那秀才的床上去?"

娇娘闻言如坠云里雾中,问道:"什么那秀才?"

... young gentleman?" Her voice faltered.

Feihong shot a sardonic glance at her young mistress. To herself, she thought, "I can read you like a book, in spite of all your phony posturing." Aloud, she said, sarcastically: "How many young gentlemen are there in the house, Miss?"

Then Jiaoniang realized what had happened. Her face turned a fiery red. The words "So he stole the shoes!" screamed inside her head. But my boudoir and his study are far apart. It seems he has the disposition of a sneak, who dare not come openly in broad daylight. Perhaps, Feihong is making up this story? But no; it rings true in every detail. Besides, she is not the sort of person to make up wild tales. But, what on earth does it all mean?"

See her young mistress sitting there, her head bowed and saying not a word, Feihong felt a sense of elation. Exulting in what she considered her victory, she said, "Well, if you didn't give them to him, and he didn't take them himself, then I must be slandering you Miss, mustn't I? All right, I'll take the shoes to your mother, and let her get to the bottom of this mystery. We can't let a shoe thief off scot-free, can we?"

So saying, she snatched the shoes from Jiaoniang's hands, and turned to leave. Frantically, Jiaoniang grabbed her sleeve to detain her. "Oh, please don't rush away like that," she gasped. "I didn't say you took them. Anyway, if anyone saw them in your hands right now, I don't know what rumors might start to flit around. Now, I'm not asking who took them; I just want you to keep quiet about this matter for the time being."

Seeing that Jiaoniang was in a conciliatory mood, Feihong changed her tone. "Very well," she said, "I won't say anything to your mother. You can have your embroidered shoes back. Just take better care of them in future, that's all."

As soon as she got the shoes back in her own hands, Jiaoniang let out a cackle: "Now you can tell my mother anything you like. I don't care. If these shoes really did find their way into the young gentleman's hands, how

飞红瞥了一眼娇娘，心中暗道："你摆着明白装糊涂，倒像真的一样。"嘴上却说："小姐想想府里还有哪个秀才？"

娇娘猛然醒悟，顿时满脸羞红，暗想道："莫非是三哥偷去的？可是我的绣阁与书房隔绝，他便是有心偷香窃玉，也断然不敢大天白日闯进来。若说是飞红编造的，可她说得有鼻子有眼，也不像是信口胡诌。这到底是怎么回事？"

飞红见娇娘低头不语，自觉胜了一着，得意洋洋地说道："不是小姐与他，又不是他拿去，定是飞红赃诬小姐的了。罢罢罢，我只把这鞋儿送与夫人，查个详细，弄个明白，省得让偷鞋贼逍遥法外。"

说着猛地从娇娘手中夺过鞋子，转身就走。娇娘顿时发慌，一把扯住飞红的袖子道："姐姐忙什么呀？我也没说就是姐姐拿去的。如今幸而落在姐姐手中，若是别人见了，还不知怎样张扬呢！我也不问是谁拿去了，只求姐姐口儿放稳些，休在人前提起。"

飞红见娇娘软了下来，也改口道："既然如此，我就不告知夫人了。绣鞋依旧还你，以后须要自家藏妥才好。"

娇娘接鞋在手，突然冷笑道："哼，你便告知夫人我也不怕。我就说这鞋既落在那秀才手中，你怎么又从他床上拿回？倒要看你这个小蹄子如何辨解？"

did you manage to get them from his bed? How can you explain that?"

This barb made the maid servant shake with anger. "You can't stop playing tricks, can you?" she yelled. "Well, I'm not going to waste time bandying words with you. I'm going straight to the young gentleman, and see what he has to say about this. And with a flurry of sleeves she stalked off.

Watching her leave, Jiaoniang suddenly felt weak in the knees. She collapsed on the bed, sick with worry. "What Feihong said was probably right, she thought to herself. "Shen Chun must have taken the shoes. But how did Feihong get hold of them? There must be some conspiracy between them. Otherwise, why did he fail to hide them properly, and just leave them out where anyone could find them? He must have bragged about stealing them to Feihong. Oh Shen Chun, my faithless Shen Chun, how could you sully yourself with a serving maid? How could you cast me aside so?" Just then, a tremendous pain gripped the girl's heart, and tears fell from her eyes like rain, soaking the embroidered shoes she held in her hands.

Meanwhile, Shen Chun returned to his quarters after noon. Entering, he carefully locked the door behind him, and quickly searched for the shoes, meaning to fondly them in solitude. First, he looked under the pillow, where he had left them. His heart skipped a beat at finding them gone. He made a thorough but fruitless search of the bed. The shoes had somehow vanished into thin air. "Someone's been here while I was out, and taken them!" was the horrifying thought that flashed through his mind.

The young man's head suddenly became heavy, and a black film seemed to descend in front of his eyes. He thought, "This is terrible! If somebody else has got hold of the shoes it will first of all ruin Jiaoniang's reputation, and secondly it will make me a laughing stock when everyone finds out that I hid a pair of girl's shoes in my bedroom. What on earth am I going to do?"

Too agitated to sit still any longer, he got up and paced restlessly round the room. But this provided no relief to his feelings of despair. To-

飞红闻言气得身子乱颤，道："小姐你倒会放刁。我如今不与你斗口，我只去问那申官人，看他怎么说？"说罢拂袖而去。

娇娘见飞红去了，两腿一软，跌坐在牙床上，心中自忖："飞红所言倒也可信，这绣鞋定是三哥拿去的。只是怎么又落在飞红手上？敢是这两人有了什么瓜葛，不然他偷了绣鞋，藏还藏不及，怎么能摆在明处？分明是他偷了去，巴巴的向飞红表功。申纯啊申纯，你这个负心郎君，连个丫环也要沾惹，又把我摆在哪里？"想到此处，娇娘不由心中大痛，泪下如雨，打湿了手中的绣鞋。

待到午后，申纯回到书房，将门关严，急急伸手去枕畔摸那双绣鞋，打算着一个人尽情把玩。谁知枕下空空如也，哪里有绣鞋的影子。心中一惊，急忙在床上翻找，才知绣鞋已经不翼而飞。心想："一定是有人趁我不在时，进来偷走了绣鞋。"

想到此处，只觉得头皮发麻，眼前发黑，暗道："不好！这绣鞋若落在他人手中，一则坏了娇娘的名声；二则自己房中藏着女子的绣鞋，传扬出去必然名声扫地。这可如何是好？"

当时急得他坐立不安，绕室彷徨，可这件事又不能声张，只好闷在心里。日暮时分，娇娘独自来到书房，进门便问道："兄长今日可曾到过小妹绣阁之中

wards evening, Jiaoniang appeared at his door, alone. She came straight to the point: "Did you enter my boudoir today?"

Shen Chun hesitated, before mumbling, "Er, yes ... yes, indeed, as a matter of fact ... I was."

"Did you take a pair of embroidered shoes from my bed?"

Shen Chun blushed to the tips of his ears, but said nothing. He just stood there gaping at Jiaoniang with a foolish grin on his face.

His awkwardness signaled to Jiaoniang plainly that Feihong had been telling the truth. Fury mounted within her. There was an icy smile on her face as she demanded, "If you took them, please have the goodness to give them back."

Shen Chun thought to himself: "Since she knows that I stole them, she must have come here as soon as she found them missing, and taken them back again. She has come here deliberately to taunt me. But since the shoes haven't fallen into somebody else's hands, there's no problem in my admitting to having taken them." He breathed a long sigh, and said, "My dear, those shoes of yours are really enchanting. I couldn't let go of them for an instant. So I admit that I did play the part of a thief. I hope you will forgive me."

"Well, since you have confessed," said Jiaoniang, "I will not pursue the matter any further. Just return the shoes, and we will say no more about it."

Looking at her outstretched hand, Shen Chun was convinced that she must be teasing him. With a jovial smile, he protested, "But, the shoes have already been returned to their owner. Why are you being so provoking?"

Hearing this, Jiaoniang concluded that Shen Chun had sent Feihong to give the shoes back, deliberately to mock her. There must be some low intrigue between the two of them, she thought. This speculation pained her, and her face clouded over. "Oh Shen Chun!" she thought. "It seems that I've found out what you are really like." She gave the young man a fero-

么?"

申纯支支吾吾,嗫嚅半晌道:"曾…曾经去…去来。"

"你可曾于帐中取了一双绣鞋?"

"这……"申纯脸烧耳热,实在无法开口,只得腆着脸对娇娘傻笑不已。

娇娘见申纯如此模样,便知飞红所言是实,心中愈发不悦,冷冷道:"若是兄长拿了,还与小妹便是。"

申纯闻言暗忖道:"妹妹既然知道是我盗了她的鞋,想必是她回房后寻鞋不见,便寻到书房,自家取了回去,现在故意来为难我。既然绣鞋没有落在他人手中,自己认了也没有什么要紧。"不由长长舒了一口气道:"妹妹的绣鞋着实迷人,愚兄爱不释手,便斗胆做了回梁上君子,还望妹妹见谅。"

娇娘道:"既然三哥认了,小妹也不追究,你还我鞋来即可。"

申纯见娇娘伸手索鞋,以为娇娘仍在逗耍自己,便嘻皮笑脸道:"绣鞋已经物归原主,妹妹还要苦苦逼索,让愚兄怎么给你变得出来?"

娇娘听到申纯已知绣鞋物归原主,便认定是他指使飞红送还绣鞋,羞辱自己。这两个如此做戏,定是背着自己有了私情。不由心中剧痛,花容惨变,暗道:"申纯啊申纯,我算是认识你了!"想到此处,狠狠

cious stare, before turning and striding out of the room. Shen Chun stretched out a hand to detain her, but he was just too late. To pursue her would be useless, he knew. So he was left alone with his anguished thoughts.

When she left Jiaoniang, Feihong was in a pensive mood. She turned the matter of the shoes over and over in her mind, and finally came to the conclusion that she had better confront Shen Chun to find out the truth. Her opportunity came the next day at noon, when the old mistress retired for her nap. Walking towards the eastern study through the willow petals falling like snow, she was reminded of her home. A feeling of sad nostalgia came over her, and she sighed, "Ah, how heartbreaking is spring sorrow! Soon the swallows will mate and build their nests together."

The words were hardly out of her mouth when she heard somebody behind her say, "Don't be heartbroken. Why not build your nest with me?"

Feihong stood stock-still, her heart fluttering. She turned her head to see Shen Chun. How long had he been following her? She didn't know, but he had certainly overheard her reciting those two lines of a poem, and found them quite amusing by the look of him! She blushed with embarrassment, and beads of sweat stood out on her forehead. "Where did you learn to sneak up on people like that?" she growled.

The young man laughed. "Have I stolen something of yours, that you think I'm a thief or something?"

"You eavesdropped on someone; that just as bad as stealing," Feihong replied.

"But when a thief is caught, you must be able to find the loot on him," countered Shen Chun. "How can words be stolen?"

"There's loot all right," said Feihong. "Where are those shoes that were on your bed?"

This rocked Shen Chun back on his heels. Recovering from his shock, he charged, "So that's what happened to them: You stole them!"

Feihong looked him with disgust. "What?" she cried. "You're the one

地瞪了申纯一眼，转身离去。申纯欲伸手阻拦，却迟了半步，又不便追出去，只好在房中干着急生闷气。

且说飞红从娇娘处出来，心中之气难消，思量再三，还得去找申纯讨个公道。第二天晌午，侍候夫人午睡已罢，飞红便朝书房走来，一路上见庭中杨花似雪，落红片片，不禁想到自家身世，心中好不凄苦，轻声叹道："春愁断肠也，何时燕双栖。"

话音未落，就听背后有人道："姐姐休要断肠，与小生双栖如何？"

顿时惊得飞红芳心乱跳，动弹不得，回转头来，却见是申纯不知何时站在自己身后，知道他偷听了自己所吟诗句，以此取笑，不由窘得腮飘红云，额角生汗，轻轻啐了口道："呸，你这人怎生这等惯作贼？"

申纯笑嘻嘻转到她面前道："我偷了姐姐什么东西，姐姐骂我是贼？"

飞红道："你窃听人言，岂不是贼？"

申纯"嘿嘿"一笑道："姐姐可知道人言捉贼见赃。窃听人言，赃在哪里？"

"要赃也有，你床头绣鞋哪里来的？"

申纯听了恍然大悟，一拍脑门道："怪不得我床里不见了绣鞋，原来是你偷去了。"

飞红轻轻啐了口道："呸！你逾墙钻穴做了盗贼，反栽赃于我，我告你到官，看不打下你的下半截去。"

who goes about clambering over walls and crawling through gaps, and you have the nerve to call me a thief! If I tell the magistrate about this, you'll be in trouble up to your neck, and you know it!"

"Tell him. I don't care." was the nonchalant reply.

"Oh, you don't care, eh? Well, what if I tell the old mistress?" With that, Feihong turned to go and carry out her threat.

Alarmed, Shen Chun detained her. "I know you are only teasing me," he said with an ingratiating smile, and an exaggerated bow. "But, please, you mustn't let this story get around."

Feihong successfully hid her glee, and stony-faced confronted the young scholar. "I thought you told me you didn't care," she said. "Why have you suddenly changed your mind? Anyway, it's too late now."

"What if I go down on my bended knees?" Shen Chun offered, with a ghastly smile still on his face, and made as if to do so.

"You can throw yourself flat on your face for all I care; it won't do you any good." said Feihong.

"What do you want me to do?" the young man pleaded.

Feihong covered her mouth to hide a smile, and said, "I want you to call me something nice."

"How about 'Sister'?"

"Pah! I'm not your sister. I want you to call me 'Miss'."

Shen Chun was taken aback. "Oh, please don't tease me," he cried. "Why can't I call you 'Sister' Since your name is Feihong, if I call you 'Miss,' I'll have to call you 'Miss Hong', won't I?"

Feihong blushed a bright red, realizing that "Miss Hong" was the name of the maid servant who was the go-between for the young lovers in *The Romance of the Western Bower*. "What impertinence!" she snapped. "I'm not the 'Miss Hong' in this household."

The double meaning in these words did not escape Shen Chun: They contained a subtle threat to expose his affair with Jiaoniang. Just as he was at a loss what to say next, he spotted a pair of butterflies. "Look!" he

申纯戏道:"随你告官去,我也不怕。"

"不怕?那我告夫人去。"说着飞红转身就走。

申纯见飞红变脸,认真起来,忙伸手拦住道:"这可吓煞了小生也,求姐姐千万不要声张。"说着便对飞红打拱作揖。

飞红心中暗笑,却将脸儿绷得铁板一般,道:"你不是不怕么?怎么这会子又没出息起来?只怕是已经迟了。"

申纯道:"那小生与你跪…跪下就是。"

说着做势欲跪,脸上却笑嘻嘻的。飞红道:"不要说跪下,五体投地也不够。"

申纯央求道:"那姐姐想怎样发落小生?"

飞红掩口笑道:"总得叫两声好听的吧。"

"叫什么?叫你嫡嫡亲亲的姐姐。"

"呸,谁是你姐姐?我要你叫娘。"

申纯道:"姐姐不要寒碜人,再说岂不把姐姐叫老了?姐姐原叫飞红,小生就叫你'红娘'如何?"

飞红一听"红娘"两字,不觉脸红耳热,白了申纯一眼道:"什么红娘?乖儿子,你是惯家的张君瑞,也不消得我来做红娘。"

申纯听出飞红言外之意,是说自己与娇娘早已偷欢成事,用不着红娘引线穿针,一时尴尬万分,不知如何是好。恰好抬头见一对大蝴蝶在花间翩翩起

said, pointing to them, "How lovely their colors are, as they caper in the east breeze, full of the delights of spring. They remind me of you."

Feihong pretended to scold him. "What nonsense!" she snorted. "But I'll tell you what: If you catch those two butterflies for me I'll give you the embroidered shoes back."

"Of course I'll catch them for you," said Shen Chun exultantly, "but don't go back on your word." So saying, he jumped over a railing in pursuit of the butterflies.

Feihong followed him, and soon the pair of them were running around among the flowers chasing the butterflies. They both squealed in delight when Shen Chun caught one, but their joy was short-lived as a harsh voice cut through the balmy air: "Have you no shame? An unmarried man and a single girl frolicking about like that!"

Shen Chun and Feihong whirled round in surprise, to see Jiaoniang standing behind them in the covered walkway, her face as threatening as a thunderstorm and her eyes blazing. Shen Chun immediately darted behind a clump of bushes, and scuttled away. But Feihong coolly straightened up and stared unabashed at her young mistress. "I was only catching butterflies, that's all, Miss," she said.

Feeling sure that the girl had been shamelessly flirting with Shen Chun, and now was relying on him to back her up, Jiaoniang forgot that she was supposed to be a well-bred young lady, and screamed at the top of her voice: "You little minx! What do you mean by wasting time fooling about here, instead of doing the needlework you're supposed to be doing?"

Instead of replying, Feihong nonchalantly opened her hand. The butterfly inside it unfurled its wings, and in the twinkling of an eye flew away. She watched it for a while, and then said, slowly: "What would you have me do for recreation on a nice spring day like this? Where was the harm in having a little relaxation?"

This enraged Jiaoniang still further, and she yelled, "Going on excursions is for the children of the gentry and scholars, not for the likes of maid

舞，心头一动，指着蝴蝶道："姐姐快看，那一双彩蝶儿，舞东风，贪春色，飞来飞去的，倒好似你。"

飞红娇声嗔道："呆子，休得胡说！你若扑了那一对蝴蝶给我，我便把那绣鞋拿来还你。"

申纯闻言喜道："姐姐可不许撒赖，小生这就去扑来给你。"说着翻身跳出栏杆，便去追扑彩蝶。

飞红也跑下台阶，绕到花间与申纯一同扑蝶。一时间二人你追我赶，绕来绕去，申纯瞅了个机会，猛地一扑，扣住一只蝴蝶，高兴得二人同时欢叫道："扑住了！扑住了！"正在这时，忽听得游廊上一声娇斥："你两个好不知羞，孤男寡女，在此做甚？"

二人急忙抬头，就见娇娘满面乌云，眼中喷火，从游廊上走了下来。申纯见了，吓得一吐舌头，忙缩头闪身躲入花丛，从旁门溜走了。飞红却冷笑一声，慢慢直起身子说道："回小姐，飞红在此捉蝴蝶玩耍。"

原来娇娘因心中烦闷，一个人到花园中散心，远远望见申纯与飞红在一处调笑，双双扑蝶，早已气不打一处来，忍不住出言喝斥。没想到飞红竟然出言顶撞，显见是仗着有申纯在后面撑腰，一时气急败坏，将往日的温柔贤良丢到九霄云外，厉声道："贱婢，你不去做针黹，在此玩耍什么？"

飞红不以为然地将手一张，那只蝴蝶扑愣愣舒展彩翅飞起来，转瞬不见了。她目送蝴蝶飞去，这才

servants such as you."

Feihong pouted. "Oh, I see," she said. "And I suppose maid servants are not people too?"

In a towering rage by this time, Jiaoniang, her face contorted with fury, spat out, "You miserable little skivvy! Your duties are to stay indoors doing needlework and arranging flowers, and don't you forget it!"

Feihong didn't turn a hair. "Anything else?" she asked, cool as a cucumber.

"Yes, there certainly is. Clean the bronze mirror on my dressing table until all the grease is off it. Who told you to go gallivanting around trying to entice our mansion's guest? Wait till my mother finds out; you'll get a thrashing with the thick club!"

This threat only drew a sneer from Feihong. "Oh, I don't think anyone can pin the label of 'entice of our mansion's guest' on me, Miss. After all, I'm just a maid servant, and I came out merely to fondle the flowers and chase butterflies ... that sort of thing. The old mistress would quite understand; nothing unusual in that. At least I don't have secret assignations with handsome young scholars like some people."

"She knows all about Shen Chun and me!" thought Jiaoniang, her heart gripped by a feeling of panic. In a softer tone this time, she said, "You are not talking reasonably. You are simply arguing for the sake of arguing."

Feihong did not want an all-out confrontation with her young mistress, who, after all, had the power to make things very awkward indeed for her if she were annoyed. So why not be tactful? She thought. At this point, she quieted the anger that had been boiling up inside her, assumed a compliant smile, and said, "I was only teasing you, Miss. A young lady of breeding and refinement like yourself shouldn't take notice of silly maid servants like me."

Seeing that Feihong had retreated from her defiant stance, Jiaoniang decided to climb down from her high horse too. "Well, I'll let you off this

慢慢地道："如此春光，教人怎不动心，就是出来玩耍一会儿又有何妨？"

娇娘恨得牙根发痒，恶狠狠地道："那游春踏青是公子王孙、骚人墨客的事，你一个丫环家，岂能整日里玩耍？"

飞红反唇相讥道："噢，难道丫环就不是人吗？"

娇娘见飞红铁嘴钢牙，一味顶撞，愈发气愤，骂道："你一个做丫环的，只配在房中刺绣扎花做针黹。"

飞红不慌不忙反问道："还有呢？"

"还有梳妆台前擦抹铜镜，清除油腻。谁叫你个蹄子游月下，笑星前，勾引府上的客人！只怕让夫人知道了，动了家法，用粗棍儿敲杀你这死丫头！"

飞红冷笑道："这勾引男人的名儿我可担不起。我一个做丫环的，偶然出来斗斗草，打打秋千，捉蝴蝶玩会子，就是夫人知道了，也是寻常小事一桩，反正又不是与哪个白面书生暗上巫山悄赴高唐做那云雨之事。"

娇娘听飞红话中有话，似是知晓自己与申纯的幽会，不免有些发慌，口气也不知不觉软了下来，道："你倒做下有理的来了？我说你两句也要争辩不休！"

飞红心中也不愿和娇娘闹僵，真的闹大发了，小姐毕竟是有头有脸的主子，最后还是自己吃亏，又何必不识趣呢？想到这里，强压心头之火，换了笑脸道："飞红与小姐戏言，小姐大人大量，不要与我们做下

time," she conceded. "But you won't escape so lightly the next time you try something like this, I can assure you."

And throwing a withering glance at Feihong, she stalked back to the rear courtyard. As she did so, her doubts grew more burdensome: Although she had come across no real evidence of collusion between Feihong and Shen Chun today, nevertheless she could not help feeling that there was something not quite right between them.

Feihong scowled as she watched Jiaoniang depart. "Who do you think you're fooling, Miss?" she growled. "You never miss an opportunity to lecture other people, do you? Well, if I tell your mother what you've been up to, you'll have a hard time talking your way out of it, I can tell you! You can't keep up this virtuous act forever; the truth will come out eventually. You think you can indulge in amorous intrigues like the heroine in *The Romance of the Western Bower*. But, unlike her, you don't have a Miss Hong to cover up for you. When your little tricks are found out it will be too late to regret having treated me so badly!" At the same time, she was already busy trying to think of a way to get her revenge on Jiaoniang.

The following day, at noon, all the servants, both male and female, gathered in the main hall to congratulate the old mistress on her birthday. Shen Chun and Jiaoniang were also present, sitting beside each other and chatting. Feihong saw her chance, and walked straight towards them. Pointing to Jiaoniang's feet, she looked sideways at Shen Chun, and said, "Master Shen, look! Aren't those the shoes you lost the other day? Now they're on the young mistress' feet!"

Jiaoniang turned deathly pale, and ducked away, pretending that she had something to say to her mother. Fortunately, the hall was crowded and the buzz of conversation prevented Wang Wenrui and his wife hearing what Feihong had just said. Shen Chun too was mortified. He even broke out in a cold sweat. Stealing a glance at Jiaoniang, he saw that she was sitting straight and composed, and didn't seem to notice his discomfiture. At the same time, it didn't escape him that Feihong was looking very pleased with

人的一般见识。"

娇娘见飞红服软，趁机下台阶道："今儿个权且放过，下次再见到你如此，定不甘休。"

说罢，撇下飞红独自回后院去了。她边走边想，疑心重重，虽说今天并未抓住什么真凭实据，可心里总觉得这两人之间有些不清白。

飞红看着娇娘走入后院，这才朝着娇娘背影恶狠狠地啐了一口，低声骂道："小姐你做的好事瞒得住谁？倒几次三番寻机找茬训人。我若是拼着去告诉夫人，看你个贱人浑身是嘴也说不明白！我倒要看看你这假清高的道学先生，怎么将你那点子私情瞒到底？待到你像那崔莺莺泄了春光，漏了底细，可没个小红娘为你包着，那时才叫你个言清行亏的蹄子后悔不迭呢。"一边骂，一边琢磨着怎么报今天这一箭之仇。

次日中午，正逢夫人做寿，阖府仆人丫环聚于中堂，为老爷夫人贺喜，申纯、娇娘也都在堂上同坐闲谈。飞红见时机已到，忽然走近，指着娇娘脚下所穿的绣鞋，对申纯一飞媚眼道："申官人你看，那便是你前日所丢之鞋，如今穿在小姐脚上。"

娇娘一听，顿时吓得脸色煞白，急忙掉头与母亲说话遮掩。好在当时人多嘴杂，王文瑞、赵夫人都没听到。申纯也冒了一头冷汗，偷着抬头去看娇娘，就见娇娘正襟危坐，目不斜视，只做看不见。再看飞红

herself as she chatted and joked with the other maid servants, shooting him sly glances from time to time. In an agony of embarrassment, he finally made an excuse to slip away. Jiaoniang had caught the glances exchanged between Shen Chun and Feihong, her mind was in a turmoil. She reasoned to herself as follows: "That faithless Shen Chun must have put Feihong up to shaming me in front of my parents. And just before he left, they were making eyes at each other. There must be some secret liaison between them. Oh, that heartless villain! How could I have been so blind as to fall for such a worthless creature? Oh Shen Chun, Shen Chun, why are there so many fickle young gentlemen in the world?"

From then on, Jiaoniang gave Shen Chun the cold shoulder. The young man was baffled: What had he done to deserve this treatment? Meeting Jiaoniang by chance in the main hall, she had uttered a curt greeting and brushed past him. Needless to say, her treatment of Feihong was even more frigid.

Shen Chun was desperate to get Jiaoniang to tell him what the matter was, but she deliberately avoided him. Eventually, being at a loose end one day, he decided to go for a stroll in the flower garden in the hope of bumping into her and being able to unburden his heart.

The willow catkins were like mounds of snow that day, and they trembled in the breeze. Suddenly, his turbulent emotions overwhelmed the young man, and he thought, "There is certainly some truth in the old saying 'A woman's feelings are as changeable as the flowing waters and the blossoms of the willow.' I have found that out for myself." Then he started to reflect upon the previous two years of his meeting and parting with Jiaoniang. Those times of bliss and times of despair — as precious and fleeting as the willow catkins he could see before him. Another proverb sprang into his mind: 'Adversaries are bound to meet.' Perhaps Jiaoniang and he had been antagonists in a previous existence, and so were fated to be lovers in this one? As he paced up and down sighing, he came across a clump of fragrant plants. Stopping to admire them and stooping to enjoy their scent, he

却面露得意之色，向自己抛个飞眼，与小慧、湘娥、绿英等丫头说说笑笑，如同无事人一般。自家好生没趣，找了个借口起身溜了出去。娇娘见申纯与飞红打个眼色，即刻起身去了，心中暗忖道："定是申纯这个负心郎，指使飞红故意在爹娘面前让自己难堪，临走时二人还打情骂俏，洋洋得意，若无私情，焉能如此？这个没良心的东西，我算是有眼无珠看错了人。申纯啊申纯，真是山川可料有难料，薄幸如君有几人！"

自此以后，娇娘便处处躲着申纯，有时在中堂遇见，勉强应酬两句，起身便走，对飞红更是不理不睬。

申纯忽见娇娘对自己冷淡，心中百思不解，苦不堪言，想向娇娘问个明白，却总也找不到机会。于是无事便在后花园中徘徊，指望着与娇娘当面碰上，也好表明心迹。

闲步当中，见柳絮杨花团团如雪，随风飘飘扬扬，一时心绪如潮，情难自禁。想道："人常言'女儿家水性杨花，情无定性'。以今看来果真如此。"转而思量这两年间与娇娘时聚时散，时好时坏，真若这风中柳絮飞落不定。也许是应了那句老话：不是冤家不聚头。娇娘与自己是否也是前世里的对头，今世里的情侣。徘徊叹息间，来到一丛丁香前，乍闻暗香袭人，不觉停步观赏。低头之际，却见花下有鸾笺一幅，俯身

noticed a scrap of paper on the ground. He picked it up, and saw that it bore some lines of verse. The composition was elegant and obviously the work of a person learned in the classics.

Moreover, it was a love poem written by a woman on the heart-tugging theme of the rapid passing away of the springtime of life. It occurred to him that Jiaoniang was the only person in the Wang mansion who was capable of writing such accomplished lines; yet the handwriting was not like hers. Surely, none of the serving maids could have written it! On the other hand, Jiaoniang had not been her normal self recently, so perhaps this had made her hand a little shaky?

In the midst of these reveries, he was startled to hear the giggling of Xiaohui and some of the other serving maids frolicking in the nearby flowerbeds. Not wanting to be discovered by the inquisitive little tattle-tales, he ducked into the covered passageway, and so made his escape.

In the meantime, Jiaoniang, who had been fretting over what she imagined was an intrigue between Shen Chun and Feihong so much that she could not put her mind to anything else, happened to be walking over to the main hall to talk to her mother. As she paced through the covered corridor which led from the rear courtyard, her head bowed in thought, she suddenly heard a voice cry "Miss is here!" Looking up in surprise, she saw that it came from the parrot in its golden cage. With a red beak and green feathers, the bird had its head on one side, and again squawked its greeting. Jiaoniang took two red beans from the sachet at her waist, and playfully pushed them through the wire bars of the cage. The parrot hopped up and down in delight, hooting, "Give me, Miss! Give me, Miss!" For an instant, Jiaoniang's gloom was dispelled, and she found herself smiling once again. Just at that moment, Shen Chun came upon the charming scene, and made a deep bow to Jiaoniang.

The young man had been attracted by the parrot's call. His heart had leapt within him when he heard "Miss is here!", despite the raucous enunciation. He hurried in the direction of the sound, and came face to face

拾起，只见上面蝇头小楷书着一阕《青玉案》：

"花底莺踏红英乱，春心重，顿成愁懒。杨花梦散楚云平，空惹起情无限。伤心渐觉成牵绊，奈愁绪、寸心难管。深诚无计寄天涯，几欲问梁间燕。"

申纯读罢，知道是一首春怨词。想这府内有此才情的只有娇娘，可笔迹却不大像。可若说不是娇娘所做，这府中的女眷并丫环婆子，又有谁有这份才情雅兴来伤春悲秋？或许是娇娘这些日子心中不畅，故笔下缭乱一二也未可知。

正在思量间，忽听小慧等几个小丫头在花园中嘻嘻哈哈地斗草，怕她们见了生疑，慌忙躲入长廊，返回书房。

却说娇娘近来日夜思量申纯与飞红的事，万事做不在心上。这一天午后，独自出来到中堂找母亲闲话。出得后院，沿游廊低头前行，耳畔忽听有人道："小姐来了。"惊得抬头看时，原来是廊下金丝笼里一只红嘴绿羽的鹦鹉，歪头正学人语。一时童心忽起，从腰间香囊中摸出两粒红豆，朝笼中掷去。那鹦鹉于笼中扑愣着乱跳一阵叫道："小姐打我！小姐打我！"惹得娇娘愁容顿改，哑然失笑。这时，申纯突然从旁侧显出身来，对娇娘深深一揖。

原来申纯正在长廊上独行，忽听梁上鸟作人言道"小姐来了"，心中一阵狂喜，当下循声找来，与娇

with Jiaoniang. They gazed at each other in stunned silence for a while, wondering if this were a dream and not knowing whether to be happy or resentful. The girl was the first to recover, and with a contemptuous look, turned abruptly away. Shen Chun asked, "Miss, why have you been avoiding me for the past few days?"

"I was not avoiding," was the reply. "It is simply a matter of etiquette that the sexes should be strictly segregated, and a man and a woman's hands should not touch when passing and receiving things."

Dismayed at her heartless manner, Shen Chun pleaded, "Oh, don't be so distant. As the old saying goes, 'A day without seeing you is like a weary three years.' These past few days I've felt as though I was dying. But this is too public a place for us to talk; please come to the study."

"It is not proper for two people with the relationship of brother and sister to share a conversation with no one else present," was the frosty response.

Shen Chun was at a loss to understand why Jiaoniang's attitude towards him had changed so drastically, so he just stood there gaping. Then he said, in a low voice: "I don't know what I have done to offend you, Miss, but whatever it is I must atone for it. Please come to my rooms."

With that, he tugged at Jiaoniang's sleeve. The girl struggled to free herself, but Shen Chun refused to let go. Afraid that someone might come along and see them tussling like this, Jiaoniang reluctantly allowed herself to be half-dragged to the eastern study.

There, at Shen Chun's invitation Jiaoniang seated herself at the desk, with her head bowed and uttering not a word, but with her mind made up to hear what the young man had to say.

But before Shen Chun had a chance to open his mouth, Jiaoniang's eyes fell on the piece of paper he had picked up in the flower garden. She picked it up, and scrutinized it closely. Seeing this, Shen Chun quickly stepped forward. "When did you write this poem, Miss?" he inquired. "And how did you come to lose it in the flower garden?"

娘正正打了个照面。二人四目相对，同时呆了，不知道是梦是幻，说不出是喜是怨。娇娘先醒过神来，冷着脸转过头去。申纯急忙又施了一礼，道："妹妹，连日来为何总躲着我？"

娇娘正色道："男女有别，授受不亲。我也不是单躲你一个。"

申纯见娇娘无情无义，又道："妹妹休说远了。古人云：一日不见，如隔三秋。这些日子来，可想煞小生了。此处人多眼杂，请妹妹屈尊到书房中一叙，不知意下如何？"

娇娘冷冷地道："兄妹之间，岂容于无人之处私会？"

申纯听了，气得目瞪口呆，暗想这花容月貌的小姐何时变成了道学先生？一时无计，只得低声下气地求道："妹妹敢是怪怨小生了，无论如何，总是小生的不对。请妹妹进房，待小生正正经经给妹妹赔个不是。"

说着伸手便去扯娇娘的衣袖，娇娘挣扎了几下，申纯却死死拉住衣袖不放。娇娘怕如此拉拉扯扯被人瞧见，反倒不好，只得半推半就跟着申纯来到书房。才一进门，申纯躬身一礼道："妹妹请坐。"

娇娘端身正坐在书案前，不发一言，心中道："我倒要听听你说些什么？"

不料一低头看见书案上的鸾笺，随手拈起瞧看。申纯见状忙凑过来，道："妹妹此词是何时所做？

Jiaoniang knitted her brows, but remained silent. Shen Chun thought that she was being deliberately peevish, and resigned himself to being patient. So, with a smile on his face, he made a courteous bow, and asked, "Why so taciturn, Miss?"

Jiaoniang turned her back on him in silent fury. Shen Chun dodged round in front of her, and made another deep bow. At this, the girl jerked her body round away from him again. This maneuver was repeated several times, until Shen Chun was completely exasperated. He couldn't for the life of him think what he had done to raise Jiaoniang's ire. "Miss, I beg you to overcome your displeasure for a little while. Such a state of mind will harm you, and it will be the death of me. Do you want to turn me into a ghost? Be so kind as to tell me what grudge you bear against me."

This pitiful appeal moved the girl to tears, despite her resolve to show him no emotion whatsoever. Standing by, wringing his hands, Shen Chun moaned, "What on earth is the matter?"

Wiping her eyes, Jiaoniang threw the scrap of paper onto the desk, and said, "This poem was written by Feihong. What do you expect me to do when I find you in possession of it?"

Shen Chun was flabbergasted. "Feihong?" he croaked. "Can she compose poetry? I would never have thought it. But it is true what I said just now; I found this piece of paper by chance in the flower garden. How can you doubt me?"

Jiaoniang sneered inwardly: "A story like that simply makes it all the more obvious that you and Feihong have been passing love verses to each other," she thought. Then, fixing Shen Chun with a stare, she asked, "Did you really find it?"

From the look on the girl's doubt-clouded face, Shen Chun knew that he would have an uphill struggle trying to convince her of his innocence. But resigning himself to the task, he said, "Of course. I was loitering in the flower garden hoping that you would appear, when I spotted a piece of paper beneath a clump of fragrant flowers. When I saw the poem on it, I

如何丢在花园里面?"

娇娘蛾眉紧锁,不作一声。申纯想女孩儿家就爱使个小性子,我且大度些,与她赔些笑脸罢了,于是恭恭敬敬一揖到地,开口道:"妹妹为何不说话?"

娇娘越发气恼,将身子转过去,给了申纯一个后背。申纯只得绕过去,再次作个长揖。娇娘却不愿受他的礼,身子又转回这边。如此三番五次,申纯心中也犯了疑,不知自己又怎么惹得娇娘这般气恼,只得道:"妹妹暂且息怒,当心气坏了身子。你就是教小生死,我也得做个明白鬼吧?乞赐明言。"

娇娘本不想搭理他,见他说得可怜,心中不由得一酸,滴下泪来。申纯急得直搓手,道:"这到底是怎么回事?"

娇娘拭着泪将鸳笺往案上一掷,说道:"这是飞红填的词,赠给三哥,又来问我做甚?"

申纯恍然大悟,道:"噢,原来是飞红的词。她还会填词?真看不出。方才我已向妹妹说过,这诗笺是小生适才在园中花下捡得,妹妹又何必生疑?"

娇娘听了,心中冷笑道:"分明是你二人赠诗和词,却来骗我,真是'此地无银三百两'。抬眼盯着申纯道:"当真是你拾的?"

申纯见娇娘脸上疑云密布,知道自己跳进黄河也洗不清,可又不甘心,便耐着性子说道:"那还有

thought that you must have written it, but there again the handwriting didn't look like yours. I was looking for you to ask you about it, when I bumped into you. It was a pure coincidence, I assure you. I didn't even know that Feihong could read, much less exchanged verses with her!"

But Jiaoniang was not convinced. With her eyes once more swimming with tears, she accused Shen Chun of deceiving her: "You went to the flower garden to meet Feihong, didn't you?" she cried, and rose to leave the room.

Shen Chun hastily stopped her, and implored her: "Miss, please remain seated for a little while longer. Let me make everything clear. I have been racked with worries, because I don't know what I have done to deserve this cold-hearted treatment from you. Tell me, have you erased the memory of our old love from your mind?"

The girl pushed him away, saying, "You can never understand the depths of my sorrow!" And without a backward glance, she hurried away, leaving Shen Chun heartbroken and weeping.

假! 方才我在花园里等妹妹，无意中在丁香花下拾到此笺，见词意颇似妹妹所作，可墨迹又不似妹妹所书，正想找你问询，正巧妹妹来了。这词笺拾得纯属偶然，小生根本就不知飞红识字，何况与她赠诗索句!"

娇娘满眼噙泪，道："你编得似真的一般，只怕是在后花园中等飞红吧?"说完，起身便欲离去。

申纯急忙扯住娇娘的衣襟，哀求道："妹妹再稍坐片刻，将一切说个明白，岂不是好? 这些日子我千思万想，不知道自己做错了什么，受你这般冷落。敢是妹妹把旧情全抛在了脑后?"

娇娘推开申纯，黯然吟道："胸中万恨千愁事，说与旁人怎得知。"说罢一抖袖子，头也不回地去了。申纯呆呆地立在当地，一时心如刀割，泪下沾襟。

娇红记

Chapter Six
More Storm and Stress

For the next ten days or so Jiaoniang spoke not a word to Shen Chun. The young man found himself able to neither eat nor sleep properly. His face became sallow and gaunt, and he visibly lost weight. He could turn his mind to nothing but praying to Heaven night and day to restore to him the affections of his beloved. At the same time, he cursed himself a thousandfold for losing the embroidered shoes, and so rousing Jiaoniang's enmity, and for picking up the slip of paper with the verses on it, and so stoking the fires of her suspicion. And so, he bemoaned his cruel fate, beating his breast and stamping his feet. Many was the time he beat his pillow in anguish.

One morning, Shen Chun rose early, and after helping his uncle with some household matter and eating lunch, he returned to the eastern study. But he found that he could neither rest nor read. Pacing up and down restlessly and muttering savagely about how slowly and tediously the hours passed recently, he finally made up his mind to have a showdown with Jiaoniang. He thereupon slipped out of the study and made his way to Jiaoniang's boudoir. He stopped before her door, and looked round to make sure that there was no one near. He suddenly remembered the time of their secret tryst here, and how joyously Jiaoniang had welcomed him. There would be no such welcome this time, he thought bleakly. He hesitated for a while, and then raised the door curtain and entered. The bed drapes were half-raised, and he could see Jiaoniang asleep, with her face turned to the wall. Shen Chun sat by the bed. Gazing at that beloved profile, he was

第六章　风波重生

却说娇娘那日将申纯撂在当地，拂袖而去，一连十几天没有同申纯说话。申纯食不甘味，寝不安席，脸儿瘦了一圈，腰腹细了一匝，万般无奈，只有日夜祷拜苍天，恳求佳人回心转意。又无数遍地诅咒自己，不该丢了绣鞋，令娇娘生怨；更不该拾那词笺，空惹娇娘生疑。翻来覆去，暗自嗟怨，以至扪胸顿足，捶床捣枕，不一而足，这也不必去提。

这一天，申纯早上起来，帮着舅父料理了一些琐事。吃罢午饭，回到书房，想睡睡不着，拈起书来却一行字也看不到心上，翻来覆去，猛地发狠道："是好是坏也说个明白，如此吊在半天，空空落落，直要把人折磨死也！"当下拿定主意，要与娇娘当面剖分明白。于是起身出门，蹑足潜踪，来到绣阁。到了门前，见四下里静悄悄的没有一个人，想起往日到此幽会，娇娘喜笑相迎；今日里冷冷清清，好生无趣。不由得心头一阵凄凉，呆立半晌，掀帘进房，只见绣帐半掩，娇娘面里而卧，想是正在午睡。申纯自行到床边坐下，从侧面瞧见娇娘花容瘦损，一时心痛泪流，伸手

overcome with emotion and tears started from his eyes. He gently stroked the girl's back, murmuring "Oh my darling, how you must be suffering!"

In fact, Jiaoniang was not asleep. Hearing Shen Chun enter, her first impulse had been to welcome him with open arms, but discretion got the better of her, and she lay still, with her eyes closed. What would the young man do? She wondered. The sound of his weeping and heartbroken words, however, caused her to turn over and confront him. "What in Heaven's name do you think you're doing, creeping into a girl's bedroom?" she cried.

Startled out of his wits, Shen Chun leapt to his feet, and made a hasty bow. "A thousand pardons, Miss," he stammered. Despair gripped his heart as he saw that Jiaoniang was still angry with him. This was replaced by a fierce sense of resentment, and he began, slowly and haltingly, to state his grievance: "I rashly came here and disturbed you today, Miss, because I wanted to tell you just one thing. That is that somehow I have unjustifiably earned your enmity. It is a matter of great dismay to me that for several days past you have been treating me like an enemy, and I know not why. Has your erstwhile deep affection for me completely vanished? I have burst in on you like this simply because I want a clear explanation."

These words pierced Jiaoniang's heart like a thousand arrows. She felt an urge to tell the young man the truth, but then the memory of Feihong suddenly came into her head, and a feeling of spite hardened her heart. She decided to remain silent, and see what Shen Chun's next move would be.

As Jiaoniang remained apparently unmoved, Shen Chun felt even deeper anguish. In utter misery, he made one last desperate attempt: "Since you have rejected me, I am overwhelmed by a feeling of my own worthlessness, and accordingly from today on I will never annoy you again. But I implore you to tell me the reason you have cast me aside like this!"

Jiaoniang could hold out no longer. With tears in her eyes, she choked over her words. "I had a special love for you," she said. "But you spurned me. How can you say that I was the one who rejected you first?"

轻轻抚摸娇娘的后背，喃喃道："我多心的妹妹，你这是何苦呀？"

娇娘其实并未睡着，听见申纯进门，不由心中狂跳，便欲起身相迎。转念一想，依旧躺着不动，要看申纯打算做什么。及至听到申纯抽泣低语，心中又气又痛，翻身坐起来，喝斥道："此乃小妹的深闺，兄长无事到此何干？"

申纯慌忙起身长揖道："愚兄得罪了，请妹妹恕罪！"说罢抬头瞧见娇娘仍是满脸怒气，摆出一副拒人于千里之外的架式，心中一酸，转而腾起一股怨气，一字一字地说道："愚兄今日贸然前来打扰妹妹，只有一言相问：此次愚兄再来，谬承妹妹厚爱，心中着实感激。可近日来不知何故，妹妹视愚兄如仇雠，全没了往日的情深意浓？务乞妹妹明言。"

娇娘听了申纯的一番话，只觉犹如万箭穿心，便欲一吐心事。转念想到飞红，怨恨顿生，当下硬着心肠，不发一言，打算着看申纯如何往下做戏。

申纯见娇娘无动于衷，愈发伤心，道："愚兄既为妹妹摒弃，自惭形秽，今后断不敢再来讨扰。但见弃之因，还望妹妹告知一二。"

听到此娇娘再也忍不住了，泪水如决堤般夺眶而出，抽噎半晌说道："妹自思往日与兄长恩情不薄，如今是兄长先将小妹弃置，小妹又何敢摒弃兄长？"

Shen Chun was astounded at this accusation. For some time, he just stood there with his mouth gaping open. Jiaoniang recovered from her fit of weeping to utter the following rebuke: "On the day we swore a solemn oath of eternal love, who could have guessed that you would break it in less than half a year? You mention changed feelings. But whose feelings have changed, I wonder, yours or mine?"

Stung, Shen Chun replied, "My heart can bear witness that my feelings have not changed since I swore that oath with you. But you have thrown me away like an old shoe. And on top of that, you put the blame on me!"

Dry-eyed now, Jiaoniang sighed, and said, "Well, have it your own way. There is an old adage which goes, 'A love-sick maiden falls for a cold-hearted man.' You are the latter kind of person; whatever oath you may swear, you will break it at a mere whim."

"When I swore that our hearts would be as one in life, and we would lie in the same grave in death, I meant those words from the bottom of my heart!" cried Shen Chun fiercely.

But Jiaoniang was not to be swayed. "I don't wish to hear any more," she said, coldly.

Shen Chun trembled with passion from head to toe. His lips quivered, and he burst out with, "May I be struck dead on the spot if I have ever been false-hearted!"

"Don't bother making ominous vows about life and death," sneered Jiaoniang. "I know perfectly well that they mean nothing at all."

But Shen Chun persisted. "Harsh words, indeed, Miss! But only tell me why you mistrust me, and I will embrace death with no regrets."

"You yourself must know the answer to that," Jiaoniang retorted. "Why do you need me to spell it out for you? You lose my shoes, and Feihong got hold of them. Then Feihong loses her poem, and it turns up in your study! Then I find you two chasing butterflies among the flowers, making merry behind people's backs and exchanging secret glances. How

申纯听了不由得万分委屈，一时张口结舌说不出话来。娇娘哭了一阵，又数落道："想当日你指天咒地，发下海誓山盟，谁料半载不到，便移情别恋，这不知是郎心变了，还是妾心变了？"

申纯闻言一怔，道："愚兄自与妹妹结盟，此心可证白日，何曾移情别恋？倒是妹妹情意不久，将愚兄弃如敝屣，如今反归怨于我。"

娇娘止了泪水，叹道："你想这么说，也随你的意。自古道：痴心女子负心汉。似你这等男子，什么结盟证日，发愿发誓，随随便便许下，轻轻易易就丢在脑后。"

申纯道："愚兄出言如金，断不违誓。昔日曾与妹妹言说生则同心，死则同穴，均是发自肺腑，绝无半点儿假意。"

娇娘冷笑道："事到如今，你还来说这话，快闭上嘴是正经，我不想听。"

申纯见娇娘如此绝情，气得浑身打颤，嘴唇哆嗦，道："愚兄若有二心，眼下就教雷劈死好了。"

娇娘哭道："你也用不着死呀活呀的发这些毒誓，有什么意思？我算是看透了。"

"妹妹且休将话说绝。我问妹妹，你到底为何疑我？现在说个明白，愚兄就是死也瞑目了。"

"兄长岂不自知，何待小妹明言？兄长遗鞋，飞红得之；飞红遗词，兄长得之。更有花前扑蝶，背人调

do you expect me then to bear the sound of your honeyed words about constancy in love? Did you think you could fool me forever?"

Hearing Jiaoniang out, the young man rolled his eyes to Heaven, and sighed, "No wonder you have been enraged at me these past few days! It was all the fault of that Feihong! As Heaven is my witness, I swear that I have been true to you. Well, I suppose no matter what I say now you will not believe me. So I intend to swear an oath before the deities, to show you what kind of a person I am."

This solemn declaration succeeded in arousing a sense of awe in Jiaoniang. She thought to herself: "Could it be that I really have wronged him?" By this time, her anger had mostly abated, and she said, "Are you serious? Do you really dare to swear an oath before the deities?"

"Of course," Shen Chun answered. "And yes, I do dare to swear so."

"Very well," said Jiaoniang, "the east side of the lotus pond in the rear flower garden faces the shrine of the Great King of Brightness. They say that this deity is wise and honest, and that he always answers prayers. If you are willing to go with me and swear an oath in front of the Great Bright Spirit King, my faith in you will be restored."

This was what Shen Chun wanted most in the world, and he would have gone to swear the oath right then and there. Seeing how eager he was, Jiaoniang found her doubts dissolving, but she arranged for them to meet the next morning after breakfast.

Sure enough, the following day found them kneeling hand in hand on the east bank of the lotus pond. They kowtowed in unison in the direction of the shrine of the Great King of Brightness, and vowed to "stay together in life and share the same grave in death."

From that time on, the love between Shen Chun and Jiaoniang was restored; in fact, it burned the more ardently for the trial that it had withstood. Shen Chun learned a lesson from this heart-rending episode to avoid Feihong as much as possible. Whenever the maid servant sought him out with the intention of flirting with him, the young man averted his eyes and

笑,暗使眼色,给我难堪,好不甜心蜜意,俨然夫唱妇随!须知瞒不过天下人的眼睛。"

申纯听了娇娘一顿发作,仰天长叹道:"难怪你近日来深恨于我,原来是为着飞红。愚兄敢说情肠匪石,苍天可鉴。罢罢罢,如今我怎么说,你也不能相信,我便于神灵面前赌下一个大誓,教你看我是如何人!"

娇娘见申纯急成这副模样,心中暗想:"或许真是冤枉他了?"说了半天,气也消了大半,于是道:"此话当真?你敢到神灵面前发誓么?"

申纯道:"怎不当真?有何不敢?"

娇娘道:"好! 后花园荷池东畔正对着明灵大王之祠。据说此神聪明正直,有求必应。三哥若是肯与小妹一同对明灵大王发下大誓,我便信了你。"

申纯急欲消解娇娘心头之疑,恨不能马上就去发誓,便道:"我如何不肯去! 妹妹现在便可随我前往。"

娇娘见状,疑虑渐释,便约申纯于明日早饭后同到后花园发誓。次日,二人如约来到花园,手牵手跪在荷池东畔,遥望明灵大王祠宇叩拜,异口同声发下了"生同舍,死共穴"的誓言。自此以后,二人言归于好,经此一场波折,情感反而愈加深笃。

申纯经了这场变故,深戒于心,再也不敢与飞红多说一句话。飞红几次与申纯相遇,或秋波暗送,或言语调笑,申纯皆视而不见,低头疾走。飞红频遭冷

hurried away, and after a few of these encounters, Feihong began to realize that her scheme had gone awry.

One day, as Shen Chun was taking a stroll in the rear courtyard, he heard someone behind him calling his name. Turning, he saw Feihong peeping through the side door and beckoning to him. He swiftly averted his eyes, pretending not to notice her, and hurried back to the eastern study.

This rebuff stung the girl like a slap across the face, and tears of rage coursed down her cheeks. She thought to herself: "He obviously saw me just now, but pretended that he hadn't. Then he vanished like a wisp of smoke! I don't know what's come over him recently; he's been avoiding me like a snake or a scorpion. He's trying to worm his way back into favor with my young mistress — that's why he's cold-shouldering me!" She then mused, "I tried every trick I could think of to win his heart. I even revealed my true feelings in that poem I left where I knew he would find it. What could I have done to offend him? Oh, fate is so cruel! I am the same age as Jiaoniang. We are both of marriageable age. I am just as intelligent and attractive as she is, and I can write poetry just as well as she can. But she is the precious daughter of a noble family, while I am of common stock. When I tried to repay the old master for his kindness, his wife became jealous, and when I fell in love with Shen Chun, Jiaoniang suddenly got peevish. It looks like I can't please either of them. What a hard life I have! Well, if you insist on making things difficult for me, why shouldn't I make things difficult for you? Jiaoniang, you're supposed to be refined young lady, but you stooped to an illicit affair with a young man. Aren't you ashamed of yourself? And as for you Shen Chun, you heartless scoundrel, I offered you my true love, but you spurned it. I am like the drooping flower pining for love while the babbling brook pays no heed. Well, all three of you had better watch out from now on!"

At this point, a fierce feeling of resentment overcame Feihong. She snapped off a peony which had just come into bloom by the railing, and squeezed it savagely. Then she rubbed it viciously, so that it fell into tat-

落,不免耿耿于怀。

一日午后,申纯独步漫游后园,忽听身后有人莺啼鹂啭地唤道:"申家哥哥,申家哥哥。"回头看时,见是飞红从角门内探出头来频频向自己招手,忙将目光收回,装作没看见,径直回了书房。

飞红遭此羞辱,只觉得脸上好似被人重重扇了一记耳光,火辣辣地烧,两行泪水慢慢地流下来。她心中想道:"申郎分明看见自己招呼他,却佯装不见,一溜烟地走了。近来,他像变了个人,见了自己如避蛇蝎,想来定是为了讨好小姐,才故意冷落自己。过去我费尽心机为他掩饰,书笺填词表露心曲,哪一点上对不起他?想想真是命苦,我与小姐同年同月生,一样的豆蔻年华,一样的聪颖可爱,一样的能诗善赋,可人家贵为千金,自己却身为下贱。这也罢了,我欲以身子报答老爷搭救之恩,夫人却在那里拈酸;我心中爱恋申郎,可小姐总是没来由地吃醋。这对母女倒教我左也不对,右也不是,活得好生艰难。哼!你们不教我舒心,我岂能让你们好受?娇娘你身为小姐,偷奸养汉,可有甚廉耻?申纯这个无情小儿,我真心待他,可落花有意,流水无情,空负我飞红的一片真情。唉,真是'春风有恨他寻我,秋月无情我恋他'。罢罢罢,申纯,小姐,夫人,咱们走着瞧!"

想到此处,心中一阵气苦,伸手将槛边一朵含苞

ters, and threw the pieces on the ground. Her anger still not assuaged, she then proceeded to stamp on them, a fierce grimace expressing her grim satisfaction. She then wiped away the traces of tears from her face, and entered the rear garden.

Shen Chun, meanwhile, satisfied that Feihong was not pursuing him, slowed his pace, and began to appreciate the scenery. It was then the beginning of summer, and the peonies were contending in showing off their finery, and the leaves of the peach and apricot trees formed emerald clouds. The young man's breast filled with a delightful feeling of relaxation. Suddenly, his glance fell upon a girl with only light touches of makeup leaning against a willow tree and gazing at the flowers. The trees, the flowers and the girl formed a perfect picture of a fairy come down to earth. Enraptured, Shen Chun stepped slowly forward, and when he drew near to the girl, said softly: "Are you enjoying the scenery, Miss?"

The girl turned to face him. It was his beloved Jiaoniang. With a happy smile, she cried, "I was just thinking how nice it would be to have you here with me to enjoy the scenery!"

"Do you know what that phenomenon is called?" Shen Chun asked.

"No. What?"

"Two hearts beating as one."

Jiaoniang lowered her head in confusion. Then she changed the subject. "The maids are all doing needlework in my mother's quarters," she said. "Why don't we go for a walk around the garden together?"

Nothing could have pleased Shen Chun more, and he assented readily.

The atmosphere in the garden was intoxicating. The lovers wandered aimlessly among the flowers, which put on their best show that day, decked out in brilliant red, purple and white hues. A warm breeze wafted the heady perfume of the blossoms, and caused a constant shower of petals to drop from the trees, like enchanted rain. Birds perched on branches in pairs, nuzzling one another, and butterflies, also in pairs, flitted among the

吐蕊的牡丹狠命掐下来，几把揉作碎片，用力摔在地上。仍然不解气，又冷笑着死命拿鞋底将残花踏得稀烂，这才拭净泪痕，进了后园。

却说申纯为了躲避飞红，疾趋书房。走了一程，估量着飞红不会追来，这才放慢脚步，观赏起景色来。时当初夏，满园芍药牡丹争奇斗艳，桃杏枝头却早已褪了颜色，碧荫似云，青实累累。不由得满心欢喜。忽见一株柳树下，一位淡妆女子正在倚树观花。那柳树垂碧千条，树前百花烂漫，再加上如同出世仙子的佳人，构成一幅妙不可言的玉女寻芳图。申纯看得如醉如痴，款款近前，轻声道："妹妹好兴致啊。"

娇娘道："今日闲来无事，便思来园中赏花，看这满园芳景，暗想若是身傍有三哥相伴赏玩，必定更添佳趣。正思量间，你便到来。"

申纯道："噢，原来如此。妹妹，你说这便唤作什么？""唤作什么？"

申纯含情脉脉道："这便唤作心有灵犀。"

娇娘听罢，低垂粉颈。过了一会儿，她转了话题，道："今日丫环们都在夫人房中做针线，你我同在园中游玩一番可好？"

申纯求之不得，朗声道："小生情愿奉陪。"

二人徜徉花间，只见嫣红姹紫，百花争妍，暖风过处，花香细细，落英缤纷。枝头鸟儿对对交颈，花间

foliage. Shen Chun gazed at Jiaoniang, at her cloud of raven-black hair, at her peach-colored cheeks, at her eyes as bright as stars. She is more wonderful than a beautiful flower, he thought, for a flower cannot speak; and more precious than jade, for no jade has such a delicious perfume. Slipping his arm round Jiaoniang's waist, he whispered, "Let's follow this path."

The girl, who had been gazing at the flowers, was puzzled at this mysterious suggestion. "Where does it lead?" she asked.

Shen Chun pointed ahead. "Further on is the Cherishing the Flowers Pavilion. It's a very secluded spot. There we can snuggle up together on a lush carpet of thick grass."

At this, Jiaoniang covered her face, and turned to go in the opposite direction, saying, "You should be ashamed of yourself. Please show a little more decorum."

Shen Chun pulled her towards him, and hurried her through the flowers and willows, rocks and vines. The girl, half protesting, half laughing, stumbled forward. The Cherishing the Flowers Pavilion was indeed a sequestered place. The grass was thick and the old trees seemed to reach up to the sky. The aspect inside could not be seen clearly without coming close to it. Deep within the trees and foliage was a springy lawn, coated about an inch deep with fallen leaves and petals. Pointing to this haven, Shen Chun said, "This makes a perfect bed." As he did so, he tumbled Jiaoniang onto the grass.

The girl struggled. "No, no!" she cried. "Somebody might come."

"Don't worry; nobody ever comes here," Shen Chun, by now consumed by steaming passion, assured her.

Her face flushed, Jiaoniang protested, "It's too shameful. Even if no person can see us, Heaven surely sees."

"Oh, my darling, I cannot conquer my passion for you," Shen Chun gasped in his ardor, as he began to untie Jiaoniang's girdle. Jiaoniang fought tenaciously to maintain the sanctity of her girdle, but as the lovers'

蝶儿双双翩跹。申纯再看娇娘，只见她层髻堆鸦，桃腮泛潮，明目如星，真正是比花花解语，比玉玉生香，不由得伸手揽住娇娘的细腰，道："咱们从这条小路穿过去可好？"

娇娘正在赏花，听申纯神秘兮兮地说话，有些不解，问道："去哪儿？"

申纯朝前方一指道："前面惜花轩畔，深幽无人，碧草茵上落红成榻，你我百花影里做鸳鸯去。"

娇娘闻言羞得把粉面一捂，转身欲走，道："羞死人也，三哥你放尊重些。"

申纯却一把将娇娘搂在怀里，穿花度柳，抚石攀藤，直向前走。娇娘似嗔似喜，半推半就，任申纯搂着来到惜花轩前。此处果然幽静，花丛密布，古树参天，不到近前，看不清里面的景致。花木深处有一块绿茵，上面落红寸许。申纯一指道："此处正好当床。"说着便搂住娇娘倒在绿茵之上。

娇娘推拒道："三哥且慢，仔细来人看见。"

申纯此时浑身血脉贲张，哪里等得及，道："此处无人，不必担忧。"

娇娘脸红如霞，噘着小嘴道："羞人答答的，便是人瞧不见，天也能瞧得见。"

申纯央求道："小生情急不能自持，就请妹妹成全小生吧。"说着便为娇娘解带宽衣。

lips locked in a frenzy of kisses her body went limp, as did her resolution, and she succumbed.

His heady zeal spent, Shen Chun carefully rearranged Jiaoniang's clothing, gave her a kiss on her fragrant cheek, and said, "Now that we have consummated our love, our relationship is that of man and wife. So let us take advantage of there being no one else present to address each other as such." He tenderly added, "Jiaoniang ... my wife."

Jiaoniang blushed and buried her face in her lover's breast. Eventually, she opened her ruby lips, and said, in an almost inaudible tone: "All right."

Shen Chun heard this with a flush of pleasure. "My wife," he encouraged her, "what do you call me?"

In a trembling voice, muffled by her proximity to Shen Chun's breast, Jiaoniang said, "My husband."

Shen Chun felt as elated as if he had just drunk a draught of fine wine. But then he perceived that Jiaoniang's head was trembling. He carefully raised her face, and saw that tears filled her eyes. "My dear, why are you weeping?" he inquired.

Jiaoniang wiped the tears away. "I am afraid that we may never actually be husband and wife," she said. "It could be that our vow will prove to be a hollow one, after all."

Hearing this, Shen Chun suddenly remembered how the matchmaker had been rebuffed the previous year, and his heart grew cold with apprehension. On the verge of tears himself, he said, "Whether our marriage comes early or late, it will make no difference to the love in our hearts. And some day, we will surely be united in wedlock."

These brave words dispelled the chill that had crept into his heart, and, wiping the last traces of tears from his true love's eyes, he said, "Anyway, on such a fine day as this, we shouldn't be talking so seriously. Let's wander in the garden for a little while longer."

娇娘死命护住裙带道:"自古风流不在成欢幸。"

申纯此时哪里听得进话去,只搂了娇娘狂吻。娇娘浑身酥软,无力抗拒,只得闭着眼睛,听任申纯摆布……

片刻雨散云收,申纯为娇娘款款整好衣裙,轻吻娇娘香腮,道:"你我已成夫妻,趁此时无人,先斯唤一声可好?"说罢,便亲亲热热地唤道:"娇娘,我的妻。"

娇娘粉面飞红,含羞将头埋进申纯怀里,轻启樱唇,微露榴齿,低声应道:"哎!"

申纯听了,高兴非常,又道:"妻,你也叫我一声。"

娇娘紧偎在申纯胸前,颤声唤道:"申郎……我的夫。"

申纯也甜甜地应了一声,只觉如饮醇酒,浑身轻飘飘的。忽然发觉怀中娇娘微微抽搐,急忙将她的脸儿托起,惊问道:"妻呀,你为何掉下泪来?"

娇娘轻轻拭泪道:"你我倾心相爱,恨不能早日成就百年之好。可只怕是这'夫妻'两字尚无准成,空负了这桩誓盟。"

申纯闻听此言,又思量起去年遣媒遭拒,心中登时凉了大半,鼻子一酸,道:"咱二人既是相爱,成婚不在早晚,各人心中将这'夫妻'二字牢牢记住,总有洞房花烛的一天。"

说罢愁容尽去,为娇娘拭去泪水,道:"今日花好风暖,咱们不提这些伤心话了,且尽情游玩吧。"

They were just setting off, huddled close to each other when the sound of Jiaoniang's mother's voice calling for her startled them out of their wits. Instantly they sprang apart, and stared in the direction the voice had come from. The old lady, escorted by Feihong, stood no more than a dozen paces away. It flashed into Shen Chun's mind that "Of the 36 stratagems, the best is flight," and he dived behind a clump of bushes, scuttling from there out of the garden by devious paths.

Jiaoniang's mind was in turmoil. How long had her mother been in the garden? Had she seen herself and Shen Chun making love? Full of apprehension, she steeled herself to approach and greet her mother.

It had happened that, after being slighted by Shen Chun, Feihong had herself gone to the flower garden to try to get over her upset, and by chance had seen Jiaoniang and Shen Chun wending their way in the direction of the Cherishing the Flower Pavilion. Her first instinct was to follow them, and catch them in a compromising act. But then, it occurred to her that, as a lowly serving maid, they could turn the tables on her by threatening to denounce her as the go-between. "Anyway, the old master and mistress would never believe her, she was sure, and this would only result in trouble for herself. No, she had a better idea: Why not bring the old mistress here, on the pretext of viewing the flowers, and let her catch them in the act? Then Shen Chun, would be driven out of the mansion in disgrace, and Jiaoniang would probably commit suicide, unable to bear the shame. What's more, she thought, gleefully, Jiaoniang's death would devastate her mother. That way she would get revenge on her three enemies — killing three birds with one stone, as it were. Then she, Feihong, would rule the roost in the Wang mansion. This prospect caused Feihong to bare her teeth in vindictive satisfaction. "By mistreating me, you have ruined yourselves," she exulted. "I will overturn the dog's dish, and then no one will eat!" Whereupon, she stealthily made her way out of the garden and straight to the old mistress' quarters.

The old lady was reclining on a couch, watching the other serving

正在二人相依相偎，情话喁喁之时，忽听远处传来赵夫人的喊声："娇娘！娇娘！"两人顿时惊得魂飞魄散，倏地分开，寻声望去，只见赵夫人由飞红扶着站在十余步外。申纯此时顾不了许多，三十六计走为上策，一矮身钻入花丛，沿着小径弯弯绕绕逃出花园去了。

娇娘心中乱成一团麻，只担心娘是何时进得花园？是否看见自己和申郎的亲密情状？事已至此，躲也躲不过去，只好硬着头皮向赵夫人走近，道个万福。

原来方才申纯躲开飞红溜走，飞红因此伤心落泪，便进后园散心，无意中撞见申、娇二人会在一处，曲曲折折向惜花轩走去，顿时想到二人必是早就约下，躲入后花园深处做那见不得人的勾当。当下就想跟去看看，一转念想道："自己不过是个丫环，当真将他二人捉住，又能怎样？人家是主子，到时闹将起来，被他们反咬一口，栽赃自己是牵头引线的红娘，老爷夫人岂能容我？不若将夫人诳了来赏花，让她亲自看见自己的女儿与情郎幽会。到时申纯出丑，必会被撵走；小姐脸皮薄，说不定就会寻死觅活。果真小姐死了，那老醋婆心裂肠断，保不准一并呜呼哀哉。那时这府中岂不是我飞红的天下了？真正是一石三鸟的妙计。"想到此处，银牙一咬，暗道："你们不让我如意，大家便一拍两散，打翻狗食盆，谁也吃不成！"于是悄悄出了花园，径向赵夫人房中走去。

maids at their needlework, when Feihong entered with a radiant smile on her face. "Madame," she said brightly, "the peonies are in full bloom in the flower garden. They are just as gorgeous as those at the Tianning Temple. And the weather is wonderful today. Would you like me to take you there?"

The old lady shook her head. "No," she said. "I've got a pain in my back and legs. Besides, I have to make sure the needlework is done properly; I can't be wasting time looking at flowers."

Feihong gave a merry laugh. "Madame, you are too conscientious," she admonished playfully. "Even without you overseeing them, these maid servants wouldn't dare to slacken their efforts and play around. If your bones are aching, what you need is a bit of a walk to relax you. It would give you an appetite for dinner, too." As she said this, she went to assist the old lady to rise. The old mistress for her part did not want to seem ungrateful for Feihong's kindness, and so she suffered the girl to escort her outside and to the flower garden.

To Feihong, the old lady's faltering steps were maddeningly slow. If Jiaoniang and Shen Chun were caught in the act, her scheme would be crowned with success. Feihong's eyes were riveted on where she knew the Cherishing the Flower Pavilion was, but the old lady seemed to take forever to make any progress. All the girl could do was grit her teeth and curse her doddering charge silently. Eventually, they got well inside the garden. At this point, while bringing the old lady's attention to these flowers and those flowers, Feihong darted her gaze here and there in search of the lovers.

The old lady sighed, and said, "I'm too old to appreciate beautiful scenery nowadays. In fact, I can't even see it properly." Then, as a gust of wind caused a shower of petals to fall, she continued, "Just as the flowers and trees fade in autumn, so does human life come to an end. The flowers bloom for a few days only, and in less than one hundred years we vanish from the earth."

赵夫人正倚在绣榻上看丫环们做针线，飞红进来，便满面春风道："夫人，后园里牡丹盛开，比天宁寺的一点儿不差，今日天气晴朗，何不由婢女陪你前去看看？"

赵夫人摇头道："我腰酸腿疼，不愿出门，再说还要督着丫环们做活计，不看也罢。"

飞红笑道："夫人就是太劳心了些，这点儿活儿您不在跟前，量这些小丫头们也不敢偷懒耍滑。您身子骨儿疼，正要散散步、宽宽心才好。还是去闲步一回，晚上也能多吃一碗饭。"说着便来扶赵夫人。

赵夫人见她如此热心，也不好驳了她的面子，只得由她扶着慢慢向后园走去。飞红心中着急，只想让赵夫人亲自将那二人逮个正着，自己的如意算盘方能成功，恨不得两步并做一步，眨眼就到惜花轩。可赵夫人年纪已大，心中无事，只是小步慢行，一摇三摆，走走停停，把个飞红急得心里直咒"老不死的"，也只好是耐着性子跟在旁边。好不容易走进花园深处，不住地四下张望，嘴里却不停地说："夫人，您看，这草绿花艳的，真个是好看呀。"

赵夫人对着满园春色感叹道："唉，老了，老了，不中用了。好景色也看不清爽。"又见微风过处，落红成阵，便道："人生一世，草木一秋。花开能有几日红，人老岂能百年好！"

Only half-listening, Feihong muttered some perfunctory reply, as she detected what seemed to be the movements of two people in a clump of peonies. Pointing towards the spot, she said, "Madame, look at those peonies over there. They really have bloomed magnificently!"

The old lady looked in that direction and saw the riot of color of the flowers, but her eyes were too dim to make out the forms of Jiaoniang and Shen Chun. "Yes, indeed," she said. "The peonies really have turned out wonderfully this year."

"Why not take a closer look, Madame?" the exasperated Feihong suggested.

Only then did the old lady see her daughter and Shen Chun walking out of the clump of peonies hand in hand. "Good Heavens!" she thought. "Jiaoniang and Master Shen, an unmarried girl and a bachelor, together in a deserted garden? And looking on very friendly terms too. What on earth is the world coming to?" She called out to Jiaoniang, who was completely taken aback at this sudden intrusion, and had no choice but to step hesitantly forward, casting a baleful glance at Feihong as she did so and curling her lip in contempt. Noticing the maid servant's smug air of self-satisfaction, Jiaoniang knew immediately that she was the author of this unseemly interruption. She thereupon determined to brazen the situation out at all costs.

The old lady frowned, and said, "What do you think you're doing here? You should be in your boudoir attending to your normal pursuits."

Jiaoniang fixed her gaze on the tips of her shoes. "But mother, I've been cooped up in that room for so long," she complained. "I just came here to refresh myself by looking at the flowers."

Her mother's frown grew deeper. "An unmarried girl like you," she said, "should not be wandering in lonely places."

Jiaoniang was a spoilt child, and responded peevishly: "What is there to be afraid of?"

This stung the old lady, who was about to ask her daughter sharply what she and Shen Chun had been doing when she suddenly remembered

飞红无心听夫人说些什么，只在口中敷衍，忽地远远瞧见牡丹丛中有两个人影闪动，便急急将手一指，道："夫人且往那边看，那些牡丹开得多艳呀！"

赵夫人顺着飞红手指的方向望去，果真一片姹紫嫣红，灿若锦屏，可是老眼昏花，却未看见娇娘和申纯，便对飞红道："今年的牡丹开得好盛。"

飞红趁机道："是呀，我扶着夫人走近些儿观看。"

说话间，赵夫人已见到女儿和申纯拉着手在花丛里行走，心中一惊，暗道："园中无人，孩儿与申家三哥儿在一处，孤男寡女，状态亲密，可莫要做出什么事来！"当下高声呼唤。娇娘尴尬万分，一步三蹭来到赵夫人面前，瞥见飞红在一旁也斜双眼，撇着嘴角，满脸得意之色，便知定是她做了手脚。事到如今，也只能抵死不认。

赵夫人见女儿过来，厉声问道："娇娘，好个不懂事的丫头！你一个女儿家不在绣房之中做女红，来此做甚？"

娇娘低头看着脚尖，说道："孩儿在房中坐得久了，身子困倦，故来园中看花消遣。"

赵夫人沉着脸道："你一个未出嫁的女孩儿，岂可独行无人之地？"

娇娘毕竟是父母宠惯了的，赌气说道："那怕什么？"

赵夫人见女儿竟敢顶嘴，心中一怒，便欲追问娇

that Feihong was standing next to her, drinking in every word that was said. To tax Jiaoniang on that delicate subject in front of Feihong would be too much of a loss of face for her daughter, so she simply echoed, "What is there to be afraid of? Dear me! In this lonely place, with not a soul about. Meandering paths leading nowhere. Sinister mists and fogs lurking around. You never know what tricks the flower nymphs and fox fairies, not to mention the willow sprites and peach goblins, might get up to. If you're not careful, anything could happen. How can you cause me so much worry?"

Seeing that her mother's temper was cooling off, Jiaoniang approached and tugged her sleeve. "Mother, I promise I won't do such a thing again," she said, soothingly.

The old lady patted her hand lightly and lovingly. "All right," she said. "I don't mean that you mustn't come to the flower garden. It's just that you should have a maid servant to attend you when you go wandering off by yourself."

Feihong was not at all pleased to see this reconciliation. She had been fully expecting to enjoy the spectacle of a thundering row between the mother and daughter. But now it seemed that Jiaoniang had cunningly wriggled out of trouble. The maid servant decided to try to stoke the fire once more. "Madame, you are absolutely right," she chimed in. "This garden is a scary place; even we maid servants are nervous about playing here, and that's when there's a group of us! Now Miss Jiaoniang here, she's the only daughter of a noble family, and of course worth a thousand times more than we lowly serving maids. She should be more careful, in case somebody comes to steal her most precious treasure."

The barb in this little speech did not fail to sting the old lady. She had long been aware that Feihong was a sly little vixen, and she still harbored resentment about the way the girl had tried to entice her husband. She thought to herself: "I know perfectly well how to bring my own daughter up, thank you very much Miss Know-It-All." She rounded on Feihong, and

娘如何与申纯在一处，转念虑及飞红在场，怕女儿脸上挂不住，便道："怕什么？这园子曲折幽深，云迷雾罩，四下里连个人影也没有，只怕那些花妖狐魅、柳精桃灵闹春思春，倘若我儿一时不慎撞上了，有个三长两短，岂不教为娘的痛断肝肠！"

娇娘听赵夫人语气缓和，流露出痛爱之意，遂走近牵着赵夫人的衣襟，撒娇道："母亲，孩儿以后再不敢了。"

赵夫人轻轻拍拍娇娘的手，爱怜地说道："女儿若想来后园中散心，为娘的岂能不允！只是你个女孩家脚小鞋弯，须得有个丫环扶持左右才好。"

飞红本以为赵夫人见了适才的情形，定会大发雷霆，将娇娘与申纯痛骂一顿。不料申纯见机溜走，娇娘母女俩越说越亲，心中的气不打一处来，便在一旁扇风点火道："夫人说的极是。这园子里阴森森的，平时我们几个丫头结着伴儿来玩还害怕呢，小姐千金贵体，比不得我们生来下贱，可千万要当心自重。若要寻芳踏草，哪里能少个梅香陪伴？"

赵夫人听出飞红话里带刺，心中顿时不快，想道："女儿是我自己的，我教训女儿岂能用你一个丫头帮衬！"况且飞红平日里妖冶狐媚，智计过人，一心打老爷的主意，赵夫人早就积了一肚皮的不满，当下打断飞红的话，阴沉着脸喝斥道："小贱人，这里岂有

snapped, "There's no call for you to poke your nose in. Now just you escort your young mistress back to the house."

Inwardly cursing, Feihong had no choice but to comply, with a pretence of willingness: "Shall we go, Miss?"

Jiaoniang cast her a withering glance. "I couldn't possibly trouble you," she said, in a voice dripping with sarcasm. "Perhaps you should accompany my mother."

With that, she excused herself to her mother, and returned to her boudoir alone. As she watched Jiaoniang depart, the old lady lost interest in viewing the flowers any further, and began to walk back, together with Feihong. As she walked along the covered corridor, she mused: "Recently, Jiaoniang has been talking and acting much differently from before. Her breasts and hips are much more ample, and manner is hazy and distracted. I wonder if she and Shen Chun have really been up to something. It is common knowledge that a girl's first amorous liaison is often with her first cousin. That's because her parents are careless about the two of them being often in each other's company. Young people are like dry tinder, ready to burst into flame. If they are often enough together, they will grow fond of each other, and then something untoward might happen. If it does, it will be too late for regrets afterwards. This incident today must not be passed off lightly. It's best to head off trouble before it starts. I won't have any peace of mind while Shen Chun is staying here, so I'll have to think of a tactful way to get rid of him."

In the meantime, Shen Chun had arrived back at the eastern study with a thumping heart. He was certain that the debacle in the flower garden had been deliberately contrived by Feihong. He was also sure that his aunt had seen him, and would have suspected the worst. If that was the case, he thought, his days at the Wang mansion were numbered, and he might as well take his leave before he was asked to leave. But he was naturally loath to part with Jiaoniang. He spent a sleepless night, tossing and turning and trying to make up his mind what course of action to take. The next day,

你插嘴的份儿?你且好好地将小姐送回绣房去。"

飞红讨了个没趣,心里对赵夫人千咒万骂,口中只得对娇娘道:"小姐,请吧。"

娇娘狠狠剜了飞红一眼,道:"我可劳驾不起,你还是扶着夫人回房去吧!"

说罢,与赵夫人道别一声,独自回绣阁去了。赵夫人见女儿走了,游园赏花的兴趣已荡然无存,便由飞红扶着回去,行走间自忖道:"近来娇娘言谈举止颇不似从前,且胸高臀宽,神情恍惚,可别是与申纯真的做出事来。想那野史传奇之中,儿女私情大半出于中表,皆因做父母的疏于防范,任其穿房入户,时时来往。青年男女犹如干柴烈火,来往的久了,难免情愫暗生,一旦出了乱子,悔之不迭。今天这事绝不可掉以轻心,当防患于未然,寻个机会,不露声色地将申纯尽快打发走,才能安心。"

再说申纯狼狈万分,逃出后园,回到书房中犹自惊魂未定。心里清楚此事定是飞红从中使坏,料想舅母看见自己,必然心生疑惑,说不得要想个办法请自己回成都去,只怕自己在这里呆不长久了。与其如此,不如主动辞行,可又舍不得娇娘。一夜辗转难眠,思量再三,终于拿定了主意。第二天,待王文瑞从衙门里回来,申纯即到中堂告辞。王文瑞见申纯突然提出要走,感到十分意外,道:"贤甥着急什么?再住些

when Wang Wenrui returned from his office, Shen Chun announced to him that he was about to depart. Wang Wenrui was puzzled at this unexpected turn of events, and asked the young man to stay for a few more days.

Wang's wife understood clearly what had happened: Shen Chun had realized that she had discovered his dalliance the previous day, and, anticipating that she would surely think of a way to expel him from the mansion, had decided to save face by taking the initiative. This was exactly what she wanted to happen, and she butted in with "But the young man has been here a long time already; his parents must be concerned about him. Besides, the imperial examinations will be held next year. The most important thing for him is to get down to some serious studying. We shouldn't keep him here tied up in our petty affairs."

The old lady had not mentioned the affair in the garden of the previous day to her husband. This was partly because she was not entirely sure that there was some illicit connection between the two young people, and partly because she feared that her husband might blame her for not keeping a tight enough rein on Jiaoniang. Shen Chun's action on this occasion was very gratifying to her, and she thought, "This young man knows how to be discreet!" And it was with a great sense of relief that she abandoned the various schemes she had thought up the night before for getting rid of Shen Chun.

Wang Wenrui, completely in the dark about the real situation, was convinced by his wife's reasoning, and said affably to Shen Chun: "Of course. My boy, your uncle very foolishly forgot that you have a great career to prepare for. Your aunt is quite right. We won't detain you. Go home and give our regards to your parents."

His wife added, "When you get back to Chengdu, devote yourself heart and soul to your studies. Set your sights high. And when you are successful, as I am sure you will be, you will not only be a credit to your parents, but a source of happiness to your uncle and me as well."

Shen Chun perceived that there was a hidden meaning behind these

日子吧。"

赵夫人心里明白，这一定是申纯因为自己在后园中见到他和娇娘形迹亲密，怕自己想法将他打发回去，到时脸上挂不住，所以主动求去。这倒正中下怀，在一旁忙插言道："老爷，三哥儿也住了一段日子了，姑老爷、姑奶奶能不惦记？何况明年又是举业之年，三哥儿必要下场，也该温习些功课。这功名之事最是当紧，岂能因咱家的琐事拖累三哥儿？"

昨日王文瑞回府，赵夫人并不曾对他提起后花园里的事，一来是因为自己也不敢肯定申纯与娇娘到底有什么事；二来也怕老爷知道了，反过来责怪自己教女无方。今日见申纯前来辞行，心里道："这小子倒还知趣。"便将昨夜里想好的一套说词搬了出来。

王文瑞不知就里，听了夫人之言，也觉得有理，便和颜悦色地对申纯道："舅舅真是老糊涂了，把你的功名之事给忘了。你舅母所言极是，老夫也就不挽留了，回去代我和你舅母问候你的双亲。"

赵夫人又道："三哥回去成都，当一心寒窗苦读，立志青云之上。到时春风得意，不但你父母夙愿得偿，就是你舅舅和我也为你高兴。"

申纯听出赵夫人话中有话，事已至此，也懒得多说，当下道："舅母放心，明日小甥便起身回成都。"

words, and was not inclined to drag the conversation out. So he simply announced his intention of leaving for Chengdu the very next day.

The young man, being a guest in the mansion, found that he did not have a great deal of luggage to pack, and this chore was soon done. Then he thought of going to say good-bye to Jiaoniang. However, he walked past the gate to the rear courtyard twice, but found Feihong and Xiang'e ensconced there, chattering and giggling, apparently on the lookout for him. Fuming inwardly, he just had to pretend to be taking a walk, and had no choice but to return. He waited until midnight, and made another attempt. There was nobody around this time, but the gate was barred. So again he was foiled. Returning to the eastern study, he sat forlorn for some time, and then finally fell asleep at his desk. After some time, he heard, hazily, the sound of a faint tapping at his door. Pricking his ears up, he made out Jiaoniang's voice urging him to let her in.

In a frenzy of delight, he opened the door. Jiaoniang slipped inside, and the two lovers held each other in tight embrace. Tearfully they whispered endearments.

"I heard Xiaohui say that you are to leave tomorrow for Chengdu, so I had to come and see you at all costs," the girl said. "It was only at this late hour that I could avoid prying eyes. Oh, why do you have to leave so soon? Is it because of that scene the other day? Has my mother forced you out?"

Drying his eyes, Shen Chun replied, "No, your mother has said nothing to me about the matter. Nor has she ordered me out of the house." As he said this, he bolted the door, and led Jiaoniang to his bedroom. The two sat down side by side on the bed, and Shen Chun explained how he had gone to take his leave; how his uncle had tried to detain him; what his aunt had said, and so on. He added, "In the afternoon I tried a couple of times to see you, but Feihong was guarding the door, so I had to turn back. Then I tried again, when it was dark, but the courtyard gate was barred, and I couldn't get in."

从中堂辞出，申纯便回房打点行囊。身在客中，并无多少行李，不一会儿便收拾停当，于是思量着到绣阁与娇娘见上一面，说明情形。可两次走到后院门口，都见到飞红与湘娥坐在那里说说笑笑，似乎是在有意监视自己，只得装作是到后园散步，慢慢返回，不由心里恨得直咬牙。待到一更打过，第三次到后院来，幸喜四周无人，举手推门，却已经在里面上了闩，依旧废然而返。回到书房，一个人形影相吊，独坐无聊，恍恍惚惚倚在案上睡着了。也不知过了多长时间，朦胧中听到有人轻轻叩门，侧耳细听，是娇娘在轻声呼唤："申郎，申郎，快快开门。"

申纯欣喜若狂，将门开了。娇娘闪身进来，两个人紧紧抱在一起。申纯道："贤妻，可想煞我了。"说着眼泪流了下来。

娇娘泣道："我听小慧说，你明日要回成都去，便打算着来看你。院门口总是有人，无法掩藏行迹，直等到二更，这才悄悄溜了出来。三哥，你为何急着要走，是否母亲因为昨日之事赶你？"

申纯拭泪道："舅母倒是不曾开口赶我，可也和下逐客令差不多。"说着，将门闩上，拉着娇娘的手进了卧室，两人并排在床沿上坐下，申纯遂将自己如何辞行，舅父如何挽留，赵夫人却如何说话等等情形说了一遍，又道："我在下午几次要去看你，都因飞红守

Jiaoniang sighed, and said, "Oh, who knows what trials and tribulations lie in our way before the enmity we forged in a previous existence is dissolved, and we become man and wife? Something is determined to tear us apart. Oh Heaven, why have I deserved such a miserable fate?"

Shen Chun dried Jiaoniang's eyes with his sleeve. "The ancients had an adage," he said, trying to comfort her. "It goes: 'The path to true love is never a smooth one.' So it is no surprise that we are encountering such obstacles to our happiness."

Jiaoniang took out a silk handkerchief, and wiped the young man's eyes with it, saying, "My dear, please look after yourself, and try not to be too upset. . . . "

But in spite of their attempts to dry each other's tears, it seemed that the flow would never stop.

Finally, making a great effort to master his grief, Shen Chun said, "My dear, we must both stop weeping like this. I must leave as soon as it is light. I do not know where I shall spend tomorrow night. I am facing a period of hardships and sorrows, and I will have no one to comfort me." He was silent for a while, and then muttered fiercely: "This is all the fault of that odious little Feihong! She is determined to keep us apart."

At this, Jiaoniang stopped crying, and breathed a long sigh. "It may be as you say, that Feihong is standing in the way of our destiny. But right now I cannot find it in my heart to hate her; I am too much worried about you."

This surprised Shen Chun. "Why are you worried about me?" he cried.

"I am worried that you may not return to me," the girl said, as if resigned to her loss.

Shen Chun hung his head, as a weighty sadness descended on him." Things being as they are, it is indeed difficult to predict whether we will meet again or not," he admitted.

"Mountains and rivers can separate people, but in the end nothing can

在门口，只好回来。最后一次去时，天已黑了，院门下了闩，不得进去。"

娇娘听了申纯一番言语，抽咽道："三哥，你我才释前嫌，谁料风波又起，棒打鸳鸯，硬生生将我二人拆散。天啊，我怎么如此命薄！"

申纯举袖为娇娘拭泪道："古人云：好事多磨。不信你我就这般儿横遭折磨！"

娇娘也举起手中绢帕为申纯拭泪，道："三哥当心身子，不要伤心……"

两个人你为我拭泪，我为你拭泪，无奈那泪水如珠如泉，滚滚滑落，一时哪里拭得干净？

最后，还是申纯强压悲痛，道："贤妻不要哭了，我也不哭。天一亮我就得走了，不知明宵梦醒何处？到时我这心中千般苦处，万种凄凉，无人诉说。"顿了一顿，咬牙切齿道："恨杀飞红贱人使坏，生生将咱们这对比目鱼、连理枝拆散。"

娇娘止泪长叹，道："虽说是飞红贱人隔断姻缘，如今我倒是顾不得怨她，只是虑着你。"

申纯闻言惊问："虑我什么？"

"我只虑你以后还来不来了。"

申纯听了，垂头丧气道："眼前事势如此，以后能否相会，又怎能预料？"

娇娘道："人道山川有隔情难隔。只要你心中有

come between true lovers, " Jiaoniang encouraged him. "So long as I am in your heart, you will find a way to come back. "

Shen Chun shook his head, and sighed, "When have you not been in my heart?" he groaned. "I only fear that if your parents are opposed to our marriage, we will only be able to meet in dreams. "

Jiaoniang was about to reply, when there came a tap at the outer door. Startled, the two young people froze, straining their ears. Then they heard the voice of the steward Wang Zhong calling Shen Chun.

Jiaoniang hurriedly signed to the young man to answer the door, while she let down the door curtain, and stayed in the bedroom, listening intently. Shen Chun went into the outer room, and opened the door. "Yes, what is it?" he asked.

Wang Zhong replied, "Have you done your packing yet, sir? The old mistress told me to inform you that her husband has some business to attend to in the morning, and she herself is not well. So they will not be able to see you off. But she has sent some traveling expenses, and says that you have no need to say good-bye; just leave whenever you are ready. Oh ... she also told me to help you pack. " So saying, he handed over a packet of silver to Shen Chun.

The young man took it, and said, "I understand. Please tell the old mistress that I intend to start as soon as it is light. As for my luggage, I've already finished packing it, and so there is no need for me to trouble you. "

"I see, " said the steward. "Well then, sir, please get some rest. " And he left.

Just as Shen Chun was bolting the door again, Jiaoniang came out from the bedroom. Shen Chun threw the packet of silver onto the table, saying, "Wang Zhong didn't come just now to give me my traveling expenses; he came to hurry me on my way. Well, I suppose there's no way I can delay my departure any longer. As soon as it gets light, I'll be on my way. "

These words were like a knife twisting in Jiaoniang's heart. She wailed, and threw herself into her lover's arms. Racked with anguish,

我，自会想方设法求便再来。"

申纯摇头长叹道："我心中何尝没有你！唉，只怕舅母从中阻隔，你我从此只有梦中相会。"

娇娘闻言，正待开口，突然听见有人叩门。二人一惊，同时侧耳静听，就听府中老仆王忠在门外唤道："申家官人，申家官人。"

娇娘急忙向申纯打个手势，示意他出去应付。自己忙将门帘放下，躲在屋中静听。申纯踱出外间，将门开了，问道："老人家何事打门？"

王忠道："申官人行李收拾好了么？夫人吩咐说，老爷明天一早有公事，夫人身子不爽，不能为官人送行，特备盘缠在此，教官人要行即行，不必告别了。又命老奴帮官人收拾行李。"说着将一包银子递与申纯。

申纯接了银包，道："晓得了，请老人家回复老爷夫人，天一亮小生即刻启程。行李已经收拾妥当，不劳老人家费心。"

王忠道："既如此，官人早些歇息。"转身回去复命。

申纯将门掩好，娇娘从卧室中迎出来。申纯将银包向桌上一掷，道："适才王忠不是来送盘缠，分明是催我启程。我如今再难停留，只得天亮上路。"

娇娘闻言心如刀绞，呜咽着扑入申纯怀中。申纯强忍悲痛，将娇娘扶入里间，道："事已至此，还望娘

Shen Chun helped her into the inner room. "You must look after yourself," he urged her, "and be brave while you wait for me."

Jiaoniang nodded, holding back her tears. She said, "Next year, in the autumn, the imperial examinations will be held once more. I hope you win high honors in them, and send a go-between again to ask for my hand. Perhaps then my parents will give their consent."

But Shen Chun was less sanguine. He was haunted by a vision of all his cherished dreams turning to ashes. He uttered a lengthy sigh, and said, "I don't care about honor and fame. I only fear that we are not destined to marry. I will depart, but I leave my heart behind. My dear, you really must take care of yourself, and not spoil your beauty by fretting. If I have to move Heaven and Earth, I'll find a way for us to meet again."

"I will endure every torment, waiting for that day," gasped Jiaoniang.

They then held each other in tight embrace, and whispered sweet endearments until the morning sun surprised them by peeping in through the window. "You'd better go back now, before anybody sees you here."

Jiaoniang nodded, but was reluctant to tear herself away. "My dear," she implored, "you must find time to send me a message."

"But you will be shut up in your boudoir," protested the young man. "How can I get a message to you?"

Realizing the truth of his words, Jiaoniang covered her face, and wept as if her heart were breaking.

The lovers were as loath to part as if they were going to their deaths, and the sun was high in the sky when Shen Chun finally rode off on his solitary way.

子善自珍重,以待重逢。"

娇娘忍泪点头道:"转年就是秋榜之期,但愿三哥一举高登,重遣媒人议婚,俺爹娘或能见许。"

申纯眼下只觉万念俱灰,长叹一声道:"我不怕功名两字无,只恐姻缘一世虚。我此去人走心留,娘子务要保重身体,勿愁损了花容月貌,我少不得掘地通天、想方设法与你重会。"

娇娘道:"妾定忍死以待。"

二人相拥相抱,切切私语,直说了半夜的情话,待到猛抬头见窗上晨色曦微,申纯轻声道:"娘子回去吧,免得被人看见。"

娇娘点点头,欲行又止,道:"申郎,你有暇可寄书信与我。"

申纯叹道:"唉,我的妹妹,你在深闺之内,我如何能寄信与你?"

娇娘掩面哭道:"真正是令人悲杀。"

二人凄凄哀哀,依依不舍,一如生离死别。无奈天色大亮,申纯只得狠狠心,单骑孤身上路去了。

娇红记

Chapter Seven
Garden of Love and Delusion

Shen Chun's journey home was a forlorn one. All the way, he wept into the wind and poured out his sorrows to the moon. When he reached home, though, he was careful not to betray his heartache. His parents were delighted to see him of course, and could not praise too highly the skill of Zhang the exorcist, who had apparently secured their son's escape from possession by demons. But in the midst of his joy, Shen Qing was mindful of the fact that his son had been away from home for too long over the previous two years, neglecting his studies. Besides, he thought apprehensively, the imperial examinations were due to be held the following year. So he lost no time ordering his two sons to put a halt to all their social activities, and shut themselves away in their study, in preparation for the examinations.

From that time on, Shen Chun never set foot outside the gate of the mansion, but, together with his brother Shen Lun, devoted himself to his books. Nevertheless, thoughts of Jiaoniang never left him. He became taciturn and gloomy. How he wished he could ride the wind and bestride the miles to be at her side once more!

Not long afterwards, Wang Wenrui was transferred to a post in Lizhou. He took his family with him, and the news of this depressed Shen Chun even further.

The following autumn, the Shen brothers took the local examinations. They both passed with flying colors, and when spring came around once more they journeyed to the capital to take the final examinations, where

第七章　情惑东园

　　申纯别了娇娘，一路迎风洒泪，对月伤情。回到家中，心中纵然千愁万苦，却又不敢有半点儿表露。申庆夫妇见儿子回来，自有说不出的高兴，直夸张师婆道法高深，使小儿避去众鬼缠附，脱了灾难。兴奋之余，申庆又想到小儿这两年在外的时间长，在家的时间短，书史荒废，学业未成，明年便是功名之会、大比之年，心中未免着急，便令两个儿子闭门谢客，在书斋中温习功课，准备应试。

　　申纯自此每日足不出户，与申纶朝夕苦读，可心中却无时无刻不在思念娇娘，整日价少言寡语，闷闷不乐，常恨不能御风缩地，与娇娘一会。

　　不久，王文瑞调任利州通判，举家赴任。消息传来，申纯更添一层惆怅。

　　第二年秋天，申氏兄弟一起赴考，同榜中举。转年春天，又联袂入京，得意春闱，双双中了进士。说不得琼林赐宴，礼部授官，申纶授绵州主簿，申纯因兼通弓马，授洋州司户。

　　不上两月，兄弟二人着了官服绶带，骑着高头大

they were again successful. After rounds of banquets, exchanges of presents and formal visits from senior officials, the brothers were given appointments: Shen Lun was made magistrate of Jinzhou, and Shen Chun, because of his martial skills, was made commander of Yangzhou.

Before two months had passed, they had arrived back in Chengdu, attired in their official robes and mounted on fine steeds. There they were to await a suitable season for traveling to their posts.

The auspicious news had preceded them, and the whole of the Shen household was in a state of excitement. Friends and neighbors came in droves to offer their congratulations. There was a constant stream of carriages and horses coming to the main gate of the mansion, and visitors swarmed all over the place. The local gentry vied with each other in preparing banquets for the young men, so that it seemed as if the whole of Chengdu was abuzz. But in the midst of all the celebrations, one person was sad. Although outwardly affable, as befitted the occasion, Shen Chun's anxious mind was as always filled with thoughts of Jiaoniang, and how he could dispatch another matchmaker to secure her hand in marriage.

One day, Shen Qing sent his subordinates out, and went to visit his wife in the inner quarters. He complained to her as follows: "You know, my dear, previously whenever we went out visiting people used to treat us rather coldly. But now, every day they are falling over themselves to pay us visits and showering us with gifts. We get a constant stream of invitations to dine with all the prominent people in the city, as if we had been a distinguished family for generations. I really can't take much more of this."

His wife said, "Well, it's true what they say: 'A poor man in a crowded marketplace has no one to talk to, but a rich man on a remote mountain finds kin visiting him from miles away.' I only hope that our sons have illustrious careers, and bring honor on their ancestors."

"Yes, indeed," said her husband. "Our family has always been noted for scholastic pursuits, and now thanks to the benevolence of our ancestors

马返回成都，只待瓜期到了，便要走马上任。

申家早已接了喜报，全家老少欣喜万分。亲朋好友和邻里乡亲纷纷前来贺喜，申家门前整日车水马龙，宾客如云。

及至二子衣锦还乡，府县衙门乡里缙绅纷纷张罗贺喜宴席，一时轰动了成都城。申家老小都在兴高采烈地迎送应酬，惟独申纯表面上应付，一心只想着娇娘，盘算如何重请媒人，再结姻缘。

这一日，申庆送出几位缙绅，回到内宅，对王氏道：

"以前就是咱去拜访，人家都不拿正眼看，如今又是亲访，又是送礼，天天都是应酬名流，听那言语如同几代的通好之家，我实在也是接应不过来了。"

王氏道：

"可不是，贫在闹市无人问，富在深山有远亲。愿孩儿们前程远大，光宗耀祖。"

"说的是呀。我家世代书香门第，如今全凭祖宗荫庇，二子争气，总算是光耀门庭，入了正道。我也算对得起申家列祖列宗了。"

老两口正在感慨不已，忽见家院来报，说利州舅老爷处派人前来贺喜。申庆令快快请进。不大功夫进来一人，正是王文瑞府上的老家院王忠，只见他笑嘻嘻地道："姑老爷、姑奶奶安好！恭喜二位相公金榜题

our two sons have proved their worth and I am sure they will embark on the right path to bring honor to our house. I am glad to say that I can now hold my head up in front of the ancestors."

Just as they were congratulating themselves, the steward announced that Wang Wenrui had sent a man all the way from Lizhou to present congratulations on his behalf. Shen Qing ordered the man shown in at once. The visitor turned out to be Wang Zhong, the steward of the Wang mansion. His face wreathed in smiles, Wang Zhong gushed, "How wonderful, my dear sir and madame, that your sons have attained the list of successful candidates! When my master heard the news, he was unable to close his eyes for happiness. The two young gentlemen have brought glory to the ancestors of the house of Shen and happiness to you both. Distressed that the great distance between you and himself made it impossible for him to pay his respects in person, he instructed me to ride post-haste and do so on his behalf. He also entrusted me to give you a token of his respect." Whereupon, he handed over a list of presents.

Shen Qing accepted the list with a few words of thanks. His wife swelled with pride and delight when she saw the lavish presents on the list that her brother had sent. "I am sure you have had a tiring journey," she beamed at Wang Zhong. Then she ordered a servant to bring refreshments for him.

Wang Zhong continued, "My master also instructed me to inform you, Your Honor, that it would bring great prestige on his humble abode and be a source of great joy for him and his good lady if the two young gentlemen could spend a few days with him in Lizhou, before they depart to take up their posts."

Shen Qing accepted this invitation eagerly. "As a matter of fact," he said, "I had been thinking of sending them to pay their respects to their uncle and aunt, but these past few days we have been swamped with invitations. Yes, they may go, and while they are there they may learn something about how to conduct themselves as officials from their uncle."

名。我家老爷看了《登科录》，高兴得一天一夜没合眼，说二哥、三哥皆登科及第，乃申家祖宗之德，姑老爷、姑奶奶之福。只恨相隔千里，不能亲自前来贺喜，令我星夜急驰送来贺礼，略表心意，请姑老爷、姑奶奶过目。"说着呈上礼单。

申庆接过礼单，连声道谢。王氏见兄弟特意派人送来厚礼，为自己挣足了面子，心中十分感激，脸上笑成了一朵花，道：

"难为你这么远赶来，实在是有劳你了。"说着令人张罗酒菜款待王忠。

王忠道：

"我家老爷还说：二位相公虽已荣授，如瓜期未及，可否到利州逗留几日？也使我们府上蓬户生辉，以慰做舅舅、舅母的欣喜之心。"

申庆忙道：

"本当遣小犬前去，只是这几日应酬甚多，原想过些天让他们去拜见舅父、舅母。一则是报喜，二则请舅父指点些做官的要诀。"

此时已有家人报知申纶、申纯，说是利州舅老爷府上来人了。申纯正在书房思想娇娘，听说舅家来人，老爷夫人有请，一颗心顿时狂跳起来，大步流星赶到中堂。王忠一见申纯，不待他开口，便起身相迎道："三官人大喜。"

Meanwhile, a servant had reported to Shen Lun and Shen Chun that a man had arrived from Lizhou, and that their parents requested their presence. Shen Chun awoke from a daydream about Jiaoniang, and with a leaping heart, sprinted to the main hall. Wang Zhong, as soon as the young man entered, rose to his feet and uttered words of congratulation.

Shen Chun thanked him, and then inquired after his parents' health. He had no sooner finished doing so than his brother and sister-in-law arrived. After a brief exchange of greetings, they all sat down. Shen Qing came straight to the point. "Your uncle wishes you both to pay him a visit. I think it is incumbent upon you to do him this courtesy. Would this fit in with your plans?"

Hearing this, Shen Chun was as delighted as a beggar who has stumbled upon a lump of gold. He was seized with a frenzied desire to sprout wings and fly to Jiaoniang's side, but had to smother his exultation with so many eyes on him. He decided to adopt a strategy of diffidence. "Perhaps my elder brother is entitled to precede me in receiving this honor," he said.

Shen Lun, however, was not eager to go. For one thing, he was not on particularly close terms with his uncle, and for another, his wife was about to give birth. Therefore, he rose, and said, "The ancients admonished: 'While one's parents are still alive, one should not stray far from home.' Of course, my uncle's request must not be denied, but as my duties lie here, may I trouble my younger brother to undertake the journey?"

His parents were quite in agreement that, in view of their daughter-in-law's condition, Shen Lun should stay at home. Shen Qing thereupon turned to his younger son, and said, "My boy, you have imposed on the hospitality of your uncle and aunt several times already. Now it is time for you to repay them for their kindness. Your brother is needed here to help us run the household; he can find time later to pay a call on your uncle and aunt."

Shen Chun could not have been more pleased at this suggestion. But he was careful to disguise his glee, lest he make a laughing stock of him-

申纯道："同喜，同喜。你远道而来，一路辛苦了。"说罢，又向父母请安。这时，申绅夫妇也来到中堂，寒暄客套了一番，大家坐定。申庆对两个儿子道："你舅父有心叫你们去他那里看看，你们理当前去拜访，不知你二人意下如何？"

申纯闻言，如同花子拣了个金娃娃，当下欣喜若狂，巴不得马上插翅飞到娇娘身边。只是碍着众目睽睽之下，不敢放浪自荐，于是以退为进，对申绅道："舅父有命相召，兄长理应前去。"

申绅听父亲之意，并非一定要去，再说自己一则与舅家不熟，二则娇妻身怀六甲即将临盆，便欠身道：

"圣人云：父母在，不远游。然舅父所命，亦不可违，长子克家，还是烦劳三弟走一遭吧！"

申庆、王氏也考虑到媳妇即将临产，申绅不宜出门。申庆便对申纯道："厚卿，你几次在舅家相扰，没少麻烦舅舅、舅母，如今理应由你去拜谢。你兄长在家中帮着父母料理些家务，过一段如有闲暇，再去不迟。"

申纯闻听，正中下怀，却不敢露出来遭人笑话，于是道：

"孩儿明白。只不过孩儿甫返故里，本欲与爹娘、兄嫂共享天伦之乐，如今又要远别，心中不免有些难

self. So he said, solemnly: "I quite understand, Father. But I have only just arrived home, and I was hoping to spend some time with you and the rest of the family. It will be a hard wrench for me to part from you so soon."

Shen Qing too was loath to see his son depart, as he knew that once the young man embarked on his official career, he would not see him again for at least three years. He did not want to disappoint him by burdening him with this chore, but there was no help for it. "Your affectionate sentiments do you credit," he said, "but in the past two years you have stayed with your uncle more than once to recuperate. Now you must express your gratitude to him. Start first thing tomorrow morning. The sooner you go, the sooner you will be back."

Shen Chun's face betrayed no hint of the waves of joy that were surging in his heart, but, as if resigned to an unpleasant task, expressed his assent.

His brother said, "Please take care of yourself on your journey, and don't worry about us here. I will take care of the family. Oh, and hurry back. Don't stay there for months like you did the last time."

Shen Chun nodded. Then a feast was spread in honor of Wang Zhong.

Early the following morning, Shen Chun bade farewell to his parents, his brother and sister-in-law, and set off for Lizhou together with Wang Zhong. After a few days, they reached the Wang mansion. Wang Wenrui, who had not seen Shen Chun for nearly two years, urged the young man to be seated as soon as he had accepted his bow, and ran his old eyes over him. He was favorably impressed by his nephew's dignified attire and bearing, and air of solid self-assurance. "My boy," he said, "I am delighted that you and your elder brother have achieved success in the examinations. Indeed, your reputation matches those of the famed scholars of old, and is rare in this day and age. Having finally achieved your long-cherished ambition, you can now soar up to the clouds and bring glory on your household and ancestors. Not only that, yours old uncle too can bask in the brilliant rays you shed!"

舍难分。"

申庆也知道儿子一旦走马上任，便要离家三年，本不想让申纯前去，可又不便驳了内弟的情面，于是道："我儿孝心可嘉，为父的心中欢喜。前两年你三番五次到舅父家养病，如今理应前去拜谢。明日你便启程，早去早归就是了。"

申纯心中激荡，脸上不动声色，道："如此我便去舅父家拜谢，爹娘、兄嫂请各自珍重。"

申纶道："兄弟自管安心出门，家中一切有我照应。只是要早些回来，莫似以往一住便是数月。"

申纯点头应允，当下申宅治办酒席款待王忠不提。

次日一早，申纯拜别父母兄嫂，与王忠启程前往利州。二人晓行夜宿，不日来到王文瑞的任所。王文瑞将近两年未见申纯，待申纯上前施礼问安坐定，便眯着一双老眼上下打量，见申纯衣冠楚楚，相貌堂堂，神采飞扬，心中十分喜悦，笑道："贤甥，你兄弟二人同登高第，除授美官，老夫不胜欢喜之至。兄弟二人同登金榜，名传六街，古虽有之，近来却不多见。正可谓读书人一偿夙愿，平步青云，门楣生辉，祖宗光耀，就连老舅脸上也增光不少啊。"

申纯谦恭地说道："小甥兄弟学识浅陋，焉有此能？皆是祖宗积德，天命安排，偶然文章顺手而已。以

Shen Chun modestly disclaimed any merit, saying, "I am afraid that my brother and I have but shallow learning. Our trifling success was due to the benevolence of Heaven, spurred by the virtues of our ancestors. We sincerely hope that you, Uncle, will extend your guidance to us."

Wang Wenrui stroked his beard, and nodded. "Your reticence is most becoming, Nephew," he said. Then he added, "But why did your brother not come with you?"

"He wished to come," explained Shen Chun, "but he had to stay behind to look after our parents. Besides, my sister-in-law is about to give birth. He hopes that you will excuse him."

As the two were talking, Shen Chun noticed the absence of his aunt and Jiaoniang. He asked about their welfare, not forgetting to inquire about that of Wang Wenrui's young son, to disguise the fact that Jiaoniang was the focus of his interest.

"They're all well, quite well," replied his uncle. "The young fellow is at his lessons at the moment. Feihong, go and fetch my wife and your young mistress here."

The serving maid, who had been standing nearby, shot Shen Chun a smile and a wink, and skipped off on her errand. Anger welled up inside Shen Chun at the sight of Feihong. He ground his teeth in rage as he remembered how the maid servant had ruined his relationship with Jiaoniang and caused his hasty departure from the Wang mansion. And now, her shameless behavior made his blood boil. In the midst of his turbulent thoughts, he suddenly heard the swish of tiny shoes and the tinkle of waist ornaments. Raising his eyes, he saw a crowd of serving maids and nurses approaching, escorting his aunt and Jiaoniang. He jumped to his feet, made a low bow, and greeted his aunt.

"I beg you not to stand on ceremony," gushed the other. "Feihong, assist the young gentleman back to his seat."

Feihong proceeded to do so. Shen Chun would have angrily thrust her hands away if his uncle and aunt had not been present; as it was, he had to

后还要仰仗舅父大人多多指点。"

王文瑞捻髯颔首道："贤甥如此谦恭，老夫实感欣慰也。"随后问道："你二哥何不同来？"

申纯道："本欲与小甥同来，只是严父慈母在堂，嫂嫂即将临盆，故留下来办些家务，还望舅父见谅。"

二人又说了几句话，申纯不见赵夫人和娇娘，于是问道："舅母、贤妹和兄弟俱好？"

王文瑞道："都好，都好。善父正在家塾读书，飞红，去后堂请夫人和小姐出来相见。"

立在王文瑞身旁的飞红应了一声，向申纯嫣然一笑，飞了个媚眼，便匆匆出门去了。申纯一见飞红，恨得二目喷火，牙关紧咬。想起上年都是她从中使坏，逼得自己仓促离去，如今厚颜无耻，尚敢飞眼调情，着实可恶至极。正思量间，就听门外弓鞋声细，环佩叮咚，抬眼望去，只见一大群丫环婆子拥着赵夫人和娇娘款款进来。申纯急忙站起，倒身下拜道："舅母在上，请受小甥一拜。"

赵夫人忙道："三哥途中劳顿，免劳下拜。飞红，还不快扶三哥坐了？"

飞红过来殷勤相扶，申纯本想甩掉她的手，又碍于舅父、舅母在前，只得由她扶了到下首坐定。偷眼看了一眼娇娘，又怕舅母生疑，便把头低了。

suffer the indignity of allowing the loathsome Feihong to steer him back into his chair. In the process, he stole a glance at Jiaoniang, but, fearing to arouse the suspicions of her parents, he quickly lowered his eyes again.

His aunt said, "We were overjoyed to hear the good news of you and your brother's success. It is an honor which our branch of the family shares, of course. The two of you are certain to become high officials, and enjoy rank and wealth. But for the present, you have had a tiring journey, and need refreshment." Turning to Feihong, she ordered her to go to the kitchen and arrange a feast for Shen Chun.

As the young man thanked his aunt, his eyes met those of Jiaoniang, who was standing beside her. Amid confusion on both their parts, they hastily averted their gaze.

Since Wang Wenrui had announced, a few days previously, that Shen Chun and his brother had passed the imperial examinations with flying colors, Jiaoniang had been in raptures. Surely, now that Shen Chun was destined for an official post, her parents would relent and allow her to marry him. But at the same time she worried lest his new-found success have caused Shen Chun's feelings for her to change. Besides, once he took up his position, it would be in some distant region, and she did not know how long it would be before she saw him again. So her mind was filled with conflicting torrents of joy and sadness. When Xiaohui brought her the news that her father had dispatched Wang Zhong to invite the Shen brothers to visit him, Jiaoniang had awaited her lover's arrival with a wildly beating heart. Now that Shen Chun was before her, and she was only a step away from paradise, it was vexing in the extreme not to be able to pour out her feelings to him. Tears of frustration welled up in her eyes, and she abruptly turned her head so that her parents would not notice, and discreetly wiped away the aqueous traitors.

Soon afterwards, Feihong reappeared, and directed the other maid servants to lay out the welcoming feast for Shen Chun. As his uncle embarked on the customary rounds of toasts, the young man absent-mindedly respond-

赵夫人道："我们听说你兄弟二人同登高第，高兴得不得了，连我的脸面上也有光彩。你们兄弟日后定能高官得做，骏马任骑，享不尽的荣华富贵。今日里三哥远路而来，一定累了，飞红快到厨下安排酒菜，为三哥洗尘。"

申纯道："多谢舅母。"说着抬眼看赵夫人，正好与赵夫人身旁的娇娘打了个照面。一时间四目相对，不知是喜是悲，忙又各自低下了头。

娇娘自与申纯分手后，无一日不在思念申郎。前些天，王文瑞从衙门回来，说起申纯兄弟二人同中进士，阖府上下喜气洋洋。娇娘更是欣喜万分，暗想申郎高中，授了官职，父母也许会回心转意，将自己许配给申郎。只不知申郎有没有变心，又担心申纯授官后走马上任，一去数年，不知何年何月才能相见。一时思绪纷乱，又喜又惧。过了两天，小慧又来告诉说老爷派王忠前去申家贺喜，还要请两位官人来府中住上一段。娇娘闻听，不禁心如揣鹿，狂跳不已，整天盼着申纯快来。如今三哥就在眼前，却如咫尺天涯，无法与他倾诉衷肠。想着想着，不由鼻酸眼潮，泪水盈盈，又怕爹娘发觉，悄悄转身拭泪。

不多时，飞红指挥着丫环们将酒席摆好，众人入座。王文瑞兴致颇高，酒到杯干。申纯心中惦着娇娘，却又无法接近，只得与王文瑞往来酬酢。一席酒直吃

ed. All through the meal, in fact, his mind was on Jiaoniang, and he took little delight in the merry-making. When the company finally broke up, at dusk, his aunt said to him: "You should retire early this evening, after your strenuous journey. I have had a chamber in the eastern courtyard prepared as a temporary study for you. Wang Zhong will show you the way."

Shen Chun bowed deeply, and said, "I am putting my uncle and aunt to a great deal of trouble."

His aunt smiled benignly. "The eastern courtyard is quiet; nobody will disturb you there. It's not like this side of the house, with its constant hubbub. If there is anything you require, don't hesitate to speak out. You're not a stranger here, you know."

As he rose to excuse himself, Shen Chun glanced at Jiaoniang. Then he followed Wang Zhong out. At some little distance, they came to a gate shaped like a full moon. This was the entrance to the eastern courtyard. The courtyard itself was a large one, thickly planted with tall bamboos. A cobbled path zigzagged among them until it came to an attractive three-roomed building with upturned eaves. The building was quite isolated, tucked away in such a spacious courtyard.

Wang Zhong pushed the door open, and lit a candle. Inside, Shen Chun saw, the room was bright and clean, and neatly furnished. After pouring tea for Shen Chun and explaining a few things that he needed to know, Wang Zhong withdrew.

Left alone in this sequestered spot, Shen Chun's happiness at being back in the house of his beloved started to turn to gloom. He guessed that his aunt still harbored suspicions that he and Jiaoniang intended to carry on their affair, and that was why she had shunted him off to this secluded eastern courtyard. He decided that if he had known this before hand, he wouldn't have come. Eventually, his oppressive thoughts teamed up with the fumes of the wine he had drunk that evening to throw Shen Chun into a deep slumber.

Living in the eastern courtyard, Shen Chun had few occasions to visit

到掌灯时分,方才散了。赵夫人吩咐道:"三哥远来劳倦,早些安歇吧。厅事东面有处园子,我已令人将园中西轩打扫干净,权做三哥的书房。王忠送三哥前去歇息。"

申纯躬身谢道:"让舅母费心了。"

赵夫人微微一笑,道:"那东园里安安静静,无人打扰,不似这边人多喧闹。三哥但凡有什么要的,尽管直言,千万不要见外。"

申纯起身道:"如此小甥先行告退。"说罢,又看了娇娘一眼,随着王忠出了中堂,向东走半箭之地,是一个月亮门,门内就是东园。这园子很大,里面遍植修竹,一条鹅卵石砌成的小径曲曲折折通到西轩。西轩一排三间,飞檐翘角,建造得十分精致,只是座落在如此大的一座园子之中,静的有些怕人。

王忠将轩门推开,点着蜡烛,申纯见轩内收拾得窗明几净,井井有条。王忠倒了一杯清茶,又嘱咐了几句,便退身出园去了。

申纯独处孤室,形影相吊,早将满心欢喜化作百转愁肠。猜到是舅母疑心未释,怕自己与娇娘私下相会,故意将自己安排在僻静的东园里。早知如此,不来也罢。想着想着,酒往上涌,昏沉沉坠入梦乡。

申纯自此在西轩住下,每天除了晨昏问省,没有别的机会到中堂来。王文瑞每天上衙门,也不像以前

the main hall, apart from the regular morning and evening greetings to his uncle and aunt. Wang Wenrui went to his office every day. Unlike before, he did not solicit Shen Chun's help in administering his household affairs, and the young man found that he had nothing much to do apart from reading and enjoying the scenery. Sometimes he would encounter Jiaoniang on his visits to the main hall, but since there were always others present, they could do no more than cast furtive glances at each other.

A dozen or so days passed like this, without Shen Chun finding any opportunity to meet Jiaoniang alone. Many times, he felt like leaving his uncle's mansion and returning to Chengdu, but could never bring himself to do so. He resigned himself to waiting for the opportune moment.

One morning he went to pay his respects to his uncle and aunt in the main hall. Finding that Jiaoniang was not present, he beat a retreat after the usual formalities, and returned to the eastern courtyard. As he entered the moon gate, he heard someone call to him. He stopped in his tracks, and turned, to see Jiaoniang emerge from behind the corner of a wall. As the girl tripped towards him the delighted Shen Chun embraced her and drew her within the gate. A careful look around informed the young man that there was nobody to spy on them, and he breathed a sigh of relief. Jiaoniang whispered, "Master Shen, since we parted I have been constantly thinking of you. My mind has been in a dizzy whirl."

Shen Chun impulsively clasped her to his breast. "I have been suffering the same torment," he said.

Jiaoniang murmured, "I was so pleased to hear that you scored so highly in the imperial examinations and have become famous. The only thing that worries me is the thought that my fate is so tragic that I will not be able to accompany you in your enjoyment of riches and honors. Now I am overjoyed that you have come all this way specially to see me. I wonder how I can deserve your sincere and kind attention."

Shen Chun hugged her tightly. "My darling, our love is as deep as the ocean," he said. "How could I ever forget you?"

那样委托申纯帮办家务，申纯除了在园内读书观景，再无事做。有时在中堂遇到娇娘，又碍着人多眼杂，两人只能眉目传情而已。

一晃十几日过去，申纯始终没有找到机会与娇娘私下见上一面。他几次想辞别回成都去，又不甘心。只好耐着性子，等待时机。

这一天，申纯到中堂给舅父、舅母问安，见娇娘不在堂上，顿时意兴阑珊，草草说了几句话，便退出来回园。刚刚走进月亮门，就听身后传来一声娇唤："申郎慢走。"申纯心中一荡，急忙停步回头，就见娇娘自墙角拐出来。此时院中空无一人，娇娘小步弓鞋飘然而至。申纯喜出望外，大步流星迎上前去，拉着娇娘躲在月亮门后。探出头来四下扫视，见无人看到，方才松了口气。娇娘柔声道："申郎，你我一别，便是经载。妾魂牵梦绕，好生思念。"

申纯动情地将娇娘拥在怀里，道："为夫又何曾不是如此！"

娇娘喃喃道："且喜郎君赴宴琼林，得了功名。只恨妾命薄一叶，不能与君同享富贵。如今郎君不以地远为辞，特来看望，妾实是感激万分。想妾何德何貌，得郎君如此至诚相待？"

申纯将娇娘紧紧搂住，道："娘子，你我情深似海，小生怎敢忘怀，又怎能忘怀？"

Jiaoniang then went on to explain: "I am sure you are aware that Feihong and I used to not get along very well. Well, as my mother's health has grown worse recently all the household affairs have been entrusted to Feihong. Moreover, she has become my father's favorite. So I had to swallow my pride and take the initiative to patch things up between us, hoping that she would be able to put in a good word for us with my parents as concerns our marriage. But we must still be careful and not risk spoiling everything at the last moment. That is why I have not been so bold as to seek you out."

There was a pained expression on the young man's face, as he said, "Oh, these past ten days or so have passed like so many years! I was on the verge of returning home. You can't imagine what a torment it was to me to have come all this way and not even exchange a single word with you. Indeed, what is the use of me staying any longer, if the situation is to continue like this? I will stay a couple more days, and then I will take my leave."

These harsh words tore at Jiaoniang's heart like razor-sharp claws, and she wept a flood of tears. There were a thousand things she wanted to say, but the words stuck in her throat, and all she could do was cling to Shen Chun, weeping silently. Eventually, mastering her emotion, she said, "It was for the sake of our long-term happiness that I curried favor with Feihong. If my plan succeeds, we will recapture the bliss that used to be ours. My dear, can't you be patient for a while longer?" So saying, she produced a small package from her sleeve, and pressed it into Shen Chun's hand. "There are 20 taels of gold here, my life's savings. I want you to have them."

When the young man tried to refuse to accept the gift, she insisted: "When the weather turns cold, you will need to buy warm clothes. Besides, you need to buy books and writing materials. If you have clothes which need mending or altering, give them to one of the maid servants, and I will see to it."

娇娘道:"妾与飞红素来不和,你是知道的。可我娘近来多病,府中事务皆委交飞红,飞红又得宠于我爹爹。所以妾只有降身屈节,主动修好,盼着她能助你我一臂之力,帮着说服爹爹妈妈,答允你我的婚事。眼下已有一些眉目,更须谨慎在意,以免功败垂成。妾这些天来不敢主动来找三哥,就是这个缘故。"

申纯一脸无奈地说道:"唉! 这十几天小生真是度日如年,欲告辞回去,却恨千里远来,未曾与娘子说上只言片语,如何放得下心! 今既若此,我就是再住下去,又有何益?索性一二日后,告辞回去罢了。"

娇娘闻听此言,犹如百爪挠心,早已泣不成声,此时纵有万语千言,都堵在喉头,只能紧紧地靠在心上人怀里。半晌,娇娘方忍泪道:"妾以为求暂时之欢,不若图长久相聚,故而屈事飞红,务要得其欢心。若能成功,你我便可重温昔日之欢。三哥,你就不能再耐着性子住上一些日子?"说着从袖中取出一包东西塞在申纯手中,道:"这里有二十两黄金,是妾数年来攒下的体己,你先收着用吧。"

申纯推辞道:"娘子这是做什么?"

娇娘道:"恐怕你有用度花销,手里没有银钱不方便。天气一天天凉了,也该加些寒衣,平时还要买些书册笔砚。日常里穿戴有什么不妥,便让丫环送进来,妾当与郎缝补修治。"

Shen Chun was deeply moved by her show of attachment to him, which was no less than that of a wife. When he thought of how, for his sake, she had humbled herself before Feihong, he was overcome with emotion, and tears started from his eyes. He hastened to apologize for causing her such heartache, and promised to remain in her father's mansion for a year if she so wished.

Jiaoniang smiled through her tears. "I am happy now," she said.

Just as the two of them were locked in a tight embrace, their lips glued together, in a transport of love, they heard the sound of someone approaching. They disengaged themselves in a flurry before whoever it was could come upon them, and Shen Chun sneaked back to his quarters by a side path, while Jiaoniang gazed after him. Then, having tidied her hair, she returned to the inner courtyard.

Back in his study, Shen Chun found his mind in a turmoil. Able neither to sit still nor stand at ease, he eventually emerged into the garden for a stroll among the bamboo groves. He had gone only a little way when he noticed, nestling in a secluded spot, a pavilion with upturned eaves. The sight cheered him up, and he quickened his pace towards it. There was a signboard hanging below the eaves of the pavilion, which read, "Emerald Bamboo Pavilion." Shen Chun climbed the steps, and discovered inside the pavilion a number of stools covered in dust, a sure sign that it was seldom visited. He was surprised to find such a charming place tucked away in the groves of bamboo. Dusting off one of the stools, he sat down to enjoy the surroundings, and after lingering there for some time, he returned to his study. From then on, Shen Chun made a habit of dropping into the pavilion every day to admire the bamboo and read. Sometimes, he would find himself in such a pleasantly relaxed mood that he would hug his knees and hum and whistle, or murmur to himself about all the things that were on his mind.

One night, Shen Chun was leaning on his window-sill, gazing at a brilliant full moon. An autumn breeze wafted sighs from the whispy bam-

申纯见娇娘想得如此周到，人家的妻子也不过如此，心中愈发感动。只是想到娇娘为了自己，竟不惜以小姐的身份向一个丫环低头，又有些不忍，鼻子一酸，眼泪淌了下来，道："难得娘子一片苦心，着实委屈你了。既然如此，我便在西轩住上一年半载，也无怨悔。"

娇娘含泪笑道："郎君如此体贴，妾便放心了。"

此时，二人相拥相抱，四唇相接，正在意乱情迷、难舍难分之际，忽听有人走近，二人急忙分开。好在无人发觉，申纯悄步沿小径回了西轩。娇娘目送申纯走远，理了理双鬟，也自回后院去了。

申纯回到书房，心中时喜时悲，整日坐立不安，见满园蓬竹凤尾森森，龙吟细细，便从房中出来，在园中漫步游玩。向东行了数十步，忽见竹林深处有一个翘檐飞角的亭子。申纯心中一喜，快步走了过去，只见亭檐上悬着一块小匾，上书"翠竹亭"三字。拾级而上，发现亭中几凳布满灰尘，想是人迹罕至。想不到在这竹林深处尚有此风雅之所，直如世外桃源，于是略为拂拭，坐下来赏玩景色，盘桓良久，方才归去。自此之后，申纯便每日里来此观竹读书，有时兴致忽起，不免抱膝吟啸，或者喃喃自语，将心事透露一二，也不在话下。

一天夜里，月明如水，秋风习习，偌大的东园中

291

boos and crickets chirped in the clumps of grass below the steps. The young man was wallowing in melancholy, wondering if Jiaoniang too was looking up at the moon and thinking of her lover.

Suddenly, from the drum tower came the sound of the beats announcing the second watch. Shen Chun listlessly closed the window, and went to lie down on the bed. He began to flip through a copy of *In Search of Ghosts.* He had just reached a particularly spine-chilling section when he heard the window paper flapping. He nearly jumped out of his skin, but then, realizing that it was just the wind shaking the paper, he relaxed again, with a sheepish grin. He yawned, and prepared to extinguish the lamp and go to sleep. But just then he heard a distinct tapping at the window. Wide-awake now, he looked at the window, and there was startled to see the shadow of a woman. In a quavering voice, he called out, "Who's there?" But there was no reply. An icy spasm of fear gripped his heart. Was it some evil spirit like a flower goblin or fox fairy? Surely, there were no such things in the whole universe; they were just parts of stories made up by witches and wizards to deceive people into believing their antics. Just like the time he had arranged for Madame Zhang the exorcist to come and pretend to chase away the devils that were supposed to be possessing him, when it was all just an excuse to get to see Jiaoniang! Perhaps it was one of the maid servants delivering a message, who had decided to play a trick on him? Or it could be Jiaoniang herself, creeping out at dead of night for a clandestine tryst. This latter thought caused him to leap from the bed and hurry to the door. Eagerly he strode to the door, and flung it open. There in the moonlight stood the lithe figure of a woman, her back to him.

At the sound of the door opening, she turned round. In a transport of delight, Shen Chun saw that it was none other than his beloved, whom he had been thinking of day and night. She was wearing her hair piled up, fixed with a golden pin and a white chrysanthemum. Over a red silk skirt she wore a dark-green gown. Her limpid eyes gazed at Shen Chun from under perfectly arched brows. Her cheeks blushed with a faint rosy tinge, and

竹影摇曳，沙沙作响，西轩石阶下草丛中秋虫儿低低吟唱。申纯倚窗独坐，对着如水月色，心中无限凄凉，也不知娇娘在闺中做甚，想来与自己一样，在一轮明月下思念心上人。

　　不知不觉中谯楼鼓响，已过二更。申纯无情无绪将窗户掩上，卧在床上翻看干宝的《搜神记》，正看得有些毛骨悚然时，忽听窗纸忒愣愣响起，吓得他心悸魂惊，半晌才知是一阵秋风刮过，不禁哑然失笑。打了个哈欠，准备熄灯安歇，窗棂上忽然响起几下轻轻的弹指声，定睛一看，窗纸上映出一个女子的身影，心中这一惊非同小可。颤声问询，却无人答话。心中一凛，暗想可不要是什么花妖狐媚仙子鬼怪吧？再一转念，想到大千世界，朗朗乾坤，哪有什么鬼怪，无非是巫婆神汉骗人的把戏。如同自家先前请张师婆驱鬼，只是为了找理由到舅父家与娇娘见面而演了一场戏而已。想来不定是哪一个小丫头来传话，故弄玄虚，或者是娇娘赁夜前来与自己幽会也不一定。想到此处，急忙下床，三步两步跨到门前，猛地将门打开，只见溶溶月光下果真有一位婷婷女子背门而立。

　　那女子听到门响，转过脸来。申纯一看，欢喜得险些背过气去。原来此女不是别人，正是自己日思夜想的娇娘。只见她头挽坠马髻，插一支金步摇，鬓侧簪一朵白菊，身上披一袭墨绿大氅，着一条暗红蜀锦

her lissom figure in the moonlight was so enticing that one would have been forgiven for thinking that the moon goddess herself had descended to earth. The young man was awoken from his fascinated stupefaction, by this vision of loveliness chiding him with, "I have tiptoed all the way here in the moonlight for a solitary tryst with you. Why were you so slow opening the door?"

Shen Chun took her in his arms, and gasped, "My darling, you've come to me at last!" Then, heedless of everything, he led her inside, and their lips met. After a long time, they loosened their mutual embrace, breathless. Shen Chun cupped Jiaoniang's fragrant cheeks in his hands, and said, "How did you manage to come here so late at night?"

"You should not be surprised," was the girl's rueful reply. "I have been thinking of only you night and day. So finally, I waited until the maid servants were asleep, and slipped away."

Shen Chun was moved to hear this. He bent down, and caressed Jiaoniang's dainty feet. Filled with tender emotion, he whispered, "How pitiful, that these little lotus feet had to endure the cold dew of an autumn night all on account of me!"

Jiaoniang slipped out of her gown, and wrapped her arms round Shen Chun's neck, murmuring, "Since I have gone to such trouble to come here, let's not waste this precious moment, but assuage our pain and longing."

Hearing this, Shen Chun felt hot all over. He bent, and untied Jiaoniang's girdle. The girl closed her eyes in bashful submission. Soon they were like a pair of butterflies dancing in the air or a pair of mandarin ducks sporting in the water.

Their first passion spent, the two lovers lay in each other's arms and whispered endearments. Several times they returned to their love-making, until, before they knew it, the approach of dawn was announced from the chicken yard. Jiaoniang rose, and began to dress. She gently fended off the over-ardent Shen Chun, saying, "Let's not jeopardize our long-term happi-

长裙。两弯蛾眉，似颦非颦；一双凤目，秋水盈盈；霞飞双腮，粉面含羞，袅袅娜娜立于月下，犹如洛妃凌波，又似嫦娥下凡，愈加风情万种，令人目乱神迷。申纯不觉已看得呆了，娇娘含笑嗔道："妾踏月而来，与郎君幽会，为何迟迟不来开门？"

申纯这才缓过神儿来，伸出双臂将娇娘搂在怀中道："好人儿，你总算来了。"说着不顾一切地将娇娘抱入房中，两人四唇相接，搂在一处。不知过了多久，才喘着气松开。申纯双手捧住娇娘的香腮道："这夜半更深的，娘子怎得到此？"

娇娘望着申纯道："郎君切莫惊讶，妾身日日夜夜只思量着你。今夜里，待丫环们睡下，这才脱身出来。"

申纯闻听，十分感动，俯身将娇娘一对娇软香柔的双弯握在手中揉捏着，充满爱怜地说道："可怜这秋宵霜冷露滑，难为这一对小金莲为我受了这般苦楚。"

娇娘解去大氅，伸臂搂住申纯的脖子道："妾冒险而来，郎君还不珍惜这千金一刻，以解你我相思之苦？"

申纯听了，顿时满身燥热，俯身为娇娘宽衣解带。娇娘羞涩地阖上眼帘，一时间，你欢我爱，恰好似双双蝴蝶花间舞，两两鸳鸯水上游。

雨罢云歇，二人相拥着说话，不觉情浓，难免再赴高唐，复上巫山。忽听雄鸡啼晨，娇娘急起身穿衣。申纯意犹未尽，将她搂在怀中不放。娇娘嗔道：

ness for one more snatched moment of pleasure. "

As he let loose his grip on her, Shen Chun murmured, "But when will we be together again?"

Jiaoniang answered, "From now on, I will come to you every night, leaving at daybreak. Will that satisfy you?"

His eyes shining with rapture, the young man cried, "Do you mean it? Oh, I must show my deepest gratitude. " Whereupon, he kowtowed to her.

Jiaoniang chuckled with mirth. "That's enough! That's enough! " She reproached him. "Now, listen to me. Since I will be coming to see you every night, there is no need for you to be popping up to the main hall looking for me. If my parents summon you, of course you must go. But if you see me there, don't greet me. If I chance to speak to you, then avoid saying anything — and at all costs, you must not make any improper or flippant remarks. That way, my parents will think that you have lost interest in me, and my mother will stop being suspicious of you. As soon as that situation comes about, and everybody is off guard, there will be nothing standing in the way of our happiness. "

Shen Chun nodded eagerly. "Since you will be visiting me every night, " he said, "what reason will there be for me to go to the main hall? But be sure to keep your promise, and don't have me waiting on tenterhooks. "

Adjusting her clothing, Jiaoniang smiled at this little admonition. "I must go now, " she said. "Get some rest now, so that you will be wide-awake tonight. " With that, she sped away.

As soon as she had gone, Shen Chun fell fast asleep. He woke late in the morning, and for the first time did not go to the main hall to greet his uncle and aunt. He spent the rest of the day reading and strolling in the courtyard. There was a high blue sky that day, with only a hint of cloud. The autumn breeze was exhilarating, and the young man's spirits soared. At last he was convinced that his trip to Lizhou had not been in vain, after all. If he was to be visited by Jiaoniang every night from now on, he de-

"郎君切不可图一时之欢,坏了你我长久团圆之计。"

申纯仍不松手,喃喃道:"谁知你这一去,何时才能重来欢会?"

娇娘道:"从今往后,妾定然每日夜来晨去,郎君还不满足吗?"

申纯听罢,眉开眼笑道:"此话当真么? 果然如此,小生先给娘子叩头了。"说着爬在床上对着娇娘便拜。

娇娘"扑哧"笑道:"罢了,罢了。你且听着,此后妾必夜至,所以郎君无事不必到中堂来寻我。若是老爷夫人招唤你去,见了妾也不必问候。妾或与你说话,你则概不答言,尤其切记不可说出狎邪调情的话来。如此则府中人皆知郎君无意于妾,夫人的疑心也就冰释了。到那时无人防范,你我欢情便可长久。"

申纯听罢,频频点头道:"娘子果然每夜必至,我入中堂内室何干? 只是娘子切不可负约,令我望断秋水也。"

娇娘整好衣裙,莞尔一笑道:"妾走了,郎君且再歇息一会子,夜里也有精神。"说罢闪身出门去了。

申纯待娇娘去后,倒头便睡,直到日上三竿,方才起床。也不到中堂拜谒请安,只在园中读书漫步,看着天高云淡,秋风送爽,心情豁然开朗。想自己这番来利州,总算没有徒劳往返。只要以后夜夜能与心

cided, he wouldn't mind staying in this backwater forever!

At midnight, sure enough, Jiaoniang glided into the young man's room, and so it went on night after night. The lovers filled the night hours by playing chess by lamplight, reciting and composing poems, and engaging in occupations involving the use of the bed.

From time to time, Shen Chun had occasion to visit the main hall. When his uncle and aunt, or Feihong or somebody else asked him why he did not drop in for a chat more often, he made the excuse that his studies left him tired and with little leisure. If he chanced to encounter Jiaoniang on these occasions, he would lower his head and scuttle away, as if he had seen a snake or a scorpion. But what struck him as strange was that Jiaoniang did not seem to be playing along with the game. Once, when there was nobody else around, she waved to him openly, while he pretended not to notice. And another time, she sent Xiaohui to ask him to go and visit her in the rear courtyard. Shen Chun stammered out an excuse, but the incident left him puzzled and angry. "What on earth does she mean by this?" He wondered. "She has impressed on me several times that we must not speak to each other in broad daylight, and yet she herself is deliberately breaking her own rule!" He thought about it for a while, and then made up his mind to confront her about it that very night.

And so he did. As they lay in bed, he said, "My dear, you told me not to speak to you outside, yet you yourself are either waving to me or making eyes at me in broad daylight. Not only that, but you even sent a maid servant to fetch me!"

"Ah, I did that specially to let other people take notice — especially Feihong," Jiaoniang explained. "I wanted to cut short her gossip. You see, the more you ignored me, the more other people would be convinced that there was nothing going on between us."

From then on, Shen Chun kept this firmly in his mind, and every time he saw Jiaoniang he would lower his head, and keep his eyes fixed firmly on the ground, seemingly oblivious to the girl.

上人在一起，哪怕在此荒园住上万载千年，也心甘情愿。

这一夜二更，娇娘果真飘然而至。自此之后，每夜二更娇娘必到，二人或于灯下对弈，或吟诗填词，床第之欢更是一夜不虚。

申纯常常数日才进一次中堂，舅母、飞红等人问起他为何不来叙话，他不是推说看书累了，便是做文章无暇。若是遇到娇娘，更是低头疾走，如避蛇蝎。有时娇娘在无人处向他招手，他也装着看不见；有时令小慧来叫他到后院去叙话，他也找个借口不去，且心中不免恼火，想道："你几次三番吩咐我白日里相互不要搭言，可你自家却不守信，有什么体己话儿，留着夜里说不好吗？"

心中疑惑，夜里床第之间便问娇娘道："娘子，你教我不要与你搭言，可你白日里见面，不是招手，便是飞眼。你不是怕人发觉么，怎么又让丫环来唤？"

娇娘道："妾那是专门做给外人看的，尤其是让那飞红看了，免得她说三道四。你愈不理睬我，旁人愈不会疑心到你我头上。"

自此，申纯牢记娇娘之言，再见娇娘，只管把头一低，眼观鼻，鼻观口，一副坐怀不乱的柳下惠模样。

Two months passed, and mid-autumn arrived. Leaves whirled from the trees, and the north-country geese winged their way southward. Shen Chun began to miss his parents, his brother and his sister-in-law. But he was too reluctant to part from Jiaoniang to consider returning. By this time, his nightly dalliance had begun to tell on his health. He became weaker and weaker, and was listless in the daytime. His visits to the main hall were few and far between.

Early one morning, he was woken by Xiaohui banging on his door. "Get up, Master Shen," she cried, "the sun is high in the sky. What are you doing lazing around in bed at this time? Get up this minute!"

Jiaoniang had left him at the crack of dawn, and Shen Chun was still wallowing in sweet dreams when Xiaohui so boisterously intruded. He hastily threw a robe around himself, and went to open the door. Xiaohui barged in. "Were you still sleeping at this time of the morning?" she demanded in astonishment.

"I was up until late last night studying; that's why I slept late," Shen Chun said. "I hope you won't find that too preposterous," he added, icily.

"Oh, is that right? You are a busy little bee, aren't you?" was the sarcastic reply.

A sense of uneasiness stirred within the young man, and something warned him to guard his tongue. "What brings you to my humble home so early?" he said, in a mocking tone.

"The old mistress wants you," said Xiaohui.

"Well, I suppose I'd better go. But why didn't she send Xiang'e, instead of putting you to all this trouble?"

The maid servant's eyebrows shot up in indignation. "What do you mean?" she demanded. "Why should only Xiang'e be fitted for such an exalted task. Am I not high and mighty enough, then?"

Shen Chun thought to himself: "This is not the sort of girl to be trifled with. She has a razor-sharp tongue. I'd better be careful." So he put on an ingratiating smile, and said, "Oh, come now, I didn't mean that at all. It's

转眼两月过去，不觉已是深秋，落叶纷纷，北雁南飞。申纯住得久了，不免思念家中父母兄嫂，可又不忍与娇娘分离，只得打算长住下去。不料因其贪恋美色，与娇娘夜夜欢会，身体渐渐瘦弱下去，后来白日里也昏昏思睡，到中堂去的次数也更少了。

这日清晨，小慧来到西轩，用力拍打门扇，连声唤道："申家官人，申家官人，阳婆晒到屁股了，还懒着不起床？快快起来！"

前晚娇娘五更方走，申纯此时尚在酣梦之中，猛听得门板山响，有人喊叫，惊醒后细听是小慧叫门，忙穿好衣衫去开门。小慧闯了进来，对着申纯没好气地说道："都什么时候了，司户大人还没有睡醒？"

申纯道："只因昨夜读书太晚，故此起来迟了。还望姐姐不要见笑。"

小慧冷笑道："是吗？官人好用功呀！"

申纯心里有鬼，不敢多说，讪讪道："不知姐姐一大早光临寒舍，有何贵干？"

小慧道："我家夫人有请官人。"

申纯闻言，道："既是夫人相召，小生这就前去。只是为何湘娥不来，反倒有劳姐姐？"

小慧柳眉一竖，道："怎么，请司户大人到中堂，必得湘娥来才行，我小慧人贱面薄，是请不动大人了？"

申纯心道，这丫头人小心大，一张嘴像刀子似的，

just that Xiang'e is attached to the old mistress' quarters, so I thought that if the old mistress wanted any errands running she would have sent Xiang'e."

"The old lady is not feeling well," the maid servant said. "She has her ups and downs, and when she got up this morning she had one of her turns. And since the old master is not at home, Xiang'e cannot leave her side for a moment. So I was sent to fetch you. I never expected you'd make such a fuss about it, I must say. Anyway, I've passed on the message; it's up to you whether you go or not."

Shen Chun saw that Xiaohui was in a huff, so he interjected, "Now, don't get all hot and bothered. Just wait a moment, while I get washed and comb my hair. Then I'll be right with you."

"All right, but hurry up. I'll be waiting for you outside." With that, Xiaohui turned and went out.

While he was making himself presentable, it struck Shen Chun that there was something fishy about this summons. Was it some kind of trap, he wondered. Had Feihong put the old lady up to sending for him to interrogate him? If the invitation had come from Jiaoniang, he would had had no qualms about turning it down right then and there. But if it really was his aunt who desired to see him, he could not, in all propriety, refuse. Well, he decided in the end, he had to take his chances and see how the wind blew. At this point, he heard Xiaohui calling sharply to him: "Aren't you ready yet? Or are you waiting for me to arrange a posse of constables to clear the way for you?"

Shen Chun did not know whether to laugh or to be angry at this. He hurried out of the door, saying, "All right, I'm coming, I'm coming. Please excuse me for making you wait."

"Oh, I'm not in a position to excuse anybody," Xiaohui said, tartly, "you're the one who should excuse me."

Shen Chun laughed. "You should curb that acid tongue of yours," he admonished her. "Otherwise, you'll never get a decent husband."

我且不与她计较。于是和颜悦色道："哪里话?我是说湘娥姐姐在夫人房里,夫人有事,自然是由她跑腿。"

"夫人身体欠佳,好一阵歹一阵的,今日起来便觉身子不爽,老爷又不在府中,湘娥在夫人身边伺候,一时走不开,所以夫人令我来请官人,没想到官人反倒有这许多话,推拖着不去。反正话我是传到了,去不去由你。"

申纯见小慧急了,便道:"姐姐息怒,待小生梳洗完毕,马上过去。"

"那好,官人快些,我在门外等你。"说着小慧一转身出去了。

申纯一边梳洗一边思量,总觉得事情有些蹊跷,不知其中是否有诈。若是舅母相召,是不是飞红在其中使坏?若是娇娘相召,我便该狠狠心不去。可万一果真是舅母有事相商,我若不去,岂不失了礼节?是福不是祸,是祸躲不过,只有见机行事,听天由命了。正思量间,小慧在门外尖声叫道:"大人还没有梳洗好吗?要不要婢子叫几个衙役来为大人鸣锣开道哇?"

申纯闻言哭笑不得,忙出门道:"这就走,这就走,姐姐快饶了我吧。"

小慧道:"小女子不敢犯上,还是大人饶了婢女吧。"

申纯笑道:"小妮子嘴巴不要这么尖酸,当心以后找不到好婆家!"

Xiaohui gave him a supercilious look. "How can we common maid servants hope to get decent husbands?" she sneered. "Anyway, it's the young mistress I feel sorry for," she continued, as if to herself. "She's such a great beauty, and the apple of her parents' eye. If even she has no self-respect, how can we maid servants be expected to behave any better?"

It was with a feeling of unease that Shen Chun sensed that there was a hidden meaning behind her words. He asked, "What do you mean by 'no self-respect'?"

Xiaohui gave a mirthless laugh. "Do you really need to ask?" she piped. "I think you know perfectly well what I mean."

Shen Chun thought to himself: "She must somehow have found out about the secret meeting between Jiaoniang and myself over the past two months. By 'no self-respect' she must mean that Jiaoniang goes sneaking off at night to her lover's chamber." This latter thought caused a crimson tide to suffuse his face.

This gave Xiaohui her cue to say, "Young master, there are many faithless lovers in this world, as I'm sure you know. I only hope that you are not one of them, that's all!"

Shen Chun was taken aback at this, but he eventually managed to assure the girl that such scoundrels could not include him among their number.

By that time, they had reached the moon gate, and Shen Chun would have headed straight for the main hall, but Xiaohui tugged at his sleeve. "The old mistress is waiting for you in the rear courtyard," she said. "Follow me."

This was the first time the young man had been in the rear courtyard of his uncle and aunt's quarters, and he noted the abundance of chrysanthemums with their heady scent, quite different from the austere western courtyard where he was staying. Before long he found himself before a small, two-storied building with upturned eaves, carved balustrades and painted beams. On the upper story, there was a lattice window, tightly closed,

小慧白了他一眼道:"我们这些丫头命贱,岂敢巴望着找个好人家?只可惜我们小姐花容月貌,贵为千金,还不被人知重,我这个小丫头又算得了什么?"

申纯听她话里有话,便道:"你家小姐如何不被人知重了?"

小慧连声冷笑道:"哼哼哼……这还用问我?大人心里明镜似的。"

申纯心想:"娇娘与我幽会已有两月,想是这小丫头有所察觉,说娇娘不知自重,夜奔情郎。"想到此,自己的脸不觉涨红起来。

小慧见申纯满面通红,便道:"官人你说,这世上负心的男子何其多哉,但愿你不是其中的一个。"

申纯支吾半晌,道:"啊啊……我不是,不是。"

说话间出了月亮门,申纯径直折向中堂,小慧却一把拉住他的衣袖道:"夫人在后院等你,你跟我来。"

申纯只得随着小慧向后院走去。他来到舅父府上两月有余,这还是初次到后院来。只见路侧金菊怒放,花香扑鼻,与自己所住的东园各有千秋。走了一程,见正面是一座飞檐翘角、雕栏画栋的二层小楼,上面一层纱窗紧闭,底下一层门扇洞开。二人来到门口,小慧侧身将申纯让入,申纯跨进门槛,就见娇娘面门端坐,一脸幽怨。申纯忙收腿撤身,意欲退出,不

while the door in the lower story was wide open. Xiaohui stood aside to let Shen Chun enter first. The first thing that the young man saw on crossing the threshold was Jiaoniang, seated stiffly and with a brow like thunder. Startled, Shen Chun took a step backwards, and was about to turn and flee, but Xiaohui pushed him back into the room, and shut the door from the outside. The bewildered Shen Chun thought to himself: "I've fallen into some trap set by Jiaoniang and Xiaohui, who want to make fun of me!" Then he appealed to Jiaoniang: "Miss, you must let me go at once. If someone were to find us like this, your reputation would be ruined!"

At that moment, from outside the door came the sound of Xiaohui's voice: "You fickle wretch, apologize to my young mistress at once!"

Shen Chun desperately shook the door. In a hoarse whisper he said, "Xiaohui, please open the door. If people find out that your young mistress and I are in here alone, there will be a scandal. Open the door this minute!"

"I'm only obeying my young mistress' orders," replied the maid servant. "There's nothing you can do about it." This was followed by the sound of her footsteps, as she distanced herself from the entire affair.

Shen Chun, in resignation, turned back to Jiaoniang. The latter's expression was frosty as she said, "Take a seat. I have something to say to you."

The young man took two steps forward. "My dear young lady," he gasped, in great agitation, "have you taken leave of your senses? Why have you had me shut up in this room in the middle of the day? You must let me go quickly!"

"You...." The girl managed to utter only one syllable before she choked with sobs, and tears sprang to her eyes.

Shen Chun rejoined, "You've scared me out of my wits! Let me go at once! If you have anything to say to me, we can discuss it later."

Jiaoniang composed herself, and said, in a stern tone: "That won't do! You will hear me out now."

料小慧在身后用力一推,将门从外关住。申纯心中暗道:"果真是小慧丫头和娇娘做下套子与己玩耍。"回头对娇娘道:"娘子,快放我走,免得让人看到,坏了你的名声。"

小慧在门外说道:"负心汉,还不快些向小姐赔礼!"

申纯摇动门扇,低声央求道:"小慧姐姐,快开门。小姐独自在堂,我二人孤男寡女于无人处相会,让人见了生疑。你还不快快开门!"

小慧道:"是小姐让我这样做的,可由不得你了。"说罢听着脚步声远去,竟然顾自走了。

申纯束手无策,只好转过头来看着娇娘,却见娇娘脸如秋霜,道:"兄长可暂坐片刻,我有话对你讲。"

申纯上前两步,急道:"好我的娘子,你不是昏头了吧? 大天白日的,你把我着在屋中做甚么? 还是让我快快走吧。"

"你⋯⋯"娇娘一时气噎,眼中泪花闪动。

申纯道:"我的心都被你吓得要跳出来了,还是快些放我走吧,有话以后再说。"

娇娘一拭泪水,厉声道:"不行! 你今日一定得听我把话说完。"

说着将申纯按在椅上,自己坐到对面,目不转

So saying, she pushed Shen Chun down onto a chair, while she took a seat facing him. Wasting no time, she said, "I have asked myself how, now that you have achieved success, you can so heartlessly discard this humble person who treated you so well in the past."

Shen Chun remained silent, thinking to himself: "Why is she making such a wild accusation? We have been together every night, so what on earth does she mean by saying that I have discarded her? This is absolute nonsense!"

Seeing that the young man said nothing, Jiaoniang spoke again. "Well then, with whom did you sit under the lamplight last night?" she asked, accusingly.

"What...?" Shen Chun could not help smiling inwardly, thinking that Jiaoniang was teasing him just to amuse herself, because she had time on her hands. He then said, in an intimate tone: "Good Heavens! How can you ask such a thing, especially after swearing me to strict secrecy?"

Jiaoniang looked shocked. "What did I swear you to secrecy about?" she cried.

The young man looked around furtively. "Are you sure there is no one in the courtyard?" he asked. "I don't want anyone to overhear."

Jiaoniang assured him that there was no one in the courtyard. "Say what you have to say," she commanded.

Shen Chun threw her a meaningful glance. "You know better than I do," he said.

"I have no idea what you are talking about," Jiaoniang protested. "It was over a year ago that we parted. But since you arrived back here, I have never once had a secret rendezvous with you. What could I possibly have told you to keep quiet about?"

Shen Chun, thinking that she was being deliberately provoking, started to become impatient. He frowned, and said, "Why are you being so stubborn? You know perfectly well that you have been visiting me at midnight every night for over two months now. And you have repeatedly enjoined me

睛、一字一句地道："妾自问昔日待君不薄，岂料你一旦贵显，便将人等闲弃置，是何道理？"

申纯心道："娇娘今日怎么尽说这些莫名其妙的话？分明与我夜夜相聚，怎么说我将人等闲弃置？真正是颠倒黑白，一派胡言！"于是缄口不作一声。

娇娘见申纯不答，又道："我且问你，前夜与你并坐灯下的是什么人？"

"这……"申纯心中不禁失笑，想娇娘是闲来无事，生着法儿拿自己取乐，于是低声说道："啊呀！娘子你怎么这样说话？是你叫我不要说出去，今日为何只管问我？"

娇娘惊问："我有何事不叫你说？"

申纯又看看左右，问道："院中可有人么？不要叫人听了去。"

娇娘道："院中无人，你有话尽可直说。"

申纯冲着娇娘一眨眼，道："娘子心里比我明白。"

娇娘道："妾不明白！自前番别君之后，至今已逾一年。兄长此次前来，妾从来不曾与郎君密会私语，又有何事叮嘱你不要说出去？"

申纯见娇娘只是一味做假，心中渐生恼怒，满脸不悦，道："娘子何苦追问不休？你自前月以来，每日夜半，必至东园西轩与我私会，又屡次叮嘱我在人前万勿与你搭言，怕飞红又生事端，坏了你我的好事。

on no account to speak to you at any other time. You said that this was to make sure that Feihong could not make any trouble and ruin our happiness. Why are you now flatly denying it?"

Jiaoniang was stunned. "You say that I have been visiting you every night?" she questioned Shen Chun closely.

"Yes," replied the young man, coolly, "for over two months now, never missing a single night. Last night, for instance, you didn't leave until dawn. Surely, you must remember that?"

"What preposterous rubbish!" Jiaoniang exploded. "I have spent every night alone and sleepless, whiling away the long, cold, weary hours. When could I have been cavorting with you, tell me that!"

Shen Chun's face was grim, as he shot back: "There is no one else here to overhear us, so why are you so adamant in denying it?"

"I think you must have encountered a ghost," replied Jiaoniang, calmly. "Your quarters are in a remote and rather gloomy part of the mansion. I have heard stories of phantoms appearing and disappearing there. I suppose one of them assumed the shape of a beautiful woman to tempt you. Meanwhile, there's something you do not know. Recently I've lowered myself to flatter Feihong, and brought her round to promising not to stand in our way any longer. I wanted to tell you about this earlier, so that we could arrange a tryst, but you always shied away. And then when I sent Xiaohui or one of the other maid servants to bring you, you always made some excuse not to come. I worried about this day and night, and finally came to the conclusion that your feelings for me had changed. Last night, I sent Xiaohui and some of the others to spy on you and find out what you were doing. Xiaohui reported that you were sitting on very intimate terms with a girl who looked exactly like me. She said the creature seemed to be a spirit or something. And so, we concocted this stratagem for getting you here. If you don't believe me, you can question Xiaohui; she will back me up."

Hearing this, Shen Chun felt his head reel and his blood turn to ice. He was speechless. It was like a horrible dream.

现在为何却矢口否认？"

娇娘惊问道："兄长是说我每夜必至西轩与你私会？"

申纯道："正是。两月有余，一天不误。昨夜灯前帐中，你我还在共效于飞之乐，五更娘子方才离去，现在就不记得了么？"

娇娘冷笑道："这话真是怪了。我在这里夜夜独对孤灯，捱不完冷夜长宵，几时与你灯前帐里效那于飞之乐来？真正一派胡言！"

申纯沉下脸来，愤愤地道："此处既无外人，娘子又何须矢口抵赖？"

娇娘脸色凝重，道："如此看来，三哥莫非是撞上鬼了？三哥所居之处幽深偏僻，久闻其中有鬼魅出没，谅必是妖物幻化成妾身形状，来迷惑三哥。三哥有所不知，妾自屈身谄事飞红，近来已得其欢心，答应不再阻扰我们。妾便急着告诉三哥，以谋相会。谁知遇到三哥，妾忙着搭话，你却不顾而去；派小慧等人去唤，三哥也总是托辞不来。小妹日夜思量，不解其故，还以为是三哥有了异心。飞红昨夜派小慧等人到东园西轩去窥探你在做些什么，小慧回来说是只见一女子相貌与妾一般无二，亲亲热热与兄对坐，想来非鬼即妖。为此今日特地编个理由，请你前来相问。三哥如若不信，可叫小慧前来作证。"

申纯听了娇娘这一番言语，只觉浑身冰凉，如坠

Jiaoniang called out, "Xiaohui, go and fetch Feihong!"

Xiaohui, who had been waiting outside, did as she was ordered, and it was not long before Feihong slipped into the room, and closed the door behind her. Stepping boldly forward, she said, "Young Master, why did you cast off my young mistress? Time and time again, you deliberately ignored her, almost driving her into a frenzy. Heartless villains like you should be boiled in oil, and locked in the eighteenth depth of Hell! I sent someone to check up on you last night, and she found you snuggling up to some pretty wench. Very nice and cosy it looked too! Was she the daughter of some important family you have eloped with, or some professional courtesan you secretly sent for? I never thought that a person like you, who seemed to be the last word in loyalty and steadfastness, would engage in such base conduct in the very house of your true love!"

This diatribe caused Shen Chun to turn a deathly pale, and sweat gathered on his brow. He stammered, "Oh Fei ... Feihong.... Is what you have just said true?"

The serving maid took great glee in the young man's predicament. "It certainly is," she said. "Now, I'm not one to believe in ghosts. But it seems that you young scholar-playboys are so amorous that even the flower nymphs and fox sprites are goaded to assume human form and dally with you."

This caused Shen Chun even more distress, and he trembled like an aspen leaf. For some time he could say nothing, and then, tearfully, he turned to Jiaoniang, and said, "If it had not been for your love for me, I would have perished at the hands of demons. Oh, how I curse the past two months, when I was led to betray you! Please tell me what I can do to atone."

Jiaoniang turned her head away, to wipe away her own tears, but said nothing. Feihong, however, laughed aloud, and said, "You have to beat a drum to make it sound, and you have to talk about things to get them out into the open. Now that this matter has been discussed, everything is all

梦中，一句话也说不出来。

娇娘见状，对着门外道："小慧，你去请红娘子前来。"

小慧应声而去。不大一会儿，飞红闪身进来，又将门扇掩住，走近前来道："官人为何抛弃我家小姐？人前几次三番装傻充愣，害得小姐神魂颠倒。似你这般薄幸之人，合当火烤油煎，打下十八层地狱。昨夜我派人打探，见你与个美貌女子勾肩搭背，好不亲热。那是谁家私奔的千金小姐，还是你从外面招来的烟花粉头？想不到你貌似忠厚，却背着人在府里养着妇人，你这艳福着实不浅呀！"

申纯听飞红也这么说，惊得额头渗汗，脸色惨白，战战兢兢问道："飞……飞红姐姐，你……你说的，可是真的？"

飞红见申纯吓得这般模样，笑道："怎么不是真的！我本来不信有鬼，想是你这风流种子，多情班头，将园中的花妖狐魅都惹得现形作祟。"

申纯听了，当下魂飞魄扬，浑身抖战，有如筛糠。半晌，方含泪对娇娘道："若非娘子见爱，则我必死于鬼魅之手。如今只恨两月以来，有负娘子深情，叫我怎生报答？"

娇娘闻言，背过脸去抹泪。飞红笑道："鼓不敲不响，话不说不明。将事情说开，一切就都好了。你二人也不必互相埋怨，不过，这后院闺阁之中，官人不可

right, and you two need harbor no hidden resentment any longer. However, as this rear courtyard is reserved for the women of the household, you had better be off back to your own quarters, young master. "

"What? Back to that desolate, haunted place?" Shen Chun bleated in dismay.

Feihong winked at Jiaoniang, and said again to Shen Chun: "How contrary you are! When we call you, you won't come, and when we tell you to go, you won't go. We were just making fun of you. Now run along, or you'll be late for your tryst with the young mistress tonight. "

Shen Chun's face was a picture of confusion. "I don't understand, " he cried. "Do you mean to say that you made up that story about a ghost. Anyway, I'm not going back there tonight; I'm going to stay right here! "

"Oh no, you're not, " announced Feihong, pushing the young man towards the door. "This is a lady's boudoir; it's no place for a grown man. Tonight, I will escort my old mistress to come and see you. Don't argue. Tomorrow, I'll see to it that you move into the main courtyard. But if the old lady asks you about the ghost, don't mention that it looked like the young mistress whatever you do. Can you remember that?"

The whole episode had left Shen Chun befuddled, but he managed to mumble, "Yes, I will remember. "

"Well, off you go then! "

In utter despair, the young man pleaded with Feihong: "All right, if I have to go back, I suppose I have to. But please come and check in a little while to make sure that I'm all right. Otherwise, you could find me an abandoned corpse. "

"Yes, yes, " the maid servant agreed, impatiently. "But what a coward you are! I don't suppose you know the meaning of the word fear when you are holding a beautiful woman in your arms, though. "

久留，你暂且回园中去吧。"

申纯急道："既然有妖精，还让我回那荒园里去？"

飞红冲娇娘挤了挤眼，又对申纯道："往日几次唤你不来，今日又推你不去。适才是哄你呢，你快快回那西轩去吧，少不得夜里小姐又去相伴。"

申纯一脸迷茫，痴痴地道："我真个疑心起来，难道说你们所说的都是鬼话？我今天哪儿也不去了，只在这里罢了。"

飞红过来推搡着申纯往外走，说道："你且出去，这里毕竟是小姐的绣阁，你个大男人呆在这里太不成话。夜间我与夫人到园中看你，别有计较。我保你从明日起住进正院，只是夫人若问起时，千万不能说那女子相貌与小姐相像，以免夫人生疑。你可记住了？"

申纯呆头呆脑地道："记住了。"

"那不快些回去？"

申纯万般无奈，道："如此我只得暂且回去。飞红姐姐，你可要早些来看我，要不只怕我死无葬身之地。"

飞红笑道："知道了。瞧你那点儿胆子，抱着美人的时候怎么不知道害怕呢？"

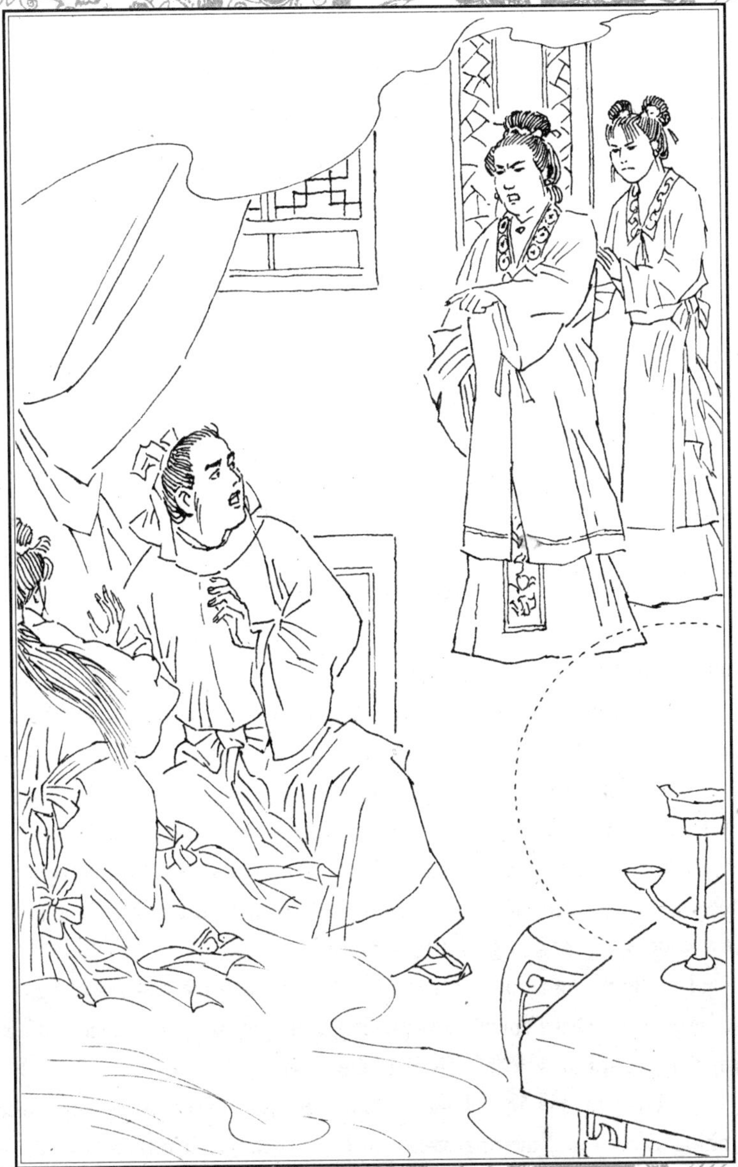

Chapter Eight
Feihong Confronts a Ghost

Previously, when Shen Chun had been waiting for his lover's visits, evening seemed to take an agonizingly long time to come. Today, he was dreading the time when the birds would seek their nests and the moon would rise. When he thought of what Feihong and Jiaoniang had told him that day, he couldn't help cold shivers running down his spine. Still, he found it hard to believe that the girl he had held in his arms every night for two months had not been Jiaoniang; her speech, her looks, her gestures had all been exactly like hers. How could it have been a ghost? Then there was Feihong asserting that his nocturnal lover really was a ghost, and insisting that he go back to wait for her next haunting. The young man couldn't make head or tail of it.

Then he heard midnight strike. A gust of wind rattled the bamboos in the courtyard, and made the iron ornaments dangling from the eaves tinkle. Shen Chun shivered, and pricked his ears up, but heard nothing more. Turning up the wick of the lamp, he forced himself to calm down, and steeled himself for the ordeal of finding out once and for all if his night visitor was a mortal or a shade. There was another gust of wind, the door flew wide open, and in glided Jiaoniang.

Despite his agitation, he was sure that this was the real Jiaoniang, and not a ghost. "That Feihong was playing tricks on me," he concluded, and stepped forward to welcome his charming visitor.

"Were you thinking of me, sitting here all alone?" Jiaoniang asked, smiling sweetly and melting into Shen Chun's arms. Just then, the terrify-

第八章 飞红明妖

往日里，申纯盼着佳人早到，只恨昼长夜短；今日里却怕金乌西坠，玉兔东升。一想起白日里飞红、娇娘之语，后背上禁不住直冒凉气。转念一想，又不由得疑惑万分，两个月里明明是娇娘夜夜前来，与自己肌肤相亲，言谈举止没有一点儿破绽，怎说是妖怪？可是就连飞红也一口咬定夜间来的是鬼，非逼着自家今夜等着鬼来。弄得自己大惑不解，也搞不清到底哪个是人，哪个是鬼了。

忽听得三更鼓响，一阵风刮过，园中竹林沙沙作响，房檐上铁马儿叮咚。申纯不由打了个冷颤，侧耳细听，却又没有了动静。他强做镇静，将灯火拨亮，横下一条心来，是人是鬼今晚定要见个分晓。又一阵风过之后，门扇洞开，申纯惊视，只见娇娘娉娉婷婷走了进来。

申纯心想："这分明是活生生的小姐，哪里是鬼？想必又是贱人飞红作祟。"起身相迎道："娘子来了。"

娇娘嫣然一笑道："申郎，你独坐于此，可是正在思想奴家？"说着往申纯怀中一靠。申纯想起白日众

ing story he had heard earlier came back into his mind. Shen Chun hurriedly pushed the girl away, and retreated behind his desk. His mind raced. "They say that ghosts have no shadows, and their garments no seams," he thought, "but that isn't the case with this one. However, one thing is very strange, and that is that she has been coming her every night for the past two months, but without even a single maid servant to attend her." Thereupon, he summoned up all his courage to say, "Miss, this courtyard is dotted with abandoned terraces and isolated pavilions. Besides, the wind is chill and the dew is cold. Yet every night you come here and depart alone. Are you not afraid? Moreover, I have heard that in this courtyard, there are from time to time sightings of ... well, er, of ghosts."

At this, Jiaoniang's face assumed a stern expression. "I long for you so much, I wish the night would never end," she said. "Every day I wait impatiently for evening to fall. No matter what frights and terrors I have to face, I cannot allow my maid servants to find out about us. Yes, of course I am afraid when I sneak here at midnight through this damp and lonely courtyard. But so that I can be with you I care not for ghosts or hardships. What you said just now really hurt my feelings!" so saying, she began to weep and wail.

This melted Shen Chun's heart, and he stepped up to comfort her.

In an instant, her tears had turned to smiles. "My dear, she said, "it's getting late. Let's not waste our precious moments in idle talk."

Seeing her so ardent, Shen Chun was convinced that this was not the real Jiaoniang. Fear suddenly overcame him again, and he flinched away from her violently, almost knocking over the lamp in the process.

"What's the matter?" Jiaoniang asked.

The young man did not reply, but stared fixedly at her. Looking into her eyes, shining with love, he thought to himself: "She must be a ghost, with the power to melt men's souls. Or perhaps she's a fairy come down from Heaven?" Involuntarily, he stepped forward, and stretched out his hand. Another thought then came into his mind: "They say that if one be-

人的言语，忙将她推开，退在书案后寻思道："人都说鬼无影，衣无缝，可看着眼前之人并不如此，怎么说也不像鬼。只有一件可疑，她夜来朝去两月有余，怎么没有一个丫头相伴？"想到此，申纯冷不丁问道："娇娘，这园中荒台孤榭，风清露冷，你每夜独来独往，心里头不害怕么？我可是听人讲起，这园里有……有鬼魅出没。"

娇娘闻言，猛地变脸道："我为你恨不得长夜无尽，每天只盼着黄昏月上，整日里提心吊胆，担惊受怕，哪里敢让丫头们知道？这园里露重苔滑，寂无一人，每逢夜半独自往来，岂有不害怕的？我只为与你相会，不惧妖魅，不辞辛劳，你却说出这样的话来，好不叫人伤心！"说着呜呜咽咽悲泣起来。

申纯见状，心中好生不忍，走近安慰道："娘子莫哭，娘子莫哭。"

娇娘顿时止住悲声，破涕为笑，扯住申纯衣袖道："申郎，夜深了，闲话少叙，咱们快歇息吧。"

申纯见她如此情急，大异娇娘平日为人，心中又害怕起来，慌忙甩开衣袖后退，险些将纱灯撞翻。

娇娘嗔道："申郎，你这是怎么了？"

申纯不答，只细细审视眼前的娇娘，见她美目传情，爱意盈盈，心中不由得想道："她便是鬼，也令人销魂，说不定是天上的仙女降临人间。"想到此处，不

comes ensnared by a ghost, one's life will be a short one. So, no matter how beautiful she is, I had better not have anything to do with her." And he immediately pulled his hand back.

Puzzled that Shen Chun was so hesitant tonight, Jiaoniang reproached him: "What on earth is the matter with you tonight, my dear? You're a completely different person. I have been hurrying to you every midnight so that we can share delight, but you have suddenly grown cold towards me. How is that?"

Shen Chun plucked up his courage again, to say: "It is not that I have lost my affection, but I fear that you ... that you are not of this world."

Jiaoniang's eyebrows shot up. She glowered, and hissed, "Not of this world? Are you trying to say that I'm a ghost? Ha! You have always been a heartless young pedant. Your heart has changed, and you have the effron-tery to call me a ghost! Well, I'm not going to let you get away lightly!" With that, she pounced on Shen Chun, tearing at his clothing. The young man dodged away in a panic. In a towering rage, Jiaoniang pointed a finger at him, and screamed, "You and I swore an everlasting oath of love, so that death will take us together and our graves will face each other. Tonight I have come for you...."

Just at this moment, the door opened, and Feihong and Shen Chun's aunt entered.

Over the past two years, the old lady's health had deteriorated. As a consequence, she had gradually handed over the handling of household af-fairs to Feihong. The latter, seeing that her old mistress had no more than a year or two to live, had done her best to inveigle herself into the affections of the old master, whom she anyway wanted to pay back for his original kindness to her. When the time came, she earnestly hoped, she would have the running of the mansion all to herself. She therefore applied herself to her duties with unsurpassed diligence, until everything in the mansion ran like clockwork. Needless to say, she paid special attention to Wang Wen-rui's needs, even going so far as to flirt with him from time to time. Wang

由自主向前跨了一步，刚伸出手去，忽地想道："人言若遭鬼缠，必促人寿。纵然此妹美若天仙，若真的是鬼，万万不可再与她交合。"于是又将手缩了回来。

娇娘见申纯今晚忽前忽后，欲进还缩，嗔道："申郎，你今夜到底是怎么了？倒像换了个人似的。奴家每日里夜半奔波，可是一心一意要与郎君做夫妻，你怎么变得这般无情？"

申纯大着胆子道："娘子，不是小生无情，是怕你……你不是人。"

娇娘蛾眉一挑，脸色剧变，厉声道："胡说！我不是人，难道是鬼吗？书生自古多薄情，你……你……你定是变心别恋，反来诬人为鬼，我今日里岂肯与你甘休！"说着扑上前来，奋力撕扯申纯的衣衫，申纯慌忙躲闪。娇娘葱指一点申纯，道："我和你海誓山盟、儿女情长一场，不能落个没结果。纵然是死，也少不得一副棺木与你两坟相向。今日里我与你这个无情郎拼了……"

正在这时，突然门扇大开，撞进两个人来，正是飞红与赵夫人。

原来这两年来赵夫人体弱多病，府中家事渐渐交由飞红料理。飞红本来就抱着报答老爷相救之心，又见赵夫人带病延年，也不过一二载的光景，只要将老爷笼络住，到时府中还不是自家的天下？因此上诸

Wenrui himself was not averse to such allurements from a girl in the bloom of youth, but tried to keep his wife in the dark about his feelings. His wife, however, was not in the least blind to what was going on under her very nose, but she was realistic enough to know that she had not long to live, and actually urged her husband to take Feihong as his concubine, so that he would have someone to look after him when she was no longer with him. Wang Wenrui made a show of abhorrence at the idea, but eventually acquiesced in his wife's wish, once again proving the truth of the old saying about the "plum blossom pushing aside the crab apple." From this time on, the whole household called Feihong "Miss Hong." Having obtained a secure station in life like this, Feihong forgot all about her resentment towards her old mistress as well as her jealousy of Jiaoniang. In fact, she and Jiaoniang became quite friendly once more. On top of that, Feihong threw herself into managing the household's affairs with even greater enthusiasm. When Shen Chun returned this time, Feihong could not help a feeling of chagrin, but, contenting herself with being the favorite of the master of the mansion, she decided not to be greedy, and so laid no more snares for the young scholar. In the meantime, Jiaoniang kept on Feihong's good side with lavish presents and polite words.

People's hearts are all made of the same stuff, and Feihong's was a particularly warm one. As soon as she had put out of her mind her previous resentment, she began to show much care for her young mistress' welfare. She was especially concerned when she heard that Shen Chun's feelings for Jiaoniang had apparently changed, and had sent Xiaohui and some other maid servants to spy on the young man. That was when she had found out about the ghost. She had straightaway formed a plan to trick Shen Chun into telling the truth of the matter to Jiaoniang face to face. At the same time, she had gone to her old mistress, and said, "Madame, something eerie is happening in our mansion."

The old lady, who had long lost interest in such affairs, and was spending her time in meditation and reciting the scriptures, asked, indiffer-

事尽心尽力，将府中料理得井井有条。更对王文瑞殷勤备至，小心侍候，且不时有意无意地飞眼传情，语涉狎私。王文瑞见飞红青春美貌，情窦已开，心里也颇中意，只是不好意思向赵夫人开口。赵夫人却将一切都看在眼里，知道自己不久于人世，老爷身边终究要个人照料，于是主动劝王文瑞将飞红收房。王文瑞假意推辞了几句，便点头默许。于是由赵夫人做主，王文瑞纳飞红为妾，正应了那句"满树梨花压海棠"的老话。从此，府中上下皆称飞红为"红娘子"。飞红有了名份，便收起了往日怨恨夫人、嫉妒小姐的心思，与娇娘相处甚好，府中之事也更加尽力。此次申纯重来，飞红虽然不免有些拈酸，可转念想到自己已经是老爷的人了，断不可得陇望蜀、红杏出墙，于是也就撒手放开。加之娇娘极力奉迎，频频致送绫罗珠宝，当面见了更是礼敬有加。

人心都是肉长的，飞红又是个热心人，竟然一变以前从中作梗的态度，反而为娇娘张罗起来。等到娇娘将申纯变心之事对飞红讲了，飞红不禁为娇娘不平，于是令小慧等人夜入东园察探，这才知晓申纯为鬼所惑。遂设计让小慧将申纯骗出东园，由娇娘当面向申纯挑明真相。自己则找了个机会对赵大人道："夫人，如今咱们府中出了件怪事。"

赵夫人早已不再过问府中之事，只是一心养病

ently, "What do you mean?"

Feihong leaned forward, and whispered in her ear: "Master Shen has been bewitched by a ghost!"

When the old lady gave a start, Feihong continued, "A ghostly woman appears every night in his study in the eastern courtyard."

"Oh, Feihong, don't talk nonsense," the old lady chided the serving maid. "I know you are only trying to cheer me up with some silly story." But her wide-eyed expression belied her nonchalance.

"Oh no, madame," Feihong protested, "I would never dare to be so impertinent

Half-doubting, the old lady asked, "Who has seen this 'ghostly woman'?"

"Old Zhao the gardener was the first person to see her," Feihong replied. "The maid servants didn't believe him, so last night they went to see for themselves. Sure enough, they saw a ghost in the form of a woman enter the young master's residence."

The old lady frowned. "The maid servants have no business snooping round the quarters of a young scholar," she sniffed. "It's most improper. You should keep a tighter rein on them."

Feihong laughed. "It's hard to rein in curiosity," she said. "Anyway, Madame, try not to be angry; it's bad for your health. Besides, you know, we really can't just stand idly by if the young master is in trouble. He is your nephew, after all. If anything bad were to happen to him in our house, how would you be able to face his parents?"

The old lady saw the point of this. In addition, she realized that if a ghost was wandering around the mansion something had to be done about it quickly. She nodded in assent. "Yes," she said. "We can't let this sort of thing go on. It will cause all kinds of trouble. Take me there tonight to see for myself. Then I'll decide what to do about it."

"Quite right, Madame," Feihong agreed. "Seeing is believing."

So at midnight, Feihong escorted old mistress to the eastern courtyard.

诵经,听飞红这么一说,淡淡问道:"可有什么怪事?"

飞红悄声趴在夫人耳边说道:"申官人被鬼迷住了。"

赵夫人闻言一惊。飞红接着说:"东园申官人的书房中夜夜有个女鬼出没。"

"飞红,这话可不是乱讲的。你不是专为要老身开心,说个笑话吧?"赵夫人睁大眼睛问道。

"不是,不是。就是借我一个胆子,也不敢与夫人开这种玩笑呀。"

赵夫人半信半疑道:"你说三哥儿被女鬼迷住,是谁见来?"

"园丁老赵最先看见,昨晚丫环们不信,也去瞧看,亲眼见一个女鬼进了申官人的房间。"

赵夫人一皱眉道:"丫头们没事到园子中偷看年轻书生,成何体统?你也该严加管束才是。"

飞红笑道:"也是好奇心使然,夫人不必动气,小心伤了身子。不过,咱们总不能见死不救吧?好歹申官人也是老爷的嫡亲外甥,若是在咱们府上出了事,将来也不好向姑老爷、姑奶奶交待不是?"

赵夫人一想也对,再说家中闹鬼,亦不可等闲视之。便点点头道:"这种事切不可乱嚷出去,今夜你陪我亲自去看看,再做定夺。"

"夫人言之有理,耳听是虚,眼见为实。"

等到二更过后,飞红就将丫头们支开,扶着赵夫

As they reached the door of Shen Chun's quarters, they heard from inside the voices of a man and a woman. Feihong hurried forward, and put her eye to a crack in the door. She saw someone who looked like Jiaoniang in the middle of the room grabbing and tearing at Shen Chun. Fetching her old mistress, she burst open the door and stepped inside.

The old lady's dim eyesight was sufficient only to make out a woman and Shen Chun tangled together. But as she peered intently at them, the woman vanished. "Who was that woman?" she demanded of Shen Chun.

The young man was panic-stricken to see his aunt standing there, and all he could do was gabble, "Nobody, nobody."

The old lady looked around carefully. Then she said, "I clearly saw a woman in here just now. Tell me the truth: Where did you sneak that woman in here from?"

Feihong, fearing that the foolish young scholar might say that it was Jiaoniang, chimed in with "There was definitely a woman here, but how is it that she suddenly vanished?"

Shen Chun looked around, and saw that the ghost certainly had disappeared. Terror gripped him as he thought, "Then it must have been a ghost, after all! How could a living woman have vanished in the twinkling of an eye like that?" He broke out in a cold sweat, and trembled from head to toe. "I ... I ... can't deceive you, Aunt," he stuttered. "There was a woman here, but how can she have simply disappeared, unless she was a fairy come down to earth and returned to Heaven as soon as she saw people?"

At this point, Feihong yelled at him: "Master Shen! Don't you understand? You have been haunted by a ghost!"

The flabbergasted Shen Chun collapsed onto the floor, mumbling in disbelief: "A ghost ... a ghost ... I've been haunted by a ghost."

Feihong quickly helped him onto a chair. "That's right," she said. "Clearly some flower fairy or tree sprite assumed human form and bewitched you. It almost took your life away. We have all been so afraid for

人来到东园。尚未到西轩门前,已听得里面有男女说话之声。飞红急趋上前,从门缝里一张,见一个娇娘模样的女子正在满室里追逐撕扯申纯,急忙回身扶着赵夫人破门而入。

赵夫人老眼昏花,隐隐约约看见有个女子与申纯缠在一起。定神再瞧时,那女子已是无影无踪。便向申纯逼问道:"适才是谁家女子在此?"

申纯见赵夫人亲自前来,心里发虚,慌慌张张地连声道:"没人,没人。"

赵夫人四下里瞧瞧,又道:"老身适才明明看到有个女子在房中,你老实说,那女子是你从何处拐来的?"

飞红站在一旁,怕申纯这个书呆子受逼不过,说出"娇娘"来,忙插言道:"刚才分明有一个女子,怎么一转眼便不见了?"

申纯这才明白过来,四下观望,果真那女子不见了踪影。心中一惊,想道:"那女子若是个活人,哪能眨眼没了踪影?"当下浑身乱颤,冷汗淋漓,战战兢兢道:"不……不敢欺瞒舅母,适才是……是有一女子在此,怎么……怎么就不见了呢?敢……敢是天女下凡,见人来了,忽然返归天上了?"

飞红大声道:"申官人,你撞着鬼了,还不明白么?"

申纯闻言跌坐在地,喃喃道:"鬼……鬼……我撞着鬼了!"

you!"

The old lady looked at her nephew in horror. "Was what we all saw just now a ghost?" she cried.

This drew a shriek from Shen Chun: "Oh no! I've been haunted by a ghost!" And he collapsed once more on the floor, with a thud, this time on his knees. Facing the old lady and knocking his forehead vigorously on the floor, he wailed, "Oh Aunt, save me! Save me! I am so afraid."

Seeing her nephew in such distress, the old lady tried to comfort him.

Feihong then said, "This eastern courtyard has long been known as a murky and lonely place. It's not surprising that ghosts have come to live here, and come out at night to harm people. Perhaps the young master should move into the main building, and then tomorrow we can arrange for an exorcist to clear all the evil spirits away. After that, he can move back again."

Her old mistress agreed to allow Shen Chun to move into the main building for a few days, until her husband returned and an exorcist could be summoned to rid the eastern courtyard of its baleful influences. She told Feihong to help the young man move out that very night.

It was with a somewhat easier mind that Shen Chun followed his aunt and Feihong to the main building. But that same night, he developed a fever and became delirious. One minute his face was radiant and charming, like a pretty girl's, and the next he was groaning and screaming, foaming at the mouth and twitching. It took several strong servants to hold him down. As a result, everybody soon got to know that the eastern courtyard was haunted, and that Master Shen had been possessed by a demon. The old lady and everyone else were scared out of their wits.

When Wang Wenrui returned, Feihong reported to him what had happened. At first, the old master was scornful of what he considered to be an old wives' tale or a story the superstitious servants had upset themselves with. If the young man is ill, then cure him, he insisted. What call was there for all this claptrap about ghosts? He sent Wang Zhong to summon a

飞红忙将他扶到椅子上坐定，又道："定是花魅树妖，照着人的模样变化，把你迷得魂飞魄丧，眼看就要了你的小命，我都为你后怕呢。"

赵夫人怔怔地看着申纯道："莫不是我们都见鬼了？"

申纯惊叫道："不好了！我让女鬼迷住了！"说着"扑通"跪在地上，对着赵夫人一个劲儿地磕头，嚷道："舅母救我！舅母救我！我好怕呀！"

赵夫人见申纯吓成了这副模样，连声安慰道："三哥儿莫怕，三哥儿莫怕。"

飞红道："这东园幽僻无人，难免有些孤魂野鬼寄居其中，乘夜出来害人。申官人且先搬出园子，待明日请个师婆，将园中的邪祟驱除，方可再搬回来。"

赵夫人点点头道："三哥儿可移入中堂暂住几日，待你舅舅回来请个师婆为你驱鬼安魂。"回过头来又吩咐飞红帮着申纯收拾一下，搬出这园子。

申纯至此心神稍安，随着赵夫人与飞红搬出东园，安顿在内院。谁知当夜申纯就满嘴胡言乱语，发起烧来，一会儿眉飞色舞媚声媚气做女儿之态，一会儿叩齿登登尖声呼救，一会儿口吐白沫抽搐不止。几个壮年家仆都按不住他，把个赵夫人吓得不知如何是好。阖府上下人心惶惶，皆知东园里闹鬼，申三官人被鬼缠住了。

王文瑞回来后听飞红禀报一番，起初还认为不

doctor. But the doctor's ministrations only made Shen Chun worse. Worried, Wang Wenrui sent for the most eminent physicians in the district, but all to no avail. His wife and Feihong pestered him to allow them to bring in an exorcist, and in the end he reluctantly agreed, as all else had failed thus far. So a woman called Yao, who was renowned far and wide for her powers in this respect, was sent for. Yao spent a whole day burning incense and talismans, and prancing about. This seemed to do some good, for the young man sank into a restful sleep, much to the relief of the whole Wang household. At night, however, Shen Chun was seized by another fit. In a panic, his aunt sent for Yao the exorcist again. The exorcist went through her routine once more, but this time it wasn't even as effective as the previous time, and Yao went away, shaking her head, having advised the old lady to find an exorcist with greater powers than hers, otherwise the young man's life would be in danger.

Jiaoniang was devastated at seeing Shen Chun's illness getting worse by the day, but she could do nothing but keep her tears to herself. Secretly she begged Feihong to think of a way to save him. The maid servant thought it over, and then suggested to her old mistress that she should put up notices all over the city, offering a rich reward to anyone who could drive out the demon that was possessing Shen Chun. The old lady agreed, and before long the whole of the city of Lizhou knew that the nephew of Wan Wenrui was possessed by a demon.

On day, a barefoot Taoist priest with unkempt hair turned up at the gate of the Wang mansion. His appearance was repulsive, but at his waist he wore a precious sword, and on his back he carried a large bronze mirror. He told the gatekeeper that he was adept at expelling evil spirits and averting disasters, so as soon as this was reported to her, the old lady ordered that he be admitted and refreshments laid before him. The Taoist did not even look at the dainties prepared for him, but strode straight into the inner courtyard, and thence to Shen Chun's sickbed. He said to the young man: "An evil influence has been dogging you, and now you are in the

过是妇人之见，庸人自扰，有病治病，哪里有什么鬼怪？于是派王忠去请郎中，诊脉开方抓药，不料几副药灌下去，申纯愈发闹得凶了。王文瑞这才着了急，将当地几个有名气的医生都请了来，仍然没有一丁点儿效验。赵夫人和飞红力主请师婆来驱鬼，王文瑞心中不信，可又束手无策，只得听任她们胡闹。于是赵夫人做主，请了一个十里八乡有名的姚师婆来府中，烧香焚符，折腾了一天，申纯这才昏昏睡去。大家才松了一口气，入夜以后，申纯如前颠狂起来。赵夫人急命将姚师婆请回，那师婆重又施为一番，依旧无效。只得摇头说是自己法力不够，要赵夫人另请高明，否则申纯小命不保。说罢出府回家去了。

娇娘看着申纯的病一日重似一日，不禁心急如焚，又不敢在别人面前掉泪，只得暗中饮泣，只求飞红设法。飞红转过来求赵夫人在城中贴出招贴，许下重赏，延请四方高人来府驱鬼。赵夫人只得允了，一时间王家外甥为女鬼所迷的消息传遍了利州城。

这一日，府门前来了一个披发跣足的道士，其貌甚丑，腰间挎一柄宝剑，身后背着一面大铜镜，自言惯能降妖除鬼，为人消灾。门子急忙报了进来，赵夫人当下令人请进，设酒款待。那道士一摇三摆走了进来，也不吃酒，径直走进内院，来到申纯病榻前道："此生孽缘深重，被一女鬼缠身，然命不该绝，合当本

clutches of a female ghost. But your life is not yet lost. You are fated to be saved by my art of the Taoism. "

So saying, he took the gleaming mirror from his back, and held it facing Shen Chun. From the mirror there flashed multi-colored rays of light, which enveloped the young man. The onlookers saw in the mirror an image of a woman dressed in red bending over Shen Chun. A look of horror sprang to every face, and a urge to flee blindly away from the sight arose in every breast. Then the Taoist cried, "Aha! You calamitous goblin in woman's form, how dare you get up to your tricks in the presence of this Taoist master?"

The bystanders saw the woman in the mirror straighten up gracefully, and sink to her knees. They marveled at what a beauty she was. The Taoist bellowed, "Whence came you, you wicked phantom? Tell me the truth at once!"

The woman's eyes brimmed with tears, as she cried, "I will gladly tell you everything. But please show mercy. Forgive me just one time. "

"Confess!" ordered the Taoist.

The woman then told the following piteous tale: "My name was Lai. From an early age I was a diligent student, and learned something of ceremony and propriety. I lost my parents when I was only ten years old. When I was 16, I was married to the son of the local prefect. I was perfectly prepared to devote my life to my husband, but unfortunately he turned out to be a good-for-nothing. He spent all day running around with a gang of young fops, gambling and whoring. I begged him to mend his ways, but all I received in return was blows and kicks. My life was so full of grief and torment that in less than a year I fell ill and died. Knowing that I had no relatives, my husband didn't even bother to give me a decent funeral, but told his servants to bury me by the Emerald Bamboo Pavilion in the eastern courtyard. Before another two years had passed, my husband was transferred. And so, I was abandoned here, and became a restless ghost. Two months ago, I was wandering in the courtyard, as usual, when

道救你一命。"

说着从背后取出那面色彩斑斓的铜镜，对着申纯一照。那铜镜刹时放出五彩毫光，将申纯罩定，众人便见镜中申纯身上伏着一个妖媚的红衣女子，面色惊惶，似欲逃走。只听得道士高声喝道："咄! 你这伤天害理的女中色鬼，在本道爷面前还想要花招么?"

众人从镜中见那女子轻飘飘地起身，袅袅婷婷跪在一侧，好一个蟑首蛾眉、滴粉搓酥的绝色佳人。道士对镜吼道："你是何方妖孽，还不速速从实招来?"

那女子秋水盈盈，珠泪滚落，泣道："妾身愿招，只求道长开恩，饶过这次。"

道士喝道："快招!"

那女子遂道："道长容禀。妾本名眯娘，自幼读书习字,颇知礼仪。十几岁上父母双亡,孤身度日。二八之年嫁与州官之子, 本以为终身有托,谁知夫婿无赖,成天价与一班纨绔子弟厮混,狂赌滥嫖,无所不为。妾几次三番苦口婆心相劝,反遭他老拳毒脚相加。妾因此郁郁不欢,日日以泪洗面。不到一年光景,便伤心成疾,含恨死去。公爹见妾家中无人,也不发丧,只命家人将妾埋在东园翠竹亭畔。不过两年,公爹调任离去,撇下妾身在此,竟成了野鬼孤魂。两个

I saw an elegant young scholar move in. He often used to come to the Emerald Bamboo Pavilion to recite and compose poetry, and to utter his thoughts out loud. I was entranced by his handsome features and his refined character, and so I set out to ensnare him. Assuming a certain appearance, I visited him, unbidden, one midnight. . . . "

When the ghost reached this point in her narrative, Feihong became suddenly alarmed that Jiaoniang's involvement in the drama might be revealed. She hurriedly whispered in Wang Wenrui's ear: "Sir, don't just stand here listening to her glib tongue. Get the Taoist to kill her quickly. It is urgent that Master Shen's life be saved!"

Wang Wenrui agreed. "Master Taoist," he said, "I think we have heard enough of this rigmarole. Be so good as to do what you have to do to drive the demon away and save this young man's life."

The Taoist nodded in assent. To the woman, he said, "Lecherous ghost, have you any other sins to confess? Seeing how you have behaved like a wicked fox sprite after death, it is clear that you were by no means a chaste woman when you were alive. Just as a married woman must observe the proprieties when alive, so she must after death also. But you, driven by lust, led a young man astray, even to the verge of taking his life. Ten thousand deaths would not expiate your crime!"

This awesome denunciation pierced the woman to the heart. She shed bitter tears as she begged the Taoist for mercy. "I admit that I gave in to temptation," she exclaimed, "and I know that ghosts and men should tread their separate paths. But I never intended the young man harm, and I certainly never wished to deprive him of his life."

"You wanton demon, how dare you continue with your quibbling?" cried the Taoist. "Have a taste of my sword!" And with that he made a sword sign with his left hand while drawing the precious sword from his waist with his right. He made one chop in the air with the sword, and the ghost fell down with a cry. Immediately, she turned into a skeleton, which then changed into a wisp of smoke. The smoke disappeared towards the

月前，妾正在园中游荡，就见一个风姿秀逸的书生住进园中，时常于翠竹亭上吟诗作词，自言自语。妾身见他年少多才，风流潇洒，遂将一缕情丝牢牢缚在他身上，幻化模样，夜半不请而至……"

飞红在一旁听那女鬼娓娓而言，生怕她扯出娇娘来，急忙在王文瑞耳边低语道：

"老爷不要听这女鬼胡言乱语，快让道士斩了她，救申官人要紧。"

王文瑞一听有理，便道："道长莫要听她鬼话连篇，请快快动手，驱鬼救人要紧。"

道士闻言点头，向那女鬼喝道："淫鬼还要为自家开脱罪名么？看你这狐媚子似的模样，料想生前也不是个安份的。你前世既为人妇，就当恪守妇道，便是作鬼也须守节。却为一点儿淫心驱使，迷惑少年，害人性命，万死不足蔽其辜！"

那女鬼见道士横眉立目，高声怒斥，不由心中伤悲，嘤嘤泣道："道爷开恩！道爷开恩！小女子实为一点儿色心所动，也是真心爱恋申生。虽说人鬼殊途，并不曾加害他性命，也不想害他性命。"

"淫鬼还敢狡辩？看剑！"那道士说着左手捏个剑诀，右手疾速从腰间抽出宝剑，当空往下一劈。女鬼应声倒地，化成一具骷髅，顷刻又散成数道轻烟，伴着一阵啾啾鬼哭向西去了。

west, accompanied by an eerie wail.

As the bystanders gaped and stared at these extraordinary goings-on, they suddenly heard a loud groan behind them: Shen Chun had woken up. Several of the servants rushed to support him, in the midst of sighs of relief all round. The Taoist priest put away his sword and mirror. Then he drew a talisman on a piece of paper, burned it and mixed the ashes with water. He directed the potion to be given to Shen Chun to drink. Soon after drinking it, the young man was able to sit up in bed, at the same time complaining that he was hungry. Wang Wenrui, marveling at the superb powers of the Taoist priest, ordered Wang Zhong to give him 20 taels of silver. The Taoist, however, smiled his refusal of the reward, and with a flick of his sleeves strode out of the hall. The others pursued him as far as the main gate, but when they got there the priest was nowhere to be seen. Thereupon, Wang Wenrui had the eastern courtyard sealed, and arranged for Shen Chun to convalesce in the main building.

The young man's health improved by the day after that, and in a matter of only ten days he was able to get out of bed and walk around. Because his new quarters were quite near to Jiaoniang's boudoir, the girl was able to sneak in and see her lover from time to time, without others knowing, and the two of them enjoyed intimacy even more than they had before.

The events of the previous weeks proved to be too much for the old mistress, however. Her illness grew worse, and before long she passed away. A pall of gloom descended on the mansion, and Jiaoniang, particularly, was devastated with grief. In this crisis, Shen Chun proved himself a tower of strength. He took care of the funeral arrangements and all the other matters that had to be attended to, as his uncle was now getting old and feeble. All the members of the family praised his diligence and devotion.

None of this escaped Feihong's sharp eyes. She decided to find an opportunity to bring about the marriage of the two young lovers. She started to casually bring up Shen Chun's good points in front of the old master when he was relaxed in the evening, and hint that Jiaoniang was now at an age

众人正在看得目瞪口呆，忽听身后申纯大声呻吟，苏醒过来。几名家人忙抢上前去扶起，众人都松了一口气。道士将剑镜收了，画了一道符，焚化之后将符灰用水调了，令人给申纯服下。不过一炷香的功夫，申纯坐起身来，只是一个劲儿地喊饿。王文瑞见这道士果真是高人，当下令王忠取二十两纹银酬谢。那道士笑而不接，一甩袍袖，大步流星出门去了。待众人追出府门，早已踪迹皆无。王文瑞当即令人将东园封了，申纯且在中堂西厢住着养病。

此后，申纯一日好似一日，不过十来天，便已能下床行走。因其所居内宅与娇娘绣楼相接，娇娘时常避人前来看望，二人欢爱更胜昔日。

而赵夫人经此一吓，身子愈加不好，没过多久，便撒手人寰。王宅一时愁云惨雾，人人悲泣。娇娘更是哀毁骨立，痛不欲生。申纯百般安慰照料，自不必说。王文瑞因年纪大了，精力不济，丧事都是申纯帮助料理，里里外外打点得滴水不漏，阖府上下无不夸奖。

飞红看在眼里，便一心想借机成全娇娘与申纯的婚事，时常在枕畔灯前有意无意地说起申纯的好处，又提起娇娘年纪已大，也该为她择偶婚配，最好是知根知底的人家，这才能叫人放心。王文瑞上次拒绝申家提婚，不过是想为女儿找一个官宦人家，如今

when a suitable husband should be sought for her. Somebody whose background and virtues were well known to the family would be the ideal son-in-law, she suggested. As a matter of fact, Wang Wenrui had begun to regret having turned Shen Chun's suit down. He had wanted his daughter to marry someone of official rank, and Shen Chun had not seemed like much of a prospect at the time. But now the young man had achieved official status, and had a brilliant career ahead of him. As a result, Feihong's blandishments found receptive ears. The two of them talked the matter over. Wang Wenrui was in favor of sending a go-between to his sister and brother-in-law of Chengdu to raise the question of marriage between his daughter and their son. But he knew that he had been stubborn the previous time, and was afraid that Shen Chun might refuse out of pique. He was also unsure of his sister and brother-in-law's reaction this time. Feihong was happy enough to see that the old man was in favor of the match, and took it upon herself to sound out Shen Chun. "Just leave it to me, sir," she chirped. "You can get the wedding streamers ready, while you're waiting for me to bring back good news."

The next evening, Feihong bounced into Shen Chun's apartment in the main building, with a radiant smile on her face. Finding the young man and Jiaoniang there matching verses, she said, "You two are pretty well caught up in highbrow pursuits, I see. But there's a piece of wonderful news for you!"

The sudden appearance of the maid servant, bubbling over with self-satisfied glee, mystified the two young lovers, who looked at each other, wondering what Feihong had got up her sleeve. Jiaoniang was the first to break the silence: "Where is this 'wonderful news' coming from?"

Feihong gave her a sly smile. "Your most ardent wish has come true," she said, "and I've come specially to congratulate you. Well, aren't you going to thank me?"

"What 'ardent wish'?" demanded Shen Chun.

Feihong pouted. "You know very well what I mean. You don't have

见申纯少年高第，前程不可限量，就有些后悔，现在听飞红的意思，无非是想与申家联姻。于是与飞红商议，欲遣媒人到成都向姑老爷提亲，可是自知先前理亏，又担心申纯要强，赌气回绝，姐姐与姐夫的意思也不知怎样。飞红听了好不欢喜，没口子地赞成，说老爷早该如此。并且一力承担，自告奋勇前去探听申纯的口风，道："此事包在妾身上，那申官人断无不允之理，老爷只须眼观旌节旗，耳听好消息。"

第二天晚上，飞红一脸喜气来到绣楼，见申纯正与娇娘灯下联诗，便道："二位雅兴不浅呀，可知喜从天降？"

飞红突兀而来，满口道喜，将娇娘与申纯弄得丈二和尚摸不着头脑，四目相对，不知飞红葫芦里卖的什么药？娇娘先开口问道："不知喜从何来？"

飞红扮了个鬼脸，笑道："你二人平生之愿成了，我特地前来相贺，还不快快谢我？"

申纯道："何愿成了？"

飞红嗔道："装糊涂，你二人有何心愿，还须问我？"

娇娘蓦地猜到，一时心跳加快，捂着胸口问道："莫非是……"

飞红见娇娘既惊且喜的样子，掩口失笑道："老爷有为你二人缔结百年之好的意思，命我前来探探

to ask me what your most heartfelt desire is. Don't pretend to be dull. "

In a flash, Jiaoniang guessed the truth. Her heart leaped within her. She covered her mouth, as if she were afraid to allow the portentous words to escape. "It must be...."

Seeing her young mistress transported by both delight and fright at the same time, Feihong hid a smile, as she explained, "Your father is willing to allow you to marry. He sent me to find out the opinion of Master Shen here. He is afraid that the young man may not agree. "

Again, Shen Chun and Jiaoniang gazed into each other's eyes. A hundred emotions jostled within them, and they said with one voice: "Heaven's goodness be praised!" Then, oblivious to the presence of Feihong, they threw themselves into each other's arms. Feihong blushed and snorted. "Shameless hussy!" she muttered, and sweeping the door curtain aside, flounced out. Shen Chun and Jiaoniang chased after her, apologizing for their thoughtlessness and thanking her profusely for the good news.

That night was a rapturous one for the two young lovers.

Feihong went straight to Wang Wenrui and reported that Shen Chun was fully prepared to marry Jiaoniang, and, moreover, the Shen family was unlikely to oppose the match. The old master was overjoyed at the prospect of such a son-in-law, and straightaway set about arranging for a go-between to call on Shen Qing and his wife. The latter agreed wholeheartedly with the plan, and said that an auspicious day should be chosen for the wedding as soon as Jiaoniang's period of mourning for her mother was over. Learning that his sister and brother-in-law bore no grudge for his previous rebuff of them, Wang Wenrui was greatly relieved. However, when he remembered that his beloved wife had not lived to see this happy day, he shed bitter tears.

申官人的口信,尚且担心官人不愿意呢!"

娇娘、申纯四目相对,百感交集,异口同声道:"苍天有眼,不违人愿!"竟不顾飞红在场,忘情地拥抱在一起。飞红见状不由心中发酸,脸儿发红,轻轻啐了一口道:"好个没羞的小姐!"说着掀帘出门去了。申纯与娇娘急忙追出,向飞红千恩万谢了一番。

这一夜,申纯与娇娘欢喜若狂,明灯燃烛,说个不停,天已大亮尚且意犹未尽。

再说飞红从娇娘处出来,便回复了王文瑞,说申纯点头应允,申家也断无拒婚之理。王文瑞听了甚感欣慰,想自家能找到这样的女婿,也算是家门之幸了。于是即刻托媒去申家议亲。申庆夫妇没想到兄弟会着人前来议亲,高高兴兴地一口应承,回复说早想高攀,断无不允之理,只待择吉日前来下聘礼定婚,等娇娘丧服一满,便为二人成亲。王文瑞见姐姐、姐夫不计前嫌,慨然相允,一颗悬着的心方才落地。转念想起赵夫人撒手西归,一对儿女成了无娘的孩子,如今只得自家又当爹又当妈为他们操劳,好不心酸,不禁老泪纵横。

娇红记

Chapter Nine
A Wedding Unites Two Eminent Families

Shen Chun was blissful beyond words at learning that his future happiness was now assured. Apart from helping his uncle with a few household matters, he spent the whole day now loitering by Jiaoniang's dressing table. He had long ago put out of his mind the idea of taking up an official post. It was fortunate for him that the court had a surfeit of officials, and so he refrained from asking for a post, nor did the court press him. While Wang Wenrui attended his office every day, Feihong took charge of the running of the mansion. She herself kept out of the way of the young lovers, and she gave strict instructions to the other servants not to mention their activities to the old master. Shen Chun and Jiaoniang already considered themselves newly-weds.

One day, Wang Wenrui took a break from his duties, and stayed at home to check on the progress his young son had made in his studies. Unexpectedly, Wang Zhong announced that two people had been sent by the regional military commander to call on him. Wang Wenrui was surprised. As a local civil official, he had seldom any dealings with such a powerful figure as the regional military commander. He was consequently not sure whether this visit boded well or ill. He ordered Wang Zhong to bring the pair into the main hall, while he hastily changed into his official robes. Wang Zhong escorted in two lavishly attired and rather haughty individuals, one tall, the other short. Wang Wenrui descended the steps of his dais to greet them with a deferential bow.

When the guests and the host were seated, a maid servant brought tea.

第九章　豪门逼婚

　　申纯见自己的终生大事已定，心中的快慰无可言表，除去帮着舅父料理些务务之外，整天里便泡在娇娘妆台之侧，早将做官赴任之事丢在脑后。当时朝廷人浮于事，官多缺少，申纯不去询问，官府乐得装聋作哑，也不来催他。王文瑞每天上衙门，府中都由飞红做主，不但不来管申纯与娇娘，反而严戒下人在老爷面前提起。申纯与娇娘身处温柔乡里，不是新婚，胜似新婚。

　　这一日，王文瑞告假在家，将儿子善父唤来书房，检点学业。忽然家院王忠来报，说现有西川节镇帅太尉府上门人前来求见。王文瑞听了心中一惊，暗想自己是地方文职官员，素来与权倾朝野的帅太尉不通往来。帅府今日来人，不知是吉是凶。忙令王忠将来人领入中堂，自己换了官服出来相迎。王忠出去不大功夫，便领着一高一矮两个人进来，穿戴华丽，神情倨傲。王文瑞降阶相迎，打拱道："二位相公，快快请进。下官有失远迎，尚祈恕罪。"

　　宾主坐定，丫环端上茶来。来人之中那个细高个

Then the tall one spoke up. "Sir, we are aides of the commander, and we have come today to bring you some news which we are sure you will regard as most felicitous."

Wang Wenrui was puzzled. "Really, gentlemen? Please be so kind as to explain," he said.

Clutching his teacup and choosing his words carefully, the same individual continued, "It has come to the attention of our master's son that you, sir, have a daughter who is both beautiful and talented. He has set his heart on marrying her. Now, I assure you, sir, that the young man would be a perfect match for your daughter; it would indeed be a marriage made in Heaven. So, you see, my colleague and I are playing the part of go-between for the commander and his son. Let me remind you, sir, that the commander is a man of the utmost influence and power, and immensely wealthy. Surely you agree that this offer is a tremendous stroke of good fortune for you and your family?" His last words were accompanied by a chuckle.

Wang Wenrui almost fell out of his chair when he heard this. The last thing he had expected when he sent his go-between to the Shens was that emissaries from the regional military commander would turn up on his doorstep the very next day, demanding his daughter's hand. What on earth was he to do. He forced himself to keep calm, fixed a smile on his face, and said, "Gentlemen, I'm afraid that there is something you do not know. This is a wonderful offer, I know. But, there is just one thing...."

The short man, who had not uttered a word since he had entered, suddenly glared at Wang Wenrui, and barked, "What is it? Speak up!"

Wang Wenrui wiped beads of sweat from his brow, and said, "The commander's family is an illustrious one, while my own is humble. There is too wide a gap in our stations. I could not dare to aspire to an alliance with such an exalted clan. I fear that this marriage that you propose would be most unsuitable."

The tall man smiled fawningly, and gushed, "Not at all, my dear sir.

道："兄弟二人是帅太尉府上的幕僚，今日专来给通判老兄报喜，为府上送一套天大的富贵。"

王文瑞道："不知有何喜事，乞道其详。"

那细高个端起茶碗，慢条斯理地说道："听说贵府有位女婵娟，才貌双全，名冠西川。我家少爷听了，顿生爱慕之情，立意非你家小姐不娶。我家少爷青春年少，与你家小姐真正是一双两美，实乃天作之合。今日我兄弟二人受太尉之命前来做冰人，专为我家少爷保媒。想那帅府权势通天，金银似海，王通判岂非喜从天降，富贵逼人？"说完打了一个哈哈。

王文瑞听了这番话，不啻于耳边炸响一个霹雳，险些从座位上跌下来。自己刚刚为女儿遣媒申家，不想今日又从半路上杀出个帅家，这可如何是好？定了定神，强颜欢笑道："二位相公有所不知，这门亲事虽好，只是有一件……"

那矮壮身材的自进府来，一言不发，此时忽然一瞪牛眼，道："有什么？快说！"

王文瑞拭了拭额头上的汗珠，道："太尉府甲第连云，下官则寒门蓬户，两下里声望悬殊，名位不称，下官不敢妄自攀高结贵，这婚事恐怕不太周全吧？"

那细高个谄笑道："这有何妨！我家太尉虽是将相蝉联，通判老爷亦是黄堂参佐，也算是门当户对了。"

王文瑞干笑两声道："无奈小女庸材陋质，实与

Although it is true that my master's family has produced generations of generals and prime ministers, your own family has had connections with the imperial court, has it not? It would be a perfectly fitting match, I assure you."

Wang Wenrui laughed hollowly. "Oh, my daughter certainly does not have the qualities required to be the consort of master's son, I'm afraid. I beg you gentlemen to go back and make my excuses to the commander in diplomatic terms, so as not to offend his feelings."

The short aide shook his head. "That won't do," he said. "The marriage must go ahead. Our young master has already prepared gold, jade, silks and jewels as the betrothal presents. They will be delivered here soon."

Wang Wenrui found himself driven into a corner. He had wanted to reveal to his unwelcome guests that his daughter's marriage was already decided upon, but, fearing the power of the commander, he dared not. So he remained silent.

The tall man spoke again. "Sir, don't you realize that all the young ladies of the best families in Chengdu and its ten surrounding prefectures would like nothing better than a chance for such a dazzling rise in the world? How can you possibly refuse?"

Wang Wenrui protested, feebly and unhappily: "It is just that my family is far too lowly to even dare to raise its eyes to such a lofty height, that is all."

The short man's face darkened with impatience. "Enough of your hypocritical jabbering!" he snarled. "Tell us right now: Yes or no!"

When Wang Wenrui, hesitated, sweating in his agony, the other crashed his fist down on the tea table, sending the cups crashing to the floor and causing a cold shiver of fear to shoot through his reluctant host. Frowning and glaring, the short bully continued, "Don't you know how powerful my master is? He could pluck the stars from the sky if he so wanted. Do you think he's going to let a poltroon like you stand in his way once he has

帅府难谐仙眷,还望二位相公回去婉言几句,劝帅府少爷打消此意。"

那矮壮身材的一摇头道:"这婚事怎能辞得?我家少爷已备下黄金千镒,白璧十双,彩缎百匹,珍珠二斛,近日就要下聘来了。"

王文瑞被逼不过,本想说出女儿已经许配人家了,可又惮于太尉府的威势不敢明言,一时张口结舌,半天说不出一句话来。

那细高个的接过话头道:"通判老爷有所不知,这成都十郡之内,多少王公贵戚的千金小姐,想高攀这门亲事尚且不能,你怎么倒推辞起来?"

王文瑞道:"只是寒门微贱,不敢高攀,别无他意。"

那矮壮身材的一脸不耐烦地说道:"你不要推三阻四、酸文假醋的,干干脆脆一句话,你是愿意不愿意?答应不答应?"

王文瑞拭汗道:"这……"

那矮壮身材的见王文瑞搪塞支吾,不肯明言,心中一股无名火冒将上来,一只大手狠狠地往茶几上一拍,茶碗应声落地,"叭"的一声摔了个粉碎,把王文瑞吓得打了个寒噤。只见他拧眉立目道:"你岂不知我家老爷的威势? 就是要天上的星星,也能摘下来。如今帅府要与你做亲,不容你小老儿不肯!"

made up his mind to forge a marriage alliance with your house?"

The terrified Wang Wenrui protested, with a tremor in his voice: "But there are lots of other families far grander than mine. Why does your master wish to marry his son to the worthless daughter of a poor family?"

The tall aide shot a glance at his companion. Then he rose from his chair, and approached Wang Wenrui. With an ingratiating smile, he explained, "Of course, there is no shortage of noble households eager for a marriage alliance with such a powerful man as the commander. But his son is bent on marrying a virtuous maiden no matter what her station in life. Now sir, as you are a man who has pursued an official career, I am sure you must be well acquainted with the significance of the word 'power.' If you consent to the betrothal of your daughter to the commander's son, the way to unrivalled riches and honors will be opened up to you."

Wang Wenrui felt as though his head were boiling. For a long time, he groped for something to say, and eventually stammered, "I ... I ... have no desire for such things."

At this, the short fellow lost his temper, and roared, "Do you think the commander can't handle a miserable local bureaucrat like you? My master enjoys the special favor of the emperor himself. So much so that he is allowed to inflict punishment first, and report afterwards! Not only that, the imperial court is filled with his relatives. If you know what's good for you, you'll refrain from annoying the commander. Otherwise, I warn you, you'll come to a sticky end! It's up to you. But if you don't make the right decision today, there will be no use regretting it later."

Wang Wenrui was well aware of the commander's reputation for ruthlessness. But if he agreed to this demand and went back on his word, how could he face his sister's family? He reflected that, as the betrothal had not yet be finalized, he would not be exactly breaking his promise. And anyway, even if it had, he could not be blamed for giving into pressure from such an overwhelmingly mighty source. Who in the western regions did not fear the commander? Besides, he certainly wouldn't be disgracing his an-

王文瑞惊魂未定，颤声道："此间豪门大户尽多，岂必寒舍丑女？"

那细高个冲矮壮身材的使了个眼色，和颜悦色地起身踱到王文瑞面前，道："若论我家老爷的威名权势，不怕没有豪门前来求亲。只是俺那少爷只求淑女，不论门第，通判老爷是仕途中人，怎不晓得'势利'二字？令爱许了我家少爷，王老爷也有了一个大大的靠山，今后的荣华富贵，又岂是他人可比？"

王文瑞脑子里似开了锅一般，半天理不出个思路，过了一会儿，面呈难色，嗫嚅道："下官倒不……不羡荣华。"

那矮壮身材的见王文瑞这一副不知好歹的模样，心中好生恼火，忍不住大声吼道："你道太尉是武将，奈何不得你这地方官么？我告诉你，太尉现有皇上恩赐的势剑铜铡，凡事先斩后奏。何况帅府上兄弟亲戚遍布朝廷，果若你不识趣，惹翻了太尉，我看你这芝麻小官是当到头了。其中利害任你挑，只怕你今日不许，以后翻悔也来不及了。"

王文瑞又何曾不知道帅太尉的厉害，只是觉得自己如果答应帅府求婚，出尔反尔，对不起姐姐一家。转念一想，好在申家还未下聘，也不能算是反悔；退一步说，即便是下了聘，帅府如此威逼，自家官低位卑，又焉敢不从？这西川一省之中，谁人不畏太尉

cestors if he married his daughter off to such an eligible young man as the commander's son, would he? He thought of the old saying: 'Necessity stifles consciences,' Surely, his sister and brother-in-law would understand that a minor official like himself could not defy the will of somebody as all-powerful as the commander, wouldn't they? Finally, with an aching heart, and wiping the cold sweat from his brow, Wang Wenrui said, "Very well, gentlemen, please give my compliments to the commander. Since he has deigned to take notice of my lowly family, I cannot but submit to his wishes. However, I am dismayed at the thought of my farmyard chicken presuming to lodge in the nest of a phoenix."

The two aides exchanged triumphant smiles, and the tall one said, "We will convey your gracious acceptance to the commander. Then an auspicious day will be chosen for the betrothal formalities."

"I would trouble you, gentlemen, to speak favorably of me to your master," said Wang Wenrui, who ordered that refreshments be brought for the two lackeys.

That evening, Feihong broke the somber news to her young mistress. Jiaoniang's response was a piteous shriek, before collapsing on the floor in a faint. Feihong and the other maid servants flocked around, and administered warm water. Eventually, Jiaoniang came round. She was so distressed that she wished to die. She couldn't believe that her father could cave in to pressure from a powerful person, thwarting her affections and ruining her prospect of marriage to her beloved Shen Chun. Fortunately, Feihong was there to utter soothing words and calm her down.

Late that night, Jiaoniang crept into the young man's room. Shen Chun was lying asleep on the bed, fully clothed. The only light was that from a guttering candle. With tears in her eyes, Jiaoniang gently shook him awake.

In his dreams, Shen Chun heard a gentle voice calling him. Opening his eyes, he was delighted to see Jiaoniang seated at his bedside. He reached out and clasped her to him, murmuring, "My own wife, you have

十分？想那帅少爷豪门公子，年少风流，女儿许了这样的人家，也算是不辱没祖宗了。古人言：良心丧于困厄。我一个小小的通判，怎能抗得过势焰熏天的帅府？姐姐姐夫将来得知，想必亦能谅解。想到此处，抬手拭去额上的冷汗，狠狠心道："既然如此，二位相公请拜上太尉，帅府既然屈就寒门，下官怎敢不奉承仰扳？只是家鸡雏燕，妄居鸾凤之巢，下官着实惶恐万状。"

那二人相视一笑，细高个的开口道："既承台诺，我们兄弟且回府禀告太尉和少爷，择日来下聘就是。"

王文瑞道："如此有劳二位相公了。此事无论成与不成，都要请二位在帅爷面前为下官美言几句。"随即吩咐家人整备酒宴款待二帮闲。

到了晚上，飞红便到绣阁将此事悄悄告诉娇娘。娇娘闻听，悲号一声，当场昏死过去。飞红与小慧等人急忙掐人中，灌热汤，乱成一团。半晌，娇娘悠悠醒来，悲恸欲绝。她万万没有想到亲生的爹爹会迫于权势，不顾自己的情感，将申家的婚约撕毁。幸亏飞红在一旁好言相劝，娇娘这才勉强止住悲声。

夜半时分，娇娘悄悄来到申纯房中，只见烛光摇曳，忽明忽暗，申纯合衣而睡。娇娘含泪轻推申纯道："申郎，申郎。"

申纯在睡梦中听得有人轻声呼唤，睁眼一看，只见娇娘坐在床边。心中狂喜，一把将娇娘搂入怀中，

come to see me so late at night!"

"My dear, I was your wife yesterday," the girl said, "but today I am no longer your wife...."

Shen Chun sat up in bed with a start. In the dim light of the candle flame, he noticed that Jiaoniang's cheeks were tear-stained. Alarmed, he asked, "My dear, what do you mean?"

"Our engagement has been broken off," Jiaoniang said in a low voice.

"How can that be possible?" cried Shen Chun. "Your father has agreed to our marriage, and just dispatched a go-between to my family. An acceptance could come from my father at any time. What has gone wrong?"

"I am afraid it is all too true," Jiaoniang replied, with tearful sobs. "Today, the military commander of the western region sent people to ask for my hand for his son. They put pressure on my father, and ... he agreed to betroth me to the commander's son."

"But he can't do that!" Shen Chun gave a heart-rending cry.

Fearing that the young man's fury might result in him harming himself, Jiaoniang tried to calm him down, first drying her own tears. "I know that my father has gone back on his word," she said, "but you mustn't blame him."

"Not blame him?" howled Shen Chun. "Then who is to blame?"

Jiaoniang sighed, "It is not that my father is faithless and inconstant. If you must harbor resentment against anything, then harbor it against our cruel fate. Perhaps it is Heaven itself that has turned its face against us, and is adamant that we should not become husband and wife."

Tears welled up in Shen Chun's eyes, and he raved, "Our fate must be a miserable one indeed! Since ancient times, how many young lovers have been united in eternal bliss? But we, despite all the trials and tribulations we have undergone, are destined for nothing but emptiness!"

Jiaoniang embraced him, and said, "If our heartfelt desire cannot come true in life, maybe it will come true after death. Do you remember the oath we swore to the Great King of Brightness, to be forever constant to one an-

道："原来是我的妻啊，难为你半夜里来看夫君。"

娇娘道："申郎，你还不知道，妾昨日做得你的妻，今日则做不得你的妻了……"

申纯听话头不对，急忙翻身坐起，烛光下见娇娘珠泪盈盈，惊问："娘子，此话从何说起？"

娇娘哽咽道："你我的婚约破了。"

"这怎么可能？你爹才遣媒人去我家，许下你我结成两姓姻亲，我家不日就要下聘，怎么又会生出变故？"

"千真万确，今日帅太尉派人前来为其子求婚，我爹爹迫于权势，已将妾身……许与他家了。"娇娘说着泪落如绳，泣不成声。

申纯大惊失色，厉声喊叫道："不会的，不会的……"

娇娘见申纯气促喘急，怕他气大伤身，自家先止住哭声，劝道："虽说是俺爹变卦，你也休埋怨他。"

申纯喊道："不怨他，让我怨谁？"

娇娘叹道："不是我爹爹负心没个始终，要怨，就怨你我命薄运穷吧。也许是老天注定咱俩今世无缘，成不了夫妻。"

申纯两眼蓄泪，痴呆呆说道："想来还是小生缘悭命蹇，不然古来多少才子佳人，都能成就百年之好，偏偏我和你受了千般磨折，万般苦难，到头来仍是一场空！"

娇娘搂住申纯道："生愿不谐，死愿却在。郎君，

other?"

In his desolation, the young man answered bitterly: "Sorrow and joy, partings and meetings — all are decided by Heaven. Now that the commander has sought you for his daughter-in-law, I expect it will not be long before that is what you become. It is best that I bid you farewell now; our relationship has now reached its end. The commander wields influence which reaches up to the skies. He has mountains of gold and oceans of silver. If you marry into his family, you will live in the lap of luxury. From now on, you are another man's wife, and must devote yourself to him. . . ."

Long before he had finished, Jiaoniang had turned pale, and was gasping with fury. Pointing an accusing finger at Shen Chun, she screamed, "A fine man you are! Have you no human feelings? After we have been one flesh for so long, how can you stand idly by and watch me taken as someone else's wife? How can you be so blind as to take me for a woman who hankers after fortune and rank. I refuse to be humiliated. Since I am pledged to you, I am yours for ever more. And even after death, I will become a ghost that haunts your house." With that, she covered her face with her hands, and abandoned herself to a storm of weeping.

Moved by this show of distress, Shen Chun clasped Jiaoniang tightly to him, and whispered, "My dear, listen to me. What I said just now did not express my true feelings. It is just that there is no way out. Since your father has consented to your betrothal to the commander's son, I can't just stay here waiting for you to be married off to him, can I? But at the same time, I cannot bear to leave you."

Jiaoniang stopped sobbing, and said, "My dear, since your feelings for me remain unchanged, I know that you will think of a way to rescue our love. I am certain that the day of our union is fated to come."

Shen Chun thought to himself, with a great deal of anguish: "Oh, my dearest darling, how can you and I stand up to the might of the commander? What can I possible do to save our love?" But, in order not to upset Jiaoniang further, he said consolingly: "My dear, just leave everything to

你可记得明灵大王前你我海誓山盟,生死相从?"

申纯此时万念俱灰,冷冷道:"悲欢离合,皆天所定。帅府既来求婚,料想迎亲也就不远了,小生自当告别。你我今生缘份,至此而尽。那帅府权势熏天,金山银海,你既嫁入帅家,自然有泼天价的富贵任你享受。今后你既为人妇,当勉事新君……"

不待申纯说完,娇娘已气得脸白气噎,手指申纯道:"好一个大丈夫,堂堂六尺之躯,怎么这般没血性!我和你早有夫妻之实,你怎能等闲看着我嫁给别人,做得全无始终?你何其忍心!你将我娇娘看成贪图富贵之辈,真是瞎了眼睛。妾身不可再辱,既已许君,则终身为君之妻;纵然身死黄泉,也是君家之鬼。"说罢掩面痛哭。

申纯见娇娘对自己矢志不渝,甘愿生死相从,动情地将她紧紧搂在怀中道:"娘子你听我说,我适才所言,不是出自本心,实在是没有法子。你爹爹已将你许婚帅家,我总不能在这里等着为你送嫁吧?若说我告别回家,又怎么舍得下你?如今我是走也不是,留也不是,好生作难呀。"

娇娘止住悲声道:"郎君既然不忘情于我,还望早早为我打算,成就你我的姻缘。"

申纯心中暗暗叫苦道:"我痴情的娘子呀,以你我之力,焉能拗得过独霸西川的帅太尉!我又如何打

me. We can discuss this later. "

The girl nodded, stoically, and urged him: "Please do not distress yourself too much, my dear; the worst that can happen is that we may die, but we can only die once. "

These words did nothing to relieve Shen Chun's despair. Just then, they heard the fourth watch sounded from the drum tower, and Shen Chun had the sad duty of sending his beloved away for what, for all he knew, was the last time.

The dreadful news he had lately received had turned the young man's innards to water, and now that he had parted from Jiaoniang — forever? — he found himself too agitated to sit or stand still. He was still pacing restlessly when dawn broke, and a servant came to inform him that a messenger from home had come post-haste and wished to see him on an urgent matter. Shen Chun had the messenger brought into his study straightaway. The man informed him that his father had fallen ill from constantly worrying about him during all the months he had been absent from home, and had sent him to urge Shen Chun to return home. "I beg that you will start without delay, sir, " the messenger concluded.

Alarmed and burning to rush to his father's sickbed, Shen Chun proceeded directly to the main hall, to take his leave of his uncle. When he explained what had happened, the latter said, "Heaven will have compassion on a good man like my brother-in-law. I am sure that your presence, my boy, will be as good as a tonic for him. There is nothing like the joy of a family reunion to heal a sickness. " He hesitated for a while, then continued, "There is one other matter. Yesterday ... er, yesterday. . . . " Wang Wenrui wanted to explain how he had been forced to promise Jiaoniang to the commander's son, but he could not help feeling that he had betrayed the Shen family most shamefully, and he found himself unable to come up with the right words.

Shen Chun fixed his sardonic gaze on the old man. He knew what was in his mind. He made a mock-elaborate bow, and said, "Please speak

算?"可又不忍再让娇娘伤心,只好暂且宽慰道:"娘子,你且容我好好想想,从长计议。"

娇娘神情坚毅,点点头道:"郎君也不必太过焦虑,大不了不就是一死吗?"

申纯闻言一怔,忽听谯楼四鼓,只得先将哀哀切切的娇娘送出房门。

且说申纯乍闻大变,五内如沸,送走娇娘后,独自一人坐立不安,彷徨无计。眼见着天光大亮,门子忽然来报,说是申家小厮飞马来到,说有急事要见申官人。申纯急命将其领至书房,那小厮一见申纯便道:"官人一走便是数月,老员外在家甚是想念,如今患病卧床,特差小的来接官人回去,请官人即刻启程。"

申纯闻听父亲染病,心中十分着急,恨不得胁生双翅,赶回家中,当下到中堂向舅父辞行。王文瑞见申纯突然前来辞行,忙问道:"贤甥何事匆匆,即刻便要启程?"

申纯道:"家父有恙,令人来召,只得告辞。"

王文瑞道:"姐夫吉人天相,定占勿药。贤甥回去后,父子相见,得叙天伦之乐,想来病也好得快些。另有一事,昨日……昨日……"王文瑞欲待将许婚帅府一事告知申纯,可虽说是逼于帅府权势,毕竟对申家于心有愧,不免甚难措辞。

申纯冷眼旁观,心知王文瑞必是要谈及许婚帅

out directly, Uncle. I am all ears."

Blushing slightly and sighing, Wang Wenrui said, "In the ordinary course of events, having sent a go-between to your family in Chengdu, I should now await a favorable reply from my brother-in-law and my sister, so that the betrothal formalities can be set in train. But, unexpectedly, yesterday the commander of the western region sent to demand Jiaoniang's hand for his son. I protested vigorously, but his emissaries browbeat me into submission. In two or three days' time, he will send the betrothal presents here. My boy, I beseech you to convey my anguish at this calamity to your dear parents, and apologize for me. Fortunately, the engagement process between our two families has not yet started. In addition, you yourself are in the prime of youth, and very talented. So, you will not be without a beautiful wife for long. I am getting old and losing my strength, and have no one by me whom I can lean on. In a couple of months, Jiaoniang will be leaving home, and everything here will be in total confusion. As cousins, you and she are very fond of each other. When your father has made a complete recovery, I hope you will come back here and help me manage my household affairs at that busy time."

Shen Chun thought to himself: "Oh you cynical old villain! You first promise me your daughter as my wife, and then give her to someone else, without a thought for propriety. And now, you have the nerve to ask me to assist you in her marriage arrangements!" But he managed a polite but stiff refusal. "Sir, I am about to return home on family business. How long this will take, I have no way of knowing. Moreover, the time is fast approaching for me to take up an official post. So I am afraid that, as my cousin's wedding is imminent, it will be impossible for me to do as you ask."

Wang Wenrui knew perfectly well that the young man blamed him for his disappointment in love, but all he could bring himself to say was, "I quite understand. Make haste, then, and put your parents' hearts at ease."

The words were hardly out of his mouth, when Jiaoniang emerged from behind a screen, and stood quietly behind him. Her tear-filled eyes

府之事，躬身道："舅父有话不妨直说，小甥在此洗耳恭听。"

王文瑞老脸微红，叹了口气道："按理说来，老夫已遣媒到成都为娇娘求亲，蒙姐夫姐姐一口应允，只等下聘。可谁想到昨日里帅府突然来人求婚，老夫再三推辞不得，迫于威势，不得不允，只在这两三日内便要下聘。贤甥回去后还望将老夫的苦衷向你父母言明，并代老夫告罪。好在一来你我两家尚未下聘，二来贤甥青春高才，不愁日后没有娇妻美妾。老夫近来精力日衰，身边也没有个得力之人。娇娘只在这一两个月内便要过门，诸事纷纭，千头万绪。贤甥与娇娘谊属中表，兄妹情深，若是姐夫不日痊愈，还望贤甥速来，帮着操持料理。"

申纯闻言心道："舅父你好狠的心肠！你先将表妹许婚与我，如今将其另聘豪门，已属不义。现在还想让我为娇娘操办婚事，何其忍心，亏你说得出口！"于是口中推辞道："小甥归侍家尊，尚不能定下期限，况且瓜期将及，须得赴任。表妹亲期已近，只怕小甥未必能赶来也。"

王文瑞知道申纯为了自己悔婚一事而心中不快，只得道："既然如此，贤甥速速上路去吧！早些到家，也让你父母宽心。"

话音未落，娇娘从屏风后闪出，悄立于王文瑞身

were fixed on Shen Chun. Feihong had sent her the news about Shen Chun's father's illness, and the urgent summons for the young man to hasten home. Thereupon, she had hurried to the main hall. Entering by the rear door, she had been just in time to hear Shen Chun's words of farewell to her father. She was overcome with grief. Shen Chun too stood there staring at his true love, not a word coming to his lips. At that very moment, the two of them epitomized the myriad sorrows fate has in store for all of us, and the anguish of final partings.

After what seemed like a long time, Jiaoniang bowed to the inevitable; covering her face with her sleeve, she slipped back behind the screen. Shen Chun, his own face ashen with grief, made a deep obeisance to his uncle, and took his leave. Still clinging to his limitless longing for Jiaoniang, he whipped his horse away from this scene of his most desolating sorrow.

From the time of her lover's departure, Jiaoniang moped and pined. With little appetite for food or drink, she sat at her dressing table all day long, tearfully watching the mating swallows and stabbed to the heart by the lonely cry of the wild goose. While everybody else in the mansion was busy with the preparations for the coming nuptials, the bride-to-be did nothing but weep night and day. Within half a month, the bloom had vanished from her cheeks, her radiant beauty faded, and she took to her bed, devoid of strength.

Her attendant Xiaohui watched her young mistress' decline with tearful alarm, and soon turned to Feihong for help. The latter, however, did not know what to do for the best, and simply whispered words of comfort to the bedridden Jiaoniang. To Wang Wenrui, Feihong explained away Jiaoniang's condition as due to an unexpected chill. Doctors were summoned, but it seemed that Jiaoniang was determined to die, for she pushed away all the concoctions that the maids prepared for her; when they forced her to take them, she vomited the medicine out again. At her wits' end, Feihong held a secret discussion with Xiaohui, who gave it as her opinion that Jiaoniang was wasting away from love-sickness. The only thing that

后,含泪凝视申纯。原来飞红听到申纯因为父亲生病要急着赶回去,急忙派小丫头告知娇娘。娇娘忙赶往中堂,从后门进来,正好听到申纯拜别父亲,心中真是苦不堪言,两眼含泪,哀怨难言。申纯也痴呆呆地说不出一句话来,二人无语凝噎,痴痴对视。真是:世间万般哀苦事,无非死别与生离。

过了半晌,娇娘实在无法忍受,以袖掩面,悄悄转过屏风出堂去了。申纯满面凄凉,一怀无奈,俯身长揖,拜别舅父,带着对娇娘的无限思恋,与小厮打马扬鞭离开了这伤心之地。

自从申纯赶回成都之后,娇娘日夜悲泣,茶饭不思,菱镜懒照,整日里见梁燕双飞落泪,闻征鸿孤鸣伤情。虽然王府上下都在为她的婚事日夜忙碌,娇娘却像个无事人似的,只是梦里哭醒,醒来哭睡,惟有滔滔不绝的泪水,犹如长流不尽的江河。不过半月光景,已是芳容尽改,艳质暗消,卧病帐中,奄奄一息了。

小慧在一旁跟着落泪,不知如何是好,只得找飞红拿主意,要她设法救小姐一命。飞红也无回天之力,只得经常来探望安慰,说些话让娇娘宽心。到了王文瑞面前,还得为娇娘掩饰,只说是偶感风寒,请医调治。不料娇娘死志已决,丫环们熬好了药送来,总是推开不喝,强灌下去,又都吐了出来。飞红无法,暗地里问询小慧。小慧答说,小姐眠思梦语,只是要

could save her would be seeing Shen Chun again face to face, she suggested. So, without Wang Wenrui knowing, Feihong wrote a letter urging Shen Chun to make a clandestine trip back to Lizhou, and dispatched it in the hands of a servant whom she could trust to Chengdu. Then she waited on tenterhooks to see if the young man would answer her plea, stationing a serving maid outside the gate of the mansion to catch the first glimpse of Shen Chun as soon as he should arrive.

Meanwhile, Shen Qing's own illness soon cured itself after the arrival home of his son. Shen Chun, however, found no joy in the reunion. The cloud of depression caused by his constant thoughts of Jiaoniang refused to lift, and he passed the days in a dispirited tedium. So when, out of the blue, Feihong's letter arrived, informing him that Jiaoniang was sick and weeping day and night, anxious only to see him, his heart leaped. In the letter, too, Feihong urged him to find a way to get to Lizhou as soon as possible, lest, she hinted darkly, the two lovers be parted for all eternity. A fit of agitation seized the young man. He wanted nothing more than to fly straightaway to Jiaoniang, but how could he explain the situation to his parents. Shen Qing and his wife had been deeply offended when Wang Wenrui had gone back on his word and cancelled the engagement. They had tried to comfort Shen Chun by saying that a young man of his outstanding talent should not be upset by the incident, and that he would not lack a wife for long. But they had also instructed him never to humiliate himself by approaching the Wang mansion again.

Shen Chun was well aware that his parents would not give him permission to go. But how could he abandon Jiaoniang to waste away on her sick bed, longing for him? Finally, he resolved to risk his parents' wrath, and that very same night, he crept out of the house and down to the river bank. There he hired a boat to take him to Lizhou. In less than two days, he arrived, and instructed the boatman to tie up a short way from the Wang mansion, while he pondered a way to slip in to see Jiaoniang in the rear courtyard. It was not long before the serving maid who had been on the

见申纯。飞红寻思着娇娘一门心思要见申纯，只是为情所迷，果若让二人见上一面，娇娘心中的疙瘩解开了，或许从此回心转意，病也会渐渐好起来。于是背着王文瑞暗自修书一封，派了一个得力的小厮送到成都，约申纯偷偷前来看望娇娘。待小厮走后，掐算日子，估摸着申纯就在这一两日内赶来，派了个小丫头到府门外打探，专等申纯消息。

且说申纯回到成都，申庆见到儿子归来，心中快慰，病情本不十分严重，不几日便痊愈了。申纯却惦念着娇娘，整日里郁郁寡欢，茶饭不思。这一日忽然接到飞红的书信，得知娇娘相思成疾，日夜悲泣，只求见自己一面，不由心中大恸。再看信中飞红催促自己设法速来利州，否则只怕永无相见之日。真是心急如焚，坐卧不安，恨不得缩地御风，胁生双翅，立刻飞到娇娘身边。可是又不敢与父母明言，原来申庆夫妇对王文瑞出尔反尔，拒亲悔婚，真是伤透了心，特意将申纯叫到跟前说："我儿乃人中龙凤，何患无妻？绝不可檐下低头，仰人鼻息，舅父家以后绝不要再去登门。"

申纯情知若是提出再去舅家，爹娘定不相允。可是自己不去，又怎能舍得让娇娘望穿秋水，含恨病榻？思来想去，狠一狠心，深夜悄悄溜出家门，到江边雇了一条小船，沿江而上，直下利州。不过两日，便已到达。申纯命艄公将船停在江畔，与王府角门不到一

lookout for him found him, and she conveyed the news to Feihong. The latter immediately sent word that he should wait in the boat, and on no account approach the mansion, in case he was spotted. She would find an opportunity to let Jiaoniang come and see him.

Shen Chun waited throughout the night, hardly able to contain his impatience. Early the next day, he peeped from the boat, and saw a sedan chair being carried from the mansion. He guessed that it was taking Wang Wenrui to his office. Not long afterwards, he saw Feihong escorting the pale and haggard Jiaoniang out of the side gate. Shen Chun forgot all about Feihong's caution to him, and leaped from the boat onto the bank. Dashing towards the girls, he threw his arms around Jiaoniang. Without saying a word, and with the help of Feihong, the young man half led and half carried Jiaoniang onto the boat. Breathlessly, Feihong instructed Shen Chun as follows: "The old master has gone as far as the suburbs to see off the local prefect. I have ordered Xiaohui to guard Jiaoniang's boudoir carefully, and make sure that none of the other serving maids enter and find the young mistress missing. I have to go back and attend to the household, so I'll leave Jiaoniang here with you. Now, whatever you do, don't let anyone else find out about this."

After the young man assured her of his compliance, Feihong alighted onto the river bank, and slipped back into the mansion.

Shen Chun held Jiaoniang in his arms, and looked at her carefully. Her breathing was shallow and weak. In alarm, Shen Chun cried, "My dear, we have been apart for less than a month; how could you fall so ill?" As he spoke, tears rolled down his cheeks.

Jiaoniang managed to smile through her own tears. "Don't shed tears, my dear," she urged him. "We are together once more. But, tell me, is this real or is it a dream?"

Choking with sobs, the young man shook his head. "It is not a dream," he said, "it is not a dream. I have come specially from Chengdu to meet you."

箭之地，思量着如何混进府去，潜入内院。结果与在外探听消息的小丫头正好打了个照面，小丫头急忙报与飞红。飞红当即传话出来，要申纯在船中等候，千万不要让府中人看见，她自会找机会安排娇娘出来相见。

申纯耐着性子等了一夜，第二日清晨，他从舱中窥见一乘轿子从王府中抬出，便知道这是王文瑞上衙门去了。不多时，就见飞红扶着瘦骨伶仃的娇娘从角门出来。此时申纯早将飞红的叮嘱抛在脑后，弃舟上岸，三步并做两步迎上前来，扶住娇娘，顾不上说话与飞红连扶带抱将娇娘飞快地架进船舱。飞红喘息着道："今日老爷到郊外送知州去了。我令小慧在绣阁中看着，不让其她丫环进入，申官人我将小姐交给你了，我还得回府中照料，千万不敢走漏风声。"

申纯道："红娘子，你去吧，这里有我。"

飞红出舱上岸，悄悄回到府中。申纯将气息如丝的娇娘搂在怀中，仔细端详，吃惊道："娘子，你我分别不到一月，你怎么就病成这般模样了？"说着眼泪滚落下来。

娇娘含泪微笑道："申郎莫哭，申郎莫哭。你我今日相见，莫非是在梦中？"

申纯抽噎着摇摇头道："不是梦，不是梦，小生专为与娘子会面，从成都而来。"

"Less than a month, you say? It seems like three years...." Tears welled up again in the girl's eyes, and stopped her saying any more.

"I have the same feeling," Shen Chun said, nodding. "But tell me what profound sorrow can have reduced you to this pitiful state, my dear. You are thinner than the proverbial chrysanthemum."

Sobbing once more, Jiaoniang said, "From the very first moment I met you, I cherished the secret desire to some day be your wife. But now all my hopes have been dashed. When I think back to the time we met in the arbor, and were as one before the flowers and the moon, how perfect our love seemed! But now we have become like the Cowherd and the Weaving Maid — two stars in the sky separated by the vastness of the Milky Way."

Shen Chun wiped away her tears, and said, "My dear, you must not take any blame upon yourself. It is my perverse fate that is to blame for our separation. I foolishly forsook the oath we swore beneath the stars and burning incense to the god."

"Since ancient times, the fate of beauties has always been a tragic one. My fate is sealed — never will I share wedded bliss with you." As she said this, she took from inside her gown the blood-stained piece of sleeve cloth that was the keepsake of their first union, and with trembling hands held it out to Shen Chun. "I am so grateful for your kindness," she said. "When I think back on our former joy, I wonder if it will ever be possible to recapture it."

Shen Chun clasped the scrap of cloth to his breast, and scenes of their first night together sprang up before his eyes one after another. When he remembered how radiant and bashful Jiaoniang looked at that time, he was shocked as he gazed upon her wan and emaciated face now. "Indeed," he thought, "she looks like one who is not long for this world. And it is all because of her deep and sincere love for me!" Then the chilling thought occurred to him: "If I continue to cling to her love, she will choose death rather than go ahead with her marriage to the commander's son. I must

娇娘道："申郎，你我分别不满一月，却胜似三秋……"话犹未了，泪水夺眶而出。

申纯点头道："我也有同感。娘子，你如今真是'人比黄花瘦'，让人看了心酸。"

娇娘哽咽道："妾与郎君初见，暗下里便以此身许于郎君，不料今日竟不能如愿。想着从前你我在荼蘼架底相逢，花前月下吟和，是多么情浓意惬，如今却成了牛郎织女，永隔天河。"

申纯为娇娘拭泪道："娘子休自嗟怨，想来这都是小生命薄所致，枉自辜负了咱们星下设誓，神前焚香。"

娇娘道："自古红颜多薄命，还是妾命不济，无福与郎君偕老百年。"说罢，从怀里取出二人初次欢好时沾染血迹的断袖，颤抖着送到申纯面前道："谢郎君厚恩，如今回想此景，怎能复得？"

申纯将断袖捧在胸前，眼前不禁浮现起二人初试云雨时的情景，一幕一幕历历在目。其时娇娘貌美如花，含羞转侧。而今病骨支离，眼见得不久于人世。想到此处，猛醒道："娇娘情深意笃，矢死靡他，全是为了自己，落得眼前这副模样。若是我依旧与她情意绵绵，她必誓死抗婚，香销玉殒。自己也应该为她着想，劝她听从父命，嫁入帅府，方可保得一条性命。"于是硬下心肠，强忍悲痛道："娘子对小生情深如海，我岂不知？但如今既迫于严父之命，复慑于帅

make a bold decision, and urge her to obey her father in this matter. That is the only way to save her life." Thereupon, hardening his heart and stifling his grief, the young man said, "My dear, I am well aware that your love for me is as vast as the ocean. But I think it would be best for you to obey your father. He has been pressed by the tyrannous commander, whom he dare not thwart. It is your duty to him to marry into the commander's family, don't you think?"

Hearing this, Jiaoniang was stunned and enraged. With her breath coming in labored gasps, she glared at Shen Chun, and cried, "I refuse to listen to such words. My heart cannot belong to two lovers. I have already told you that if I fail to have you for my husband, I will repay you for your love with my death. Although, as a helpless girl, I may not go against my father's wishes, I am also mindful of the sanctity of an oath. Do you not forget either, my dear, that we swore a solemn pledge together."

Shen Chun gave a long sigh, and with tears in his eyes, begged Jiaoniang not to remind him of the oath they had sworn.

Then, choosing her words carefully, Jiaoniang said, "My mind is made up; nothing will change it. Do not be distressed, my dear. Some day, you will be a high official and pursue a brilliant career. But my destiny is an unhappy one, and I am resigned to it. I dare not aspire to sit with you on the dizzy heights. There is only one thing that worries me, and that is that your constitution is not a robust one. You often fall ill. You must take good care of yourself, and not fret about me."

Shen Chun hugged her tightly to him, and in a voice trembling with emotion, said, "My dear, how can you think only of my welfare when you are gravely ill? The whole of Heaven knows how much I appreciate your care for me. How can I ever enjoy riches and fame without the happiness of having you for my wife?"

The two of them clung together for a long time, weeping streams of silent tears.

This was how Feihong found them when she returned to the boat. At

府淫威，娘子莫若屈从，嫁入帅府也罢。"

娇娘闻听此言，真是又怒又惊，凤目圆睁，气喘连连道："申郎，此话休要再提。我岂能做得两鞍鞴一马，单轮碾双辙？当初妾与郎君曾言：事若不济，当以死谢君。妾虽为女子，三络梳头，两截穿衣，老父之命，断不敢违，但那从一而终、誓不改节的道理却也牢牢记得。郎君莫要忘了你我共同发下的誓言！"

申纯长叹一声，泪眼婆娑道："盟言虽在，休要再提。"

娇娘一字一句道："妾主意已定，绝无更改，郎君不必挂怀。郎君他日青云万里，鹏程高远，妾命薄福浅，今生不敢奢望攀附。只有一件放心不下，郎君气质孱弱，自来多病，今后务须善自将养，万毋以妾为念。"

申郎紧紧抱住娇娘，颤声道："娘子，你眼下一身尚且难保，心里还挂念小生。小生此心，苍天可证：此生若是无福娶你，还要什么富贵功名？"

二人相拥相抱，相依相偎，泪水交汇在一起无声地流淌。飞红匆匆上船来，见申纯与娇娘和泪相拥，难舍难分，心中不由的一阵酸楚，实在不忍将这一对相亲相爱的人儿分开。可是时辰已久，王文瑞随时都可能回来，若是发现事情真相，立时就会生出一场大风波。踌躇良久，还是硬着心肠上前道："小姐，官人，不要啼哭了，老爷快要回来了。千里搭长棚，没有不

first, she felt a pang of sorrow, for she could not bear to part the young lovers. But the day was well advanced, and if Wang Wenrui returned and discovered them there would be a terrible row. She hesitated, before steeling herself to say, "Miss! Young Master! Dry your eyes. The old master will be back soon. It's time to part company for now."

Shen Chun still clung to his beloved, as if fearing that Feihong intended to steal her away from him. He pleaded with her, saying, "Miss Hong, you have known about our love all along. I am only afraid that if I part from my beloved today, it may be the last time I will see her. How can you have the heart to tear us asunder?"

Feihong fought back scalding tears. "The course of true love is never predictable," she reminded him. "How can you be sure that you will never meet again? What is important now is for my young mistress to take care of her tender body and recover her health. What need is there to suppose that you will never meet again?"

Jiaoniang sobbed, "The fact that we have broken our vow means that it will be difficult for us to meet again. But even if Heaven decreed that we should be reunited, I am so wasted by illness that I have not long to live anyway." She then wept against Shen Chun's breast so violently that she collapsed in a swoon.

This caused both the young man and Feihong to call out to her in a panic.

After what seemed like a long time, Jiaoniang gave a groan, and slowly came to, wailing "Master Shen, abandon all thought of our ever being reunited in this world. . . ."

With tears constantly streaming down his cheeks, Shen Chun cried out, "O Heaven! What heinous crime did I commit in a previous life that I have had to pay the penalty of losing my true love in this one?"

The lamentations of the three of them was so heart-rending that even the boatman, sitting outside the cabin, shed tears into the fast-flowing river.

Feihong was the first to master her grief. "Your father will soon be

散的宴席,该分手时且分手吧!"

申纯紧搂着娇娘,央求道:"红娘子,我与你家小姐的事,首尾你全清楚。今日一别,恐成永诀,你怎忍心教我们就此分手呢?"

飞红强忍热泪道:"姻缘成毁,辗转无常,安知此后不可复合?只要小姐善自将养身子,保全玉体,何愁日后无见面之机?"

娇娘气喘吁吁道:"休道盟言中变,难以再合。便天教再合,我身子狼狈如斯,性命不久,又如何再合?"说罢哭倒在申纯怀里,一时气噎,昏厥过去。

申纯摇晃着娇娘唤道:"娘子!娘子!"

飞红也连连惊呼:"小姐醒来!小姐醒来!"喊着喊着,眼泪扑簌簌地滚落下来。

半晌,娇娘呻吟一声,慢慢苏醒过来,放声哭道:"申郎啊,休要再想今世里相逢了……"

申纯泪落如绳,绵延不绝,喊道:"天也,天也!前世里我申纯究竟是造了什么孽呀,今世里罚我受尽磨难,难结良缘?"

三人哭作一团,大放悲声。艄公在舱外听在耳中,也不禁泪水纵横,一串串落入奔涌的江水中。

最后,还是飞红先止泪道:"老爷就要回来了,小姐快些上岸吧。"说着挽起娇娘要走。

娇娘悲痛欲绝,死死扯着申纯的衣襟不放,道:

home, Miss," she reminded Jiaoniang. "Let's go ashore quickly." And she took her by the arm to lead her away.

But Jiaoniang clung desperately to her lover. "Master Shen, we have parted several times before, but we always met again," she said. "But I am afraid that this time our parting is permanent. You must find yourself a beautiful wife, and not let thoughts of me spoil your happy future. . . ."

Choking on his tears, the young man was not able to speak for a while. Then he stammered, "My dear . . . if you die for me . . . how can I go on living . . . alone? . . . With whom . . . in the whole world . . . could I find joy . . . as man and wife?"

"Don't say that," Jiaoniang admonished him. "How do you know that we may not meet in the next life?"

Seeing that the young lovers were unwilling to break away from each other, Feihong hardened her heart, and pulled Jiaoniang away, off the boat and onto the bank.

As she was being hurried away, Jiaoniang kept turning her head, and calling, "Master Shen . . . we'll meet in the life to come . . . won't we?"

The young man took a few faltering steps, as if to follow her, but was restrained by the boatman. He struggled in vain in the other's strong grip, hoarsely gasping, "Jiaoniang . . . Jiaoniang . . . my darling. . . ."

As he watched the figures of the two girls diminish in the distance, Shen Chun's knees buckled under him. The boatman, filled with pity at the sight, helped him back into the cabin. "Sir, there is a favorable wind for our return to Chengdu," he told Shen Chun. And without more ado, he set about casting off from the bank and hoisting the sail.

Meanwhile, as she drew near the Wang mansion, Jiaoniang suddenly found the strength to shake off Feihong. She tottered back towards the river bank, but was soon halted by the maid servant. The two of them, through tear-filled eyes, watched the boat disappear over the horizon, leaving behind the lapping waves and soaring gulls.

"申郎，从前你我几番离别，总还有相见之期；今日这一别，却是永诀。愿君早寻佳偶，休为我误了你一生的锦绣前程……"

申纯早已泣不成声，断断续续道："娘子……为小生而死，小生……岂忍独活……放眼世上，又有谁能与小生……同欢共悦，再结……姻缘……"

娇娘哭道："今生休提，不知来生你我能否相会？"

飞红见二人互相扯住不放，只得狠心掰开娇娘的手，拉着就往外走，边走边道："千别万别，终须一别。老爷就要回来了，快快上岸吧。"将娇娘连拉带扯搀出船舱，登上堤岸。

娇娘一步三回头，哭道："申郎——来世重逢——吧！"

申纯踉跄追出舱外，却被艄公紧紧抱住。他用力挣扎，嘶哑着嗓子喊道："娘子——娇娘呀——"

眼见娇娘被飞红扶着走远了，申纯腿一软瘫了下来。艄公将他扶入舱内，拭泪道："相公，此时风顺，正好开船回去。"说着手脚齐忙，解缆升帆，顺风而去。

飞红扶着娇娘上得岸来，临近府门，娇娘不知从哪里来了一股劲儿，奋力挣脱飞红，跌跌撞撞向江边奔去。飞红急追两步，一把将她揪住。两个泪人伫立在江边，目送一叶扁舟顺风而去，但见波浪翻涌，彩鸥急飞，转眼间，那小舟便消失在水天相接处。

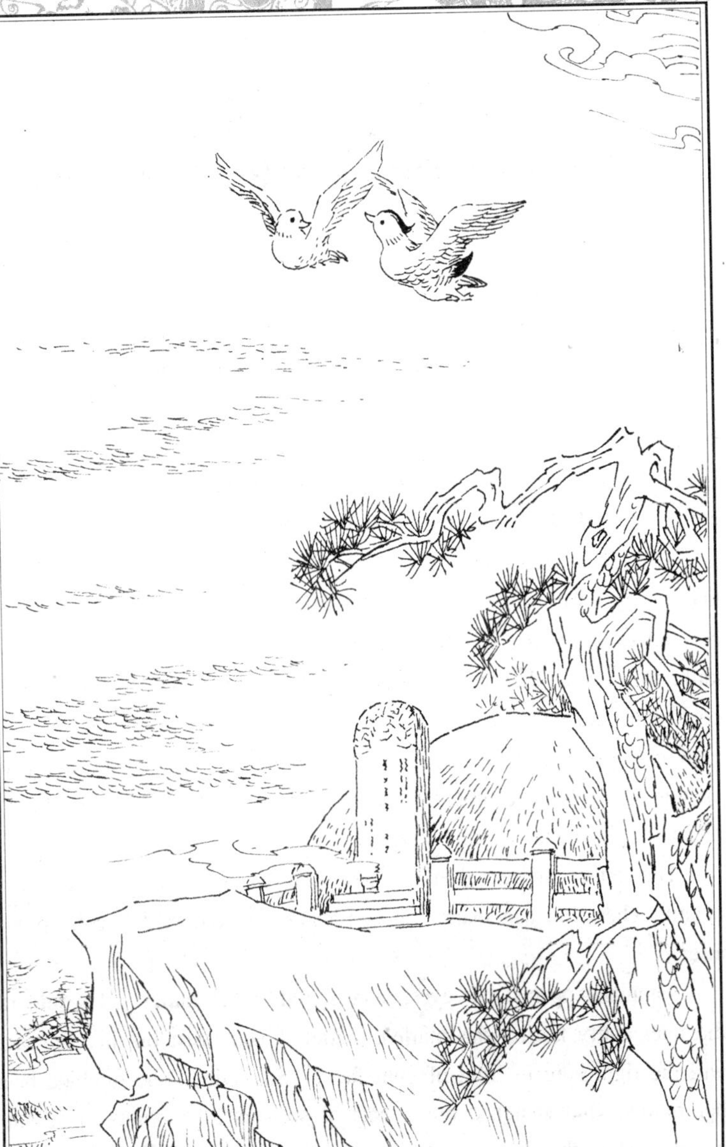

Chapter Ten
Leaving This World Together

Jiaoniang's condition grew inexorably worse. For ten days or more, not a sip of water nor grain of rice passed her lips. She was in a constant state of drowsiness, awaking occasionally struggling and crying out that she did not want to be married into the commander's family. Wang Wenrui viewed this situation with extreme exasperation. Any day now, he thought in consternation, the commander's men will be here to arrange the wedding procedures. How can Jiaoniang become a bride in this state?

One day, Wang Wenrui entered his daughter's boudoir. He observed that her eyes were tightly closed, her hair bedraggled, her eyes sunken and her cheeks shriveled. Her face was the color of wax. It cut his heart like a knife to see that her beauty was almost completely gone. The old man could not hold back his tears as he murmured to himself: "Oh, my child! How can that wonderful girl that I used to know have become this pathetic creature?" As he said this, he noticed a large teardrop roll from the corner of one of Jiaoniang's firmly shut eyes.

Her father addressed her: "My dear child, you must restore your health. Then you can marry the commander's son, and live happily ever after!"

Jiaoniang opened her eyes, and glared at her father. "I would rather die than marry him!" she snarled. "And if you insist on this marriage, I will die right here in front of your face!" So saying, she fumbled beneath her pillow, and snatched out a pair of scissors, the points of which she pressed to her throat. But before she could do a mischief to herself, Xiao-

第十章　双逝合冢

　　娇娘自从与申纯在江边诀别后，病情愈发重了，十几天来水米不进，整日里只是昏睡。偶尔清醒，便吵着闹着要与帅府退婚。王文瑞看在眼里，气得长吁短叹，心烦意乱，眼看着帅府就要前来迎亲，女儿这般模样，又如何能做新娘？

　　这一天，王文瑞到绣阁看望娇娘，见女儿双眼紧闭，凤鬟雾鬓，眼陷腮削，面似黄蜡，昔日艳丽早已丧失殆尽。一时心如刀割，老泪纵横，道："儿呀，你这是为了什么？好端端的一个人儿，怎么就成了这般模样？"说到这儿，就见娇娘紧闭的眼角淌下一滴大大的泪珠来。

　　王文瑞又道："儿呀，你快些将养身子，高高兴兴地嫁到太尉府中做少奶奶，今后的好日子长着呢。"

　　娇娘猛地睁开眼道："女儿死也不嫁帅府。倘若爹爹不肯答应，女儿这就死在爹爹面前！"说着猛地从枕侧摸出一把剪子向喉间刺去。多亏立在床边的小慧、飞红一齐扑上去夺下，方才没有出了大事。

hui and Feihong leapt at her, and wrested the scissors from her hand.

Horrified, Wang Wenrui stood there speechless. He was so agitated that his beard wagged up and down. Finally, he turned to Feihong, and said, "Take me away from here."

Feihong whispered a few urgent words to Xiaohui, and hurried to escort the old master back to the main hall. Wang Wenrui seated himself in a chair, trembling uncontrollably. Feihong brought him a cup of hot tea, and personally put it to his lips. Wang Wenrui gradually calmed down. He glanced at Xiang'e, who was standing nearby, and the girl immediately left the room, knowing that the old master wanted to have a word with Feihong alone. When she had gone, Wang Wenrui turned to Feihong, with a cold expression, and remarked, "Your young mistress is of age to be married. Yet, she expresses no desire to marry. When a desirable match is arranged for her with the son of the commander of the western region, she is adamant that the engagement be cancelled. What can be the reason for her odd behavior, I wonder?"

Feihong thought to herself: "You muddle-headed old goat! You deliberately tore apart two lovers who were made for each other, and now you have the effrontery to cast suspicion on other people." But aloud she explained, "Sir, I urge you to calm yourself. In my opinion, the young mistress does not care for fame and wealth. In her heart she hankers after a simple scholar for her soul mate, so that they can live in harmony and mutual respect. Just think of those sons of noble families — most of them are dull fops who spend their time gallivanting around the courtesans' quarters. The young mistress would rather sleep alone and live quietly as a spinster than spend the rest of her life married to one of those dim-witted coxcombs."

Wang Wenrui thought that he understood. "Ah, so that's it, is it?" he said, feeling enlightened. "The silly girl! She doesn't realize that the commander's household is far wealthier than that of any ordinary rich family. And his son will inherit a noble title. The young man is a fine, upstanding

王文瑞被女儿突如其来的举动惊得险些背过气去，半晌吐不出一个字来，气得胡须乱颤，指着飞红道："你……你给我出来。"

飞红叮嘱小慧几句忙跟出来，扶着脸色铁青、浑身颤抖的王文瑞回到中堂。进了中堂，王文瑞坐在椅上，仍旧抖个不停。飞红令湘娥端过一杯热茶，亲自送到老爷唇边，给他喝了两口，王文瑞这才慢慢定下心来。他看了一眼湘娥，湘娥知道老爷和飞红有话要说，便知趣地退出门外回避。王文瑞转过头来，冷了脸问飞红道："我且问你，小姐年纪已大，难道就不要嫁人了？如今既许帅家，却执意要退婚，这究竟是何缘由？"

飞红心中道："好个糊涂的老爷，是你生生拆散了她的美好姻缘，还理直气壮地兴师问罪。"口里却说："老爷且消消气。我想小姐么，她倒不求富贵，心中只要一个相知相重的书生为伴，小两口儿青灯共守，举案齐眉。您想想那侯门富家子弟，多是些愚笨不堪、拈花惹草的纨绔之辈，若是与这等蠢才厮守一生，倒不如一世孤眠到底，还落个清净自在。"

王文瑞恍然大悟道："原来如此，这个傻孩子，她还有所不知，那帅府的富贵，岂是寻常人家可比？帅公子承袭世爵，人材端方俊拔，不类凡儿。你去说与小姐，教她休要自寻烦恼，好好将养身体，高高兴兴

fellow, and talented too. Now you run along and tell your young mistress to stop making all this fuss. She should get well again, and then enter into this happy marriage I have arranged for her. "

As Feihong was about to carry out his instructions, the old man added, "Oh, and you can tell her that when she marries into the commander's family, she'll be presented at the imperial court, wear court robes and be surrounded by opulence and luxury. It's something that most people couldn't even dream of. If she were to marry a poor scholar she'd spend her life with thorns for hairpins and a sack for a dress, and eat nothing better than rotten cabbages. By the way, there's a portrait of the commander's son here. Show it to her. I bet she'll be pleased. "

As he said this, he took a rolled-up scroll out of a cupboard, and handed it to Feihong. "Oh, and another thing," he told her. "You can remind her that ever since time immemorial marriages have been decided in the previous existence. Everything must follow the course of nature, so she should recognize what is best for her. Anyway, I am her father: Would I wish her any harm?"

Feihong took the scroll to the rear courtyard. As soon as Jiaoniang saw her entering the bedroom, she struggled to sit up in bed. The maid servant hurried to support her. She sighed gently, and said, "Oh, Miss, you are so foolish! What did you try to do to yourself just now?"

Jiaoniang sank back, listlessly, against the pillow, and said in a weak voice: "So many people struggle to prolong their lives in vain. But death will not come to me even when I seek it. "

"Your father is only anxious for you to recover your health, and then to be married," said Feihong. "Why on earth do you keep talking of macabre things like death?"

"Nobody else knows what is in my heart," replied Jiaoniang, "But I cannot hide my secrets from you. Tell me what my father said to you just now. "

"He said that the commander is incomparably wealthy and exalted, and

地嫁过去才是。"

飞红只得应下。 王文瑞又道:"你再告诉小姐,她一进帅府,便是夫人县君,朝廷命妇,凤冠霞帔,荣华富贵,多少人家想还想不到呢! 强似嫁个穷酸女婿,做那寒士之妻,荆钗布裙,一辈子只能吃些酸黄菜。这里有帅府下聘时带来帅少爷的写真图卷,你拿了去,让小姐看看,她必定喜欢。"

说着从柜中取出一轴画递与飞红,"你再说与她,自古男女婚姻,都系前生注定。一切当顺其自然,劝她好自为之。我是她嫡亲的爹爹,岂能害她?"

飞红接了画轴,便到后院去看娇娘。娇娘一见飞红,便要挣扎着起身。飞红急上前按住,轻声叹道:"哎,好个糊涂的小姐,看你刚才都做了些什么呀?"

娇娘倚在枕上,少气无力地吟道:"人欲求生生不得,我今求死死偏难。"

飞红道:"老爷一心只盼着小姐的病好转起来,完成亲事。小姐到底是何主意?怎么口口声声只说要死?"

娇娘道:"我心中之事,他人不知,怎瞒得过你?我且问你,爹爹适才唤你说了些什么?"

飞红道:"老爷说帅府的富贵非常人可比,小姐嫁过去便是朝廷命妇,凤冠霞帔。又说那帅公子人才

that if you marry into his family you will be presented at court and wear court robes. He also said that the commander's son is outstandingly talented, upright and dignified in his behavior, and his prospects are limitless. Finally, he said that all marriages are decided by Heaven, and that you should stop being stubborn and bringing ruin on your own family. The commander is eager to get the marriage arranged, and so you should do what your father tells you and get well again in preparation for the happy day."

Before Feihong had finished, her young mistress was already glaring at her with eyes that flashed fire. Through firmly gritted teeth, Jiaoniang growled, "Don't mention the commander again. The very sound of his name makes me want to die." As she said this, she groped under her pillow again, produced a small silver knife, and placed it against her throat.

Quick as a flash, Feihong snatched the knife from her, and threw it on the floor. Turning to Xiaohui, she yelled, "You useless baggage, Xiaohui! Haven't you got an ounce of brains in that thick skull of yours, that you allow the young mistress to put herself in danger?"

The startled Xiaohui hurriedly rearranged the bed curtains, and then removed Jiaoniang's needlework box with its pins, needles, gimlets and scissors. Feihong turned again to Jiaoniang. Tears choked her as she implored, "Miss, why are you seeking to end your own life?"

The other uttered a long-drawn-out sigh. "Long ago, Shen Chun and I pledged ourselves to each other for the past, present and future. We even swore a solemn oath before the Great King of Brightness. Even now, the words we uttered on that occasion still hover around my ears. How can I forget? All I want to do now is to die."

"Die? Die?" cried Feihong, exasperated. "All you seem to think about is death. What's so good about death? I think that if you really were dead, you would regret it, but by then it would be too late, so there!"

This rather incoherent diatribe had no effect on Jiaoniang. "I certainly wouldn't regret it," she said. "Returning to the Yellow Springs of the

俊拔，行止端方，将来前程不可限量。最后说婚姻皆为天定，小姐休得固执，枉送了自家性命。帅家目下就要成婚，要小姐听爹爹的话，好自将息，以待佳期。"

娇娘不待飞红说完，早已二目喷火，咬牙切齿道："不说那帅家罢了，说起帅家，我恨不得即刻就死。"说着从枕下摸出一把小银刀来，抹向喉间。

飞红奋力将刀夺了过来，掷在地下，回头向小慧怒道：

"小慧，你个无用的东西！小姐若有个三长两短，摸摸你腔子上有几颗脑袋！"

小慧吓得忙过来收拾床帐，将针线盒儿、锥子、剪刀等一并收了去。飞红转过头来又对泣不成声的娇娘说道：

"小姐何必如此，只是一而再、再而三地寻死觅活？"

娇娘长叹一声说道：

"我往昔与申郎定下三生之约，曾在神灵前发下重誓。如今誓言尚萦绕耳际，岂能转头便抛在脑后？我只要拼得一死……"

飞红抢白道："死！死！你就知道个死，死是什么好事！我看你若真是死了，只怕后悔也来不及了。"

netherworld is all that my heart desires now. "

Seeing her young mistress facing the prospect of death so calmly, Feihong was at a loss what to say. She wanted to hold Jiaoniang in her eyes and weep a storm of tears, but when she remembered the wish of her white-haired old master in his twilight years, she stifled her emotions, and said, "Miss, you are an educated young woman, and versed in the tenets of etiquette. You surely must know that a woman before she marries must obey her father. Your pig-headedness is causing your father much heartbreak. How can you call yourself a filial daughter?"

The word "filial" brought on a flood of weeping from Jiaoniang, who of course had been anguished at the pain she was causing her aged parent. "Feihong," she wailed, "you mustn't tell him about Shen Chun and me. We consider ourselves man and wife, even though we have not obtained our parents' permission. I dare not wait until this important secret becomes leaked to others. Since ancient times, how many maidens have there been who lived lives of misery and came to tragic ends, all because they were thwarted in love? I often think that if it is possible to regret one's love choice later, one wouldn't make that choice in the first place. I have pledged myself to Master Shen. Twice we have tried to get married, and my father finally gave his consent. But now he has gone back on his word, and promised me to the commander's son. This faithlessness should be laid at the door of my father; it is no fault of mine. In olden times, when Miss Xun marred her beauty and cut off her hair to foil her father's marriage plans for her, subsequent generations did not label her as unfilial. So why should I be forced to follow my father's wishes, and betray my oath of love?"

Feihong replied, "When you fell in love with Master Shen, Miss, it was only his good looks and talent that attracted you. But the commander's son is not only just as cultivated and handsome as Master Shen, he comes from an extremely wealthy and exalted family. I hear that he yearns for you like a starving man, and thinks of nothing else. If you marry into his fami-

娇娘道:"我绝不后悔。果然早归黄泉,倒了却一桩心事,我还求之不得呢。"

飞红见娇娘一副视死如归的架式,心中不辨是何滋味,只是想抱着她大哭一场,可转念想到白发苍苍、桑榆晚景的王文瑞,便又忍泪劝道:"小姐知书达礼,岂不闻女子未嫁,当从父命?如今你这样执拗,伤了老爷的心,难道说得上是孝吗?"

娇娘又如何不心疼白发老父,听飞红提起"孝"字,顿时泪如雨下,道:"红娘子你不要说了⋯⋯我与申郎之事,虽说未获父母之命,但自念婚姻兹事体大,不敢等闲视之。看古来多少佳人,匹配匪材,一生悲痛,郁郁而终。我常想与其悔之于后,岂若择之于始?因此上与申郎私订终身,以身相许。至于中间两次婚议,爹爹业有成言。而今他又悔约,将我改许帅家,这才是负义之举,错不在我。昔荀氏毁容截发,以抗亲命,后人不谓不孝。我又安能强从父命,自背初盟?"

飞红道:"小姐与申官人相遇,最初也只是爱其才貌。今帅家富贵至极,帅公子又端方俊拔,不让申纯。听说他欲得小姐之心,如饥似渴,其他皆所不问。小姐若能改从帅家,上既无逆亲命,下亦不乖凤志,岂不是两全其美之举?"

娇娘听了飞红的话,却不答言,只是摇头。

ly, you will not only be obeying your father but you will also be making the best possible match for yourself."

Jiaoniang made no answer, and simply shook her head.

Feihong tried another line of persuasion: "Since ancient times there have been generations of beauties who have fallen in love with handsome and talented young men. But have they always married them? Lovers are like birds in the forest; when it comes time to part, they fly off on their separate ways. Now, you and Master Shen are not really man and wife, because you did not obtain your parents' permission, nor has a go-between made the proper arrangements. Wouldn't it be better for you two to make a clean break, and find your own spouses? My advice to you, Miss, is to stop feeling sorry for yourself, do what your father tells you, recover your health and marry the commander's son." With that, she unrolled the portrait of the commander's son, and held it up for Jiaoniang to see, saying, "Your father told me to show you this."

Jiaoniang turned her face to one side, at the same time pushing the portrait away. "I refuse to look at it," she protested. "That man is a dissolute wretch. What can he have to do with me? You were quite right when you said that it was Master Shen's good looks and talent that won me at first. But now, I love him for his pure and loyal nature too. Our hearts are entwined, and we have sworn an unbreakable oath of fidelity. Ours is not the ordinary love in which mere talent and beauty bond. I would not find a shred of attraction in the commander's son even if he were more talented than Song Yu, handsomer than Pan An, higher in rank than a prince or marquis, and as rich as Shi Chong!"

Feihong was taken aback by this show of steely resolution, and for some time did not know what to say. Eventually, an idea came into her head. "You are resisting your father, Miss," she said, "just because of that pledge you and Master Shen made long ago. But I have heard recently that the young man's parents arranged a marriage for him with the daughter of a rich family as soon as he got back to Chengdu. The engagement is about to

飞红接着劝道："自古佳人代出，莫非都找到才貌双全的夫君，才肯出嫁么？夫妻本是同林鸟，大限来时各自飞。何况小姐与申纯并无父母之命、媒妁之言，有夫妻之实，无夫妻之名，如今撒手放开，两下里干净，各择良配，岂不是好？我劝小姐不要与自己过不去，还是听从老爷的话，养好身子，嫁去帅府，才是真的。"说着拿起画轴解开丝绳，举在娇娘面前道："老爷让我带来帅官人的图影在此，小姐不妨看一看。"

娇娘别过脸去，一双手奋力推开画幅道："不看，不看。那人便是风流绝世，又与我何干？你说得不错，当初我是被申郎的才貌所吸引，可如今我不单是爱他的才俊貌美，更爱他那一片赤诚之心。我们二人心心相印，誓同生死，并非常人所说的郎才女貌、才子佳人。那帅府公子纵然才欺宋玉，貌过潘安，贵为王侯，富如石崇，我也没有丝毫艳羡。"

飞红见娇娘痴情如铁，心似磐石，一时不知该如何劝解，沉吟半晌，忽然计上心来，又道："小姐不从老爷之命，皆因昔日与申官人有约在先。可前两日听人说起，申官人回去后，他家已为他议亲豪门，不日便要下聘。小姐独个儿在此痴心苦守，生死不计，岂不枉然？"

娇娘摇头道："申郎不会如此。"

be formally made any day now. Isn't it foolish of you to be pining your life away here when he has abandoned you?"

Jiaoniang shook her head. "I can't believe that Master Shen would do such a thing," she said.

"How can you be so blind?" cried the exasperated Feihong. "It's obvious that Master Shen has decided to forget his old life and start a new one. He has completely renounced the oath he swore together with you, while you sicken and pine away here, hovering between life and death, foolishly being constant to that unfaithful scoundrel! As the old saying goes: 'If you won't be true to me, I won't be true to you.' So, since he was the first to break your promise, I don't think that you can be blamed for going back on your word if you marry the commander's son."

"That makes no difference," Jiaoniang rejoined. "Even if he has been unfaithful to me, I will never be unfaithful to him."

This drew tears of frustration from Feihong. "Oh, Miss, why are you making things so hard for yourself?" she pleaded. "If Master Shen had any feelings for you at all, he would remain a bachelor. But do you really think that if you were to die of grief, he too would be unwilling to live? He would be married to someone else within a year and a half! And then, while you were drinking the bitter waters of the Yellow Springs of the netherworld, he would be cavorting on the marriage bed. But it would be too late for you to repent then, wouldn't it?"

"Do not fret over me," said Jiaoniang. "I would gladly seek death, with no recriminations and no regrets. If Master Shen found a soul mate after I were gone, I would gladly languish at the Yellow Springs."

Feihong realized that it was no use any longer trying to change her young mistress' mind. Sobbing, she cried, "But, Miss, if you are determined to die for your lost lover, why didn't you tell your father when he promised you to the commander's son? Why did you wait until now?"

Jiaoniang said, with a sigh: "I tried to explain to my father that he had gone back on his word, but he wouldn't listen to me. Of course, I couldn't

飞红道："小姐怎么如此执迷不悟！如今申官人眼见得就要弃旧迎新，早将当初与小姐的海誓山盟抛到九霄云外去了。你却在这里发痴害傻，为他守身不渝，寻死觅活。俗语说：他不仁，我不义。申官人既然违誓在先，小姐出嫁帅府，也不算是负约了。"

娇娘道："休道申郎不是那种负心的人，即便是他负我，我也绝不负他。"

飞红忍不住落泪道："唉，小姐你怎么就是想不开呢？即便申官人眼下还在惦念小姐，独身不娶。可倘若小姐果有不幸，难道他还当真也不活了不成？一年半载之后，一样娶妻成亲。到那时，小姐孤单单黄泉下饮恨，人家乐陶陶绣帐里追欢。小姐地下有知，悔也悔不迭了。"

娇娘道："红娘子不须过虑。是我自家甘心赴死，无怨无悔。申郎果若另寻佳偶，鱼水欢爱，我在黄泉之下也只有为他高兴。"

飞红见娇娘说出这样的话来，心知再也劝不转她，不由哽咽道："小姐既然矢死靡他，当初老爷将你改许帅家之时，为何不当面明言，而必出此下策？"

娇娘叹息道："爹爹背弃前约，我便明言于他，他亦不肯听。况且我与申郎私下里以身相许，也羞于向爹爹启齿。违逆父命为不孝，背誓另嫁为不贞，我惟有一死以明志。娇娘我生为女子，空负才貌，有此不

tell him that Master Shen and I were already united. To defy one's parent is unfilial, while to betray one's pledged love is unchaste. So, I can do nothing but vindicate myself through my death. My talent and beauty have been nothing but curses. They have brought heartache to my father and disappointment to my lover. The best way for me is to seek an early death."

"Oh, please, Miss," howled Feihong, "think again! Once you're dead, you can't come back to life again. Even crickets and ants cling to life. While you are alive, there is still a chance that things can change for the better. But once you're dead, that's it!"

But Jiaoniang was unmoved. "I will have no regrets," she assured the serving maid. There are two poems under my pillow. After my death, please deliver them to Master Shen. If you do that, all will be well for ever between you and I."

Jiaoniang had been fasting for over ten days. Moreover, she had her mind set on dying, so the spark of life was fast dying within her. She found the conversation with Feihong draining, and her last words were uttered in a barely audible whisper. Then her eyes closed and she fainted away.

In a panic, Feihong ordered Xiaohui to run to the main hall and fetch the old master. At the same time she told another maid servant to run to the kitchen and bring back a bowl of hot water.

Hearing the distressing news from Xiaohui, Wang Wenrui came staggering and stumbling as fast as his old legs would carry him to Jiaoniang's bedside. At the sight of his daughter's tear-stained and apparently lifeless face cradled in Feihong's arms, he felt as though a dagger had pierced his heart.

He called to his daughter, but all in vain. Jiaoniang was not breathing. The old man wailed, beat his breast and stamped his feet. "My child, my child!" he howled in agony of mind. "It is I who deprived you of life in the prime of your youth. Now it is too late for regrets. . . . "

"Don't despair, sir," Feihong urged him, "the young mistress is weak

祥之身，上使老父伤心，下令申郎失望，如今只盼速死。"

飞红痛哭道："当初不说，如今想说也迟了。小姐啊，人死不可复生，蝼蚁尚且贪命。留得性命，凡事还可回旋，若是死了，后悔也难。"

娇娘道："我如今也没有什么后悔的。我有两首诗在枕下，我死之后，烦请红娘子替我寄与申郎，便是你对我的情了，也不枉你我相处相知一场。"

娇娘十余日水米不进，心中死志已决，此时油尽灯枯，与飞红说了这半天的话，一直在勉强支撑。到了最后，气如游丝，每说一个字都要使出全身的力气。待到这一句话说完，再也支持不住，两眼一闭，昏厥过去。

飞红心叫不好，忙令小慧到中堂去请老爷，一边命小丫环速去厨房端一碗热汤。

王文瑞听得小慧哭禀，踉踉跄跄、跌跌撞撞来到绣阁，只见女儿满脸泪痕，不醒人事，歪在飞红怀里，真是心如刀绞，三步两步扑上前去，连声唤道："孩儿，孩儿，你这是怎么了？"

却见娇娘毫无动静，气息仅属。王文瑞老泪纵横，捶胸顿足道："罢了，罢了，孩儿呀，都是为父把你青春断送了。如今悔也迟了……"

飞红道："老爷且勿惊慌，小姐连日饮食不进，以

from hunger and grief. If we feed her some hot water, she may revive."

At this moment, the maid servant who had been sent to the kitchen arrived with a bowl of hot water, and handed it to Feihong. The latter carefully pried open her young mistress' teeth with a silver spoon, and poured some of the hot water down her throat. Choking and gasping, Jiaoniang came back to life. She slowly opened her eyes, and when she saw her gather standing over her, she gave a ghastly smile, and said, "Father, I have caused you much pain."

"Oh, please don't say that, my child," Wang Wenrui begged, wiping his eyes, "you must get a grip on yourself."

Jiaoniang sighed, and said, "No, Father, I have failed to be a filial daughter to you. The only thing for me to do is to join my mother under the ground. That is the only filial act that is left for me to perform. ..."

"What are you saying, Miss?" shrieked Feihong. "Your father said just now that he wants you to get better. It is not what you want that counts. Your father depends entirely on you, don't you, sir?"

Wang Wenrui's only concern was to save his daughter's life, so he nodded his head vigorously. "That's right," he said. "My daughter, tell me whatever is in your heart. You know that I am completely dependent upon you."

But his appeal fell on deaf ears. Jiaoniang shook her head, and said, "There is no point trying to dissuade me, Father." Then, turning to Feihong, she said, "Feihong, our lives have been entangled together through fate. I want you to do two things for me: One is to look after my father when I am gone. The other is. ..."

Feihong, seeing that she wanted to say more, but was afraid to speak out loud, bent close to her, and said, "Miss, if you have something else to say, please speak out what is on your mind. You don't still harbor some distrust of me, do you?"

A faintly rosy glow appeared on Jiaoniang's waxen cheeks, as she whispered in Feihong's ear: "Whatever you do, you must not reveal my

致闷绝,快取热汤来灌下去,或许还得苏醒。"

此时小丫头飞跑着从厨房端来一碗热汤,递与飞红。飞红小心翼翼用银匙撬开娇娘的牙关,灌了几口热汤下去,就见娇娘喉间蠕动,呻吟一声苏醒过来。她微微睁开双眼,看到爹爹守在面前,凄然一笑道:"爹爹,女儿让您费心了。"

王文瑞拭泪道:"儿呀,快休说此话。你可要挺住些,我的儿!"

娇娘叹道:"爹爹,女儿我不能在您老人家膝前尽孝了,只能追陪母亲于地下,略尽女儿的孝心……"

飞红哭道:"小姐,你说的是些什么呀?老爷方才说过了,只要你好起来,无论你要如何,老爷俱依你的。老爷是吧?"

王文瑞此时救女心切,顾不得许多,忙点头道:"是呀。女儿啊,你有什么心事尽管对爹爹说,爹爹一定依你。"

娇娘摇摇头道:

"此话休要再提。飞红,你我相处一场,也算有缘,请你答应我两件事:一件是爹爹老了,善父年幼,以后父子相依为命,你须好生看待,尽心照料;第二件……"

飞红见她欲言又止,于是俯下身去问道:"小姐有话但讲无妨,你还信不过我吗?"

secret. "

The maid servant knew exactly what she meant. With tears in her eyes, she promised, "Miss, you may rest assured that I will keep your secret. "

Jiaoniang gave a long-drawn-out sigh, nodded, and said, "Only Heaven and Earth must know. . . . "

Wang Wenrui grasped his daughter's emaciated hands tightly, and cried, "My child, if you will only get better, I will cancel your engagement to the commander's son! "

But Jiaoniang could feel the end approaching, and her mind was overcome with bleak despair. With a trace of a frown and a gentle sigh, she said, "It is too late, Father. Everything is now too late. Please do not say any more. " Raising her eyes to the window, she saw the dead leaves tumbling down amid the sighing of the harsh autumn wind. With a ghastly grimace, she said, "Father, your child is leaving you. . . . "

Her eyes closed, and her soul departed. At the very same time, black clouds gathered from all four corners of the sky. Heaven and Earth blenched. Lightning flashed, and thunder rolled, and a howling gale brought torrents of rain.

In the meantime, ever since his parting from Jiaoniang on the riverbank and his return to Chengdu, Shen Chun had been in a piteous state, tearful and distraught. The rest of the household guessed, quite rightly, that his woebegone condition had been brought on by the breaking of his engagement to Jiaoniang and the promising of her hand to the commander's son. They tried everything they could think of to cheer him up, but nothing seemed to work. The young man's parents bitterly blamed Wang Wenrui for their son's distress, but decided that as things had come to this pass, the best thing they could do was arrange another marriage for Shen Chun as quickly as possible. Perhaps with a new person to love he would then forget Jiaoniang, they thought. They thereupon sent for Flowermouth Li, and with the promise of a handsome reward urged her to fix up a match for Shen

娇娘腊黄的脸上微微一红，对她耳语道："切记休在人前提起我生前之事。"

飞红知道娇娘的心事，含泪点头道："小姐放心，我答应你。"

娇娘长出一口气，点点头道："此事只有天知，地知……"

王文瑞将女儿纤瘦的双手牢牢握住，泣道："儿呀，你果然身子好起来，爹爹便回了帅家的婚事也罢。"

娇娘此时万念俱灰，大限已到，微微皱眉叹道："爹爹，如今一切都已晚了，休要再说了。"抬眼看看窗外秋风瑟瑟，落叶乱飞，凄然一笑道："儿去也……"

双眼一闭，香魂出窍。就在此时，只见乌云四合，天地失色，电闪雷鸣，风雨大作。

申纯与娇娘在江畔诀别，回到成都之后，便失魂落魄，整日以泪洗面。家里人猜到他必定是因娇娘改聘帅府而心中不快，于是百般开导，却无济于事。急得申家二老直骂王文瑞害了儿子，可事到如今，只得商议快快托媒另寻姻亲，指望着新人进门，申纯或许就会将娇娘忘记了。于是将李花嘴叫来，许下重赏，要她在这几天里为申纯寻一门亲事。李花嘴使出浑身解数，东奔西走，还真的找到一两个人才出众的女孩儿家。没想到任凭李花嘴磨破嘴皮，申纯只是摇

Chun within a few days, if possible. But although Flowermouth Li ran herself ragged seeking out and introducing eligible maidens, Shen Chun turned them all down, one after the other. Meanwhile, he himself refused to say a word about his own marriage preferences. Shen Qing was completely stumped as to what else to do in this direction, and so, after consulting with his elder son Shen Lun, he spread largesse in government circles to try to solve the problem by obtaining an official post for Shen Chun. Perhaps, after immersing himself in his new duties he would pull himself together.

One day, Shen Lun entered his brother's bedroom to inquire after his health. He found Shen Chun prostrate on the bed, his eyes glazed, looking as though he were in a trance. His right hand was making motions in the air, as if he were writing something, and his lips were moving as if he were talking to somebody. Seized with apprehension, Shen Lun asked his brother: "What are you doing in such an odd posture?"

Shen Chun rolled his eyes, and replied, "Forgive me, Brother, I did not notice your arrival. My illness has left me muddled." As he said this, he tried to rise to bow to Shen Lun, but the latter restrained him gently.

Shen Lun said, "It is my guess that the reason you have not touched food or drink for the past few days and have grown weak and ill is that little word 'love.'"

Shen Chun nodded silently, and tears streamed from his eyes. His brother sighed. "This is driving our parents and myself to distraction," he admonished Shen Chun. Just think, you are now a famous scholar; you will not long be without a wife. You must not keep on punishing yourself like this, throwing away your future."

It was Shen Chun's turn to sigh. "Ah, Brother, you do not understand what is in my heart," he said.

"Well, even though you haven't told me, I think I do understand," was Shen Lun's reply. "You cannot rid your heart of Jiaoniang."

Shen Chun nodded his confirmation. "It was love at first sight," he admitted. "And we pledged to be true to each other for life. But now, we

头,对自己的亲事竟然一个字都不愿意说。申庆万般无奈,与申纶商议一番,又用重金托人到官府去打通关节,求衙门里尽快给申纯下文书,安排他赴官上任,到时政事繁冗,申纯也许就会振作起来。

这一日,申纶前来探病,进门看见兄弟倚在床头,神情恍惚,双目无神,右手对空指指画画,像在书写什么,口中念念有辞,又似与人交谈。心中不由一惊,问道:"三弟,你痴坐在此做甚?"

申纯眼珠转了一下,道:"小弟病中恍惚,不知兄长到来,望乞恕罪。"说着便要起身施礼,被申纶轻轻按住。

申纶道:"我猜兄弟近日来茶饭不思,恹恹成病,都是为了婚姻之事,有一个'情'字作怪。"

申纯点头无语,泪流不止。申纶叹道:"三弟,你真真令父母和兄长失望!如今你已是功名在身,还怕鸳帏里少了如意之人?万万不可自暴自弃,断送了前程。"

申纯长叹一声道:"二哥,你不明白我的心。"

"虽然你不曾说起,二哥我却也明白。你心里只是放不开表妹。"

申纯点点头道:"小弟与娇娘一见钟情,相恋相慕,私订终身。不料如今被人无端分开,这教小弟如何能无动于衷?"

have been cruelly separated. How can you expect me to remain indifferent?"

This caused Shen Lun to ponder: "My brother has had several bouts of illness — all probably caused by his longing for Jiaoniang. Originally, our family approved of their marriage, but attempts at arranging a match twice came to naught. The first time, the go-between we sent met with a rebuff, and the second time, the betrothal was called off. This caused much displeasure on the part of our parents. But I never thought that Shen Chun would admit to their having pledged to be true to each other for life. Now that I come to think of it, he has frequented our uncle's mansion several times over the past few years. There, he must have come into close contact with Jiaoniang. As time passed, they must have fallen in love. But now, she is engaged to be married to the commander's son, and the day of the wedding is surely approaching. That will cause our uncle's family to rise in the world, far beyond our station. No wonder Shen Chun is pining and torturing himself like this!" Aloud, he said, "But you are still in the springtime of youth. You have all your life ahead of you. You really must take a broader view of things."

Before Shen Chun had time to reply, a servant announced the arrival from Lizhou of Wang Zhong. The news their uncle's steward brought burst over Shen Chun's head like a clap of thunder. Wang Zhong had come to announce the death of Jiaoniang two days previously. The world spun around the young man, and he swooned away on the spot, with a cry of anguish. Shen Lun hastened to support him, and Wang Zhong and the servants dashed forward to help. Some pummeled Shen Chun's chest, some massaged his back, and others pinched his lips and poured hot water down his throat. Eventually, much to everybody's relief, Shen Chun regained consciousness.

They all started to babble at the same time, urging Shen Chun not to do harm to himself in an excess of grief. But the young man writhed frantically on the bed, moaning through gritted teeth: "My darling! My darling!

申纯闻言想道:"兄弟三番五次生病,看来都是为了表妹娇娘。这件事家里本来极其赞成,可是先后两次议婚,一次遣媒遭拒,二次成约被毁,爹娘心中也十分不悦。可是万万想不到三弟动了真情,口口声声与娇娘已经私订终身。想来是这几年常在舅家走动,与表妹耳鬓相磨,日久生情,做下事来。可如今娇娘已经许聘帅府,亲期将近,眼见着王家攀高附贵,兄弟却一人在此苦苦相思,岂不是自己折磨自己?"想到此处,开口劝道:"兄弟,岂不闻人言'命里有时终须有,命里无时到头无'?你正当青春,来日方长,万事还须想开些。"

申纯正待答言,忽有家人来报,说是利州舅老爷府上王忠到申宅报丧,娇娘小姐于前日身亡,那王忠道要与三官人叙话。申纯闻听娇娘玉殒,宛若身遭雷殛,顿觉天塌地陷,大呼道:"天呵天! 痛煞我也!"当时昏晕倒地。申纶急忙将他扶到床上,申宅家人及王忠也都拥上前来,当下捶背抚胸,掐唇灌汤,半晌方才悠悠醒来,众人这才舒了一口气。

诸人当时七嘴八舌劝申纯不要过于悲痛,以免伤了身子。申纯却泪如泉涌,反来覆去只在口中念叨:"娘子,娘子,尔之薄命,一至于斯!"

王忠走上前来,递给申纯一封书柬道:"三官人,人死不能复生,还望顺变节哀。这是红娘子托老仆带

Your tragic fate has worked itself out to its dreadful conclusion!"

At this point, Wang Zhong proffered a letter he had brought with him. "Young master," he said, "the dead cannot be brought back to life. On such an occasion as this, it behooves us to restrain our sorrow. The maid servant Feihong entrusted me to deliver this letter to you. She said that it was written by her young mistress just before she died."

Shen Chun seized the envelope with trembling hands, and tore it open. He pulled out a piece of silk upon which were written verses in Jiaoniang's delicate hand. In the lines of the poem, she bade him farewell, lamenting for their lost chance of happiness.

When he had finished reading, Shen Chun cried out, "My darling, you have been snatched away from me, and have gone to a far-off realm. Oh, how can I meet you again? Where can I go to find you?"

Shen Lun, fighting back his own tears, tried to comfort his brother. "Try to lay aside your sorrow," he urged. "The dead are dead, but the living must go on living, so as to be able to console the souls beneath the ground."

Shen Chun made no reply, as he struggled to compose himself. Eventually, with a tremor in his voice, he said, "A fine piece of writing is hard to come by. Since Jiaoniang bade farewell to me with a poem, it is only fitting that I mourn the loss of her in verse." So saying, he got out of bed, and strode to the desk. Arranging his writing materials, and hardly pausing for thought, he began to write. His wrist moved as swiftly as the wind, and ink rained down on the paper. In no time at all, the whisking sound of the brush had ceased, leaving the sheet of paper covered in writing.

Looking over his brother's shoulder, Shen Lun gasped, "But why have you used such words of ill omen? Those who have been taken from us cannot be reunited with us. The dead cannot be resurrected. Besides, you must remember that you and Jiaoniang were first cousins. Twice your attempts to marry her were thwarted — that must have been the hand of fate! So isn't it perverse to be torturing yourself like this? As an educated and cultured

给官人的,说是小姐的绝笔。"

申纯不顾一切挣扎起来,抖索着双手拆开书束,抽出里面一幅素绢,展开一看,娇娘隽秀的笔迹便映入眼帘:

"如此钟情古所稀,吁嗟好事到头非。

汪汪两眼西风泪,犹向阳台作雨飞。

月有阴晴与圆缺,人有悲欢与会别。

拥炉细语鬼神知,挤把红颜与君绝。"

看罢,申纯哭道:"娘子,你今朝死了,魂向楚天。让我到哪里去寻你?到哪里去看你?"

申纶见三弟悲痛欲绝,忍泪劝道:"兄弟切莫悲伤。死者已矣,生者犹存,当勉力上进,以慰死者于地下。"

申纯不答,忽地勉强支撑起来,颤声道:"佳构难再得。娇娘既然以诗诀别,我当以词吊她。"说着下床来到书案前,取了一支笔,展开纸笺,不加思索,挥笔而书。只见他运腕如风,洒墨如雨,纵横起落,沙沙有声,转瞬墨渗满纸:

"蜀下相逢,千金丽质,怜才便肯分付。自念潘安容貌,无此奇遇。梨花掷处,还惊起,因共我拥炉低语。今生挤两两同心,不怕傍人间阻,此事凭谁处?

对明神为誓,死也相许。徒思行云信断,听箫归去,月明谁伴孤鸾舞。细思之,泪流如雨。便因丧命,甘从地下,和伊一处。"

person, you should know how to control your grief and protect your precious body. " He then turned to Wang Zhong: "Please come with me to inform my parents of this tragedy, and arrange to send representatives of the family to the funeral. "

Urging Shen Chun not to take his bereavement too hard, Wang Zhong followed Shen Lun outside.

When they had gone, Shen Chun thought to himself: "How could you know how deep our love was? It was a love that would last till the end of time. She died for my sake, so how can I go on living without her?" Thereupon, he dried his eyes, and mumbled aloud: "Father, Mother, Brother — please don't think me ungrateful for your kindness. But I am mindful of the righteous heroes of old, who never hesitated to choose death rather than break a promise. Long ago, Jiaoniang and I pledged that if we could not be together in life, we would be together in death. Now she is waiting for me by the Yellow Springs of the netherworld. How can I break my oath? Anyway, I don't think Heaven would allow it. My darling, if you can hear me, wait for me a little while longer. Your Master Shen is coming to you. " As he said this, he reached under his pillow, and drew out a silken girdle. This had been a present from Jiaoniang, and he had intended to wear it on his wedding night, but today it was to serve as his passport to the land of dead souls.

Holding the girdle in both hands, he wept for a while, and then, steeling himself for the deed, he attached it to the door lintel. He brought a stool. Mounting the stool, he cried out, in a tear-choked voice: "Oh, cruel Heaven, why did you not allow us to unite? My darling, wait! Your husband is coming!" Thereupon, he made a noose with the girdle around his neck, and kicked the stool from beneath him. Just as he did so, his parents, escorted by his brother approached the room. They had come to comfort Shen Chun. At the sight of the young man dangling in the doorway, his mother fainted on the spot, while Shen Lun rushed to support his younger brother's body, and his father fumbled to untie the noose round his

申纶在一旁看了惊道："兄弟为何出此不祥之语？却不道断者不能复续，死者不能复生。况且兄弟与娇娘义为中表，两次言婚不遂，定是缘份不到。岂得过于伤心，有乖大义？三弟读书知礼，宜自节哀，以保千金之躯。"说罢，转头对王忠道："老院公且随我来，告与我爹娘知道，打发人前去吊丧。"

王忠说道："三官人，请节哀保重。"便拭泪跟着申纶去了。

申纯见二人去了，心中道："唉，兄长，你怎知我与娇娘情深义重，万劫难改。她既为我而死，我岂能独生于世！"于是拭干眼泪，喃喃道："爹爹，娘亲，兄长，不是我不念深恩，忍得半路相抛。想古来仁人烈士，不惜杀身践诺。我昔与娇娘发下誓言，生不同辰，死当同夕。如今她既待我以九泉之下，我怎忍悔背前盟，谅老天也断不相容了。娘子，你若有知，且等着我，你的申郎来也。"说着到枕下取出一幅锦香罗，此物本是娇娘所赠。原想待到洞房花烛夜用它牵绣幕，结锦裙，可今日却只能将它做了追魂的牒子，索命的幡儿。

申纯手捧锦罗，泪下如雨，最后横下心来将罗帕悬系于门楣之上，掇了一条短凳站了上去，含泪道："苍天呀，我好恨呀，你为何不肯成全我们？娘子慢走，夫君来也！"遂引颈投缳，脚下一蹬。正在此时，申纶扶着王氏和申庆来到房前，本是要来劝说申纯，一

neck. The two men then laid Shen Chun on the bed.

Shen Qing pinched his son's lips, and called to him over and over again. His wife picked herself up from the floor, hobbled over to where Shen Chun lay, and began to wail distractedly.

It seemed now that the whole household was crowding around, everybody agitated and at a loss what to do. Presently, they heard a gurgling sound in Shen Chun's throat. Shen Lun hurriedly opened his brother's gown, and applied his ear to the young man's chest. "His heart's still beating!" he cried in excitement. "My brother has come back to life!"

But, with his eyes still closed, Shen Chun sighed, and said, "I was about to follow my true love. Who summoned me to return?"

At this, Shen Qing and his wife cried out in unison: "My son, your loving parents are here. Why are you trying to end your life? Please open your eyes, and look at us."

Shen Chun did open his eyes. Beholding his white-haired parents anxiously watching over him, he said, "Father, Mother ... there is something I want to explain. My elder brother is quite capable of inheriting the family line, and bringing glory on our house. I am a worthless wretch who has failed to carry out his filial duties. If only you will reject the ties of affection which bind us, and refuse to grieve for me when I am gone, then I will be able to rest in peace."

Shen Qing and his wife wept silent tears of anguish at hearing this. The former said, "My son, don't speak such ill-omened words. All we want is for you to get better, preserve your life, and embark on your glorious future career."

The young man, however, shook his head weakly, and said, "I am afraid that it is not possible for me to recover." With that, he grasped Shen Lun's hand, and sobbed, "Brother, I am not long for this world. I entrust the care of our parents, now in the evening of their lives, to you. I am sure that you will look after them with the utmost care. I have been an unfilial son and an undutiful brother. I beg you to forgive me."

进门，却见申纯晃晃悠悠吊在里间门楣之上，惊得王氏大叫一声："儿啊！"便跌坐在地。申绾顾不了许多，抢上前去先将申纯托住，申庆忙着将其脖子上的绳扣解开，二人合力将申纯抱下，放回床上。

申庆此时倒还能定住心神，狠掐申纯的人中，唤道："孩儿！孩儿！"王氏从地上爬起来，踉踉跄跄扑到申纯身上嚎啕大哭道："我的儿呀……"

众人正在乱成一团，忽听申纯喉咙咕噜响了一声。申绾急忙解开申纯的衣襟，俯耳贴在申纯的胸前听了听，道："心还在跳，兄弟醒来了！"

就见申纯呼出一口气，闭着双眼悠悠道："我正待要相随娘子而去，是谁又把我唤回？"

申庆、王氏同声道："孩子呀，爹娘在此，你怎么这等短见？快睁眼看看我们吧。"

申纯慢慢睁开双眼，看了看守在床前的白发爹娘，叹道："爹娘在上，孩儿今有一言禀明，承继宗祧，光耀家门，有兄长一人足矣。孩儿不孝，不能终侍膝下，半路上将双亲别去，惟愿大人割不忍之爱，休为孩儿哀痛不已，则孩儿死也瞑目了。"

申庆、王氏闻听此言，不由得肝肠寸断，泣不成声。申庆道："儿呀，休说此不祥之语。父母只愿你好自将息，保全性命，直奔锦绣前程而去。"

申纯无力地摇摇头，道："要想孩儿转好，谅也不

"Why are you uttering such foolish words?" wailed Shen Lun. "A true man takes a broad view of the world. How can you end your life just because of fondness for some girl? Already at an early age, you have made a name for yourself, and the world is at your feet. What need do you have to wallow in a trifling dalliance? Besides, there are plenty of beautiful women around; why restrict yourself to one? Is it worth betraying our parents' hopes and destroying yourself just for her?"

Standing at his side, Shen Qing nodded in agreement. "My boy," he said, "your brother is right. You must put a stop to this folly immediately."

His wife chimed in, wiping her eyes: "When you are an official, you will be bound to get a good wife. You despair of life right now because your marriage plans have been ruined. You must not throw away your youth and desert your parents. Please try to bear your sorrow...."

"I know that what you say — all of you — is correct," Shen Chun said, in a tear-choked voice. But I am no longer master of my own fate. My earnest wish is that you will not mourn too much for me, and I promise that in the afterlife I will repay you for your boundless kindness to me in this one."

His brother felt emotions of pain, anger and anxiety well up inside him. He cried, "You disgraceful whelp! Can you not see the agony you are subjecting our white-haired parents to? How can you allow them to say farewell to their son forever?"

Shen Chun burst into tears. "Father, Mother, Brother ... please don't blame me too much for my lack of family feeling. You can detain my body, but you cannot detain my heart. My soul has already gone to join Jiaoniang. No matter what you...."

He was interrupted by his mother, who wept and beat her breast. "Don't say such things," she howled. "You are breaking my heart to pieces! This is all the fault of my wicked brother. Wenrui ... by standing in the way of the marriage, you sent your daughter to her death. And now

能够了。"说罢，抓住申纯的手，哽咽道："兄长，我将不久于人世，白发父母，全托付给你一人，还望尽心侍养。我对父母不孝，对兄长不义，乞望兄长恕罪。"

申纶道："兄弟，你怎么如此糊涂？大丈夫志在四方，岂能为儿女私情而自绝？你少年高第，青云足下，何必区区眷恋一女子。况世间美妇人尽多，又何止一个娇娘？你今为她一人而死，上负双亲之望，下殒六尺之躯，值得么？"

申庆在一旁忙点头道："孩儿，你兄长说的话句句在理。你快休发痴了。"

王氏也拭泪道："儿呀，你做了官，还怕没有好媳妇？你如今只为亲事不就，便寻死觅活，断送了自家青春，抛下爹娘不管，你好生忍心啊……"

申纯含泪道："爹爹、娘亲、兄长之言，孩儿岂不晓得？但事到如今，儿即欲自主，也不能够了。只望爹娘休要为死伤生，哭损了身子，爹娘无极之恩，待孩儿来世再报吧。"

申纶见状，又痛又气又急，摇晃着申纯的身子道："好个不争气的兄弟！你不顾别的，你也该看看白发父母为你痛断肝肠，你就忍心让白发人送黑发人么？"

申纯哭道："爹娘、兄长，休怨我绝情，你们便是留住我的人，也留不住我的心。我的魂灵早随娇娘去了，顾不得你们了……"

you are depriving my son of his life too!"

Shen Lun seized his brother, and shook him violently, crying, "Sit up! How can you simply die right in front of our parents?"

Shen Chun's brows were knitted, and he was barely breathing. With a great effort, he managed to open his eyes. "Father, Mother, Brother," he gasped, "please do not mourn; it will be all in vain. Now I am going to follow Jiaoniang. Since we were fated not to be united in life, it is fitting that I go to seek her in death...." Before he could finish, he spat out a huge quantity of blood, and shortly afterwards expired.

A few days later, notice of Shen Chun's death reached Lizhou. Learning that the young man had died for love, Wang Wenrui was overcome with excruciating remorse, realizing that he had wronged two young people who were perfectly matched in beauty and talent, and had caused them to choose death. He brooded for a long time, and then wrote a letter to his sister and brother-in-law. In the letter, apart from expressing his condolences and regrets, he suggested that the bodies of the lovers be buried together, so that although "in life they did not share a quilt, in death they would share a grave," which had been their long-cherished desire. Shen Qing and his wife thought the matter over carefully, and in the end agreed. The two families then chose an auspicious day for the funeral, when the two young lovers were interred on the bank of the Zhuojin River. Soon after, a pair of mandarin ducks appeared by the riverside near the tomb, flying backwards and forwards together and nestling close to each other. The local people said that the souls of Shen Chun and Jiaoniang, forever united and eternally faithful, had turned into the ducks. So they named the grave the "Mandarin Duck Tomb." Its remains can be seen to this day.

王氏捶胸大哭，道："快不要这么说。儿呀，为娘的心快要碎了，这都是你那狠心肠的舅舅做的孽。文瑞呀，你拒婚背约，自家断送了女儿的性命，又来夺我儿的性命。"

申纶将申纯抱起，用力摇晃他的身子，喊道："兄弟，你挣扎着坐起来！我不信你就这样死了，爹娘在此，你怎么放得下心？"

申纯此时双眉紧蹙，呼吸将绝，奋力睁开眼道："爹娘，兄长，你们不要哭了，哭也枉然，我就要随娇娘去了。今生无缘与她完聚，死也要寻她而去……"话语未竟，吐血不止，须臾气绝。

几天以后，凶讯传到利州。王文瑞得知申纯殉情而死，想起女儿与申纯两人正值青春，才貌相当，皆为自己所害而命殒黄泉，一时不禁肝肠寸断，悔恨难当。思之良久，主动写信给姐姐姐夫，信中除了深自悔疚之外，又提出将两个孩子合葬，以了其"生不同衾死同穴"的夙愿。申家二老见到王文瑞的书信，思量再三，应允下来。王申二府遂择吉日为娇娘和申纯出殡，将这对有情人葬于濯锦江边。坟茔之畔，从此有一对鸳鸯相偎相伴，上下飞翔。人们都说是申、娇二人魂魄不散，精诚所至，化为鸳鸯，遂称之为"鸳鸯冢"，至今遗迹犹存。

图书在版编目(CIP)数据

娇红记/(明)孟称舜原著;张雪静改编.
–北京:新世界出版社,2001.10
(中国古代悲剧故事)
ISBN 7–80005–645–7

Ⅰ.娇… Ⅱ.① 孟… ② 张… Ⅲ.英语–对照读物,
小说–汉、英 Ⅳ.H319 4:I

中国版本图书馆 CIP 数据核字(2001)第 075494 号

娇红记

原　　著:孟称舜(明)
改　　编:张雪静
审　　订:刘幼生
翻　　译:保尔·怀特
封面剪纸:于平　任凭
绘　　图:李士伋
责任编辑:张民捷
装帧设计:贺玉婷
责任印刷:黄厚清
出版发行:新世界出版社
社　　址:北京阜成门外百万庄路 24 号
邮政编码:100037
电　　话:0086–10–68994118
传　　真:0086–10–68326679
电子邮件:nwpcn@ public. bta. net. cn
印　　刷:北京龙华印刷厂
经　　销:新华书店　外文书店
开　　本:850×1168(毫米)　1/32
字　　数:226 千
印　　张:13.5
印　　数:1–5000 册
版　　次:2002 年 1 月(汉英)第 1 版第 1 次印刷
　　　　　ISBN 7–80005–645–7/I·074

¥60